The Apprentice to Zdrell

By

David K. Bennett

Published by Ergoface Imprints
Simi Valley, CA 93063
www.zdrell.com

Publisher's Note: This is a work of fiction. Names, characters, places, and incidents are a product of the author's imagination. Locales and public names are sometimes used for atmospheric purposes. Any resemblance to actual people, living or dead, or to businesses, companies, events, institutions, or locales is completely coincidental.

Apprentice to Zdrell, The / David K. Bennett – 1st ed.
ISBN 978-1-949704-01-3

Prologue

Jelnick watched from his concealed position in the rocks of the mountainside as the wizard called Mlandress tiredly rounded the bend in the steep rocky path. Mlandress was walking instead of flying, that alone showed how tired the ancient zdrell master must be. Jelnick still smarted over the two failed attacks on Mlandress in the last four days, but today he would not fail.

Jelnick initially grinned in triumph as the three demons lords appeared and attacked the unsuspecting wizard. It had been a lot of work on his part to goad these three into attacking a zdrell master, but even Mlandress could not withstand alone three of the strongest demons.

His feeling of triumph turned to silent cursing as instead of being overwhelmed, Mlandress threw out a wave of energy, absorbing the forces from the demons' simultaneous attack. He invoked the power from a ring and cut the lifeline of the center demon, following immediately with a burst of energy, causing the now defenseless demon to explode in a cloud of dense orange vapor.

The other two demons paid no apparent heed to their companion's demise and again attacked from either side. Mlandress was only just able to deflect the energies of the demons' assault. Jelnick dove for additional cover as rocks on both sides of Mlandress exploded from the force of the diverted power.

Jelnick knew he had to act; Mlandress was readying another counterattack. The ancient wizard was so intent on the two demons that he did not notice the poisoned dart Jelnick shot at him until it was nearly to him. He attempted to divert it, but was too late to keep it from embedding in his side.

The poison was very fast acting. Jelnick knew Mlandress could neutralize it in the three seconds before it killed him. Unfortunately, for Mlandress, it would require his full attention. During his preoccupation, the demons struck again. This time he was not able counter their attack, and his body instantly charred from the force and heat of their attack.

Mlandress' body stood smoking for moment, and then fell over as another pair of explosive bolts impacted, causing it to rupture and partially disintegrate. There was no question about it; Mlandress was dead.

§ § §

Emerging from his concealed position, Jelnick dusted himself off and addressed the two hovering demon lords.

"Well, that's it then. Mlandress was the last of the zdrell masters. There isn't another wizard left alive who can do more than the most trivial zdrell magic. Your position in this world is secure, Lord Kelf."

"You are certain he was the last?" the demon called Kelf asked.

"Most certain," Jelnick said firmly. "I have searched the world over, as have you. There are no others. The eventual dominance of demon magic is assured."

"That is good, for now," Kelf said. "But what about when other wizards arise in the future? My brothers have fought and died, for this cause. How can we know we will not soon have to fight it again?"

"I am most sorry for the loss of your brother, Lord Kelf. I had no idea Mlandress could counterattack so quickly. I thought three demon lords would be enough to put anyone, even him, on the defensive . . .," Jelnick sounded much less sure of himself now.

"I care not for what you thought, *mortal!* You cannot even imagine what the loss is for one of my kind to die! You have still not answered my question," the demon thundered. "How likely is it another zdrell master will arise?"

"Not likely at all," Jelnick said regaining some of his composure. "At least not for several hundred if not several thousand years. The ability to directly manipulate the forces which bind the world as zdrell masters and you do is very, very rare in humankind. Less than one in a thousand can do any sort of magic at all and only one in a thousand wizards can do any real sort of zdrell magic. It is only because they are so long lived and have been cultivating new students that this crisis came at all. Did you know Master Mlandress was over two thousand years old?"

"Two thousands of your years are nothing to me and my kind. My brother was old before your sun began to shine. Now he is dead. Since you mortals cannot understand this, it will be left to my kind to watch for another zdrell master, and stop him before we are threatened again."

The demon lord, Kelf, turned in the air. He gestured and an opening appeared in the air before him. He entered the opening and disappeared, along with the opening.

Jelnick turned to address the second demon lord.

"Well, Karf," the wizard began, "it looks as if the end of this war only means a long vigil to prevent another. Can your powers keep me alive two thousand years?"

The demon regarded Jelnick with sharp-toothed grin. "As long as you can keep your end of our contract, Master Jelnick, I can keep you alive till your sun grows cold."

"I don't think that will be necessary, but I do look forward to outliving all my contemporaries, to watch demon magic fill the world. The power that will be mine, now there are none of those pompous zdrell masters to interfere, is more than even my considerable ambition requires."

"You still must destroy any remaining line cutters in existence," Karf said.

"Yes, that will be my next task. That and ending all the petty wars on this continent, but with your assistance it shouldn't be difficult."

It took Jelnick nearly three hundred more years to find and destroy the last zdrell line cutter artifact. Demon magic grew unchallenged to eclipse all other magic the world over, for more than twelve hundred years.

Chapter 1 - The Reluctant Apprentice

Jashoc dunked his head again into the cold water of the fountain on the edge of the city bazaar. He still could not get the stink out of his stringy red hair. At least now it was not quite so greasy, and it helped cool the midday heat. He hated it when he had to clean the flues at the confectioner's shop. They were always filled with rancid grease that got all over his face and arms. He could wash those easily enough, but it never seemed to get out of his hair, and the smell, though rank, only made him hungrier.

The day was unseasonably warm, for early fall, and the head baker had been in a foul mood and had not even allowed him to take stale scraps. Usually, he or the other bakers allowed Jashoc to eat as much of the castoffs as he wanted, but not today. His stomach grumbled, reminding him he had eaten nothing since his scanty meal last night.

He wandered wearily along the edge of the bazaar, wondering how long he could stay out of sight before his master, the slave trader Murdoc, or one of his apprentices, found him and put him on the next assignment that needed a small boy.

As he passed the brass shop, the merchant's son, one of Jashoc's few friends in the market, gave him a half-eaten, wormy, apple out of sympathy. Jashoc thanked him. As he turned to go, the boy told Jashoc that Gareselin, the slave trader's head apprentice, was looking for him.

Jashoc started jogging for the back alleys at the edge of the bazaar. The sun was now high, and the market bustled with activity. Jashoc could smell the heavenly scent of kabok cooking two shops over, causing his stomach to rumble again. The air was only slightly clouded with dust, not like the thick haze of mid-summer.

If Gareselin was looking for him this early, it could only mean he had another ugly job he wanted done today. Murdoc was usually content to get one job out of Jashoc a day. It meant Jashoc missed supper most days, but he felt that not working an extra six hours a day was worth it.

He tried to look in every direction as he headed for his new hidey-hole in a burned out stall at the edge of the market. His heart sank as he saw Foresel, another of Murdoc's apprentices moving through the crowd, clearly looking for someone. He ducked out of sight just in time, he hoped.

Things were going from bad to worse.

If Foresel was looking for him, Ryalor, the other apprentice slave trader probably was too. They obviously wanted Jashoc for something, and every possibility he considered seemed worse than the previous. With all three apprentices looking for him, he had little hopes to escape, but he would try anyway, he had almost gotten away twice before. He was nearly to his new hiding place, and he felt confident that once he got there they would never find him.

He moved through the crowd, alternately following close behind larger shoppers or merchants, and then crouching behind carts or the edges of stalls. He could easily have eluded one pursuer with these tricks and his small size, but with all three apprentices following, they would eventually find him unless he could go to his secret place.

He almost made it.

Just as he started down the back alleyway that led to his hiding place, he saw Foresel running after him.

Once again, he cursed the fates who seemed to have decreed that nothing go right for him. It was not his fault his parents had died and left him with almost nothing. It was not his fault that the judge had made him a ward of Murdoc, nor that Murdoc seemed to think Jashoc a slave, and not merely a ward. It might be his fault that he did not work as hard as Murdoc wanted, but who would? Why should he work hard for a man who fed him little and treated him like a worthless slave? He knew he was nothing, but he did not have to like it.

Jashoc moved faster, his breath burning in his lungs, only to see Ryalor turn into the alley at the other end. Trapped, but there was one chance left. The wall of the alley had a hole in it about midway down. It would slow his larger pursuers much more than it would him, and maybe give him a chance.

Jashoc ran hard for the hole. He could hear Foresel gaining on him from behind.

He dived through the hole and only just saw the wagon wheel before his head hit it and exploded with pain. The world spun. He tried to get up off the ground where he had fallen, beside a wagon parked just that side of the hole, but he could not seem to make his legs move.

Just as his vision cleared enough and he started to get up, he felt a hand grab his leg. Foresel pulled his leg out from under him and sent him sprawling. Jashoc felt a knee in his back as his arm was twisted up behind him. He heard Gareselin and Ryalor arrive while he lay contorted, his face pressed into the dirt and dung on the ground.

Gareselin was still puffing hard from running, and had a nasty sneer on his face, as he motioned for Foresel to let Jashoc up.

"I ought to pound you to a bloody pulp, you little nit-brain. You've had us running you down for the last hour. The Master is going to be very angry," he huffed. "If he didn't have a very important client who wants a look at you right now," he paused for effect, and for another breath, "I'd kill you here myself. You're not worth the effort of keeping. The Master is always saying that, and I more than agree.

"You're coming with us right now, and you'll come quietly. If you try to run off, like you did last time, I will just have to forget myself and club you one. Bring you in like the sack of meat you are."

Jashoc could tell by the look in the boy's eye that Gareselin really wanted him to try to run so he would have a reason, with witnesses, for bringing him back damaged.

The three boys were all in their early teens and should easily have been a match for the ten-year-old, but they had been overconfident other times and allowed him to escape. The look on Gareselin's face told him this would not be one of those times, so he went along without resistance.

§ § §

They arrived at the slave master's quarters to find Murdoc pacing up and down the street with a panicked look on his face. He caught sight of them and his look rapidly shifted from panic to relief, and then to an ugly rage. Before anyone had a chance to say anything, Murdoc shouted so that the whole street could hear. "Gareselin! You pitiful excuse for an apprentice! I sent you off over two hours ago to collect this little sewer rat. Where have you been amusing yourself all this time instead of doing your master's bidding?"

"Please, Master, it's not our fault," Gareselin said in his most simpering tone. "This nit-headed snot brain knew we were looking for him and had us chasing him all through the market square and half of town trying to catch him." As he spoke, his voice shifted from cringing and whining to anger.

"We just now caught the little carp and didn't even give him the beating he deserves for making us chase him over half the town, since you said he was to be in the best shape possible. Here he is." Gareselin finished the last with a flourish, to prove he had not disobeyed at all.

Murdoc looked at Gareselin and the nodding faces of Foresel and Ryalor, and seemed to come to the conclusion they were telling the truth, this time. He turned to Jashoc, his lips curled into a sneer as he regarded him. "So you've been up to your old tricks again. You finished the bakery job hours ago, and you just disappear. You are truly the most worthless slave I've ever owned!" Jashoc considered trying to correct him, since he was only a ward of the city, not a slave, but Murdoc over-rode him. "And I don't care a flea's whisker if you're a real slave or not! You'll soon no longer be my problem!"

This last statement made Jashoc's head snap up. The effect was not lost on Murdoc, who barked out a short harsh laugh. "Yes, you heard me right, guttersnipe. I have a man here who is interested in acquiring a boy of your age, and if you do something which causes him not to take you," he said with a leer and a nod towards Jashoc's captors. "Then I might just let Gareselin and his friends here beat on you till you cannot walk, and see if you bring in more money as a crippled boy beggar than as a useless boy worker."

Looking in his eyes, Jashoc could see Murdoc was dead serious. Gareselin smiled evilly at the prospect of turning Jashoc into a permanent cripple.

The ugly sneer on Murdoc's face slowly turned into a grimace of pleasure as he saw the color drain from Jashoc's face. He laughed. "That's right, boy, now you see how things really are. I've put up with more than I can stomach from you, and if I can't be rid of you one way, then I will another."

He pulled Jashoc roughly into his counting room and whispered to him. "Now mind, boy. This is one of the most important men in the land. You will do exactly as he says and answer any questions he puts you to with no back talk or other foolishness. If he likes you, he'll be taking you and that's what I want, so don't you dare be doing anything to mess this up."

As they came to the far side of the room, Jashoc saw the stranger standing there. He was tall, dark haired, and seemed to be middle aged. He was dressed in dark blue robes with gold brocade at the sleeves and collar, a sure sign of nobility. There was little expression on his face as he turned to face them, other than the intensity of his gaze.

Murdoc was exuding his "humble trader" persona, which Jashoc had seen him use any time he dealt with persons of position or authority. He practically groveled in front of the man. "Here he is, Lord Feldor. The boy, just as I promised. You can see for yourself he's in fine physical shape even if he is a little dirty," Murdoc said, bowing towards Lord Feldor. "He's just what you asked for, ten years old, and stronger than he looks.,"

Jashoc thought furiously. He had heard the name Lord Feldor before, but he could not remember where. This man was obviously important, the clothes alone told that. What could he want with Jashoc? He was a nobody, Murdoc and the last two years had taught him that.

Lord Feldor came closer and stared at Jashoc. He slowly circled around him, looking him up and down as though appraising the value of a piece of a sculpture or horseflesh. "He looks like he does not get much to eat," Lord Feldor said with a tone of a trader in the bazaar trying to get a lower price. "I would wager you feed him as little as possible, though . . . the red hair is nice. His parents were not from Alavar, were they?"

"No, no, my Lord, his parents seem to have been from the hills of Caravain, and only came here to try and better themselves. Instead, they had the misfortune of getting Farthigs blight and dying."

"So you said, so you said. Does he mind well?" Lord Feldor asked.

"No, my Lord, he minds abominably. Truth to tell, I'd be asking twice what I was for him if he minded any better. No, he's a quick little snipe, but only when he's avoiding work. But then again, he doesn't need to mind all that well for what you have in mind for him now, does he?" he said, with a nod and wink, as though he had just told a dirty joke. "A sorcerer's apprentice either learns his task or ends up feeding demons, isn't that the way of it?"

Jashoc flinched as he realized Lord Feldor was the chief steward for Master Magician Silurian, the ruler of Salaways, and reportedly one of the greatest wizards in the whole world. Lord Feldor was one of the most powerful men in the land, possibly second only to Master Silurian. Jashoc had seen him before at public events, but never up close and had not recognized him. Jashoc now understood just what was going on here.

He was being sold as a sorcerer's apprentice.

Chapter 2

Becoming an apprentice should have been an improvement over being a virtual slave, but it was not.

In other trades, if you showed some talent and worked hard you were very likely to make journeyman and eventually, after some years, become a master of your trade. Jashoc had heard that for every thirty or more apprentices to a sorcerer, only one was likely to become a journeyman wizard, let alone a master sorcerer. People said those who failed to become journeymen simply disappeared, and they were fed to the demons sorcerers used to do their magic. Jashoc was more afraid now than when Murdoc had threatened him in the courtyard.

If Murdoc's comment had caused Jashoc to flinch, the effect on Lord Feldor was nearly as dramatic. A dark shadow passed over his face and his eyes burned brightly as he rounded on Murdoc. "You ignorant stuffed pig!" he glared at Jashoc's now cowering master. "It is enough for foolish gossips to say such things, but to imply in front of him that you are selling the boy to be eaten by demons is intolerable! I am of a mind to recommend to the city council that we have one slave trader too many in Alavaz!"

Murdoc retreated before his words as though struck by an invisible lash. "Oh no, my Master, my Lord, I meant nothing by it. It was only a jest, a poor one no doubt, but only a foolish jest. I know you and your master would never feed the boy to demons, else I couldn't possibly sell him to you, even as much as I loathe being his master." He cringed and stared at the floor, unwilling to meet the burning gaze of Lord Feldor.

Without taking his eyes off the floor, Murdoc said, "It truly was a poor jest, my Lord, and for my lack of manners, I'll gladly take another ten silver off the price we'd agreed on, just to show you how very sorry I am and to apologize for any insult, though none was meant."

Lord Feldor looked at Murdoc with undisguised loathing. They both knew that what Murdoc had said was no jest. It was his true opinion of what would happen to Jashoc once he was "apprenticed."

Lord Feldor looked up to the ceiling, sighed, and said shortly, "Well accepted. Done and done." He reached into a pouch at his belt, counted out a number of coins, and slammed them onto the desk.

"Has he clothes or other possessions?" Feldor asked.

"Just what's in his loft," Murdoc replied. "Go and get your stuff, boy. Be quick about it, and don't think about running off again. I've got Gareselin watching to make sure you don't try."

Jashoc did think fleetingly about running, but figured it would do no good, so he went to the loft and collected his few belongings. It took almost no time. He had so little, only a coat for the colder season he had owned since before his parents died, a brass coin from a far kingdom said to be of no value here, and a small plain dagger that had been his father's. All of the other family possessions had been sold, before he became a ward of the city. Murdoc had bought him no more than one new shirt and set of trousers in the year and a half he had been his slave and then only bought those when all of Jashoc's old clothes were too small, and worn to rags.

He gathered all his things quickly and came down from his loft to find Lord Feldor and his master, now his former master, already out on the street. Jashoc looked to Murdoc, who grinned and said, "Off with you now. And mind the lord here better than you've minded me. You're his problem now." So saying, he turned his back and walked back inside the shop and could be heard yelling for Gareselin.

Lord Feldor wasted no time in setting off, walking rapidly. Without looking back, he said over his shoulder, "Hurry on boy. We have no time to waste, and this distasteful errand has already cost me two hours I could ill afford to spare."

Jashoc hurried to catch up with the Lord Feldor's long strides, nearly having to run in order to keep up. Again, he thought of running away, but dismissed the idea very quickly. Lord Feldor would just call out the city guard if he ran. That could only make things worse. He shivered as he thought about what Murdoc had said. He desperately hoped Lord Feldor had been telling the truth that he was not going to his death.

Soon they had left the center part of Alavar and were moving to where the wealthy traders lived, a part of town Jashoc had rarely visited. When they turned into a small open plaza with a fountain in its center, he was certain he had never been there before.

Lord Feldor looked back to Jashoc and said, "Wait here, boy. I have some business to conduct and then we will be off shortly."

Jashoc stood alone for several moments, unsure of what to do. Just as he decided he would take his chances running, Lord Feldor came out again. As he walked out, another set of gates swung wide and a closed carriage pulled by two horses emerged. The driver got down and opened the door. Lord Feldor motioned for him to get in and he followed. Jashoc noticed the crest of the kingdom of Salaways was on the door. Jashoc looked up at the sky as he climbed into the carriage and wondered if he would live to see it tomorrow. He wished he had run.

Chapter 3

"So is Jashoc the name you were presented with?" Lord Feldor asked, after they had settled, facing one another in the carriage.

Jashoc thought it an odd question, but answered as best he could. "I don't know I was ever presented, my Lord, but Jashoc is what my parents always called me. It's the only name I've ever had."

"Well, we will have to change that, right here and now," Lord Feldor said with a thoughtful look on his face. "Yes, we must have a new name for you now if you are to be an apprentice. It would not do for you to be known by your true name. Even you must understand that."

Jashoc did understand, or thought he understood, what Lord Feldor meant. It was common knowledge in the markets wizards were never known by their true names. Knowing a wizard's true name was necessary for another wizard to be able to cast certain spells, which would have a hold upon him. So Jashoc reasoned that if he were really to be an apprentice sorcerer, he would need to be known by a new name. That the lord was attending to this detail made Jashoc believe being an apprentice might not be as bad as he feared.

Lord Feldor sat and stared out the window for a time as the carriage reached the edge of town and started on the road that led to the great castle. Suddenly, he turned and looked down at Jashoc and smiled and said, "We will call you Jonny. Yes, that is your name from now on. Do you like the name well enough?"

"I suppose," Jashoc, now Jonny, replied. "I've never heard it before as a name, but I guess I can get used to it."

"Good. That is settled then. Only you, Master Silurian, and I will know your true name in the castle, and you will not be going back to Alavar any time soon. Do not respond to any other, and do not let the other apprentices trick you into revealing your true name. It is the most important thing you possess right now, outside of life itself."

This thought was more than a little unsettling to Jonny. It brought home to him how he had absolutely no idea what he was getting into. If even half of the stories he had heard in the market were true, he had just gone from one form of misery to one infinitely worse.

By the way Lord Feldor had reacted to Murdoc's insinuations, he knew he was not going to be the first course in a demon's meal this evening, but, he was still scared and unsure. He desperately wanted to ask Lord Feldor questions, but at the same time, he was scared of the possible answers.

Lord Feldor must have seen his discomfort, "You really must not believe anything you have heard in the markets about being a sorcerer's apprentice. All the people know there are lies and rumors."

Jonny knew Lord Feldor was trying to put him at ease, but he could not keep from asking the question that had been tormenting him. "But sir, my

Lord, um, ah, . . . isn't it true thirty boys become apprentices for every one who makes it to journeyman?"

Jonny could see this question had not been what Lord Feldor had been expecting. He said "Well of course, my boy, there are at least thirty apprentices who fail for every one who makes it to being a journeyman. It is very difficult to become a wizard, and only a very few have what it takes to be able to perform magic consistently. Much of it cannot be learned; you must be born with an innate talent for it."

This answer did not help Jonny at all. In fact, it made him even more nervous than he had been before, he was no one, he could not possibly be the one out of thirty, but he felt he had to ask the question burning inside him. "So, so, um, ah . . . what, ah, . . . what happens . . . what happens to the, the thirty who, ah, um, . . . don't, um, become journeymen?" There he said it.

The whole time he had been asking the question, Lord Feldor had been scowling as though he was going to have to say something unpleasant, but when Jonny got to the end of his question, he smiled and laughed.

"So that is what you are worried about?" he said with a chuckle. "You are still worried about being killed and offered on some altar to a demon?"

"When you say it that way it does sound a little simple-minded. But, what does happen to the apprentices who don't make it? Everyone says they never come back to town. What happens to them?"

"Well," Lord Feldor began, "they are right about that. Any of the boys who apprentice here are almost never sent back into town. Their failure would mark them for life. So, after they have served a sufficient time to show no aptitude for magic at all, they are sent to other cities to apprentice in other trades. Many of our former apprentices have gone on to become quite prosperous tradesmen, traders, and scholars. All apprentices can read and write before they leave, that alone is a great benefit to them."

Lord Feldor had looked a little uncertain, as he had begun his response, but looked increasingly confident as he finished. "In fact," he said with enthusiasm, "one of the reasons sorcerer's apprentices start so young is so that if they fail to show aptitude for The Arts, they will still be able to be sent off to apprentice at a useful age. Usually, we send them off at around thirteen or fourteen, which is only a year or so later than they would be apprenticed normally."

Jonny sensed he was not being told everything, but he also thought Lord Feldor was telling the truth. It made him feel better, but he was still far from being at ease.

§ § §

The carriage turned as it left the flat of the valley and headed up the winding road leading to the castle, and Jonny got his first close look at it. In the past, he had only seen it as a clump of buildings on top of a hill. Now he could see it clearly and appreciate just how very large it was.

Jonny had heard Castle Salaways had protected this part of the country for at least five hundred years, maybe more. For the last ninety years it had been the home to the master wizard and ruler of Salaways. He had united the cities of Alavar, Kenton to the north, and Sharafleg to the south and created the land of Salaways by driving off the competing armies from the three adjacent lands.

The three cities lay in the long valley of Sharafleg, bordered on the south by Lake Sharafleg, and on the north by the Crags of Glondor. The land of Salaways had known mostly peace for the last ninety years, but had been a prize fought over for centuries. The castle was heavily fortified, and well positioned for defense.

Salaways' location, and its relative peace since Master Silurian united it, made it a prosperous trading nation. Though far from the sea, its fertile fields and open society made it a crossroads for the trading routes on the continent of Skryla.

The road wound back and forth up the hill. As they climbed higher, Jonny saw both the castle grow ahead of them, and the city of Alavar, his home for the last two years, spreading out below them. He had never seen the city from this height and was amazed at how big it really was, though the buildings were looking smaller and smaller.

The closer they got, the more ominous the castle seemed. Its huge walls of dark stone were covered with gray-green moss that made it appear as if the whole structure had somehow grown out of the ground. There were six tall towers in the outer walls with arrow slits evenly spaced up them and the tops of all the walls had crenellations, the square toothed top that allowed defenders to take refuge while raining down death on their attackers. Jonny had heard the castle was big enough for half the town of Alavar to be housed in case of a serious attack. He had never believed it, until now.

From the top of the tallest tower flew a single white flag bearing the same seal that adorned the door of the carriage, the Seal of Salaways. The seal was a circle of red. In the center of the circle was a smaller gold circle, a book, lightning bolt, and a sword, all done in black, were arranged in a triangle within the circle itself. Jonny thought it looked like a large demonic eye as the flag waved in the strong breeze.

Lord Feldor had been content to allow them to ride in silence until they entered the outer gate of the castle. Jonny had been so intent on the panorama unfolding as they climbed that he had not paid attention to the time it took to get there.

It had been early afternoon when he was caught and this whole adventure had begun. Now he noticed it was getting late. The hillside already blocked the sun from the castle as the carriage took them into the main courtyard.

Jonny was struck by just how dark and foreboding a place like this was. His fear, which had nearly left him for the last hour, now redoubled. What would become of him?

Chapter 4

Lord Feldor leaned close to Jonny just before they exited the carriage and reminded him, "Do not forget what I said about your name, Jonny. From now on, that is your only name. The old name, and the person it belonged to, are gone. You are Jonny, the newest apprentice sorcerer, understand?"

"I guess so," Jonny replied. "Will they really try to get me to tell them my real, I um, mean my true name?"

"Oh yes, it is a game all apprentices play at. But remember, it is a very deadly game. If even one of them finds out your true name, he could cause you considerable harm. Some of the most powerful spells are easily done if you know your victim's true name, so keep a watch out."

Jonny wondered how all the people in town would be kept from telling his true name, but he dared not ask. Besides, he thought, he would not be one of the lucky ones who made it to journeyman; he was no one after all, so it would not matter.

They were met at the carriage not by liveried servants, as Jonny had expected, but by three boys, two of them looked hardly older than Jonny was. The third looked to be around twelve, and addressed Lord Feldor directly. "My Lord, The Master wishes for you and the new boy to proceed directly to the north study. He desires to see him before dinner. I am to ask you if there are any urgent matters you need to communicate to the staff."

"No, that's quite all right," Feldor said. "Any information I have for the staff can wait till after dinner, or I will discuss it directly with Master Silurian. Just make certain the horses and carriage are seen to. I will almost certainly need to leave early tomorrow." He turned to Jonny and said, "Let us not keep Master Silurian waiting."

As they headed off, Jonny looked over his shoulder and saw the two younger boys leading the horses and carriage off while the older boy spoke with the driver. He felt terrified to think he was about to meet the ruler of the land, but even more terrified as to what might happen after. He turned and ran to catch up with Lord Feldor, who was disappearing through a door up the stairs from the courtyard.

Just as Jonny passed through the door, he thought he heard something that sounded like a child screaming in pain coming faintly from the opposite side of the courtyard. A shiver ran up his spine, how he wished he had run away when he had the chance. Now, instead, he had to run just to catch up with Lord Feldor. He felt as if he was going to vomit.

§ § §

After some time he caught up with Feldor just as he knocked on a door at the end of the corridor. Jonny heard nothing, but apparently, Feldor did, for he opened the door and stepped in. Jonny followed slowly.

They entered a large room, easily as big as the home he had been born in, with a high ceiling, which nevertheless felt crowded. The walls on three sides of the room had bookshelves that reached nearly to the ceiling, all filled with books, small wooden boxes, gleaming silver orbs, and other strange objects. The fourth wall had a large window that reached the ceiling as well, flanked by two smaller bookshelves that were, if anything, more crammed than the others with books, papers and writing implements. The faint glow from the nearly dark sky cast an eerie light over the unlit parts of the room.

Two large candelabras stood with squat candles burning to either side of the large desk that sat in front of the window. Behind the desk littered with papers and large books, one of which he was studying, sat the legend Jonny had never seen before, the ruler of Salaways, Master Magician Silurian.

The Master looked up from the book and said, "Ah good, Feldor, you're here. And you have the new boy with you. Excellent. What are we calling him?"

"I have decided to call him Jonny, Master Silurian," Lord Feldor replied. "Unless you have something else in mind for him."

"No, Jonny, Jonny, that will do just fine. Bring him up closer where I can look at him better and see if the feeling I have had the last couple of days is right, or if it is just indigestion."

As Jonny stepped forward at Feldor's urging, he got his first look at the legendary ruler of Salaways. He had stood as Jonny approached, and Jonny saw a very tall thin man, well over six feet. He had a fringe of pure white hair that ringed his mostly bald head and came together into a long ponytail going down his back. His mustache and closely trimmed beard were white as well.

Master Silurian's piercing blue eyes seemed to bore right through him. Jonny was surprised to see Master Silurian did not have the lines and wrinkles Jonny associated with older people. In fact, Jonny had seen many men in their forties who had faces that looked older than this man, who he had heard was at least a hundred and fifty years old, and was possibly much older. But for the hair, Jonny would have assumed him to be a man in his early thirties, the age Jonny's father had been when he died.

The Master motioned for both Feldor and Jonny to sit in two chairs set in front of the desk. He turned to Lord Feldor. "Were there any problems finding the boy and securing his release?"

"Not really. That odious swine of a slaver kept me waiting for over an hour, but I understand I have young Jonny here to thank for that," he said motioning towards the boy, who was now trying to shrink into non-existence in his chair.

Silurian raised an eyebrow. "Don't be afraid. I am not mad at you. I am sure you had good reason for making it hard for that rogue, Murdoc, to track you down."

Jonny was surprised that the Master was not upset. His fears eased slightly, but he said nothing.

Master Silurian turned back to Lord Feldor.

"If you do not need me further," Feldor said, "I have several matters I would like to attend to before dinner."

"Well, go then. Jonny and I can have our chat here, just the two of us. And he can show me all the magic tricks he knows," Master Silurian said with a twinkle in his eye.

Feldor got up to leave, and Jonny wanted to beg to go with him. His heart was pounding wildly, while his chest was so tight, he felt he could hardly breathe. He did not know any magic. He did not know much of anything. He could just barely read, and that only because his father had started teaching him at a very young age.

Jonny pulled his legs up to his chest and said in a small voice, "But I don't know any magic tricks."

The Master smiled as he then got up and came around the desk and sat in the chair Feldor had just left for him.

"There is no need to be afraid. I know you have not been doing any real magic tricks or things you think of as such, or I would already have heard of it. But do you have something you can do, something you would do to amuse the other boys when you had time to play in the bazaar?"

For some reason he could not explain, Jonny relaxed a little bit. This man seemed to be truly a kind sort, and Jonny sensed no threat behind his words. Unlike his time with Murdoc, Jonny did not think he would be punished if he failed.

He thought for a moment and said, "Well, there was this one game we sometimes played in the bazaar that I could always win," Jonny began. "Till no one would play me any more. It's not much . . ."

"Show it to me, Jonny. I am most anxious to see it."

"Well, first you have to have a big coin, like this one." Jonny dug in his bundle for his old brass coin. "This one's not worth anything here, but it works great for this game."

Jonny got off his chair, knelt down on the floor, and set the coin on its edge, holding it upright with his left index finger. "First you take a coin, like this . . ., and you set it spinning," he said as he flicked the edge of the coin with his right index finger. "Then you see who can keep the coin from falling over the longest."

As he spoke, the coin spun, winking in the light from the candles. After a few seconds, the spinning slowed and it fell to the floor.

"My trick," Jonny continued, "is that I can keep it spinning longer than anybody else can."

He set the coin up again and flicked it as he did before. Only this time he hit it harder and spun it faster. Jonny put his hands on his knees as he knelt before the coin and stared at it with intense concentration. Initially, the coin slowed as it had before, but then the spin began to stabilize. The coin continued to spin, and it neither sped up nor slowed down, but stayed spinning in the same place, at the same rate, for a very long time.

After several minutes of this had passed, the Master spoke up, "That's enough, Jonny. That is a very good trick. You can let it fall down now."

Jonny let out a sigh of relief. He had not moved a muscle since he placed his hands on his knees, and there were beads of sweat on his forehead. As soon as he relaxed, the coin began to slow and wobble. Within seconds, it fell to the floor.

"Wow, that was hard. I don't think I've ever kept one going that long before."

"That was very good, Jonny," the Master said. "May I see the coin that you used?"

"Sure. Everyone says it isn't worth anything here. That's the only reason I've got it."

The master picked up the coin and examined it very carefully. "Can you do it with other coins, or is it only this one?"

"Uh, I can do it with just about any coin," said Jonny. "But it's easier if it's bigger and heavier. I did a gold piece once. It was really easy, but I only got to do that once."

"Well Jonny, you may not know it, but you have just made me a very happy man."

"Why?"

"Because you have just proven to me that my feelings were right. You can do magic. And if you can do it with this with no training, I have great hopes for what you can do once you have received some."

"You mean I just did magic?" Jonny stared at Master Silurian with disbelief.

"Yes, yes you did, Jonny. Not only that, but you did it in a way I never would have thought to do. I could not have done it the way you did, until I saw you do it just now. You have already just shown me something new. I thank you."

Jonny was stunned. He had done magic. He had also done something the greatest wizard in the land said that he could not have done.

"You really mean you couldn't have done that trick I just did?"

"Jonny, I could have made the coin spin. However, the type of magic I would have used to do it would have been completely different from the way you did. It would have taken me more to get set up. Of course, the way I would have set it up, it would still be spinning there now. Once I started it spinning, I would also not have had to concentrate on it as you did, but, as I say, that would have been a completely different kind of magic. What you did, I have never seen done that way before. You truly are a natural magician."

Jonny sat back on his heels, amazed and confused. He had no idea that he had been doing magic. It made him feel the best he had felt since before his parents died. It made him feel, for once, happy.

The Master got up from his chair and headed for the door. "Come, it is time for dinner. We will eat and see if we can't get some flesh on those bones of yours. I will also introduce you to the other apprentices and the journeymen."

With that, he held the door for Jonny. The Master locked the door behind them. They walked down the corridor towards the sounds of many voices and the smell of food that made Jonny's mouth water.

Chapter 5

As hungry as he was, Jonny was only barely aware of the path they took to get to the great hall where several tables were already piled high with food. He had actually done magic! He felt as if he were floating. He hoped this would not all turn out to be a dream where he woke up to the reality of life as a slave.

As they entered the hall, the babble of conversation died down and all heads turned in their direction.

"I want you all to look over here and pay special attention," The Master began. "This is our new apprentice, Jonny. He has just showed me a magic trick the likes of which I have never seen before."

As he said this last part, the attention of everyone in the room focused on Jonny. He could feel their eyes examining him. Not all the attention was friendly.

"He will be under my special tutelage," The Master continued. "And . . ." he paused, sweeping his gaze around the room, "He is not to be bothered or molested in any way. He has just been freed from slavery. I will not countenance *any* improper behavior from any of you towards him. I am sure you all know what I mean. You are all warned, so you will be without excuse."

As he delivered these words, Master Silurian glared meaningfully towards certain of the older boys. His look was fearsome, not the kindly look Jonny remembered at all.

The Master scanned the assembled faces, nodded, then the fierce look left his face as it relaxed into a smile. "Jonny, let me introduce you to the boys and staff," The Master said, pointing to various people and naming them, and what they did.

It was all too much for Jonny to take in; there were over seventy people in the room in total. He smiled and returned the nods of the boys and young men who were introduced to him, but their names simply did not register. He was still too giddy. The Master introduced him as if he was some visiting wizard from a far country, to be given special care and consideration. Only The Master, Lord Feldor, Jonny and one other Journeyman wizard were seated at the head table. There were three other long trestle tables with at least twenty boys at each.

Several of the boys looked at him with barely concealed hostility and resentment. He had seen the look before. Many of these boys were *not* going to be his friends. Some of them might already be his enemies. If he were not already feeling so disconnected, their looks might have scared him.

He knew in the back of his mind that this would not all be easy, but he also knew The Master had extended his special protection to him. He hoped it would be enough.

There was more food at this meal than Jonny had seen in the last two years: meats, breads, potatoes, apples, pastries, and pies. He was sitting next to his new master, being offered anything he wanted.

He ate so much he thought he would burst. Twice Master Silurian had to caution him to slow down the speed he was stuffing food in his mouth. The last two years had taught him to eat fast, before someone bigger came to take the food he had. In the end, when he could eat no more, he sat back. He was so full, he was not sure whether it felt good, or if he was going to be sick.

Smiling, the master turned to him and said, "So, you can be filled." He laughed. "For a moment I was unsure of whether you would ever stop. I have seen boys twice your size not able to eat as much as you have. I just hope this is only because of how little you've eaten recently."

Jonny happily nodded his agreement and blinked and yawned.

"Ah, I see the food has got you feeling sleepy," Master Silurian chuckled. "Well then, it's best if we get you a place to sleep." He looked over to one of the other tables where several boys were talking. "Roald, is there a place for Jonny in your room?"

"Yes, Master," replied the tall, thin shyly smiling boy.

"Good, show young Jonny here the room and the privy while you're at it so he can get to bed. He has had a long day, and he will need his strength for tomorrow." The Master turned to Jonny and said, "Go with Roald. He will show you where things are and what to do. I will see you tomorrow, and we will see if you have any more tricks you can show me."

With that, The Master stood up and started walking towards a different door than the one by which he and Jonny had entered. Just before he left the room, he turned and smiled back at Jonny, shook his head and then said to Feldor, "Come, Feldor, we have much to discuss." Feldor, who had been talking with two of the young men in the room, immediately got up and followed him.

"Wow," began Roald. "I've never seen The Master treat a newcomer like that. You must be something special." Roald looked amazed and impressed. "I mean, really, The Master usually doesn't even see new boys for a few days after they arrive. After they've, uh, um, . . . been broken in. But you, he might as well have said if anyone even touches you, he'll flay them alive. *Prodigious.*"

This whole outburst only puzzled Jonny. He knew what The Master had done must have been unusual, but Roald's reaction made it seem like it was a once in a lifetime event. The confusion on his face must have been evident.

"But you don't know what I'm talking about, do you?" Roald said. Then talking more to himself he said, "Of course you don't, and it's really better you don't." A calculating look came on his face, and he brightened. "I bet that's why The Master put you with me. I'll show you how to stay out of trouble. Yes I will," he said, now looking at Jonny again. "And we'll be the best of friends! Come on. I'll show you where the privies are and then get you set up for bed."

They left the great hall heading down a corridor and out and across into the main courtyard to where the privies were located. As soon as they had been mentioned, Jonny knew he very badly needed to relieve himself and was glad they stopped there first.

After they finished in the privies, they walked to the opposite side of the cobbled courtyard and climbed a winding set of stairs that opened out onto a narrow corridor. They walked past several doors, until Roald opened one up and said, "Here we are, my own little home."

The large room looked like it had seen better days. At some point in the castle's history, it had probably been officer's quarters. It had two racks of solid bunk style beds with posts extending to the ceiling with three beds in each stack. There were clothes and other items strewn on the floor and dust coated nearly everything. Of the six available beds, only one looked to be in use. The others were without bedclothes. Two tall dusty and mostly empty bookshelves stood along opposite walls, with two large scarred wooden tables each with two chairs in the middle of the room.

"There used to be three others in here with me," Roald began. "One made Journeyman, Diego he's now called, and the other two, they, uh finished their apprenticeships and, um, left. So, I've had the place all to myself for the last two weeks. It's been great." Jonny could see what Roald considered great. It certainly wasn't cleanliness.

Just then there was a sound behind them, and they both turned to see another boy coming in with blankets, sheets, and a pillow. "Feldor said you would be needing these things," the blond-haired, freckled boy, said as he walked into the room, working to balance his load. "Where do you want me to put them?"

Roald said, "Just set them anywhere. Jonny hasn't decided where he's going to sleep yet."

The new boy ignored Roald's remark, snorted, and gave Jonny a questioning glance. "Uh, just set them on that empty bunk over there," Jonny said, indicating the one across from the one Roald was occupying.

"That's probably best," the new boy said. "If you sleep over here there's a chance Roald's screams in the night won't wake you." He laughed. "That's why he's been in this room alone. No one else can get any sleep around him."

"You didn't need to tell him that, Larin," Roald muttered.

"Yes I did. He might have thought there was something really wrong, when you woke him up with your screaming. Now, he'll know that's just what you do most nights."

"Do not!"

"Do too," Larin replied, not at all put off by Roald's protest. "Only you don't know it, because you sleep right through them, not that anyone else can."

Jonny found the whole conversation amusing, but was already too tired to care. "I think right now I could sleep through just about anything."

"Yeah, well that's good enough. And don't let Roald's screams worry you. They don't mean anything," Larin said. He had already been working on putting the covers on Jonny's bed the whole time the conversation had been going on. "There, I think you're set. They didn't give me a nightshirt for you, but I'm sure there's one in the cupboard," he said pointing to a cabinet beyond the bed. Jonny had failed to notice it earlier. "Have a good night. I'll see you at breakfast." With that, Larin smiled at Jonny and left, closing the door behind him.

"He didn't have to tell you about that," Roald said, scowling at the closed door. "I'd have told you. But he is right. That's why I've had the room to myself. I hope it doesn't bother you too much." He stared at the floor.

"Naw, I doubt I'll even notice," Jonny said. "I'm so tired right now, I doubt a stampede would wake me up."

Jonny went to the cupboard and found there indeed was a nightshirt, as well as other clothes, inside it. It also looked like Roald did not use this cupboard, because aside from the dust it was orderly inside. He changed and got into bed. Roald, who had been hunting around on the floor for his nightshirt, put it on and went over to the candle on one of the tables.

"Are you ready?"

Jonny said, "Sure," and Roald blew out the light.

Chapter 6

Jonny woke up to the sound of screaming.

It was still dark. At first Jonny was not sure where he was or what was going on, but it soon all came back to him. He rolled over and looked towards Roald's bed. The moon was shining in through the window and Jonny could see Roald was sitting up in bed and screaming. It was a piercing wail without words. It seemed like he would go on forever, and Jonny wondered if he was ever going to breathe. Roald paused just long enough to pull in a deep breath and then continued.

After a few minutes, though it felt like years, the sounds coming from Roald changed. Now he was sobbing, and muttering something between the sobs. Jonny had known there was no way he could go back to sleep while Roald was wailing. Eventually, the sobs were quiet enough he thought he might be able to get back to sleep. Then the words Roald was saying started to register with Jonny, and he was suddenly more scared than he had been waking up to the screams.

"Please, oh please . . . don't do that again . . . not again. I can't take it," Roald moaned. "Isn't that enough, please, oh pleeasse, not again, no . . . no. I'll do anything, no, no, nooooooo." He kept crying and repeating the same things over and over. Then he began again.

Now Jonny was scared, not of something that would happen, but scared of whatever had happened to Roald. He was obviously reliving something very bad that had happened to him. Jonny had been beaten, starved, lost his family, and had experienced other horrible things in the last two years, but nothing gave him such terrible dreams or made him feel the kind of pain that Roald was dreaming now. Jonny trembled at the thought of the horror Roald had been through, whatever it was.

Then, as suddenly as it had begun, Roald simply stopped screaming, lay down, and was quiet except for the sound of his rhythmical breathing.

Jonny however, was too upset to get back to sleep. He lay there for a long while before he finally started to relax. He deliberately avoided thinking about anything that might have caused Roald that pain. Instead, he thought of how he was no longer a slave. Tomorrow he was going to eat well and learn magic, and that brought him some peace, and he finally relaxed. Just as he was drifting off to sleep, he thought he heard what might have been someone screaming in the distance, but the sound was too faint. Jonny wondered muzzily, as sleep claimed him, if this was just his imagination, or the wind or if maybe Roald wasn't the only boy here who screamed at night.

Chapter 7

"Feldor, we are going to have to make some changes in the arrangements here," Master Silurian said, as he and Feldor sat in his north study. The predawn light faintly illuminated the window. The candles were once again alight.

"How so, Master?" Feldor said, still writing down the items they discussed would be secured on the next supply run into Alavar.

"I want to isolate Jonny, especially from the normal routine of apprentice and journeyman demon summonings."

"Is that wise?"

"I believe it is essential." He paused, glancing around and then continued. "Jonny has no need to go through the standard initiation to magic by being a demon offering. The process is so injurious, not just to the body, but to the soul. If there were any other way to identify those with the talent, I would dispense with it altogether. Jonny has already proved his talent. I do not wish for him to be warped unnecessarily."

"Won't that not alienate him from the other boys?"

"Yes, that cannot be helped. In some ways, I believe it will be best if he becomes accustomed to the isolation. I fear he will bear it much of his life."

"What exactly is it that makes him so special? You seemed so excited about him last night. I cannot recall when I've seen you so affected."

"Feldor, I believe he has the native talent to be a zdrell master."

"But I thought all the zdrell masters were killed in the Great War?"

"They were. There were a few wizards left who could do some of the simpler zdrell manipulations, but those true masters were always rare, and they were all killed in the war.

"It has always been my suspicion, though I know of no way to prove it, that eliminating the zdrell masters was the reason for the war. The Grimoridans withdrew after the last zdrell master was killed and they made no serious attempts to keep the lands they had conquered."

"The histories make no mention of that connection."

"No, they do not. They claim the Grimoridans could no longer maintain their troops against constant attacks from the varied forces here. Nevertheless, they make no mention why after nearly ninety years of continuous struggle the Grimoridans would simply give up and withdrew. None of the traditional explanations can give reason for the timing. However, the death of the last zdrell master occurred just prior to it.

"If they had been fully committed to conquering Skryla, it would have made more sense for them to have pressed the attack. Without the zdrell masters, our continent of Skryla was much more vulnerable. But what did they do instead? They withdrew."

"I see your point, Master. But how does this involve young Jonny?"

"Only those with great power in zdrell could reportedly do it without training. If Jonny is the first new zdrell master in over a thousand years, he could become as great as some of the legendary ones in the sagas. I do not want him to be spoiled. Not all the zdrell masters were good. I need him to become a good, honorable man. I cannot have him twisted by whole demon initiation process, just so the other apprentices' sense of fair-play is upheld."

"So what do you want changed then?"

"I've already talked with some of the journeymen. I need you to talk to all of them and all the apprentices. Jonny is not be involved in any way in summonings. He is not to know the secret of how apprentices are used, nor to know any other part of demon magic."

"That could be difficult, Master. You know only those who have known the secret have been allowed to stay in the castle for more than a pair of days, for that very reason."

"I know, I know, but I believe it is essential."

"How long will we have to keep him from learning the truth?"

"I am not sure, but it should be months, if not years, until he is ready."

"It will be difficult to keep him from being able to hear the screams," Feldor said, shaking his head.

"Yes, we will have to make certain the doors to the dungeons are closed whenever a summoning is in progress. The boys are too careless with that as it is."

"Have you spoken to Jonny's roommate, Roald?"

"No, but I will have you do that after lunch. I doubt Roald has said anything to Jonny yet. He is too embarrassed by his reaction to his own initiation."

"Indeed. I will talk to Roald, the apprentices, and the journeymen. Is there anything else?"

"No. I need to begin my morning exercises. Once I have completed them, get Eleander to bring Jonny and Roald to me."

"As you wish, Master."

Chapter 8

As Jonny awoke in the sunlit room, his first thought was he had overslept and if he did not move fast, he would be beaten. Then he remembered where he was. The fright left, only to return when he remembered the previous night. He looked over to the other side of the room just as Roald began to stir. Jonny got up and looked through the cupboard, where he had found his nightshirt the previous evening, to see if he could find some clothes that fit. He did not know what clothes were there, but they could not be worse than the ones he had been wearing non-stop for the last year.

He found a plain, but clean tan shirt that fit, a brown woven vest that was a bit large and a pair of black trousers that were too long, but otherwise fit well enough. As he was putting them on, Roald woke up and started to search the floor near his bed for something to wear.

He sat to put on his trousers and looked at Jonny and said, "Did I . . . Did I scream much last night?" As soon as he asked, he looked down and was very intent on the task of putting on his shoes and socks.

Jonny waited for a second, and then said, "Yeah, I guess you did, uh scream, a bit."

"I woke you up?" Roald asked, still not looking up.

"Uh, yeah . . . But, but I was able to get right back to sleep after," Jonny lied.

"I'm sorry," Roald said looking up. "I really can't help it, and I never even remember I do it, but everyone says I scream really loud. I hope I didn't keep you awake long."

"Not long. No, uh, not long, really," Jonny said. Now, he was the one who did not want to make eye contact. "But, Roald," Jonny continued. "What *happened* to you? I mean, you were begging someone to stop something. That part was worse than the screams."

"Happened?" Roald asked. "Nothing . . . Nothing *happened*. I just, I just have bad dreams, that's all. That's all, really. You'll probably understand soon enough." Roald said all this while staring at the floor. He had finished dressing and was deliberately looking away. Jonny was sure he was lying.

"Anyway," Roald looked up brightening. "It doesn't matter, and I really need to get to the privy fast." Roald jumped up and headed out the door. Jonny figured he had until at least that evening before he had to worry about how he was going to sleep through those screams again.

§ § §

Jonny got down to the main courtyard and after visiting the privy himself headed back into the main building where they had eaten the night before to look for breakfast. When he finally found the great hall, he found it empty and cleaned. He was just coming back out to the courtyard when he saw Roald running up to him.

"There you are. Where did you go?" Roald asked.

"Well, I just thought we would be eating in the same place as last night."

"No, we only eat there on special occasions, and never for breakfast."

"Oh, so where do we eat breakfast, and what was the special occasion last night?" Jonny asked.

"You, you were the special occasion last night. The Master said he'd be bringing a new boy, and we were all to be there to greet him," Roald answered, as they walked through a doorway going back into the part of the castle where their room was located.

They turned down a corridor and entered a room with a long table going down the center with benches on either side. It was not a particularly large room and the table nearly filled all of it. There was another doorway at the far end.

Jonny dimly recognized several boys from the previous night sitting at the table. They glanced at Jonny and Roald as they entered but quickly returned to their conversations and eating. Roald led him down to the opposite doorway that led into a kitchen.

"This is the kitchen and the servant's mess. This is where all the apprentices eat normally. We eat in shifts because we can't all fit in at one time," Roald said, pointing at the cramped space. That's why we had to be in the main hall last night, so everyone could be together."

"How many apprentices are there?"

"I think there's about forty five of us right now," Roald replied, moving over to a large pot. "This is the morning porridge. You can get some of it, and there should be bread over there," he said, indicating a table to the side where several large loaves sat.

Roald scooped himself a bowl of porridge and Jonny did likewise, then Roald cut them both a large piece of bread and motioned for them to head back out into the mess. He paused just as he was about to go out through the doorway and pointed with his bread at a large slate board on the wall beside the door.

"That's the chore list. I doubt they have you on it yet, but that's where they post what chores you're assigned to each week. This week I have to clean out the stables. See there," Roald pointed to a box labeled stables. Roald's and three other names were listed there. "That tells you what you have to do. You'll find out what you're assigned to soon, I'm sure. C'mon, let's eat." With that, he went into the other room.

Jonny lingered and studied the board. He quickly saw why he had not seen any servants last night. Looking at the board, he could see that the apprentices handled nearly all the operations of the castle. They were not only there to learn magic, but to act as the serving staff that kept the place running. It made sense, but Jonny had thought being a magician's apprentice would be more, well, magical.

He asked Roald as he sat down beside him, "So the apprentices do pretty much all of the dirty work around here?"

"Yeah, you've got that right," Roald said, with food in his mouth. "If there's a nasty job that needs doing, you can bet it will be an apprentice doing it."

"So how much of your time do you actually spend learning to do magic?" It seemed like a simple question, but as soon as he asked, he could tell Roald did not want to answer.

"Well, in the beginning," Roald said, suddenly very intent on finishing his porridge, "we spend a lot of time watching others do magic and, uh, assisting them. You have to spend a fair amount of time around magic before you can really start doing it. But maybe it won't be that way for you," Roald said, his look of wariness lifting. "The Master last night said you had already shown him some magic tricks. Is that true?"

"Well," Jonny began, feeling more than a little embarrassed by the question. "I only showed The Master one trick, but he seemed really excited about it. I don't know why. It's really no big thing." Now he was looking down.

By this point, several of the other boys at the table were listening to their conversation. One of the older ones turned to Jonny and said, "Show us the trick, Jonus. We want to see what the master's new pet can do."

"My name's not Jonus, it's J—."

Jonny suddenly stopped. He was about to use his old name, his true name.

Jonny's ears burned red with shame. The mocking tone in the boy's voice said clearly he did not think Jonny could do any sort of magic. And now he had nearly tricked Jonny into giving away his true name. He wanted to sink under the table, out of sight, but knew he could not get away with that. The other boys joined in, "Yeah, c'mon, Jonny, show us all," they taunted. It was just like when Jonny was a slave.

The boy's comments had the opposite effect on Roald. Jonny could see him getting mad.

"You all just better watch out," Roald said, challenging the other boys. "I bet Jonny can do more magic now than any one of you stinking *dulls*!"

Jonny had no idea what a *dull* was, but it was obvious the other boys did not like being called that. Two of them started to get up, but the boy who had made the first comment, who seemed to be some kind of leader, motioned them to stay put.

"Well, if he's so powerful good, then he should prove it," the boy sneered.

"No problem. Go on, Jonny, show them your trick," Roald said, with the confidence of someone introducing a talking dog.

Jonny did not feel half as confident in himself as Roald seemed to be, but he figured the only way out of this situation was to show his trick. "It's not much," he began, as he dug his coin out of the pocket in his new trousers. "I just take a coin like this," he said, placing the coin on its edge on the table.

"Then I set is spinning," he said, while flicking the edge of it to start it rapidly spinning on the table.

"That's your trick?" asked the boy who had started it all. "Anyone can do that."

Jonny was staring intently at the coin, not letting it slow down. In fact, he wanted to show the boy up so much he tried to see if he could make it spin faster, and it did. After a few seconds, all the boys were staring intently at the coin as they could see it was not slowing down as they had expected it to. Instead, defying logic, the coin was spinning faster and faster. It slowly traveled across the table and stopped in front of the boy whose jaw was hanging open in amazement where it continued to spin.

"Anyone can do that," Roald mocked, sarcasm dripping from his words, "Can't they, Frank? Why, I'm sure you could show Jonny here a thing or two about how it's done, right?"

Jonny heard his cue and stopped concentrating on the coin, which immediately began to slow down. "Sure," Jonny said, trying to make it sound sincere. "Uh, Frank, could you please show me how I could do it better?"

Now it was Frank's turn to have his ears burn. He stammered for a moment then finally said, "You both just better watch out, especially you, screamer boy." He glared at Roald. "I know you and where to find you. Maybe I'll see if I can't find a reason for you to scream some more." He turned from them and got up, ears and face still bright red and headed for the door, as the coin rattled to a stop on the table. He nodded at his friends and said, "C'mon, let's go," and he left the room.

After Frank and the other boys left, Roald could not contain his happiness. "Well, you sure showed them, didn't you," he said, pounding Jonny on the back. "Did you see their faces? You'd have thought they saw a demon coming to eat them or something. They never believed you could do that, but I knew you could. I knew."

Roald bubbled on in this vein for several minutes while Jonny ate in silence. He was still embarrassed by the whole thing, and even more embarrassed by Roald's reaction to it. It was as if Roald had done the magic, not Jonny. Finally, he had enough.

"Look. It was no big thing," Jonny said, putting his coin back in his pocket. "It was just a trick. I didn't move a mountain, or blow up a castle wall, or something. I just made a coin spin. That's all. Now leave it alone."

"You just don't get it, do you?" Roald said, shaking his head. "That was serious magic. And, you did it without any props, or a demon, or anything. You made that coin spin just by looking at it. I doubt if there's anyone besides The Master in this castle who could do that the way you did."

"But what good is it?" Jonny sighed. "It's just a stupid little trick."

"Jonny. If you can do that, there are probably all sorts of other things you can do once Master Silurian shows you how. Most of the guys here will never do *any* magic on their own. Only a few can make it work at all. I can't. You can already do it, and you haven't even been taught. No wonder The Master made such a big deal about it."

It still did not seem all that amazing to Jonny, but he now saw a little of what Roald was getting at. Big or small, he had already proved he could do magic. He was just starting to believe it might be something special. But it felt so much like he wasn't doing anything strange. He just made a coin spin. No big thing.

Maybe.

Chapter 9

Roald and Jonny were just getting up to leave when a young man poked his head in the room. Jonny recognized him as one of the journeymen from the dinner the previous evening. He saw Jonny and Roald and said, "There you are. The Master just got back from his morning exercises and wants to see you both in his north study. Hurry up, and I'll go with you."

Jonny looked at Roald to see if he had any idea why he was being called back to The Master so soon. Roald just shrugged, and they both quickly put their dishes back in the kitchen and hurried out to walk with the journeyman, Eleander, over to the same study where Jonny had first met The Master.

When they got there, the door was open and Eleander walked right in and called, "Master, I found them, right where I should have looked in the first place, eating breakfast."

"Yes, yes, well that's fine, Eleander," The Master replied distractedly from his desk where there were several more books piled than Jonny had seen the previous evening. The Master was reading from a passage in one of the large dusty volumes and looked up towards Jonny.

"My boy, I have spent a good deal of time thinking and reading about that trick you showed me last night, and I believe I finally understand just what was going on."

Jonny was once again feeling embarrassed over the large fuss from his simple bit of magic.

"Jonny," The Master continued. "I need you to do your trick again for me while Eleander and I observe you, and you too, Roald. I am fairly certain what I will see, but I need to have this confirmed. It could change the way I do quite a number of things." He looked at Jonny, smiling, "Can you spin the coin and have it stay in a certain place on the table?"

Jonny nodded.

"Good, good, then please do it." He motioned for Jonny to place the coin on a large table Jonny did not remember being in the study the night before.

Jonny placed the coin and flicked it to start it spinning, but hit it wrong. It shot across and off the table. He was so nervous at having everyone watching, he was not sure he would be able to do the trick again. He muttered, "Sorry, sorry," and went to pick up the coin.

Master Silurian looked at Jonny and smiled, "It's alright, Jonny. We know you can do the trick. We just want to see how it is done. You are fine. Just go ahead."

Jonny set the coin on the table again and deliberately did not look at anyone as he started it spinning. Seeing the coin spin was enough to allow Jonny to go back to the task.

He stared at the coin, and felt the familiar feeling he associated with the trick and focused on making it spin well. After a few seconds, when he was feeling more confident, he did as he had done earlier; he concentrated on making the coin speed up. It was easier the second time. The coin was soon spinning so rapidly that it looked like a golden ball.

"That's excellent, Jonny," The Master said. "That's even better than what you showed me yesterday. Can you make it move around the table and still keep it under control?"

"Yeah, I guess so," Jonny replied, and started thinking about having the coin move across the table, as he had earlier. Slowly the coin edged to the side of the table. Once it got close to the edge, Jonny willed it back to the center.

"Wonderful, Jonny, perfect, just perfect," The Master exclaimed. "It is just as I understood, though I'd never have figured this out without seeing it. Eleander, do you see it?" he asked, turning to the journeyman.

"Alas, no, Master," Eleander said, sadly. "I see he is bending force lines, but I cannot see how he is doing it. He has no tools or props, uses no gestures, and makes no incantation. I don't understand it, but I see it happening," he said, frustration in his voice.

"His mind is the tool, my boy. Don't you see? He is moving the force lines with his mind. It is phenomenal. He is using the lost magic of Zdrell. And now I see how he is doing it, I think I could do the same."

Jonny had been listening to this exchange while still keeping the coin spinning. When he heard the last thing The Master had said, he momentarily stopped focusing on the coin and it flew across the room and bounced on the floor, rebounding off of books and chairs before it finally came to rest.

"You really didn't believe me when I said you had taught me something new, did you, Jonny?" The Master asked, chuckling. "Yes, it is true. Even one as old as I, still feel like I have so much to learn. And you, yes you, will be my teacher, as I will be yours."

"But, Master, it is only a coin, a trick . . ." Jonny pleaded.

"Only a trick?" Master Silurian snorted. "Jonny, Eleander here is one of the more talented journeymen I've had in the last several years, and he could not duplicate your *trick*. He has enough talent to see what you are doing, but he has no idea how he would go about doing it himself, do you, Eleander?" The Master said, turning to look at the journeyman.

Eleander bowed his head and said softly, "No, my master. I could not do this myself and can see no value in creating an incantation or invoking a demon to do it for me."

"You see?" The Master said turning back to Jonny. "Eleander is a competent wizard, nearly ready to become a master, and he couldn't do what you already can. This is most significant."

"Roald," The Master called to Jonny's friend who had been sitting at the side of the room. "Fetch Jonny's coin from the floor over there. It is time I put my enlarged understanding to a test." He turned and winked at Jonny. "We'll see if the old man here can do as well as his apprentice. Maybe I can even teach you a thing or two," he said laughing.

He was laughing, but Jonny sensed there was an edge under the joviality, and it worried him.

"Now set it up on the table and get it spinning like Jonny did," The Master said to Roald.

"I can start it, Master, but I don't know anything about keeping it going," Roald said, with a quaver in his voice.

"That's all I ask, boy. I should be the one to keep it spinning this time," The Master said. He paused as Roald set the coin up. "Start it spinning, boy. Spin it fast," The Master said, excitement in his voice.

Roald flicked the edge of the coin and it spun true. Suddenly without warning, the coin slued sideways and shot off the table as if it had been kicked.

"Arrgh, I almost had it," said The Master, with disgust in his voice. "Well, I suppose it wasn't a bad first try." He grunted. "Roald, set it up and let's try it again."

Jonny was awe struck. Here was the greatest wizard in the land, and he was having trouble with Jonny's trick. Not only that, but he did not get it on the second or the third tries either. On the fourth attempt, it spun for a moment and then fell. Finally, on the fifth attempt the coin spun in place for over a minute.

"There, I believe I've got it now," The Master said, panting slightly. "Yes, I think I have this now. Let me rest a moment and we'll see if I can repeat it." He got up from his chair, walked to the window, and stared out for a moment.

"Jonny, I foresee great things for you, and great danger as well," The Master said, still looking out the window. "Yes, I will have to train you as I've not trained anyone in over one hundred years. There is no time to waste, none at all."

He turned from the window and sat in his chair again. "All right, Roald," The Master sighed. "Let's do it once again." Roald started the coin spinning and The Master closed his eyes. "Yes," he said. "I should have thought of this earlier." He smiled. "Yes, I do have it now."

The coin, which had been spinning, now began to speed up. It initially stayed in the same spot then slowly started moving around the table. First, it moved in a circle. Then it described a square. Then it started to move in a figure eight. Master Silurian chuckled. "Watch this, boys." As he said this, the coin continued spinning as it left the table. It moved slowly higher and higher until it was more than four feet above the table.

"Hah," The Master chuckled, now obviously enjoying himself. "I told you I could show you a trick or two there, Jonny." The coin now moved in the air until it stopped in front of Jonny. "Hold out your hand."

Jonny slowly reached out his hand and held it palm up in front of him. The coin, which had been spinning in front of him abruptly stopped spinning but continued to hang suspended as if by some invisible wire. Then, suddenly, the coin dropped into Jonny's hand. He nearly dropped it he was so startled.

"There you have your coin back, Jonny," The Master said, opening his eyes and smiling warmly at him. "I would have paid many gold coins to have learned that trick years ago. Ah well, better late than never, right?"

No one said anything. The three young men seemed stunned by what they had witnessed. The Master looked at each of them and laughed. "You are all so solemn. You look as if someone died. This is a time to celebrate. It's not every day I come across something this wonderful," he said with real feeling.

"No, I know what you need. You need to get out and play a bit, yes that is it," The Master said to Roald. "Roald, you and Jonny are released from any duties for the rest of the day. Go and show Jonny all the places you boys play when you should be doing your lessons or chores. Get out now, the both of you. Eleander and I have things to discuss."

He motioned for them to leave. Roald did not hesitate, and Jonny followed.

Chapter 10

"Was that really zdrell, you and Jonny did, Master?" Eleander asked, after the younger boys had left.

"It was indeed, Eleander." The Master stared off into space.

"But, I thought it was a lost art."

"It is, or was until now."

"How is it, you can do it now, Master, when you couldn't before with all your studies and experience?"

The Master chuckled, tiredly. "I can do it, because I've seen it. It is not so terribly hard, once you see it, but you are mistaken if you think I can really do it."

"But that coin, it just flew."

"The coin was nothing, Eleander. With no training, Jonny could do nearly as well, and I doubt those boys knew how much energy it cost me to do that. I shall have to rest the remainder of the day, just to recuperate. I doubt Jonny felt tired by it at all."

"So what does this mean, Master?"

"What indeed? This changes many things, and it could not have come at a better time. Yes, it changes many things," he said, still staring into space.

§ § §

"Did you see that?" Roald said excitedly as soon as they left the room. "The way that coin just flew up off the table like it had wings. And then, the way it stopped spinning right there in front of you and dropped. Wow!"

"Yeah," Jonny said, though not with the enthusiasm Roald had. "That was really great."

Jonny was not thinking about the last part. He was still thinking about the four times The Master had tried before he got the hang of Jonny's trick. It still amazed him that The Master had needed to work to learn the trick.

In a way, it scared him.

Roald was oblivious to Jonny's discomfort. "This is the best, Jonny," he began. "Not only do we get to spend the morning watching some of the most prodigious magic I've ever seen, but we get the rest of the day to play!" He practically danced down the steps out into the main courtyard. Then he suddenly stopped. "We better go tell Lord Feldor The Master gaveus the day off, or we'll be put to work."

They went to the steward's office where Feldor sat at his desk. He looked skeptical as Roald told him what The Master had said. Then he looked at each of them for a moment and said, "Very well, I accept your story, Roald. But you know what the penalty will be if you are making any of this up."

Roald started to look a little bit worried, but then he brightened. "Sir, I swear to you, The Master truly did give us the day off. You can check with him if you want."

"I shall not trouble Master Silurian with this now. He has other concerns. Nevertheless, that does not mean I will not talk to him about it eventually. You have both been warned," he said, with a stern stare at each of them. "Go on, both of you. Get out before I change my mind," he said as he looked down to the papers he had been reading when they entered.

"C'mon, let's go," Roald said, and they both ran out of the office.

They spent the rest of the day, with Roald showing Jonny all the different parts of the castle and then the woods up the hill from the west side of the walls. Twice older apprentices, who obviously wanted to put them to work, challenged them. Roald clearly loved telling them how they were at liberty on The Master's order and that Feldor would verify this. Both times when The Master and Feldor's names were invoked, the boys backed down. The two had a thoroughly fun time all afternoon and into the evening. Feldor only required Roald to run some errand without Jonny at lunch time. Jonny took the opportunity to take a nap.

Finally, Jonny asked, "Don't you think we'd better get back or we'll miss dinner, won't we?"

"Nah," Roald replied. "Dinner's not usually a formal affair like last night. Unless you get invited, you eat in the mess just like we did for breakfast. That means scut boys like us eat last, after the big fellows have eaten and cleared out. It's easier to avoid trouble if you wait till later."

"Do you get into trouble very often?" Jonny asked. He was still curious about some of Roald's dark hints.

"Not very often now," Roald replied. "When I first got here, I swear that was all I got into. I didn't have anyone to tell me what to do or anything and it was . . . bad, for a while," he said with a shudder. "But that's all past now. And I'll make sure things go well for you, Jonny. Friends?" he asked, grabbing Jonny lightly by the forearm.

"Friends forever," Jonny replied, grabbing Roald's forearm as well.

"Let's go eat," Roald said. "I'll make sure no one messes with you."

"Sure," Jonny laughed. "You can do the fighting for us both," he joked as they walked slowly back into the castle.

§ § §

Dinner was uneventful. The food was mostly gone, but there were more than enough scraps for them to eat their fill. For Jonny, even those scraps were wonderful. For the last two years, he could not recall two days in a row when he went to bed with a full stomach.

As they headed up to their room, Jonny's thoughts turned again to trying to sleep with Roald's screams. "Do you, um, scream, ah, every night, Roald?" he asked as they entered the room.

Roald did not look happy to have to talk about it. "Really, I don't know. I know I wake everybody else up, but I almost never wake up myself. As a matter of fact, it's usually when I don't scream that I wake up." He turned away and looked at the floor. "On the nights when I don't scream that's usually because I'm having nightmares, and they wake me up, but I usually don't scream."

"Roald, what happened to you?" Jonny asked, unable to contain the question any longer. "I mean, you don't just scream. You beg for someone not to do something to you. What happened?"

Roald spun around and looked at Jonny for just a moment with hate in his eyes, then the look faded, replaced by some kind of shame. When he spoke, Jonny could tell he was holding back tears, and the effort made him sound mad at Jonny. "I—don't—want—to—talk about it! I, . . . there's nothing anyone can do about it now. It's in the past. Just leave it alone."

"Alright," Jonny said, holding up his hands. "If you don't want to talk about it, that's Okay. I just thought, since we were friends, we could talk about those kinds of things. But if you don't want to, that's okay. I didn't mean to get you mad."

Now Roald did begin to cry, not loud, just little shuddering gasps. "I'm sorry, Jonny. I didn't mean to get mad at you, but I can't even think about it. It just hurts too much."

"That's all right," Jonny said, unsure of what to do. "If I'd have known it would get to you so much, I wouldn't have brought it up." He sighed, "But if you ever do feel like talking about it, I'll listen."

"Thanks, Jonny," Roald said, now mostly over his tears. "You're the best friend I've ever had. Someday, I probably will tell you. Some other time, yeah." He started throwing off his clothes. "I guess we better get to bed. Who knows what tomorrow will be like? I doubt it will be half as much fun as today."

"Yeah, that's probably true," Jonny said as he started to change his clothes. "I sure hope we get to see more magic tomorrow. That was great."

"Well, don't get your hopes up, Jonny. Today we saw more magic than I've ever seen in a single day except for once when one of the apprentices was performing to become a journeyman. Most days you're lucky if you see any magic at all," he said as he got into bed.

"Huh. I never thought of it before exactly, but I thought wizards went around doing magic all the time. I mean, they're wizards, that's what they do, right?"

"Maybe the master wizards do stuff all the time, but not from what I've seen," Roald said scrunching down in his bed. He yawned. "After all, magic takes effort and there's a price to pay to do anything by magic. So you're not going to run around just doing it for no reason, are you?"

Jonny was puzzled. "What do you mean, a price to pay? There's no price I pay when I spin a coin," Jonny said with an exasperated tone.

"Well, that's different," Roald said, clearly not wanting to talk about it right then. "Your magic's different, not like most others, but I'm sure there's some way you pay." He rolled over in bed. "You'll see what I mean soon enough. Now I *really* want to go to sleep. Good night."

Jonny lay there very puzzled by the whole conversation since dinner. It seemed every time he asked a simple question Roald got upset and did not want to talk about it. So far, his whole experience here had been as if he was living in a dream. He felt like at any moment he would wake up and find himself back as a slave again.

On the other hand, there was much here he just did not understand. He guessed that was to be expected. After all, he had never even thought about what it must be like to be a wizard. Now, he was training to be one.

Nevertheless, there were all thesestories in the market place. After the way Feldor had reacted, he had first thought they must all be just stories made up to frighten people. Now, he was not so sure. What if there was some truth to the stories and, they had just been exaggerated. How do you exaggerate being eaten alive by a demon? Every question he asked just left him with two more questions. He guessed he would just have to wait and watch.

By the time he had finally come to this conclusion, Roald had been asleep for some time. Jonny decided he would just wrap his pillow around his head and hope he could get more sleep this night than he had the last. As soon as he had made up his mind to do this, he fell asleep.

Chapter 11

He woke the next morning to Roald shaking him. He had not stirred the entire night.

"Come on, get up," Roald said, pulling on Jonny's arm. "We've got to get down to breakfast fast before the older apprentices get there!"

"I thought it was best to wait them out," Jonny asked as he threw back the covers and started changing into the clothes he had worn the previous day.

"That's for dinner," Roald said, while putting on his shoes. "For breakfast you have to get in fast, eat and get out before they show up, or you'll get nothing. And just as likely you'll end up having to do all the dishes." Roald stood up and looked impatiently at the door. "I'll head down now. Follow quick and I'll save us both a space. But don't waste time or we'll be too late." Jonny watched Roald go as he hastily finished putting on his clothes.

Jonny hurried out and down the stairs as fast as he could. He got into the mess just as Roald was moving out of the kitchen with two bowls loaded with food. "There you are," he said, setting a bowl down in front of him. "It's a little late, but if we eat fast we should be able to get out of here before, . . . oh no, not again," Roald said as he looked over Jonny's shoulder at the door he had just entered through.

Jonny turned to look, and saw why Roald was so distressed. The boy who had challenged Jonny the previous morning, Frank, and his cronies were just coming in.

"Have a good scream last night," Frank said laughing to his companions. "No?" he continued. "Well maybe he just wet himself and did it quietly." Frank's friends laughed as Roald's face turned bright red. "Yep, that's it," Frank continued. "Just look at his face, he wet his bed again. That's our little Rolly boy. He either screams enough to wake the dead, or he pisses all over himself. I *almost* feel sorry for his roommate," he said, shaking his head in mock dismay.

Roald had gotten more and more red in the face. Jonny could see he really wanted to say something cutting back to Frank, but he just did not have the words. Or maybe he was so mad he could not say anything at all. Jonny thought that if Frank's friends had not been there, Roald would have tried to fight him, even though Frank was more than a foot taller than Roald and probably outweighed him by more than forty pounds. As it was, Roald's obvious frustration just gave Frank and his friends more to talk about.

"Let's just eat and ignore them," Jonny said to Roald. "They're just blowhards anyhow." Jonny held Roald's gaze until he nodded and started to eat, still without having said a word. Jonny looked down and started to quickly eat his food when he heard a sound and saw Frank come up to stand beside him.

"I heard what you said to your bed wetter friend," Frank said with a dangerous quiet tone. "You said me and my friends are blowhards," he continued, still quietly. "If you take that back real fast, say you're really sorry, and promise to do our dishes for the next month, we might just forget your having said that. Otherwise," he paused dramatically. "we're going to have to pound you and your screaming little friend till you won't be able to walk. And don't think spinning a coin is gonna save you."

Jonny looked up at him and was strangely unafraid. This was just like his life had been as a slave. The insults and threats were nearly identical

He looked up at Frank and smiled. Trying to sound more confident than he felt, he said to Frank, "I don't think so, Frank. I don't think I'll apologize, since what I said was true. You and your friends are a bunch of blowhards. You're just like the bullies I knew in the marketplace before I came here. Except, they were usually a bit more creative with their insults."

Now, it was Frank's time to turn red, not from embarrassment, but in anger. "Not quick enough with the insults, am I?" he growled. "I'll show you an insult all right, you little squirrel face," he said as he grabbed at Jonny's arm.

Jonny expected the grab and threw his bowl into Frank's face just as Frank was reaching for him. It was still half full and splashed Frank full across his head and chest. He screamed with rage and lunged for Jonny who was already running for the door.

Jonny ran for all he was worth in the confined space. He just cleared the door when his shirt pulled him to a stop. Frank had hold of it. He yanked Jonny halfway through the doorway and wrapped a large arm around Jonny's throat, when he suddenly loosened up.

"What's going on here?" a voice boomed.

Frank let go.

Jonny turned to look and saw Eleander, the journeyman from yesterday's session, standing there.

"I said, someone better tell me what is going on here," Eleander said with an edge to cut metal.

"We were just playing a little game is all," Frank began, but Eleander would have none of it.

"Really, Frank? You'll have to tell me what kind of game this is where you get porridge all over your head and then choke new apprentices. I played a lot of games when I was an apprentice, but I don't recall a game like this one. Do tell me how it's played," he said, sarcasm coloring every word.

"Well, I, . . . ah," Frank stammered.

"Don't even bother, Frank. I know just the sort of game you're playing. And it looks like young Jonny here managed to give you a lot more than you expected. But I don't have time to deal with this. You're on scullery duty for the next month. And don't protest, or I'll talk to Feldor, and he'll see you get something worse. Jonny and Roald are to come with me right now. The Master doesn't like to be kept waiting.

"Clean up this mess, and you would be wise to not pick on young apprentices again or you may have to deal with me," Eleander said, with a low dangerous tone.

The whole time Eleander had been talking, Frank had been seething. Twice he had opened his mouth to say something, but Eleander never gave him a chance. Jonny knew that as soon as Frank had a chance, he would be out to even the score.

Chapter 12

For the second time in as many days, Jonny found himself personally escorted to The Master. From what Roald had told him, this was very different from what normally happened to new apprentices. Jonny could also tell that The Master seemed pleased to have an apprentice who came with talent. Jonny got the distinct impression it was unusual.

Eleander talked to Jonny as he escorted both boys to a different part of the main keep than Jonny had been in before. "It looks to me like Frank really has it in for you, Jonny." He grinned. "It also looks like you might have been able to handle him, even without my help," he chuckled. "Frank is used to being bigger than the other boys and hasn't had anyone to put him in his place for a long time. A pity. I used to do it regularly when I first came to the castle as a journeyman. But, you should watch out for him. He's going to be looking for an opportunity to come after you again. He won't be able to attack directly, but you had best watch your back."

"Why won't he be able to attack directly?" Roald asked. Jonny had been wondering the same thing.

"Because you two are now under a *special status*," Eleander answered. "All the boys will hear about it tonight. It won't make you any friends, but it will ensure the usual bullying and such that go with being an apprentice will pass you by."

Jonny did not know what special status meant, but evidently, Roald did. He looked stunned. "But why?"

Eleander laughed as they came to a landing in the long spiral staircase they had been climbing. "Well, it's not because of your good looks, Roald. No, The Master has special plans for Jonny, and you have the good luck to be his only friend here right now. He wanted Jonny to have a friend so of course you're covered too."

"What does special status mean?" Jonny asked.

"It mostly means you will do what The Master asks of you, and nothing else, it is normally only applied to The Master's brightest students," Eleander said with a grimace. "It means you won't do the chores or scut work most apprentices do. But trust me, that just means you'll work even harder for The Master, and I should know," he snorted.

Eleander opened the door at the edge of the landing, and motioned the boys to go in. Inside was another study similar to the one where Jonny had met The Master previously, but it looked like it had not seen nearly so much use. It had one long window looking out on the hills. There was only one bookcase, partially filled with books and a large dark wooden table with four chairs around it. Master Silurian sat in one of the chairs, reading. As the boys entered the room, he closed his book and stood.

He took the book and placed it in the bookshelf, and then pulled a long plain dagger from his robe and placed it on the table. "Good morning, boys. I hope you are ready to work. You had your fun yesterday, so now we will make you pay for your fun," The Master said with a grin.

Jonny turned to Roald. He had heard a sharp intake of breath from his friend when The Master said they would have to pay. Roald's eyes were glued on the dagger and even in the light of the room, Jonny could see he had gone pale and was breathing in short gasps.

The Master noticed this too. "Calm down, Roald," he said smiling at him. "No pain for you today. In fact, unless you can do better than Eleander here, you may have a very boring day in front of you. Though, I think you'd prefer that to shoveling out the stables, ah?"

The Master turned to Jonny. "Up till this point you have been the teacher here," he began. "That all changes today. I have read quite a lot about the type of magic that you are doing. It is called *zdrell*, an old and almost lost art. I am now clear on how to proceed in training you. We will get to see how quick a study you are. It should be interesting, though I think it could be the hardest thing you have ever done."

"I'm ready, Master," Jonny began, "or at least I think I am."

"Sit down, all of you," The Master said. "Jonny, you are to sit in the end seat." After everyone sat, The Master picked up the dagger and said, "Jonny I want to show you a variation on your coin trick and see if you can do it." Jonny nodded.

The Master took the dagger and placed it point down on the table, holding it vertical with one finger on the end of the hilt. He then took hold of the end flange of the guard and flipped it rapidly setting the dagger spinning on its tip in a similar fashion to which Jonny had spun his coin. The point of the dagger dug slightly into the wood, but the wood seemed hard enough to keep it from doing more than making a small divot.

The Master sat concentrating on the spinning dagger and it continued to spin for nearly a minute. Suddenly, it stopped, but continued to stand on its point, motionless. Then, just as suddenly, it fell and lay with its point facing towards Jonny.

Everyone stared at the knife as if it might suddenly sprout legs and walk across the table. Jonny said, "Master, that was amazing. That was so much better than my little trick."

"Jonny," The Master replied looking at him steadily. "I expect you to be able to do that and better, soon."

"What? No, no," Jonny stammered. "I couldn't possibly do something like that."

The Master banged his hand down hard on the table. Everyone jumped in surprise. "I will not hear such talk. What you just saw is essentially the same thing you can do with a coin. You *can* do it, and you *will* do it!" The Master's voice grew even more intense. "You will not leave this room until you can at least get this knife to spin. Have I made myself clear?" he asked, pinning Jonny with his stare.

Jonny gulped, at first unable to make a sound. He nodded his head and then stammered, "Yes, ah yes, Master. I understand. I will try," he said staring at the table.

Again, The Master was not happy with Jonny's response and his voice showed great displeasure. "No. You will not *try*, Jonny. You will *do* this. You are completely capable of *doing* this, so you will not leave until you can. Do—you—understand?"

"Yes, Master . . . I will, I will work at it till I can do it," he said, still not wanting to meet The Master's gaze.

"Good," The Master said. He stood up and nodded to Eleander. "Come, Eleander. We have much to do." Eleander rose and followed The Master out of the room. Jonny and Roald both sat staring at the dagger dumbfounded of what to do.

Chapter 13

Outside on the landing The Master sagged against the wall. He was breathing in gasps that slowly returned to normal. "Eleander, how did it look in there?"

"Very good, Master," Eleander replied, trying not to stare at The Master's weakness. "I couldn't tell at all how much effort it was taking for you to do that, and I knew it must be costing you. I'm sure those boys don't have any idea how difficult it was for you to make it look so effortless."

"They must not know," The Master said, starting to regain some of his composure. "If Jonny does not think effort should be required, then he will strive to work at it until it is easy for him. If he saw how much this cost me, he would never achieve his full potential.

"Everything I have found out about wizards who have had zdrell talent is that they can do truly amazing things with virtually no effort, no cost, on their part. I want Jonny to develop his talent this way. If he can do this, he has the potential of being one of the most powerful wizards of this age."

"Yes, Master. I agree," Eleander said. "Still, talent or no, you did amazingly well in there."

"Yes, I suppose I did," chuckled The Master. "I wish I'd learned this trick years ago. It changes everything. However, I also see why so few can do it. It is hard to learn, and well-nigh impossible to teach."

"Master," Eleander asked. "Why didn't you share what you've learned in your research with Jonny? Surely it would speed up his learning."

"Not at all. Everything I have learned about this is that those with talent work best if they are *not* told how to do it. Can you explain to a baby how to walk, how to sit up, or stand? No, he has just seen it *can* be done, and that is all he needs. He will have to work out how to do it for himself, and I have every confidence that he will.

"Do make sure lunch is brought up to them, and dinner if need be. Check on them every hour or two. Make sure they are actively working on the problem and not just sitting around. I believe I am going to lie down for a few hours. I have been getting too little sleep of late, and that demonstration wore me out."

"I will do as you ask, Master," Eleander replied. "Do you mind if I stay in there and watch some of the time?"

"You may stay and watch if you say nothing other than to let Jonny know he has to work it out for himself. Till later, Eleander," Master Silurian said, and left for his bedchamber.

§ § §

"So what do we do now?" Roald asked.

"I guess we work at it till I can make it spin," Jonny said. "Either that or we learn to sleep on a stone floor."

"Can you really do it, Jonny? I mean that was amazing how The Master made that thing spin and then stopped it cold. And the way it fell down pointing at you. That was just sooo prodigious."

"I don't know. I mean, The Master said I could, so I guess I should be able to do it, though I don't have any idea how. I guess we just set it up and do it like he did."

Jonny set up the dagger and flicked the guard. The dagger barely moved. "Hmmm, I guess that's why he grabbed the edge of the guard to make it spin." Jonny grabbed the guard, tried to flip it, and only succeeded in knocking it loose from his hand and sending it spinning across the table at Roald.

"Hey, watch out what you're doing," he said as he jumped back from the table.

"Fine," Jonny said. "If you think you can do better, then you try it."

"But I'm not the one with the talent."

"Yeah, then why don't you just back off and let me try."

He picked up the dagger and tried again with equally poor results. He tried five more times without any more success. He sighed.

"Roald, what am I doing wrong? I can't even get the thing started to spin. This isn't working."

"How should I know?" Roald asked, obviously frustrated as well. "You're the one with the trick. I can't make anything spin. How do you do it when you spin the coin?"

"Well," Jonny replied, thinking. "I sort of feel the coin. Not really like you feel it in your hand, but like I feel it in my head, and, then I just . . . kind of push it in my head and it spins."

"So can you feel the dagger?"

"No," Jonny said, clearly perplexed. "I guess I never really tried to feel it, or anything else for that matter before except for coins. I wonder if I can." He squinted at the dagger. "Hmmm, hmmm . . . No, I just don't feel anything. What am I going to do?"

"I don't know Jonny, but I don't want to be sleeping on the floor up here tonight, so you need to figure it out."

"Yeah, but *how* do I do it?"

"If I knew that, I'd be the one The Master was in love with," Roald replied, sadly.

Chapter 14

An hour later when Eleander came into the room to check on them, Jonny and Roald were no closer to making the dagger spin. They were scarcely talking to one another. He knew unless something changed they would never make any progress.

As he watched Jonny and Roald, he knew he had to do something; he just had to make sure he did not give him any direct *help*, or he would incur The Master's wrath.

"So how's it going?" Eleander asked, trying to sound cheerful, even though things looked bad. Jonny sat looking at the table, toying with the dagger and did not answer. "That well, huh?" Eleander said, trying to at least get him talking.

"Oh, it's going just swell," Roald answered from the floor where he sat toying with some loose grout between the stones. "See how Jonny's got the knife spinning?" he said, gesturing to the table. "It spins so well, it looks like it's just sitting there."

Eleander could see that they were stuck, but he was starting to be frustrated with the boys' attitude. "I told you this wouldn't be easy work. I warned you that working for The Master directly would be about the hardest thing you have ever done in your whole life."

"But you didn't tell me he'd ask me to do an impossible thing and then walk off and not bother to give me any idea on how to do it," Jonny said, looking up at last.

"He might as well have asked me to move the whole castle with a spade. I don't know how to do this! I don't even know how I do it when I spin the coin. I just do it. How am I supposed to make a dagger spin when I can't even get it to spin without magic?" Jonny shouted in exasperation.

Eleander knew he had to tread a fine line here. He decided asking a question could not be construed as giving him an answer. "Jonny," he asked. "Do you have any idea how you make the coin spin?"

"No," Jonny answered gruffly. "I just do it. That's it." He glared at Eleander.

"So, don't you think it might be a good idea to forget about the knife until you've figured out how you make the coin spin? Then you might be able to see how the coin and the dagger are alike and use that knowledge to make it spin too?" Eleander asked carefully.

"But how can I figure out how I do it, when I don't know?" Jonny moaned.

"You told The Master you could spin different coins, didn't you?" Eleander asked, hoping he was not being too obvious.

"Yeah, I can spin different coins," Jonny answered, with slightly less belligerence. "What difference does that make?"

"Well," Eleander began, trying not to let Jonny see he was leading him. "I can't do what you do, but if you could compare what it's like to spin several different coins and see what they have in common, it might help you see what it is that lets you spin them."

"Yeah," Jonny said, starting to get excited. "Maybe if I—"As quickly as he had become excited, Jonny lost the spark. "But I don't have a bunch of different coins to use," he sighed. "That won't work."

"Maybe you could take something shaped like a coin and spin it instead, Jonny," Roald said. He started to get excited too. "I've been playing with these loose bits of stone here and trying to spin them cause I was so bored. Some of them spin pretty good even though I've got no magic to keep them going."

"Sure," Jonny said, excited again. "That could work. My biggest problem with this dumb knife is I can't get it to spin on its point at all, magic or no magic."

Eleander felt like they were past the roadblock and decided to get out before he influenced them any further. But he had to try one more thing. He reached into his pouch. "That's a really good idea there, Roald. Jonny, you should try it, and," he brought out four coins of different sizes and metals and set them on the table. "You might also want to try using these too, if the stone idea doesn't work out."

"Wow, thanks Eleander," Jonny said.

"Just make sure you don't lose them. That's a lot of money for me. I'll expect it back later."

"Sure, sure," Jonny said, staring at the money. "I'll guard it with my life. This could be just the thing. Thank you, thank you so much."

"That's all right, Jonny. We may not even have to tell The Master about this, if you figure it out fast enough. Good luck," he said, and went out the door before Jonny could even ask him any questions.

§ § §

When he came back nearly two hours later, Eleander was very anxious to see what had happened. He was a little concerned he had gone too far in leading Jonny to see what to him was an obvious approach to figuring out how to accomplish the task The Master had set him.

One of the reasons Eleander had ended up staying in magic was he could see the kind of method needed to solve a problem. His logical attitude had won his previous Master's interest and eventually with that and a little talent, though not much, he had progressed until he was a journeyman. Now he was nearly ready to go before the board of wizards to become a master.

The atmosphere when he entered the room this time was completely different. The boys both excitedly started talking to him at once as soon as he came through the door. He had to calm them down in order to figure out what either of them was saying. "Slow down both of you," he said, waving his hands. "One at a time."

Jonny nodded at Roald. "Well, we did what you said, and Jonny tried spinning a bunch of things. We started with the rocks I'd been messing with. I would spin them and then Jonny would keep them going."

"Yeah," Jonny continued. "It took me a bunch of tries before I could get one of the rocks to spin like a coin, but finally, I figured it out."

"And then," Roald picked up the story. "Jonny started to spin those coins you let us borrow, and boy he could really make those spin!"

"After the rocks, the coins were really easy," Jonny enthused. "Each of them feels different, but sort of the same."

"Yeah," Roald jumped in. "Jonny even got so he could keep two of them spinning at the same time!"

"Hmm," Eleander said. "I'm sure The Master would like to see that."

"But the best part," Roald said, "happened just before you came in. Jonny got the dagger to spin!"

"Really," Eleander said, impressed because he had just thought it would take longer. "How did you do it, Jonny?"

"It was really Roald's idea," Jonny began. "He should be the one to tell you."

Eleander turned to Roald, who suddenly looked bashful. "So what was your idea, Roald?"

"Well, after Jonny spun the coins and the rocks, he said he could kind of feel the knife to make it spin, but the problem was we didn't know how to make it spin at all. We tried all kinds of ways of holding it, but when you flip it, it just falls over. It's not like a coin. It won't stand on its point. That was what gave me the idea; it was like some of the rocks I'd been playing with. You have to put it with one point down and hold the top with just the tip of your finger Then you can rub your other finger on the edge to get it to spin fast enough to stand.

"So we tried that with the dagger, but it's flat on the sides so you can't spin it by rubbing against it like my rocks. We couldn't make it spin fast enough so when we let it go it would still stay up."

"Then Roald had an idea," Jonny jumped in. "He asked me if it had to already be spinning for me to make it spin. I'd never tried before, but I had let coins get real slow and then sped them up so that was what we did. Roald held the dagger really light with the tip of his finger and I started it spinning while he held it. Then when it was going fast enough he took his finger off and it stayed up!" Jonny beamed and so did Roald.

"So show me," Eleander said. He was really hoping they were telling the truth. Their excitement was contagious.

"Okay," Jonny said, pointing. "Set it up, Roald."

Roald eagerly took the knife and put it point down in the center of the table. He held it up with only the tip of his index finger. "Ready!"

Jonny took a deep breath and stared intently at the knife. For a moment he closed his eyes then said, "That's it," and opened them. Almost immediately, there was movement from the dagger. It began to turn under Roald's finger. It started slow, but soon turned faster and faster. It kept accelerating until it was only a blur. As it had sped up, Roald had placed less and less force on it, until now he took his finger off the knife entirely and it stood spinning in place.

It continued to spin, not moving because it was cutting a small indentation in the surface of the table. Eleander let out a breath he had not known he had been holding. "Wow, Jonny," he said beaming. "That's great. The Master is going to be very impressed. How long can you keep it going?"

"Not much longer," Jonny replied, still gazing steadily at the knife. "This is harder to do than coins, but I think it's easier this time than the last. Roald grab it so it doesn't go shooting out like last time."

Roald moved forward and put his hand directly above the spinning hilt of the knife, then reached down and grabbed it in a quick gesture as Jonny signaled, "Now!"

Jonny relaxed his gaze and stretched. "Last time when I stopped concentrating, it was still spinning pretty fast and it shot off the table and bounced off the wall."

"Yeah, it nearly killed me," Roald griped. "If I'd been two feet to the left of where I was, I think it would have gone right through me. I wish it weren't so sharp." He stood looking at the knife, shook his head and sat down.

"So what do you think?" Jonny asked anxiously.

"I think The Master is going to be very impressed with both of you," Eleander said. "Yes, I'd say he's going to be very pleased indeed. I think you exceeded anything he expected. You've been working at it no more than half the day and you already accomplished what he wanted, and I think more.

"I fully expected to be coming up here tonight with your dinners and bedding, but I guess I won't be needing to do that now," he laughed. "Could you show me that bit where you spin two coins at once, Jonny? I think The Master is going to be interested to see that one too."

"Sure, it's not really all that different than doing one. I just kind of focus back and forth between the two." He took a coin and started it spinning. "Roald, start one of the others," he said still looking at the coin he had started and making it spin faster and faster.

Roald took one of the larger coins and flicked it spinning. "There you go, Jonny."

Jonny glanced over at the second coin and it began to accelerate. He looked back at the first coin and made it speed up again. He continued to look back and forth between the two coins, shifting his attention from one to the other. After a couple of minutes he sighed and let both of the coins slow down and drop.

"Oy, that's work," he said. "When we did it the first time they were closer together and it wasn't so hard. When they're that far apart it's a lot harder."

"I'd say you both have more than earned your lunch," Eleander said as he brought a sack up to the table that the boys in their excitement had not seen. He started to take bread, cheese and sausage out of the bag. As soon as they saw the food, they both started eating quickly.

Roald, with his mouth full of cheese said, "I'll show you what this knife is really good for." He took the dagger and started to cut the sausage into chunks so he could more easily get them in his mouth.

"Slow down you two," Eleander said chuckling. "If you eat too fast, I'll have to explain to The Master how I let his prize apprentice die choking on a piece of sausage. Don't worry. I've already had lunch and there's no one else to eat the food so you might as well enjoy it. You've earned it."

§ § §

After they had finished eating and sat for a few minutes relaxing, Eleander looked at them both and said, "The Master will be very interested in seeing this, but he said he would be busy all afternoon. He let me know that in the unlikely event you two figured out how to spin the dagger before dinner you could go to the creek and swim, after you've practiced to be sure you can perform after all."

Roald jumped up and shouted, "Yes! That's great. I never get liberty when the weather is good."

"Didn't we have liberty just yesterday?" Jonny asked, smiling.

"Not like this," Roald replied. "Anyway, don't you want to get out of this stuffy castle and have some fun?"

"Sure."

"Then I would suggest you *practice* a bit more," Eleander said. "Then go off to the creek and have your swim. The Master will want to see you after dinner." He paused, then added, "And dinner will be in the great hall again tonight. Someone very important is visiting, and The Master wants everyone there. You both are lucky enough not to have to serve. I wish I'd been that lucky when I was an apprentice," he said, with a sigh.

He turned to leave, "Just be sure you can do it *well* Jonny. You may have more of an audience than The Master tonight." He left the boys looking a little more concerned, but still happy.

Chapter 15

Jonny practiced for more than an hour, with Roald's help. He got so he could spin the knife easily, but always had to have it held to start. He tried holding it himself, and having Roald do it. He even managed one time to keep the dagger spinning while spinning a coin. After he tried it one last time, with Roald yelling and running around the room and banging on the table to try to distract him, Jonny decided he was ready and they went off to swim.

By the time they got to where the creek that ran by the castle widened into a swimming pond, they only had about an hour to swim. They both thoroughly enjoyed playing in the water and were refreshed and hungry when they headed back to the castle. They changed into fresh clothes to be ready for dinner and headed down to the great hall to see who The Master's guest would be.

§ § §

"What's the matter, Silurian?" Alira, the wizard's wife asked. "You're stomping around here like someone put sour milk in your tea."

"I can't figure out why Boregond is here," he said as finished taking off his work robes.

"He said we were just on the way, didn't he?" Alira sat mending one of the apprentice's shirts.

"Yes, he said that, but I think there has to be more to it. He might be trying to poach some of my journeyman." He stood in front of his wardrobe deciding what to wear. "Or maybe he's trying to size up the support I'm getting from the other local wizards.

"Who knows, he might even be trying to see if he can find or create some discord in Salaways?" Silurian finished putting on the robe he selected and started looking for suitable hose.

"But I thought he was one of your favorite journeymen, when he stayed here?"

"He was." Silurian bent to put on his hose. "One of the most talented journeymen I've seen in the last hundred years, but that was before he threw in with the demon wizards; more go to them every year. What a waste." He stomped as he put on his shoes. "He is too talented to be working with that lot. I don't understand it, and I don't trust him any more. I'm not sure I ever should have."

"Well, he's here now. Try not to antagonize him. Show him the courtesy you would any visiting master. I doubt he'll stay long."

"No doubt, my old weidge," Silurian said, as he leaned down to peck his wife on the cheek. "He will stay just long enough to accomplish whatever underhanded deed he must be planning. I'll try not to irritate him too much, but I think I might just make him think a bit when he sees Jonny tonight." He grinned at himself in mirror, adjusting his neck bow.

"You're not going to have the boy perform in front of Boregond!"

"I am. Maybe when he sees a genuine zdrell trick it will give him pause. But I would wager he won't believe. Even as a journeyman he was adamant that zdrell was just a legend, even with all the evidence to the contrary."

"I hope this new boy, Jonny, can perform," she said, shaking her head and continuing with her mending.

"So do I, dear, so do I." Silurian looked thoughtful as he left the room.

Chapter 16

As Jonny and Roald entered the great hall, they noticed they were almost late. Most of the seats were filled, and the boys doing the serving were already bringing in plates of food. They looked around for a place to sit.

Feldor grabbed Jonny by the arm. "There you two are," he said, scowling. "You both are to sit at the head table with The Master." He guided Jonny up towards the table at the center of the room. "You had both better remember to be on your best behavior as well, spinning trick or no," he added with a glare as they arrived at the only two empty seats at the table.

Feldor hurried away and The Master noticed them as they sat down. "Jonny, Eleander tells me you have good news," The Master said, smiling. "Eat now, we'll talk later."

Jonny and Roald sat down and could not help but notice where they were sitting. The Master sat at the head of the table. On his right sat a large, distinguished looking older man. Resident journeyman wizards filled the other five seats separating where Jonny and Roald sat from the head of the table. Eleander sat directly across from the special guest. The other boys at the table were older apprentices.

Roald whispered to Jonny that everyone at the table was a journeyman or would be made one soon. He looked even more intimidated by their favored location than Jonny felt.

As Jonny looked around, he saw even more people stealing looks at him than on his first night. The looks were not all friendly; in fact, some were downright hateful. He doubted, after tonight, he would ever have another friend than Roald.

After a few moments, Roald seemed to be enjoying the attention much more than Jonny. He whispered, "I bet Frank and his buddies are eating their hearts out now." He laughed, "The head table! This is so *prodigious*. You don't sit at the head table unless The Master really likes you or is going to make you a journeyman or something like that," he said still whispering in an excited tone. "I wonder who the visitor is? I bet he's some kind of big wizard or something."

Jonny had been eating quietly. Listening to Roald go on, but noting that except for Eleander and The Master, no one at the table was looking at either he or Roald. The two boys directly across from them had been engrossed in a quiet conversation when he and Roald had sat down, and had given them only the briefest of glances before going back to whatever it was they were discussing. The room was so noisy you had to deliberately talk loud just to be heard even across the table.

The Master was talking to the guest and Eleander, while the journeymen looked on. Jonny could not hear what was being said, but at one point The Master said something and pointed down at Jonny. As he did, the visitor and the journeymen turned and looked down at Jonny. The Master continued talking and everyone looked back at him, but for the rest of the meal Jonny noticed the visitor glancing occasionally at him. The look on his face was unreadable, but Jonny felt like a fly about to have its wings torn off every time he saw the visitor staring at him.

Roald kept whispering things to Jonny during the dinner, but Jonny did not hear him. He was too concerned with what would happen after dinner. The food was the best Jonny could ever remember having in his life, but he got very little enjoyment out of it because as the meal wore on he became increasingly nervous.

Finally, Roald turned to Jonny and said, this time not at a whisper, "Jonny, you haven't heard a word I've said the whole meal." When Jonny did not respond, he tried again, a little louder still, "Jonny, look at me, this is great. You should be enjoying this. Why aren't you? Is it because of the visitor with The Master?"

Jonny nodded. "Yeah Roald, I'm really scared. What if I can't do it? Every time I look at The Master, I just feel like I'm going to forget all I know. And if the visitor is there too . . . What if I can't do it?"

Roald stated confidently, "Jonny. We practiced."

"But did we practice enough?"

"Jonny, I ran around and banged the table and yelled at you the last time. I did everything, except slug you in the arm, and you still did it fine. This will work. Trust me."

"Maybe. I hope you're right."

"Look Jonny," Roald said, holding his gaze. "I don't know a lot about magic, but there's one thing I have learned in the last six months. You have to believe in yourself and that you can do your magic. If you don't believe, it won't work. So you've *got to* believe. If you don't, we're both in big trouble. You know you can do it. I know you can do it. So when the time comes, we just do it, right?"

"I guess you're right Roald, but I'm still scared."

"So what," Roald said, now sounding frustrated with his friend. "I'm scared too, but I know you can do it. What's the worst thing The Master will do to us? Probably he'll just make us clean out the privies for a few months. That's nasty, but I've done it before. You get used to it," Roald sighed. "But that's not going to happen, cause you are going to impress The Master and the visitor so much they'll want to make you a master wizard right then and there!"

Jonny had to laugh. The absurdity of him being made a master wizard was too much even for Jonny's present gloom, so he joined in. "And right after that they'll make you the Lord Mayor of Alavar."

That set them both off laughing and earned them some looks from the other occupants of the table. This time Jonny did not care, so he continued the joke, "Oh yes, my Lord Mayor." Jonny pretended to bow to Roald. "I have the season's crop reports for your approval," he said, pretending to hand him a stack of paper.

Roald fell right in with the game. "Yes, yes my good man," he said, in a stuffy voice, sitting with his nose in the air. "Put them over there on the table next to the three chests of gold," he gestured with an imperious flourish, then they both broke down laughing so hard they nearly knocked their plates off the table.

As Jonny and Roald were starting to get over their attack of the giggles, Jonny noticed The Master and the visitor both stood up. The Master was calling for attention.

"I hope all of you have enjoyed this dinner," The Master began. "I want to introduce you to our honored guest this evening, Master Boregond. He is a most accomplished master of The Arts, and will be staying here for the next two days. He and I have been acquaintances for many years. I want you all to treat him with the same respect and deference you treat me. Answer any questions he asks of you. If you're lucky, he may even teach some of you something."

Both Master Silurian and Master Boregond smiled. The Master whispered something to Master Boregond who only shook his head in reply. The Master looked over the crowd and said, "Carry on then. Enjoy this food and don't ever let it be said I don't feed you boys properly."

He turned and left the room with Master Boregond. Just before they went through the doorway, Master Boregond glared over his shoulder at Jonny. Jonny looked down, but not before their eyes met, and he felt a shiver go down his spine that brought back all the gloom he had been feeling earlier.

As soon as The Master left, the noise in the room resumed its previous level. "Did you see the look he gave you?" Roald asked.

"How could I miss it? I don't know why he looked at me like that, but I don't like it."

"Yeah," Roald continued. "I don't know anything about him but that wasn't a nice look. I don't like him already."

"But we have to still be really polite to him. He's The Master's guest, and besides that he'll be gone in a couple of days." Jonny paused, and then continued, "I think there's more going on here than we know about."

Roald snorted. "You can be sure there's lots more going on here than we know about. There always is, but maybe this time we'll find out a bit of it."

As Roald finished speaking, Jonny saw Eleander, standing by the door where The Master had recently departed. He gestured for them to come, and Jonny's stomach filled with butterflies again at the prospect of what was to come.

Chapter 17

The three of them entered the same office where Jonny had first met the Master--had it only been two days ago? The Master and Master Boregond sat on either side of the Master's desk. Boregond's back was to them as they entered the room, but he turned his chair sideways and stared at Jonny on hearing them. Jonny's fear became a physical pain. His heart beat so fast it felt as if it were a caged animal trying to escape. He stared down at the floor trying to ignore the piercing gaze.

The Master spoke. "Jonny, Eleander tells me you have something to show me. I mentioned your little talent to Boregond, and he expressed an interest in seeing it as well. Are you ready?"

"I g-guess so," Jonny stammered, still looking the floor.

"Well then, you can use the same table where we worked with the coin the other day," The Master said, seeming not to notice Jonny's discomfort.

Jonny looked up at The Master who smiled at him and gestured towards the table. He deliberately did not look in Master Boregond's direction as he walked over to it.

Roald put the dagger, pointed down, on the table and held it with his finger, waiting. Jonny looked at the knife and the tension in the room mounted. He reached out with his mind as he had that afternoon, but as he stared at the dagger, he could feel Boregond's gaze on him. Nothing happened. He could not concentrate.

Jonny turned to Master Silurian. "I'm sorry, Master," he said nearly in tears. "We worked on it all afternoon, and practiced and it worked then, but . . . but I just can't . . . can't make it work now."

The corner of Boregond's mouth quirked up in a leer. The Master looked quite irritated.

"Jonny," he said with an edge to his voice Jonny had not heard before. "*Can't* is a word I will not hear! If you were able to do it this afternoon, you should be able to do it now. Being nervous is understandable, but failure is *not acceptable!*" His eyes burned as he held Jonny's gaze. "Do you understand?"

"Yes, Master, yes I'll do it," Jonny said, feeling even worse than before. He fleetingly wondered if The Master would kill him if he tried to run for the door, but was unwilling to find out. He stared back down at the dagger.

Roald said, "Come on Jonny. You can do it. You did it lots this afternoon. Just do it again."

Eleander joined in, "Just like earlier, Jonny. Just do it."

Jonny stared at the knife, trying to recapture the feeling he felt that afternoon, but it would not come. Sweat trickled down his forehead and from his armpits. His knees trembled. Nobody said anything. He strained and strained but nothing happened.

Master Boregond broke the silence. "Well, what did you expect Silurian," he snorted. "He's barely out of diapers. You're asking too much of him," he said with a dismissive tone. "I know very few masters who could do what you're asking without demon assistance, and just look at him, a baby. Is it any wonder he fails?"

Both Jonny and Master Silurian colored at the words. The Master's jaw set and Jonny could see that The Master and Boregond were probably not the best of friends, maybe even rivals. This only served to deepen Jonny's shame. He said nothing, what was there to say? He had failed.

Roald spoke up breaking the tension, "C'mon Jonny. This is stupid. You know you can do this, I know you can do this, just do it."

The Master spoke, "No, Roald. If Jonny cannot perform, then we will take no more of Master Boregond's time. He and I have more things to discuss tonight. You three can go now. I will deal with you tomorrow," he said, turning back to face Boregond.

Even if Jonny was ready to leave in defeat, Roald was not so easily put off. "Wait, Master," Roald said, earning him a sharp glare from The Master. Even so, he continued, "Master, please let Jonny have one more try, please. I know one more thing that will make it work."

He did not wait for The Master's response. He ran over to Jonny and gave him the dagger. "You hold on to it to start with, then we'll do it just like we did at the end of the afternoon, just like we did it before," he said, winking at Jonny.

Jonny could not figure what Roald was talking about, but he went over to the table and placed the dagger pointed down and held it. As soon as it was in place Roald started yelling nonsense words at the top of his lungs and running up and down in the room. Everyone stared at him, stunned by his bizarre behavior, including Jonny. Roald could see Jonny still had not caught on, so he stopped for a moment and said to Jonny, "Just like at the end of the afternoon, remember?"

Now, Jonny understood. Jonny did remember how Roald had done the same thing that afternoon trying to distract him, and how Jonny had been able, eventually, to spin the dagger no matter what strange things Roald did to distract him.

Jonny smiled. The tension in him broke and it was just like that afternoon all over again. He ignored Roald, just as before, and he focused on the knife. It immediately began to spin. Within a few seconds, it was spinning rapidly and he took his finger from it.

"Now, see here," Master Boregond began to protest. "This has gone on for long enough," he said, not having seen the dagger spinning because of how Jonny was standing blocking his view. "Clear these children out of here and let's get back to our work, Silurian," he harrumphed.

"Certainly, Boregond," The Master said, smiling now because he could see the dagger spinning. "But you really ought to look and see what this *child* is doing," he said, with obvious relish.

"Jonny, could you move so Master Boregond can see."

Jonny, feeling more comfortable now he had control of the knife said, "Certainly, Master." He moved out of the way and the color drained from Boregond's face. He did something with an amulet he wore around his neck and became even more alarmed.

"That's right, Boregond," The Master said with triumph in his voice. "No demons, no charms, no constraints, no glyphs or incantations, and yet it spins. Disconcerting, isn't it?"

Master Boregond said nothing.

After keeping the dagger spinning for over a minute, The Master turned to Jonny and said, "I think that's enough for now Jonny. You've accomplished what I asked you for today. By the way, what happens when you stop making it spin?"

Roald did not wait for Jonny to reply and jumped in, "He can make it come to a stop pointing wherever he wants, Master."

"Really?" The Master said, amusement plain in his voice. "Okay, Jonny why don't you stop it, and have the tip pointing at Master Boregond."

"Yes, Master," Jonny said as he concentrated on slowing the knife down. As it slowed and began to wobble Jonny gave it a push with his mind and if fell over and landed spinning now flat on the table on the hilt. It spun more and more slowly, finally coming to a stop pointing directly at Master Boregond.

When it came to a complete stop, Jonny let out a large sigh of relief. Only then did he look up at Master Boregond who was looking at him with a glare of undisguised hatred. Jonny did not understand why he would look at him like that, but did not dwell on it as The Master smiled broadly when Jonny looked at him.

"Well done, Jonny," The Master said beaming. "And well done for you too, Roald. You did a very good thing helping your friend out like that. Yes, well done both of you." Roald positively glowed with the praise from The Master. Jonny felt warm inside too.

"That's enough for now," The Master said. "Eleander, take them back out now. Master Boregond and I still have some things to discuss."

Eleander motioned for Jonny and Roald to go. They were only too happy to leave. As soon as they were out in the hallway Roald started skipping up and down.

"Did you see the look on that fat pig's face," Roald almost shouted.

"Keep your voice down," Eleander said sternly, then started to grin. "But he did look like he was going to explode didn't he?" Eleander said laughing.

For a moment, Jonny could not say anything. Finally, he said, "Roald. Thanks. I couldn't have done it without you. You saved me."

"Awww, it was nothin'," Roald said, becoming much more subdued. "You just needed a little help getting started. I knew you could do it. You only needed to remember you could."

"Well, he's right," Eleander said. "You have as much to be proud of today as Jonny, Roald. You helped make it happen."

For the second time in as many minutes, Roald looked like his fondest desire had been granted. He did not say anything, but Jonny could see how happy the kind words had made him.

Eleander then turned and said seriously to Jonny, "You better not let anything like that happen again. If your friend hadn't bailed you out, you would have been in very big trouble with The Master. I told you to practice till you could do it with no hesitation. What happened?"

Jonny's sense of elation dropped significantly. They stepped out into the dark courtyard and Jonny stopped. "We did practice, Eleander," Jonny began. "I could do it without even looking at the knife, easy. But, that Master Boregond, when he looked at me, I . . . I just couldn't. I forgot everything."

"Well you better not let it happen again, but I don't blame you," Eleander said. "Master Boregond is a fearsome character, but you can't let him get to you like that."

"Why does he hate Jonny so much?" Roald asked.

"I don't know, Roald," Eleander replied. "He's a powerful wizard in the north countries. Don't tell anyone, but I don't think The Master likes him very much; but he has to give him courtesy as a fellow wizard. He is a powerful demon worker, so that might be why he didn't like what Jonny did. I know that's why The Master doesn't like him much. Master Silurian doesn't have much respect for wizards who rely too much on demon magic.

"Either way, I don't think you'll have to do anything more around him. He is just on his way back to the north. He will be gone in a couple of days. So just steer clear of him, and you should be fine. Both of you ought to head up to bed now. You've had a busy day. I will find you tomorrow at breakfast and tell you what The Master wants done. So you better get some rest."

Roald and Jonny headed up the staircase that took them to their room. They recounted the whole thing back to each other a couple of times whenthey got ready for bed.

Once in bed, Jonny turned to Roald and said, "Thanks, Roald. You really saved me. You're the best friend I've ever had."

"Thanks, Jonny," Roald replied quietly. "You're the best friend I've ever had too. G'night."

"Good night, Roald," Jonny said, and drifted into a dreamless sleep.

§ § §

"Well, Alira," Master Silurian said as he entered his bedroom suite. "I believe we gave Boregond a bit of a shock tonight."

"Silurian," she said with mock indignity, while she sat in the high-backed chair embroidering, her long gray hair in a braid down her back. "What have you done now, my foolish husband?"

Master Silurian smiled mischievously as he began changing into his nightgown. "I only let our new little Jonny show him what a real wizard can do."

"Do you think that's wise?" she said quirking an eyebrow at him.

"Yes, I believe it is more than wise. Boregond has no business being here. He claims he is only taking customary hospitality as he journeys back north. Such an obvious lie. I've heard him claim he never travels by carriage if he can avoid it. He prefers to have demons cart him here and there in the blink of an eye. He has always said no self-respecting master should even own a carriage."

Master Silurian finished tying the draw string at the neck of his nightgown and began pacing. "My guess is that the pack of demon wizards he associates with decided to send him through to test my mettle again. They are like a pack of vultures waiting for me to weaken enough for them to move in and take over Salaways."

"Dear, don't work yourself into a state, or you'll never get to sleep. It is already quite late." Alira locked eyes with him for a moment, and then he lowered his gaze.

"You are right, dear. But, oh you should have seen his face when little Jonny had that dagger spinning. I thought he would die of apoplexy," he said chuckling.

"But will he guess the truth? Couldn't that pose a threat to Jonny, and you too?"

"No, he won't," The Master said as he came to kneel by her chair. "You see, he didn't believe his eyes. He will infer I have come up with some new spell and a way to activate it and only used Jonny as a ruse. The man is incapable of believing the boy is a future zdrell master." He stood, and walked slowly to the bed they shared, and lay back.

"His own pigheadedness protects us. He does not know what he saw, and so he will report that I am still too strong, and we will be left in peace for another few years. I only hope it is long enough to get Jonny ready. When they finally do believe he is a zdrell master, they will stop at nothing to destroy him."

§ § §

As Roald and Jonny were finishing breakfast, Eleander came and sat down with them. "I wonder if you two might be interested in a bit of news," he said, stealing a piece of bread off Roald's plate. Both boys looked at Eleander expectantly. After chewing on the bread for several seconds to see if they would beg him to tell, he continued. "It seems our visitor, Master Boregond, who was going to be staying for two days, changed his mind and left early this morning. He didn't even have breakfast before he was in his carriage and on his way."

Roald and Jonny looked at each other, then back at Eleander, who had a faintly amused expression on his face.

"You don't think that had anything to do with us?" Jonny asked, sounding worried.

"I don't know . . . ," Eleander said coyly. "But unless The Master said something to offend him after we left last night . . ."

"Do you think The Master will be mad at us?" Roald asked, beginning to tremble.

"No, I don't think so," Eleander said smiling. "In fact," he stared straight at Jonny. "He might even be happy. I don't think he really wanted to host Master Boregond all that much in the first place. If you two gave him a reason to want to leave in a hurry, I think he'll welcome it."

Roald looked very much relieved that The Master would not be upset with him. He let out a large sigh. "That's not nice Eleander. You really had me worried. I don't know what I'd do if The Master was mad at me."

"Well, it's still not certain he isn't, but you'll both find out soon enough. He just sent word he wants to meet with both of you this morning. This time, I think he's going to work directly with you, Jonny. So, you both better finish up so we can get going."

Jonny and Roald looked at each other again. Jonny shrugged, then they both set to work quickly finishing off what was left of their breakfasts.

As soon as they left the mess, they had to walk fast to keep up with Eleander who was plainly in a hurry. He took them to a back part of the main keep that neither of the boys had visited before. The room they finally entered was the largest Jonny had ever been in. The ceiling arched more than twenty feet up, and a skylight in the middle of the ceiling went much higher.

Several large work tables spread around the room. Not one of the tables was empty. They were piled with books, cauldrons, blocks of metal, wood and other substances Jonny couldn't identify.

In some parts of the room, the dust was thick, as though no one had walked there in months or years. Other areas showed recent use, including one table covered by a slowly spreading smoking puddle that was dripping onto the floor. Several journeymen occupied different parts of the room. All of them made a show of not noticing Jonny.

From the doorway, Jonny looked around the room in wonder. After several moments Eleander said, "Come on. I know it's a bit much the first time you see it, but you two don't know how lucky you are. This is The Master's main workshop. Most apprentices never see it. This is where The Master does all of his real work, and he wants you close at hand, Jonny."

Eleander led them over to a table, which only had a couple of books on it. When they got closer, Jonny saw that next to the books was the dagger he had spun the day before. Eleander pointed towards it, noticing Jonny had seen it. "I bet you can figure what you need to do with that," he said grinning. "I'm not sure what else The Master wants you to do, but I'm sure he'll tell you soon enough himself."

No sooner had Eleander spoken than Master Silurian came in. He was carrying a canister, which he opened as soon as he got to the table with the spill, and began sprinkling its contents over the smoking puddle. He continued, ignoring the boys for several moments, then said, "That's about got it. Nasty stuff acid potions, especially when they are done wrong, which this one was, eh, Alexander?" He nodded towards a young man who had been sitting at one of the tables reading a large book ever since they had come into the room. "I swear I had everything in the right portions according to this book, Master. I've just gone over it all again and I did everything exactly as it's written here," he said gesturing harshly at the book. He was a tall young man, who appeared to be in his early twenties or very late teens. His hair fell in a loose mop that was beginning to recede at the forehead. He stood up and walked over to The Master.

"Well, I've warned you often enough, Alexander," The Master began. "Most of these books are copied by scribes who haven't the foggiest idea what is in them, and who frequently seem quite careless about numbers. I have had enough problems myself with that sort of thing. This is why I am always telling you that you must always check the numbers yourself to see if they make sense. Too big or too small, and it can all end in disaster. This was only a small explosion. Imagine if it had been bigger. There have been more than a few wizards and alchemists who have lost a hand, an eye, or even their lives over this sort of error."

The Master glared at Alexander, who looked stricken. He motioned at the now congealing dust covered puddle and said, "Now clean this up, and do be careful. This neutralizing agent has slowed it down some, but that acid is still potent. You know how, right?"

"Yes, Master," Alexander sighed.

"Then get on with it," The Master snapped. Then he wheeled on Jonny and barked, "And what are you doing here standing and gawking? There's work to be done!"

Jonny started to stammer something, but The Master cut him off. "Yes there's work to be done, but at least now that windbag Boregond is gone, it can be useful work. And I suppose I have you to thank for that," he said smiling. "But don't think it will get you out of any work. Why, if your friend here hadn't bailed you out, you would have ruined my little surprise for Boregond." He paused and looked thoughtful, "Though it did end up being very dramatic in its own way, didn't it?

"After what he said when he thought you couldn't perform, he couldn't stay around much, could he?" The Master chuckled, "Just thinking of the look on his face does my heart good."

The Master walked over to the table where both Jonny and Roald were standing, afraid to say anything. Neither had seen The Master in this type of a volatile mood before, and they did not want to say anything that would get his anger directed at them. He balanced the dagger on its tip and held it with one finger. He looked directly at Jonny and said, "Make it spin, now, no hesitation!"

Where the previous night Jonny had been afraid of not being able to perform, now he was afraid of disappointing The Master. This had just the opposite effect on Jonny. Without even pausing to think, he reached out with his mind and immediately started the dagger spinning rapidly. The Master had to remove his finger hastily because of the friction building up between the knife and the tip of his finger. He laughed.

"Just as I thought! All you needed was the appropriate motivation. I knew if your mind wasn't allowed to dwell on your fear, you could perform." He stared at the dagger for a few moments, and then looked up. "Eleander tells me you can spin a coin while keeping the dagger spinning."

"Yes, Master," Jonny said not looking up from the dagger. "But it's easier if the coin is where I can look at it and the dagger at the same time."

"Oh, it's easier if it is . . . ," The Master said with a tone Jonny was beginning to dislike. "Then we'll have to make sure it isn't very close then, shan't we?"

The Master extracted a coin from his belt pouch and put it down on the table at the opposite end from where the dagger was spinning. Jonny was alarmed at the distance, but said nothing.

"Roald," The Master began. "Come over here and spin this coin for your friend. And I want you to stand right here," he said indicating a spot where Roald's body would hide the coin almost completely from Jonny's gaze.

Jonny grew more alarmed by the second. It was bad enough The Master wanted him to spin the coin while he was spinning the dagger. It was even worse that he placed the coin so far from the it, but now he had Roald standing so he could barely see it. How was he going to make it work? The dagger started to wobble.

"Concentrate, Jonny," The Master said, taunting. "We wouldn't want to make the dagger fall, especially when we haven't started the coin. Come, Roald. Spin the coin for Jonny so we can see if he really can do as advertised."

Jonny did not like the edge in The Master's voice. This whole thing had seemed like a dream come true just moments before, but now it was starting to feel like a nightmare. He wished he could find someone to wake him. Roald flicked the coin with practiced ease and suddenly Jonny did not have time to be afraid.

He shifted his focus momentarily to the coin and sped it up quickly, then shifted back to concentrating on the knife, which had already begun to slow. He kept up the effort for several moments, shifting his attention back and forth between the two, keeping them both in motion. It was tiring, but he was doing it.

"Good, Jonny," The Master said. "This is well done, but now we need to make it more interesting." The Master took a large square piece of leather from another table and gave it to Roald. "Roald, my boy, hold this on its edge right here," he said indicating a spot just past the coin.

"But, Master," Jonny blurted out. "If he puts it there I won't even be able to see the coin."

"That's the point, Jonny," The Master said with a kinder tone. "You can barely see it now with Roald standing where he is. I want you to see if you can still spin it, even when you can't see it with your eyes."

Jonny's fear, which had receded when he had gotten the two objects under control, now came back with a great rush. "I can't do it, Master. I have to be able to see it."

"Nonsense!" The Master roared at him. "Boy, you don't even understand what you're doing here. How do you know you *must* see the coin in order to make it spin? You know nothing of the sort. You only know you have always needed to see it before, but before yesterday, you would have said you could not spin two things at once. Today you are spinning them both and you will learn to spin something without seeing it. Put the panel where I showed you, Roald."

Roald placed the leather panel down while looking helplessly at Jonny. Jonny did not see the look. He was desperately trying to get the coin to spin as fast as he could while he could still see it. Then the panel came down.

Jonny shifted his focus to the dagger to get it spinning faster as well, and then tried to focus back on the coin. He tried to touch it with his mind and thought he did. He asked, "Is it still spinning, Roald?"

The Master did not give him a chance to answer. "Say nothing to him, Roald. What do you think, Jonny? Is it still spinning?"

"I don't, I don't know," Jonny said. "I'm trying to spin it just like always, but I can't tell if I can't see it."

"See it with your mind, boy," The Master commanded. "Feel it. You have to feel it to make it spin in the first place. Use that same feeling to let you know what it's doing."

Jonny continued to work at keeping the coin spinning, but was starting to panic at not being able to tell if it was working or not. Suddenly he was distracted by the sound of the dagger falling down. He had been concentrating so hard on the coin he had forgotten about it.

"Ignore it, Jonny. The dagger is unimportant. If you can figure this out, then you will be able to do two again. This is just a matter of practice. Now, is the coin still spinning?"

"I, I think so," Jonny moaned. "But I'm not sure. I just don't know."

"Lift up the panel, Roald," The Master commanded. "Let Jonny see with his eyes for a moment."

Roald lifted the panel out of the way, and the coin was spinning right where it had been before, only now it was spinning much faster. Jonny was so happy, but The Master left him no time for celebration.

"Now, make it move a little closer towards you," The Master said.

Jonny concentrated and the coin moved several inches closer.

"Now, put the panel back down, Roald," The Master said dashing Jonny's hopes that the ordeal was over.

"Move the coin back to where it was before, Jonny," The Master said, staring straight at him.

Jonny said nothing. He knew complaining would do him no good. He tried to move the coin back to where it had been before. He did it totally by feel. After a few moments The Master said, "Roald, lift up the panel and let Jonny see."

Roald lifted the panel out of the way again, and Jonny saw the coin was nearly back to where it had started. He laughed, "It worked, it really worked!"

"Yes, it did," The Master said, obviously pleased. "Now let it drop. Rest for a few moments and then we'll work up to more difficult things."

Jonny did not know whether to be happy or sad. He had already done more than he would ever have thought possible, and here was The Master telling him it was only the beginning. Now he knew what Eleander meant when he said The Master would make him work harder than he had ever dreamed possible.

Before the day was over, Jonny could spin both the coin and the dagger at the same time while blindfolded. It was the start of The Master's relentless program to develop Jonny's talent.

Chapter 18

The next day, and the days that followed settled into a routine. In the morning, Jonny worked on his *tricks:* spinning more and different things with variations in the combinations and complexity as suggested by The Master. Roald was there to assist Jonny and function as a gofer for The Master and any of the other journeymen, if Jonny did not actively need help.

In the afternoon Jonny and Roald were tutored in another part of the castle by one of the journeymen, on reading, writing, and figuring. Sometimes this happened with other apprentices, other times it was just Jonny and Roald.

In the late afternoon, or evening, Jonny and a few select apprentices were tutored by The Master, or senior journeymen on the theory and practice of the various forms of magic. Jonny soon discovered that the other apprentices were those The Master and the journeymen referred to as "brights." When he asked, Jonny was told that the brights were apprentices who showed some aptitude for magic, and had a real chance of becoming journeymen.

There were never more than two or three brights with Jonny, even though there were nearly fifty apprentices at the castle. No one would answer when Jonny asked how they figured out who was a bright and who was not.

§ § §

"A message arrived while you were at the city council meeting, Silurian," Alira said, as she sat knitting by the fire. The Master was changing out of the formal purple and gold robes he used for government functions.

"It must be important, dearest, or you wouldn't be teasing me with it. Out with it, why should this message be any different than the other twenty I'm sure are sitting on Feldor's desk?"

"I wouldn't know, but it's written in Klathar, and sealed with a master's ring." She smiled at his excited reaction, and before he could protest further pointed with one of her needles at the sealed scroll on the night stand beside the bed. "It's over there."

Silurian picked up the scroll, opened the seal and quickly began to read. His excited expression faded as he read. He was soon frowning.

"Bad news?" she asked gently.

"Yes. My old friend Beldereth is dead. He was probably one of the finest materials magic practitioners alive, and now he's dead, and who knows how much knowledge lost with him."

"How did he die?"

"It says he died exactly the way he always cautioned me about. He was alone and an experiment went awry, and he asphyxiated. If he had had an assistant with him, he probably would have been saved, but he was working late in the night, alone. Oh, what a loss."

"His passing strengthens the demon camp, doesn't it?" she said, staring into the fire.

The Master, too, stared into the fire and answered slowly. "Yes, it does. Nearly all the younger masters have been thrown in with them. In some ways I can't blame them, demon magic is so much simpler and the rewards are greater, if you can stomach the price to be paid." Silurian's expression turned grave. "It makes me sick, to see what demon magic does to its wielders. They don't even think of their sacrifices as human, they can't afford it. I'm not sure how human they are after years of it."

"They are quite human, my dear Silurian, and that is why you loathe them so completely."

Chapter 19

Jonny never would have believed that learning could be more work than being a slave, but sometimes he found himself longing for the simplicity of cleaning out a crawlspace. He was learning a lot, but it never seemed to be enough for The Master. He learned reading and writing in Herglish, the common language of the continent, figuring, geometry, and history. All of this, in addition to time he spent spinning objects in more and varied combinations, and learning the theories and history of magic.

When Jonny asked why he was learning so many things, so much faster than any other apprentice or journeyman in the castle, The Master replied, "Because there is little time, and because you can learn these things, and because you must learn them soon, before there is no time."

The response puzzled Jonny even more, but before he could ask again, The Master continued. "No more delaying. Tell me the five major branches of magic, with each of their sub-branches."

Jonny sighed and recited, "The five major branches of magic are: Material, Demon, Divination, Power manipulation, and direct manipulation, also called sleight of hand."

"Good. Continue," The Master said, and Jonny did.

§ § §

One day, during history class, taught by Feldor, Roald asked a question that was to have great significance.

"Sir," Roald said, raising his hand to interrupt Lord Feldor's detailed explanation of a battle in The Great War. "Sir, why do we spend so much time studying The Great War? It happened over a thousand years ago. There have been lots of wars and battles since, so why do we spend so much time on it?"

"Roald, I could ask you the same question, but I won't. The Great War was unique. It was the only time the Grimoridans attacked our continent of Skryla. It was the only time in the history of Skryla that all of the seventeen city-states of Skryla have been at war with a common enemy. And it lasted a very long time. How long did it last, Larin?"

Larin suddenly became very interested in his feet. Feldor looked around. "Jonny?"

"Twenty years?" Jonny answered uncertainly.

"No. Roald?"

"Ninety three years?"

"Correct, Roald. In the more than one thousand years since that war, there have probably been fewer battles fought, put together, than in The Great War alone."

"How did it finally end?" Larin asked.

"Does anyone know?" Feldor said, scanning the room.

"No one knows for sure," Jonny said quietly.

"Correct, Jonny. The exact cause is unknown, though there are more theories than you could know in a lifetime of study. The simplest reason is that the Grimoridans simply could not hold their land here and couldn't forever supply their armies across the sea. That explanation does not explain how they could maintain the war for nearly a century and then suddenly not be able to.

"That will be enough on this topic for now. Now, who will tell me why *this* battle," he said indicating the diagram on the wall, "was lost by the Grimoridans?"

§ § §

The next morning, both Jonny and Roald were surprised to find the coins, rocks, knives and the other objects on Jonny's worktable were gone. In their place, there was single, large, very ancient book, and a basket filled with small river rocks. Jonny examined the book, and could not figure out any of the strange curled script that adorned its cover and pages. He did not recognize the letters, let alone the words.

The Master came in as Jonny was closing the book in puzzlement. "I would wager you are wondering what happened to all of your things, Jonny, and why this book is here," Master Silurian said with a small smile.

Jonny nodded.

"It's there because it is one of the few books I have that was written by a wizard who could do zdrell, and was trying to explain how it all worked. It is very old, and is written in Klathar, the old High Wizard tongue. It is still the best reference I have. This copy is over five hundred years old, but it is what I need to help you, Jonny."

"Boys, as of today we are done with spinning things. It is time to move on to the next level."

Both Jonny and Roald were shocked. It seemed to Jonny that spinning things was all he would ever do. In the first days he had been there he thought The Master would rapidly run out of things to do with spinning, but nearly two months later he still seemed full of variations for Jonny to work on. Now, suddenly it was all over. Jonny was both amazed and relieved, but not for long.

"Jonny, as of today you begin learning how to make things fly," Master Silurian said simply.

Jonny looked at Roald who only shrugged his shoulders. "Master," Jonny began. "How does making things spin have anything to do with making them fly?"

"I thought you might ask that," The Master said, grinning. "Jonny, when you spin a coin, or a knife, or a book, what are you doing?"

Jonny was confused by the question. "Uh, spinning it?"

"Yes, Jonny," The Master said still grinning, but obviously less than pleased with the answer. "But, Jonny, when something is spinning is it moving or still?"

"Moving, Master," Jonny replied, still not getting where The Master was leading with these questions.

"That's right, Jonny, it's moving. When you spin something you make it move, and you even know how to make it stop and start again, don't you?" Jonny nodded. "So, you already know how to make things move. Flying is just a particular type of movement," The Master said, as if that settled everything.

Jonny stuttered, "But, but, but flying and spinning are lots different, Master. I couldn't possibly," he began, but The Master cut him off.

"It's all right, Jonny. I know you could not just go right out and start to make things fly, but I believe that soon you will be able to do it. I have the progression all worked out. Just as you started by making one coin spin, and now you can spin twenty. This is the same thing."

Jonny was not convinced, but he had learned that The Master did know more about this stuff than he did, so he did not object. "So what do we do, Master?"

The Master grinned. "First, we take this and put it here," he said, taking a large basket he had been carrying and putting it in the middle of Jonny's work table. "Then, we see how good a shot Roald is," he said, taking a handful of small stones out of the basket and handing them to Roald, who was looking very concerned.

Roald was relieved to find out that all Master Silurian wanted was for him to practice throwing stones into the basket until he could do it reliably from ten feet away. While Roald practiced this, Jonny practiced getting the *feel* for the same rocks by rolling them around on the table, so he could move them the same way he spun coins. When he thought no one was looking, he tried to make the stones lift off the table, but rolling was the best he could do.

In just under an hour, they were both ready for the next step. The Master had Roald throw the stones, and all Jonny had to do was to make them miss the basket. For long minutes, a frustrated Jonny could not divert the stones even a small amount, but then he managed to push one. By lunch time, Roald was the frustrated one because Jonny would not let a single rock go where he threw it.

Master Silurian had been supervising some of the journeymen in the other side of the cavernous workshop, but he kept glancing over and occasionally walking by to gauge their progress. He could see Roald's growing frustration and told the boys they could break and go with him to lunch. This was unusual, as The Master usually ate alone or with Lord Feldor. To their greater amazement he casually mentioned that their old tormenter, Frank, would be serving them.

Roald and Jonny were both shocked. Roald recovered first and started laughing. "Oh this will be sooo good! Thank you, Master. I just want to see the look on his face. Thank you!"

The Master chuckled. "Now, Roald, don't be too hard on him, at least no more than he deserves."

"You can be sure of that, Master. Yes, you can be sure he'll get no more than he deserves," Roald added with an evil snicker.

Chapter 20

The lunch they ate was as good as Jonny had ever eaten. It tasted all the sweeter for seeing their previous tormenter forced to play the part of servant to them. Roald seemed to be even more clumsy than usual. He knocked plates on the floor two different times requiring Frank to clean up the mess. He might have even done it again except The Master made it clear enough was enough. While they were eating, The Master asked Jonny about his family and how he ended up with Murdoc. It didn't take long for Jonny to tell the story. The Master then asked Roald about his family. Jonny was very interested since Roald had always been reluctant to talk to Jonny about his family.

Roald said his father was a land owner on the northwest edge of Lake Sharafleg. Roald was the third son and there was nothing for him to inherit. He had been apprenticed to The Master because it was hoped The Master would find a noble profession for him, not because they had thought he was in any way magical. He had been at the castle for six months before Jonny arrived, and during that time had only shown an aptitude for horses. Now working with The Master, he confessed he found all the books fascinating and really enjoyed organizing the workshop.

Finally, Jonny mustered his courage and asked The Master about his past and his family. The Master answered. "Boys, it has been so long, I can scarcely remember what I was like at your age. It seems I have been an old man forever. My parents have been dead over three hundred years."

"How old are you, Master?" Jonny asked timidly.

"Well," he paused, "you will turn eleven this week, won't you?"

"Yes, Master, tomorrow."

"Well, Jonny, next month it will have been three hundred and fifty two years since I turned eleven."

"Wow," both boys said simultaneously.

"Yes, it is true. I have been around for a long time. Boys your age think anyone over thirty is old, but in my case, I really am ancient. There are wizards out there older than I, but not more than ten in all of the continent."

"Tell us, Master," Roald said. "Have you seen many battles? Is it true you led the armies that drove out the northern chieftains, and created Salaways as a kingdom of peace?"

"Yes, I had a hand in the creation of Salaways, Roald. And yes, I've seen many a battle, and found glory in none. No, truth be told, I only created Salaways as my kingdom because I was tired of war and political intrigue interfering with my studies. Never forget boys, there is never glory in war. It is to be avoided at all costs, and won quickly when it must be fought." He looked out the window thoughtfully and then continued speaking. "Yes, Salaways has been the best thing I have ever built, and I certainly cannot claim credit for all its creation. Many good men have died to make this country, but it may indeed have been worth it.

"Now, if we can just convince the madmen from the north it isn't worth their while to try and take it from me." He sighed, "But that is no concern of you boys. You have other concerns. Let's finish up here, and then we can see if we can enlarge your talent a bit more this afternoon, eh, Jonny?"

"Yes, Master," Jonny replied happily and they left Frank to clean up as they went back to the workshop.

§ § §

When they got back to the workshop, The Master let Jonny and Roald know his plan. Now that Jonny could make the rocks miss the basket, The Master wanted him to miss in a single direction. When that was mastered, he would have Jonny work until he could change direction and height, and even hold the rock suspended in the air.

The next day when Jonny and Roald came to the workshop, The Master said that since it was Jonny's birthday, as soon as Jonny could demonstrate making rocks miss to any side he asked for, they would have rest of the day off. Now it was Roald's turn to pressure Jonny. The weather was cold, clear, and the sun was out for the first time in weeks. Roald really wanted to go outside, and so did Jonny.

As usual, Jonny was able to pick up work at his best performance the previous day. In fact, Jonny felt things were coming much easier that day. Within two hours of arriving, Jonny was ready to demonstrate for The Master. He knew Master Silurian would try to throw him off, but he was ready. He had spent the last half hour going over everything; having Roald try various tricks like throwing the rocks quickly, or unexpectedly.

When he called The Master over to watch it was actually rather anticlimactic. The Master called off directions and Jonny diverted rocks off in the requested direction. He made no mistakes, and The Master did not seem surprised. His only comment was that if he had known Jonny would get done this early, he would have made the task harder. However, he smiled and sent them on their way.

§ § §

Jonny and Roald spent the rest of the day out playing in the woods near the castle. They tramped around, chasing each other, squirrels, and birds. Even though the water was icy cold, they tried a few times to catch fish with their bare hands. They had no success, and soon decided throwing rocks in the water was more fun. They could not catch the fish, but they could scare them. Jonny even secretly tried pushing some of the rocks Roald was throwing to see if he could make them go where he wanted. Roald soon figured out that something was going on, and told Jonny to stop, which he did.

Jonny started to think of some interesting uses for being able to change the direction of something being thrown, but he did not mention it to Roald. He tried to make a rock fly without being thrown, but had no success than he had had previously. He still could not get the right feel for the rocks.

At the end of the day, they came back to their room at the castle, tired and cold but very happy. They took the time to bathe, since they had both gotten quite muddy from all their play. When they went to bed that night they both fell instantly asleep. For once, Roald did not wake up in the middle of the night screaming.

Chapter 21

Things went back pretty close to what Jonny had come to think of as normal, except now instead of spinning things he was pushing around rocks when he wasn't involved in his other studies. At first, his control increased rapidly, but after four weeks, he was still only able to move rocks after they had first been thrown.

Jonny was feeling frustrated, both because he had not made much progress with the rocks, and because The Master was driving him hard to learn Klathar so he could read the book on zdrell. So far, Klathar made no sense to him, half the words didn't even seem to translate to Herglish.

One day Jonny was making more embellishments on the flight of a rock Roald had tossed, when he noticed The Master standing and watching with a scowl.

"Jonny, I think it's time you stopped playing around and started to really use what you can do."

"Don't look so startled, Jonny," The Master said in an almost soothing fashion. "I think it is time to let Roald get on with his studies, and for you to give up this silly notion that you need your rocks thrown for you."

Jonny was confused. He asked, "What do you mean, Master?"

"Jonny, I just watched you take a rock Roald threw to the right, you curved it to the left, then send it higher, and then dropped it straight down into that basket. If you can do that, you do not need to have Roald throw the rock at all."

Could it be true? He had been playing lately at making a rock go up and down and then up again before he let it drop into a basket, but it had always been with a rock that was already in the air. "Do you mean I should throw the rock myself," he asked, deliberately avoiding what he thought The Master meant. He had tried to get rocks to fly by themselves, but they had stubbornly stayed on the ground.

"No I most certainly do not mean that, and you know it, Jonny. I want you to take a stone that is sitting on this table," he said pointing, "and make it go into that basket. If you can make a stone spin around like you have in the air, you can make it take off too!"

This was just what Jonny had feared, and he started to stutter how he couldn't, but The Master cut him off roughly.

"No excuses, Jonny. I know you are just a child, but you simply must stop pretending you can't do it. Here," he said, placing a stone on the table, "let's see you make this stone leave the table. I don't care where it goes, just get it up in the air, even for a second, and I will leave you alone."

Jonny knew he had no choice when Master Silurian looked at him like that, but he just did not think he could do it. He had tried just yesterday, but had gotten nowhere. He stared at the rock but he could not even get a feel for it, though he could feel The Master's gaze burning through him.

After waiting for several moments while Jonny stared impotently at the rock on the table, The Master must have decided drastic action was required. He grabbed Roald roughly and twisted his arm up behind his back. Roald cried out in pain.

"Sorry, Roald," The Master said in a tight voice, "but Jonny needs a little help here, and you are going to give it." He turned towards Jonny. "I did not want to do it this way, Jonny, but we do not have all the time in the world. You need to get past this NOW!"

He took the little finger of Roald's trapped hand and started to slowly twist it. Roald screamed in pain.

"Now, Jonny," he said staring intently at him. "I am going see that stone lift off the table, or I am going to twist Roald's finger here until it breaks. Roald is extremely sensitive to pain, as you can see, and it will hurt him a lot. So either you get that rock off the table, or your friend is going to suffer quite a bit for your fear."

Jonny wanted to scream. The Master was asking him to do the impossible. He could not make the rock move, and if he did not, Roald would be hurt. The Master had hardly done anything to him, and Roald was already crying and screaming. Jonny knew that scream; it was the one Roald made at night. Seeing Roald in pain made Jonny want to lash out, but he was just a little kid. What could he do? If only that stupid rock would move he could save his friend, but he could not do it.

The Master glared at Jonny. He started to twist Roald's finger. Roald screamed louder. Jonny was sure any moment he would hear the sound of snapping bone.

Jonny started to get mad, madder than he had been since his parents had died and he lost everything. This was not fair. Roald should not have to suffer, just because Jonny could not move some stupid rock. As Master Silurian continued to twist Roald's finger, causing him to scream even louder, something broke inside Jonny. His anger for this and all the injustices in his life was directed at The Master.

So, he wanted the rock to move did he? He would make it move all right!

Jonny looked down at the rock now with the fierce focus of his hate. The rock glowed in his mind. He looked up and stared at The Master, and without any conscious effort on his part, the rock flew off the table and right at him. Master Silurian had been watching Jonny and not the rock so he did not see it until too late. It was only a small stone, the size of an acorn, but it struck The Master's shoulder with great force, knocking him to the ground. As he fell, he released Roald, who jumped away and then looked to The Master, who was on the floor on all fours moaning.

"Jonny," Roald said, awe and fear in his voice. "What did you do?"

"I had to make him stop hurting you, Roald," Jonny said, now feeling more than a little unsure about what had just happened. "I couldn't let him keep hurting you like that, and well, he said he wanted the rock to fly, so I made it happen. He deserved it," he said with a petulant tone. "It's his fault it happened."

"I do believe you are right," The Master said, slowly getting to his feet. He was rubbing his shoulder where the stone had struck. "It was my fault, and I do not blame you. I half expected you to do something like that, but I never thought you would hit me so hard."

Master Silurian's reaction was just the opposite of what Jonny had expected. He thought The Master would be upset at him for attacking him, but amazingly, Master Silurian was grinning as he rubbed his shoulder. As soon as The Master had gone down Jonny had felt remorseful for having attacked him, but the Master's reaction first puzzled him, and then slowly rekindled the rage that had caused him to attack in the first place.

The Master saw the look change on Jonny's face, and spread his hands to placate him, wincing as he moved the injured arm. "Jonny, Jonny, don't be angry."

But Jonny was mad, and the more he thought about the whole thing, the madder he got. The Master had been right that Jonny could do as he said, but he had no right to hurt his friend just to get what he wanted. He was no better than a slaver when he treated Jonny and Roald like that. No, he was worse because he pretended to be their friend. The whole time these thoughts were going through Jonny's head he had said nothing, but The Master could see the building rage.

The Master changed his tactics. He had been trying to jolly Jonny out of his mood, but when that did not appear to work. His voice became hard and his look harder.

"So you're mad at me are you, Jonny, when it is I who should be mad at you? You have been holding out on me boy, and that makes me not at all happy. I have been trying to accommodate you since you are so young. You have been making progress, but not fast enough. You have no idea what is at stake here, or who or what you are, but I do! Do you think I took any pleasure in hurting Roald? Do you?"

"I, uh, don't know," Jonny stammered.

This was not what The Master wanted to hear. Jonny could see his face turning red and he looked like he was about to yell something, but then thought better of it. With great effort, he calmed himself.

"No, Jonny. I take no pleasure from hurting Roald, or anyone else. I am sure that is why I have never been able to stomach demon magic. However, you had all of the technique, yet you refused to use it. I had to act. You forced this on yourself."

Jonny wondered if The Master was right, but he refused to believe it. He was still very mad. "No, Master, I did not!" he said, surprising himself both with the strength of his tone and that he would dare contradict The Master. Even so, he pushed on. "You didn't have to hurt Roald. I didn't make you hurt him. You just hurt him because you knew it would make me mad. You didn't care about his feelings. You still don't."

The silence that graced Jonny's outburst was a palpable thing. No one seemed to even breathe to break the tableau.

Once again, The Master surprised Jonny. Instead of getting madder with him, he just looked at Jonny as if he had never seen him before. The silence held for several seconds, with Jonny and The Master just staring at each other.

Finally, The Master looked down at the floor for a moment, and then he looked up again at Jonny with something like wonder in his expression.

"You are right, Jonny. I was wrong. What I did to Roald was wrong. I am sorry." The Master looked at Jonny carefully to gauge his reaction.

Jonny did not know how to respond. He did not know what he had expected The Master to do when he said what he did, but he certainly had not expected him to apologize. That was beyond amazing. Then The Master threw another twist at Jonny.

"From now on, Jonny, if someone needs to suffer for your fear, it will be you." The expression on The Master's face was grim. "You have just shown me how you have more courage and moral strength than most men three times your age. I will not treat you like a child again, nor will I allow you to hold out on me again either. You cannot have it both ways, and you have chosen. So be it." The Master turned and walked out of the workshop.

Jonny was stunned, but Roald was frantic. "Jonny, you can't talk to The Master like that!"

"Roald, what I said was true. It wasn't fair what he did to you."

"Yeah, you're right, Jonny, but so what? He's The Master. He could have killed you right there. No one, and I mean no one, talks to him like that."

"Well, maybe they should."

Eleander came over to them. He had watched the whole confrontation from the other side of the workshop. No other journeymen were present. He looked at Jonny and shook his head. "Jonny, that was either the bravest or the stupidest thing I have ever seen, maybe both. Roald is right. The Master has killed men for lesser insults before. Somehow, you pulled it off. You really are something," he said, still shaking his head.

"But I was right," Jonny protested.

"It doesn't matter if you were right, Jonny," Eleander said. "The Master could have killed you anyway, but I'm sure the only reason you are still in one piece is that The Master agreed with you. But I wouldn't try that again, ever, if I were you. You heard what he said about you suffering for your own fear from now on; I think you should be more than a little worried about that."

Jonny was worried about that statement. Eleander's and Roald's reactions did not make him feel any happier either. "Yeah, you're right. I guess it was kind of stupid. It's just . . . he made me so mad, the way he used Roald and didn't even care how he hurt him."

Roald and Eleander exchanged looks that showed they were both thinking about something Jonny could not understand.

"Look Jonny, it wasn't all that bad," Roald said "My hand doesn't even hurt now."

"It's still not right, Roald," Jonny insisted. "The way you guys are reacting you'd think I did something wrong. See if I ever stick up for you again."

"It sounds to me like you won't have to," Eleander said. "From now on The Master will go right after you if you don't perform when you should. Think about that."

"You're not helping, Eleander," Jonny said.

"Look I probably shouldn't tell you this," Eleander said lowering his voice. "But you don't understand, Jonny, just how special you are. The Master told me that in all his years he has never seen anyone with talent like you have. He also said it was a good thing because of what is coming. I don't know what he is talking about there, but I do know he wants for you to be ready, for what I don't know, but it must be big from the way he talks about it. He is also worried at how young you are, even though I get the impression this 'thing' is still a long ways off. I think he is really worried about whether you will be ready. Everything he is doing is because he wants you to be ready."

This was all news to Jonny. Coming as it did after all the emotional shocks, he had experienced over the last half hour it left him stunned. No one said anything for several minutes.

"Okay, Eleander. I will try to remember that. I want to make The Master proud of me, and I want to be ready for whatever's coming."

"All right then, let's see you lift a rock off the table without Roald screaming like a stuck pig," Eleander said grinning.

"I did not scream like a stuck pig," Roald said indignantly.

"No, more like ten pigs," Jonny said with a smile. Roald just harrumphed.

"One more thing, Jonny," Eleander said taking a rock from one of the baskets and putting it on the table. "Try not to hit anyone with it this time, okay?"

Now it was Jonny's turn to be indignant. "The rock will go just where I want it to go. So you better not make me mad." His tone showed he was only kidding.

Strangely, for Jonny, now he had made his breakthrough with the first rock, this one was easy. He looked at the rock and saw it in his mind's eye easily. He picked it up and flew it flawlessly back into the basket Eleander had taken it out of.

"Good," Eleander said, clearly impressed. "So can you make it just hang there in the air?"

Again, Jonny had never thought of doing that before. He looked at the rock in the basket and made it fly up in front of Eleander's face and stop there. He held it, but after several seconds, it started to waver around in the air. The longer he held it the more slippery it seemed. After a few more seconds, he gave up and let it drop to the floor.

"That was a really good start, Jonny," Eleander said with a twisted smile. "But of course you know The Master will keep wanting more, but it is a good start."

§ § §

"Alira, I'm going to need a bruise poultice," Master Silurian said as he walked into his private quarters.

"Did some of the boys get into another tussle?" Alira said, getting up from her chair.

"No. It's for me. Jonny finally made his breakthrough and got a rock to fly, rather dramatically, I might add. The rock hit me in the shoulder."

"What aren't you telling me, old man? Why did the rock hit you?"

So, Silurian was forced to explain the entire encounter, while his wife got the poultice and applied it to his already purple shoulder. After he had finished, she sat back and thought for a moment.

"Well, I suppose you had it coming. You're pushing him so hard. He's only just turned eleven and you are working him like a fourth year journeyman."

"I know, I know, but there is just so little time. I doubt I have three, maybe four years at most before he will have to be fully trained and able to stand up to wizards with decades, if not centuries of experience. Once the demon wizards accept that he is what he is, no place will be safe for him. As it is, there are a couple of journeymen I'm going to have to send on their way this week. They are too partial to demon magic to have around here observing Jonny."

"Won't that raise more questions?"

"No. They all think I'm capricious. As it is, those two should have gone weeks ago, they aren't learning anything more from me, too dense."

"Who? Trudil and Maxtor?" she said as she finished putting away her herb supplies.

"See, even you knew who they were. I am going to have to be a bit more careful about which journeymen I accept from now on, this gets more complicated every day. With care, I can hope Jonny will live to realize his potential."

"Do you really think he could be a zdrell master like Mlandress? The stories of him were always so incredible."

"Yes, I do. He could even be greater, if only he can live long enough to understand and master his gift."

"Well," Alira said, sitting down on the bed beside Silurian, "let's hope you can survive him as well." She chuckled softly, as did Silurian.

Chapter 22

Eleander was right. The Master did want more each day. First, he had Jonny work on keeping things in the air for longer periods. As everything with Jonny's talent, the first time he would try something it would be hard, but became easier and easier with practice. The new practice was work, but Jonny found it easier than the other sessions he still attended in history, writing and figuring.

After a month of work, Jonny was able to keep a stone in the air for over five minutes. The Master then shifted the focus to the weight of objects. He kept having Jonny lift bigger and bigger stones until after three nine-day weeks Jonny was lifting stones bigger than a boy's head. Jonny thought that with more practice, he could have lifted even bigger stones, but The Master again shifted tactics.

Now he wanted Jonny to lift more than one stone at a time. As with spinning multiple coins, it was very hard to divide his attention at first, but he kept working at it for weeks, until, as spring became summer, he could easily keep three stones up, and could keep five in the air with effort.

Once he could reliably do five, The Master said he should have some fun with the several stones. When Jonny asked what The Master meant, he only laughed at Jonny.

"Jonny, I'm surprised at you. You are the child here. Play with them. If you can't think of anything fun to do with them I am sure Roald can, can't you, Roald?"

"Yeah, Jonny," Roald enthused, happy to be included. "Why don't you make them move like you're a juggler, only don't use your hands."

"Okay, I get it," Jonny said thoughtfully. "Let me try this."

Jonny looked at the table and three of the stones went up into the air. They started off in a line and then the middle one dropped slightly forming an open triangle. Jonny focused fiercely and then all three began to move in a circular pattern. Each stone was chasing each other around an imaginary circle. They started slowly, but as Jonny got the hang of the concept, he was able to make them move faster and faster until it was hard to see the individual stones. It looked like a blurry ring hanging in midair.

Roald let out a whoop. "That is so *prodigious*, Jonny!"

Jonny looked at Roald and smiled, but almost as soon as he did, his expression changed.

"Oh, no! I'm losing them," he yelled. The three stones suddenly lost their circular pattern and each flew off in a different direction. Everyone ducked for cover. The Master was laughing.

"Oh, Jonny, that was very good," The Master said, still laughing. "But do try to not get distracted. We might not be able to get out of the way in time."

"Sorry," Jonny said, blushing.

"Why don't you try it again, Jonny," The Master suggested. "This time using four stones. I have something I want you to try."

Jonny nodded and one at a time four stones rose from the blanket where he now had a large assortment of stones of different sizes. They were all river stones, smooth and mostly round. The four he lifted were all about the size of a walnut. Once he had them up, he arranged them into a rough square and once again slowly started them chasing one another in a circle.

"Good, Jonny. Do not make them go too fast. I want you to try a few different things."

Jonny nodded without taking his eyes off the stones.

"First, I want you to see if you can make the circle go flat, so that the stones are spinning like a plate laid flat. Do you know what I mean?"

"Yes, Master," Jonny said still focusing on the stones. "I'll try."

No one said anything as the stones continued to circle. Slowly, the imaginary hoop the stones followed began to tilt.

"Wow," said Roald, as the tilt became greater and greater. "This is so prodigious!"

"Stop saying that, Roald," Jonny muttered as the stones assumed a flat circle. "This would have been easier if I had started with them like this, Master."

"I know," The Master said. "I wanted to see if you could do it. Well done. Practice it several more times and then you are released for the day."

§ § §

The next day was no different. When Jonny and Roald arrived at the workshop, The Master was already there and from the expression on his face, Jonny could tell he had something new for him to try.

"You have done well with multiple objects Jonny. Now I think you are ready for the next area of your training to begin. Lift a medium stone and hold in the air for me, will you."

Jonny did not know what The Master intended, but complied. He selected a stone the size of robin's egg, lifted it into the air, and held it hovering above the worktable.

"Good. Now don't drop it when I tell you what to do next," The Master said, with the grin Jonny was coming to loath.

Jonny did not say anything, just nodded his head to indicate he understood.

"Okay, Jonny, what I want you to do is close your eyes for just a second."

Jonny did not look at The Master, but he was glad he had been warned. Jonny opened his mouth to protest, but The Master did not give him a chance.

"This should not be so big a thing, Jonny. You look away from a single stone when you start to lift a new one all the time."

Jonny had to admit he was right. The more he thought about it, the more he figured that lately he had not really so much looked in the basket for a stone as felt for it with his mind.

He closed his eyes but kept his mental focus on the stone. He kept his eyes shut for several seconds and was not sure what was happening with the rock so he opened his eyes. The rock was still hanging right where it had been when he closed his eyes. Jonny smiled.

"Good, Jonny," The Master said, his lips turning up just slightly. "Now close your eyes again and keep them closed."

Jonny was a little worried, but the stone burned brightly in his mind. He closed his eyes and focused on his mental image of the stone.

"Good. Now make the stone go up and down in a line."

"But how will I know how high or low it's going?"

"Don't worry about that, Jonny. I am not concerned with accuracy right now. I just want to see you move it without using your eyes. I will tell you if it is working."

"Okay," Jonny said, concentrating on making the stone go up and down. He had mastered doing that with his eyes open days earlier. He pushed at the mental image of the rock just as he had done with his eyes open. It seemed to work the same as before, but he was not sure.

"Is it working, Master?" Jonny asked nervously.

"You tell me, Jonny. Does it feel like it usually does?"

"Yes, but I can't be sure."

"Well, it is working just fine, Jonny. It is going up and down just the same as you have shown me previously."

Jonny wanted to open his eyes to see, but he could tell Master Silurian did not want him to.

"Now, bring it to hover again."

Jonny stopped it in place.

"Good. Now here is the hardest part. I want you to slowly drop it down till it is just barely off the table."

"But how can I do that when I don't even know how high it is?" Jonny moaned.

"Just do your best, Jonny. I think you will do better than you suspect," The Master replied evenly.

Jonny did not feel like he had any other option, so he tried to bring the stone slowly down to just above where he thought the table was. When it was where he thought it should be, he stopped lowering the stone.

"How is that, Master?"

"Open your eyes and see."

Jonny opened his eyes and looked. The stone was hovering about four inches above the tabletop. Jonny had thought it was closer, but still it was not too bad.

"Pretty good, Jonny. Let's do it again."

And work they did. By the end of the day Jonny could bring a stone into the air, hover it, and make it run in circles, then stop it less than an inch from the surface of the table, all without opening his eyes.

As they finished, The Master asked him a question.

"Do you know why I am having you do all this, Jonny?"

"Not really, Master."

"I'm trying to help you develop your zdrell sight. I know you've read about it in some of my books."

"Yes, Master, but they never talk about anything like this. They talk about second sight in dealing with demons and foretelling the future. This isn't anything like that, is it?"

"Yes and no. Jonny, most of the wizards for the last several hundred years were ignorant of the type of things you are able to do. You are doing zdrell, a type of magic I had mostly only read about until I met you. For that reason, the books you have been reading don't mention the sight in the way you use it.

"When you move a rock, you see it in your mind first. Right?"

"Yes, I guess so," Jonny said, wondering what The Master meant.

"So you *see* it in your mind." Jonny nodded. "That is a type of the second sight, zdrell sight. Really, the second sight is not one thing. It is just a term we use when we are talking about a way to see things you do not see with your eyes. Do you understand?"

"I guess . . ."

"Herglish really is very imprecise when talking about magic. That is why you need to learn Klathar. It is the language of magic and only it really has the words necessary to describe the different types of 'second sight' as well as other aspects of magic. Only when speaking Klathar can these things be properly discussed. Only now, as I watch you and see you perform, do I understand some of the words I learned when I first learned Klathar. How can you describe blue to someone who has never seen a color?" he said, staring off into the distance.

"Enough of this," the old wizard said, shaking his head.

"So now, names aside, how did you know where the tabletop was? Did you see it in your mind?"

Now Jonny had to stop and think. How did he know? Until that moment, he really had not thought deeply about it. He just did. "Well, I guess, I just sort of sense where it is. I don't see it like a picture. It's more like when you're in a dark room and you kind of know where the furniture is, but you have to feel your way around. You can't see anything, but you sort of guess where things are. I guess that's the best way to describe it."

"That is a good way to describe it. Right now, it is not clear to you because you are not used to thinking of it as a way of seeing, but with practice you should be able to see at least as clearly with your zdrell sight as you do with your eyes."

Jonny marveled at the idea, to be able to see and not use your eyes. "You really think so, Master?" he asked hopefully.

"Yes I really do, but it will be work. It will be more work than anything you have done before. Moreover, while we are developing your zdrell sight, I am going to have to teach you to read in Klathar, the High Wizard's tongue. This book here," he said, pointing to the heavy volume which had been sitting unopened on Jonny's worktable for weeks now, "is the only one that talks about the types of things you can do and it is written in that language. You also will not be a proper wizard until you can read it. There may be some masters who would let a boy become journeyman without learning Klathar, but I am not one of them. It might even do you good to learn one of the Grimoridan languages as well."

"But, Master," Jonny protested. "That will take years!"

"Yes," The Master replied gravely. "Yes it will. Best we get started."

Chapter 23

The Master kept Jonny working hard through the whole summer. As the weeks passed, so increased the abilities of Jonny's zdrell sight. The Master took to having Jonny blindfolded, first when he was working with Jonny, and gradually more and more, until Jonny was using his zdrell sight to see all the time except when he was studying in a subject where he had to read.

As Mid-Summer's day came and went things changed around the castle. Eleander left to attend the annual wizard's conclave and be tested and awarded his master's rank. New apprentices came, and others left, apprenticed out in other trades, because they lacked the talent to be wizards. Journeymen were consistently coming and going. Because of Master Silurian's reputation as a powerful wizard, many journeymen came to study with him, though only a few stayed for more than a month. The Master would not allow any to stay who did not work hard and study harder.

The Master continued to push Jonny on studying the various forms of magic. Jonny showed no aptitude for materials magic, or divination, and he drove the journeymen who tried to teach him incantation or gestures to distraction. He would pronounce spells incorrectly, or move incorrectly with his gestures, and yet, sometimes the spells would still work. His other teachers did not understand, but Master Silurian knew that with Jonny's increased understanding of zdrell, he could do with his mind what other wizards could only do with complicated chants and movements. The Master was content to allow the journeymen to be puzzled over Jonny's accomplishments.

The two areas The Master concentrated on tutoring Jonny personally were learning Klathar, and in developing his zdrell sight. The two skills developed apace, and The Master proved once more correct, as time and again, Jonny found that Klathar let him describe things he saw with his improved sight, where Herglish would not.

Chapter 24

"Master Silurian," Feldor said, as they were coming to the end of another planning meeting, "do you intend to personally appear in stage events at the Harvest Festival?"

"Feldor, let's not start this again," The Master said with a sigh. "You know I have no intention of appearing. Yet every year you ask."

"I only ask, sir, because I am asked repeatedly by members of the city council and merchant guilds. It is difficult, to come up with reasons why you as the ruler of Salaways, and a wizard, fail to perform, year after year."

"We've been over this, Feldor, magic is not amusement for the masses." He put up a hand to forestall Feldor's response. "I know, I know, the people don't understand, but after ninety years, you think they would have learned." He sighed. "You shouldn't have to make excuses, Feldor, I will address the issue at the next council meeting. And besides, I will be in meetings with the trading guild for most of the festival."

Feldor sighed.

Silurian, pretended not to notice. "So do we have anything else to cover today?"

"No, sir."

"Good. I'll see you at dinner."

Feldor gathered his books and left Master Silurian who was already muttering as he read from one of the many volumes on his cluttered desk.

§ § §

By the end of summer, Jonny had greatly improved his zdrell sight. He reached the point where he could walk around blindfolded all day and still function nearly normally. He could even do things with his sight he could not do with normal eyes. He could see through walls that weren't too thick. It did not matter if a room was dark or light either. He could see behind and to the side without turning his head. He also learned to see what he was now reading about in "his" book, lines of force. He saw them everywhere. He now realized that when he lifted an object, he did it by bending the lines of force, which normally held the object down.

As his sight improved a whole new world opened up to him. Jonny found that inanimate objects, things of simple composition, were clearer to see with his second sight. A rock, a coin, or a pot, were all simple objects, but to his zdrell sight, even the smallest bug was a mass of confusion. As he understood the differences, he discovered why lifting a small twig was much more difficult than lifting a large stone. Living matter, or things that had once had life, were much more complicated, harder to see, and harder to manipulate.

During this same time, Jonny and Roald's friendship continued, but like all things, it changed. Jonny spent more time with The Master or the various journeymen, following his lessons. The Master decided Roald's talent for organization and numbers should be cultivated. He had Roald continue organizing the workshop. At the same time, he started having him spend time with Feldor learning more math and bookkeeping tasks. Roald turned out to be almost as good at these things as Jonny was at magic. Master Silurian decided his talent was not to be wasted.

Jonny had a standoffish relationship with the other apprentices and journeymen in the castle. The apprentices were mostly in awe of him. They knew he was The Master's prize pupil and that he could do incredible magic in ways they could not understand. The journeymen were even more puzzled by Jonny. Here was a young boy, eight or ten years younger than they were who could do amazing things that they could not duplicate, and yet he was only an apprentice.

Traditionally apprentices were held in contempt by journeymen, since only a very small fraction of them would ever succeed at magic. The journeymen took great pleasure in lording it over the apprentices; bullying them was a popular pastime.

With Jonny, all that was different. While Jonny did not complain when a journeyman asked him to do something demeaning, the knowledge had a way of getting back to The Master. When it did, that journeyman quickly found themselves engaged in menial tasks that were normally an apprentice's job. The journeymen learned to steer clear of Jonny, and Jonny did not try to make friends with them. Many of them may have resented Jonny, but they made sure they did not talk about it where The Master could hear.

§ § §

The night before the Harvest Festival found both Jonny and Roald together in their room, getting ready for the next day's festivities. It was the first time in several days that they were together for more than a few minutes. Jonny's studies and Roald's had been going in increasingly different directions, and though they still shared the same room, they saw little of each other.

Roald had gradually over the near year they were together stopped waking up in the night screaming. Jonny had adjusted to it, learning to go back to sleep, in spite of it. Roald would never explain what caused it, and would get mad at Jonny whenever he asked. He had gotten even madder, when Jonny tried asking one of the other apprentices. That apprentice wouldn't talk either, and Roald had found out and had yelled at Jonny about how it was none of his business. Jonny hadn't pursued it further, but he still wondered, and feared what the secret might be.

Jonny sat fiddling with the new robes Master Feldor had given him earlier in the day. The Master wanted all his apprentices looking their best at the Festival. Roald sat at the desk making some annotations in a book, which appeared to be one of Feldor's ledgers.

"So what are you going to see first at the Festival, Roald?"

"I don't know," Roald said, distractedly, still focusing on book.

"You work too much, Roald. Is that one of Feldor's ledgers? Has he got you doing his work for him?"

During these questions, Roald had continued writing until Jonny had asked the last question, whereupon Roald slammed down the quill, carefully avoiding the book, and turned angrily to look at Jonny.

"Yes, Jonny, this *is* one of Master Feldor's ledgers. And I am doing a small part to help him with his work. I feel privileged to be allowed to help." He glared at Jonny, who sat looking puzzled at the outburst.

"Do you have any idea how important Master Feldor is?"

Jonny shrugged. "He runs all the stuff around the castle Master Silurian doesn't want to deal with, supplies, chores, and stuff."

"That's nothing, Jonny. He runs all the stuff in the *entire kingdom* that Master Silurian doesn't want to deal with. He handles most of the administrative and governing in the three cities that isn't handled by their city councils. He answers requests and settles most matters, so that The Master can spend most of his time concentrating on magic, and not on running the kingdom. He's the second most important person in the realm."

Roald glared at Jonny, who sat back, face blank, and said nothing.

"So, if I can do a little work to help Master Feldor, I do. You have no idea how much extra work there is putting on the Harvest Festival."

"Roald," Jonny said, interrupting what looked like it would be another tirade, holding up his hands in surrender. "I'm sorry. I was only joking. We hardly ever see each other anymore. I was just trying to be funny, you know?"

"Sorry, Jonny. I guess I'm just cross. Working with Feldor is great, but I never knew before how much work there is, and now I'm getting to be part of it. I just wanted to get this done so we can have fun tomorrow."

"That's okay, Roald. Finish your work. I was just trying to have some fun. It seems like we never get to do anything together anymore."

"Yeah, I know what you mean. We can have fun together tomorrow, at least most of the day. I have to do an errand for Feldor in the middle of the morning, then I have the whole rest of the day free. So what do you want to do?"

"Oh, I don't know. Everything. Nothing. I just can't wait to actually spend a Harvest Festival when I can do what I want and actually have some money to buy something. I can't really remember what my first festival was like when my parents were still alive, but I have no trouble remembering the two after they died. They were miserable. I had to work while everyone else played." Jonny looked down at the floor shaking his head.

"Well, I think we are gonna have a lot of fun, don't you, Jonny?"

"Yeah," Jonny said, looking up with what might have been a tear in his eye. "Yeah, this is going to be the best Harvest Festival ever." He smiled.

Chapter 25

Both boys woke early the next morning.

The harvest festival was the biggest celebration of the year. The festival was not so much about the harvest as about the abundance found at this time of year. There was food and entertainment and every merchant in town tried to find some way to celebrate in a grander fashion than his neighbor. Food, drink and lodgings could be found freely and even slaves and servants were allowed to celebrate, though they were still expected to work some of the time.

Nearly the entire complement of the castle went to town. Jonny and Roald were both dressed in their apprentice robes. The wizard's apprentice robes were very plain. They were made of a medium gray cloth and came well below the boys' knees. The only thing that marked them out was the band of bright red satin cloth at the bottom hem and at the end cuffs of the long sleeves. Jonny's robe was new, as he had outgrown his last one.

They caught one of the large open wagons heading into town and rode with the other apprentices. The journeymen had their own wagon and Master Silurian and Feldor rode in the carriage Jonny had once arrived in. There was much excited talking and joking among the apprentices as the wagon traveled down the road. For once, the other apprentices included Jonny and Roald in the banter.

They arrived at Alavar and everyone went in separate directions. Jonny and Roald headed towards the central market. Neither of them had much money, but during the festival that did not matter much. They ate their breakfast from the fruits vendor. Fruit that other days would have been expensive was free during the festival. There were many street performers playing instruments, telling tales, or performing acrobatics. The crowds would show their appreciation by throwing small coins at the performers.

The two boys slowly walked through the market, taking in the unusual sights and sounds. In the afternoon, there would be various sorts of competitions. Jonny also knew from his time as a cresdin that there was also non-stop gambling, drinking, and womanizing for those who preferred those sorts of entertainments.

North of the main market a stage was set up for formal performances. There were plays and singing groups, and occasionally there would be a magician who would perform wonders for the crowd. Much of the *magic* performed was what Jonny now knew as sleight of hand, or "manipulation." It was not true magic, but the crowds did like to see it. Occasionally one of the journeymen from the castle would perform, but The Master never did. He claimed he had grown bored with that sort of thing centuries ago, and had never performed in a Harvest Festival in Salaways, nor did anyone expect him to do so. He was much too important to be involved in such petty things, or so everyone said.

After wandering the whole of the market area where the main part of the festival took place, Jonny came back to the stage to watch the performers. Roald said he had to run off to do the errand he had promised Master Feldor but that he would meet up with Jonny later at the soldier trials. Jonny hardly noticed him leave. He was engrossed watching a master of sleight of hand doing coin tricks.

Jonny found now that he could see using his zdrell sight as well as his eyes. much of the wizard's deception did not work on him. He could clearly see when a coin was palmed or pocketed unobtrusively. He even spent several minutes with his eyes closed watching purely using his sight. He was really enjoying seeing the world through different eyes and was so captivated he did not even notice trouble until he felt a rough hand on his shoulder.

"Well what have we here?" a voice Jonny knew all too well chortled. Jonny opened his eyes as he was spun roughly around to face a young man who he probably would not have recognized but for his mocking voice. It belonged to his old nemesis Gareselin.

In the year since Jonny last saw him, Gareselin had gotten much bigger, and in Jonny's opinion much uglier. He now stood over six feet tall and weighed well over two hundred pounds. He was already missing one of his front teeth and Jonny could smell the strong scent of ale on his breath. His same two sidekicks, Foresel and Ryalor, flanked him. They too were much bigger than Jonny remembered them, but neither of them approached the size or bulk of Gareselin.

"If it isn't the little sewer rat we got rid of last year," Gareselin taunted. "Come to see the sights have you, nit for brains?" He had a firm grip on Jonny's shoulder and shook him by it. "What, you got nothing to say?"

Jonny glared up at the hideous face of his old tormenter, but was unafraid. "Let go of me," was all he said.

"Oh ho! He wants me to let go of him," Gareselin laughed. His accomplices laughed too. "Why should I do that?" he sneered, not laughing now. "What are you going to do, *apprentice*? Turn me into a frog?"

Ryalor and Foresel laughed at the suggestion. "Yeah," Ryalor laughed, "why don't you turn him into a big toad if you can?" This earned him a glare from Gareselin who did not like the idea of being compared to a toad.

Jonny ignored the comments. "Turn me loose or you'll be sorry."

"What will you do, nit head," Gareselin taunted, "call your mommy, I mean your master to save you?" He hooted derisively.

Jonny could indeed have invoked The Master's help but he did not want to do that. This was his battle. Whether they were drunk or not, he was not going to let them make a fool of him, not again.

"No, I won't bother my master with pitiful slime like you. But you do know he has killed men for less than you're doing now," Jonny said with a low hard voice.

Gareselin momentarily was taken aback by Jonny's quiet defiance, but only for a moment. "Oh he does know how to talk tough don't he," he said laughing, but with a little less confidence in his manner.

"Your master isn't here now and you don't want to trouble him, so we don't have anything to worry about then, do we?"

"You do if you don't let me go right now," Jonny replied, still serious.

"I think I've had just about enough of this out of you nit head," Gareselin growled.

Just as he was about to pull Jonny closer to him, Jonny squatted and twisted sideways releasing Gareselin's hold on his shoulder. He jumped to the side and yelled.

"Catch me if you can. Toad breath!"

The chase was on. Jonny was still fairly small and could worm his way through the crowd much faster than the older boys. He knew that in time they could spread out and corral him as they had done when he was younger, but this time his objective was not escape. He headed for a wagon in the middle of the square that was loaded with large summer melons. He made sure he did not get there too fast. He wanted them close, so he could use the plan that had popped into his head as soon as Gareselin had grabbed him.

He worked his way around to the far side of the wagon where there was a pile of bruised and cracked discarded melons. He stopped deliberately making it easy for Gareselin to see him, and then he jumped up on the side of the wagon and yelled loud enough to be heard over the din of the crowd.

"Gareselin, you fat pig. You're so fat and slow I could have gotten away from you ten times if I'd wanted. In fact you're so fat, I bet you couldn't hit me with one of those melons if your life depended on it!"

Gareselin's face flamed red. He roared, further catching the attention of the crowd, "I'll get you, you little swamp monkey. Think I can't hit you with a melon, well you're about to find out how wrong you are."

Jonny's challenge and Gareselin's angry reply had attracted a fair amount of attention from the crowd. The area separating Jonny and Gareselin quickly cleared of people, as they understood that pieces of rotten melon would soon be flying. People also stopped to watch the confrontation. Fights between drunken revelers were a common spectator event during the festival and it was early enough in the day that this face off was one of the first.

Gareselin noted the attention of the crowd and grabbed a partially rotten melon from the pile and yelled "Here, sewer rat. Have a rotten fruit to go with your rotten brains!"

He drew back to throw, but the melon shifted further backward and fell out of his hand, then burst on the ground. The crowd roared with laughter as Gareselin's face turned purple with rage.

"Hands a little slippery there, frog face," Jonny taunted loudly from his perch on the side of the wagon.

"I'll show you, you little . . ." Gareselin grumbled. He picked up another melon, drew back, and threw it right at Jonny who was no more than twenty feet away. This time he completed his throw, but instead of flying at Jonny, it looped up, over twenty feet in the air, and came back down and burst on Gareselin's left shoulder. He screamed in rage and embarrassment, but his scream was lost in the midst of the roaring of the crowd who found the whole thing funny beyond words.

Now Gareselin picked up two melons, one in each hand. He threw them both at Jonny with great force, but both went hardly four feet before they went straight into the ground, exploding their contents in every direction.

"I told you, you couldn't hit me if your life depended on it," Jonny taunted. The crowd watching had grown quite large and was greatly enjoying the spectacle. There were even bets being placed by some at the edge of the crowd as to whether Jonny would be hit.

Gareselin raged as he picked up melon after melon and tried to hit Jonny, but none of them came close. Finally, after the third melon he threw had somehow gone straight up and then come down on his head, he gave up. The crowd hooted their derision at him. He tried to leave and melt into the crowd, but Jonny was not done with him yet.

"Are you going to slink off like the frog scum that you are then?" Jonny yelled. Gareselin glared at him with impotent rage. He knew he could not attack a boy less than half his size with the crowd watching, so he only turned his back and began to walk into the crowd.

"Wait!" Jonny yelled. "I have one more present to give you!"

Gareselin looked back at Jonny, but then noticed what was happening below him. At the edge of the pile was a tremendous melon, easily two feet across, it was cracked but now it was slowly starting to lift up off the ground. Jonny was still hanging from the side of the wagon but now his eyes were closed. The cracked melon continued to rise until it was nearly fifteen feet in the air. A hush fell over the crowd. Jonny opened his eyes and looked at Gareselin who was staring dumbfounded at the melon hanging in the air.

"I just wanted to give you something to remember me by," Jonny said with a touch of harshness in his voice. "A little gift for all of our old times together."

Gareselin's eyes opened wide as he saw how the melon was coming to hover directly above him. He turned and started to run as the crowd scattered wide on either side of him. He made it only two steps before the enormous melon crashed down on the back of his head spilling its putrid contents all over him and knocking him to the ground. He lay on the ground groaning as the crowd laughed at him.

Jonny used the crowd's distraction to leap down from the wagon and head off in the opposite direction. He felt happy about finally being able to pay Gareselin back for years of torment, but he was a little worried about what The Master's reaction would be. He was sure The Master would not mind what he had done to Gareselin, but he was not sure The Master would approve of his having done so publicly. He actually had not thought he would make it so obvious he was using his magic. He originally just wanted to make him miss badly and look like a fool, but as he had done it more and more he just could not stop with making him look like a buffoon. He had to completely humiliate him so he would never try to come back against Jonny again, so he did.

Jonny tried to melt back into the crowd and continue moving through the festival as he had earlier in the day. But while most people did not notice him among the throng, every now and then he would see someone pointing at him and would hear muttered comments of "Look! That's him." After some time, it felt too uncomfortable so he left the main festival area and wandered the alleyways he had known as a slave.

§ § §

Jonny wandered through many areas and saw how little things had changed in the year, but he had changed. Everything seemed smaller, smellier, and dirtier. He decided he was glad he did not have to go back and live in the city again. He headed out to the fields east of town where the soldier trials would take place.

The soldier trials were one of the biggest events of the Harvest Festival. The professional soldiers of Salaways were a small but very efficient group. The Master had set it up so only those who wanted to be soldiers were admitted, unlike armies in most other kingdoms where mostly conscripts formed the armies. The trials were a way for serving soldiers to demonstrate their prowess and buck for advancement. They were also a way for young men who aspired to be soldiers to prove they were skillful enough to join the service.

The trials included many contests, individual combat with blunted weapons, wrestling, knife and unarmed combat as well as full scale mock battles where the soldier commanding the troops proved his skills in tactics and strategy. The trials started early on the afternoon of the first day of the festival and went on round the clock until the morning of the third day, which culminated in the largest mock battle. On the afternoon of the last day of the festival, the latest recruits to the army were announced.

Since all of the individual competition and some of the smaller battles were open to anyone who wanted to participate, there was a warm competition between soldiers and townspeople. Occasionally soldiers were bested by men of other trades who happened to be particularly skilled in some area of combat, but the soldiers or would be soldiers, nearly always won.

It was exciting to watch and was accompanied by much wagering on the part of the spectators. The crowd had clear favorites, and several of the squads had fans who watched and cheered for them at every event.

Jonny had always loved to watch the trials. He felt no desire to be a soldier, but he marveled at the skill and grace of these deadly men. Walking through town had been a partially depressing experience to him, but his spirits lifted as he watched the beginning matches of the trials.

He was watching two men fighting with long sword and shield when Roald came up to stand beside him.

"It sounds to me like you had a fun morning," Roald snickered.

"What do you mean?"

"What do you mean?" Roald mocked, waving his hand dramatically. "Does dropping a melon on a journeyman slaver's head ring any bells?"

"Oh yeah, that."

"Yeah, that. I wish I could have seen it, Jonny. That must have the funniest thing in the world."

"How did you hear about it if you weren't in the crowd?"

"How did I hear?" Roald asked incredulously. "Everyone's talking about it: how some young apprentice was making melons fly around as if they were birds and dropping them down on the head of the big oaf who was throwing them at him. They don't know your name but they know it was a magician's apprentice. As soon as I heard, I knew it had to be you. Who else could make things fly like that? I sure wish I had seen it."

"Yeah, well don't worry. It was no big thing."

"Jonny, you dolt. No big thing huh? You just don't get it. You're famous. I heard the manager of the big stage has been trying to find you. He wants you to do a performance. He'll even pay you to do it!"

"I'm not sure that's such a good idea. If The Master finds out, I'm afraid he'll be mad."

"Why would he be mad? You being so good and only an apprentice, *his* apprentice, you only make him look better."

"I don't know . . .," Jonny said, feeling worried.

"Think about it. I know the manager. If you decide you want to do it, we can talk to him anytime."

"Okay, I'll think about it," Jonny replied reluctantly. Jonny was not sure at all what to do. It had felt good to have people applauding him, really good. Roald's reasoning made sense to him. Jonny reasoned that showing what he could do would only enhance The Master's reputation, but he was still afraid Master Silurian might not agree.

The more Jonny thought about it the more he thought he would like to perform on the stage. He had not felt at all nervous, as he had pelted Gareselin. The cheering of the crowd had only encouraged him to go to greater and greater lengths. The vision of having a large crowd cheering for him while he stood on stage was very powerful. His only concern was whether The Master would approve. He decided he would try to find him and ask his permission.

That turned out to be much harder than he thought it would be. He told Roald what he planned, and Roald was excited, but neither of them knew where to look for The Master. His only public appearance would be the last day of the festival, at the same time the new soldiers were announced. Jonny thought maybe he would be at the government building Jonny had visited with Feldor on the way to the castle. They headed to that part of town and when they finally found the building, it was locked with a sign saying it was closed until the end of the festival.

Roald thought maybe the manager at the big stage would know where to find The Master, and that would give Jonny a chance to talk to him about performing. Jonny thought that would be a good idea, but was nervous about committing without Master Silurian's permission. They went over to the stage and found the manager. His name was Hanzel. When Roald introduced Jonny to him, he became quite excited.

"No, no my boys, I'm so sorry to say I have no idea where Master Silurian keeps himself during the festival. He just randomly appears at places and then disappears. Then again, he is a wizard and is expected to be mysterious. But, I can't think of any reason why you shouldn't be able to perform here Jonny. I've had several of Master Silurian's journeymen perform here in years past and have never had any problem with it. No, I can't think of any reason he would be against it at all. The only problem I think we have is where I can fit you in the schedule. Hmmm," Hanzel said as he consulted a parchment with many things scribbled on it.

"Well, it looks to me that if you want to perform, and I do want you to perform, it will have to be in about half an hour, right after the Carlenian choral group and right before the Festival Players nightly farce."

Jonny was impressed. The farces put on by the Festival Players were one of the biggest attractions of the big stage. They drew enormous crowds because they took place after the majority of the soldier trials for the day had ended and when people were in a partying mood. If he were put on before them, there would be an even bigger crowd than he had envisioned watching. The thought sent a thrill through him, but then he realized there would be no time to find The Master and get his blessing.

Hanzel saw Jonny wavering. "Can you be ready that soon?" he asked nervously.

"Yes, I'm sure I could," Jonny answered distractedly. "I just really wanted to ask The Master . . ."

"Jonny, my boy. I don't see how this should be a problem," Hanzel soothed.

"Yeah, Jonny, it would be really fun!" Roald joined in.

"Ah . . . Okay, I'll do it," Jonny said without enthusiasm.

Roald's enthusiasm more than made up for Jonny's lack.

"This will be great, Jonny. You'll see! Why don't you start off with some coin spinning, and maybe a dagger, and then juggle the coins without using your hands," Roald gushed.

"That sounds good," Hanzel said. "I'll give you ten minutes, fifteen if the crowd really likes it. Can you do that?"

"Yeah, I can," said Jonny starting to warm up to the idea. This would make all the practice for the last year pay off.

Hanzel showed them where they had to be and at what time, then he hustled off and Jonny and Roald spent all the time discussing what Jonny would do. Jonny did not actually practice any of the tricks since there were too many people around, and anyway he had had a year of practice.

The time came and Jonny was suddenly nervous. He stood at the edge of the stage as Hanzel announced him to the crowd. Many people were annoyed that they would have to wait through another act before the farce could begin, but when Hanzel announced that Jonny was the apprentice who had given an impromptu show by the fruit wagon a murmur spread through the crowd. By now, everyone had heard of Jonny's performance and wanted to see it for themselves.

Jonny stepped out onto the stage. A chill went down his spine when he saw how very many people there were. For just a moment, he wondered if this was all a mistake and wanted to run back off the stage, but then scattered people through the crowd started to applaud. Jonny took courage and started the dialog he had worked out with Roald, who was now watching from the wings.

"Uh, Hello, uh my name's Jonny, and uh, I guess a few of you might have seen it today when I, uh 'helped' an old 'friend' of mine learn why you have to be careful when you throw fruit at people," he began nervously. The crowd did not really react, so he rushed on. "Anyway, when I was done, uh, 'helping' my 'friend' no one threw me any coins to show their appreciation. Would any of you like to do that now?"

The crowd was getting restless. Jonny realized he did not really know how to talk in front of lots of people, but a man in the middle of the crowd came to his rescue.

"If I throw you a coin you won't make it fly back and hit me in the head will you?" the man yelled.

The crowd laughed and so did Jonny. He felt the tension that had been building in him begin to relax. The man made a big show of throwing a large coin onto the stage. As soon as he had done so, several other coins followed from other parts of the crowd. After the coins had landed Jonny bent to scoop them up and set them up on a table on the stage.

"I thank you for your kind donations," he said in a stronger voice, trying to imitate the way the stage manager had talked when introducing Jonny. "And I want to use these tokens to show you the magic my great Master Silurian has been teaching me as his apprentice."

A hush fell over the crowd. Jonny took the largest coin, and just as he had first learned, started it spinning. He stepped away where the crowd could see the coin. They were obviously waiting for something more so he bent and set four more coins spinning on the table.

"I know it might be hard for some of you to see," Jonny said again addressing the crowd. "But I now have five coins spinning on this table, and they will spin for as long as I want them to keep spinning."

This was not the great event the crowd had been expecting, but there was some courtesy applause.

"Thank you, thank you, but I'm sure that isn't what you wanted to see."

A murmur of agreement swept through the crowd.

"So, how about if I make it easier for those of you in the back to see," Jonny said, gesturing at the spinning coins. As he pointed at the coins, all of them slowly lifted off from the table, still spinning. They rose slowly until they were about eight feet above the stage. The crowd began to clap and shout their approval. This was more like what they had been expecting.

"But there are more ways for a coin to spin than that," Jonny said, when the crowd had quieted. He looked at the coins that suddenly ceased spinning and hung motionless in mid-air. Then slowly some coins rose and others dropped until they formed a rough circle hanging in the air. The crowd ooohed in approval. Then he started the coins chasing each other around the circle. They moved faster and faster until the individual coins were scarcely visible. Then Jonny allowed the circle to widen, larger and larger until they were describing a loop over ten feet tall.

Without warning, the loop ceased to be a loop and all the coins shot straight up into the darkening sky, then came back down and spun in a horizontal loop around Jonny. He stood for a moment with the coins circling and then turned to the side and said "Catch Roald!" and the coins flew off to the side of the stage where Roald was waiting.

The crowd went wild. Hundreds of coins rained on the stage from the crowd, so many that Jonny had step back and shield his face. Jonny waited until the crowd had quieted and was about to begin the next part of the act that he and Roald had worked out when there was a loud explosion and burst of smoke from the left-hand side of the stage. The loud concussion caught the crowd and Jonny equally by surprise.

Master Silurian stepped from the center of the smoke and strode quickly to Jonny's side. To Jonny he quickly whispered in a short harsh tone, "That will be quite enough. This little show is over." He then turned to crowd, all smiles, and said, "Another round of applause for my apprentice!" He gestured grandly to Jonny. The crowd echoed their approval.

When the applause began to die down The Master once again addressed the crowd with a booming voice, "I truly am proud of this boy, and one day we expect great things of him, but right now he doesn't need all the coins you all so graciously gave him so now I'll have him give them back." He turned to Jonny who was confused by the turn of events and said, "You heard me boy, send them back!" Comprehension dawned on Jonny and he quickly began sending all the coins lying on the stage back into the crowd. The crowd roared its approval while many of them scuffled to get the coins flying back.

As soon as Jonny had cleared the coins off the stage, The Master took him firmly by the arm and walked him rapidly off the stage, all the while making it look to the crowd like it was Jonny who was trying to escape the sudden fame. Hanzel was beaming as they left the stage and he entered to introduce the first act of the evening farce.

Master Silurian was all smiles as well till he had taken Jonny and Roald nearly a quarter mile away from the stage at a brisk walk, then he let go of Jonny's arm and turned to face them.

The look on The Master's face alone told Jonny this was going to be bad. His eyes, which just moments before had twinkled with mirth now shown with an intensity that made Jonny want to hide in the depths of the earth.

"What did you think you were doing there, Jonny?" he asked with a whisper that felt like a shout. He did not wait for Jonny to respond. "Did you actually think you could perform on the big stage and I wouldn't hear about it?"

Jonny was on the verge of tears but he tried to defend himself. "Master, I tried to find you. I tried all afternoon to find you to ask your permission," Jonny pleaded.

"We did try, Master, but no one knew where you were or how to find you," Roald added, trying to help his friend.

This did not help. The Master turned on Roald and said with even more venom in his tone, "And you, you, should know better than Jonny that you never, ever, do something of this nature without permission. You should have stopped him, but now I see you wanted to bask in his reflected glory didn't you?"

Roald wilted under the attack from The Master. Jonny nearly sprang to his friend's defense, but The Master had once again swung his piercing gaze at Jonny.

"What made you think that if you found me that I would ever allow a *display* of this kind?"

"I, well, ah, Hanzel, the stage manager said he'd had other of your journeymen perform there before, and he'd always wanted you to perform, and that he didn't think you'd mind . . ." Jonny tried to continue but the glare from The Master dried the words in his throat.

"He didn't think I'd mind, did he?" The Master asked menacingly. "I'll just have to have a talk with him when the festival is over, then, but that is still no excuse for you. Yes, I have allowed *journeymen* to perform there before, but that was when things were very carefully planned and staged, not just thrown together in an afternoon. And you were just getting started weren't you? You were probably going to spin a knife or a sword or something else weren't you?"

Jonny gulped because that was exactly what he had intended to do, and he could tell The Master knew it and was not happy about it.

"Jonny I have not spent all this time teaching you, training you, so you could perform at a simple show. You still have no idea what talent you have or what is at stake here. You *cannot* afford to draw attention to yourself like this, not at this time, not at this place, not now!"

The Master was shaking with what Jonny at first thought was rage but then realized was frustration. Jonny now began to see things in a different light, and it made him even more afraid than he had been of The Master's rage.

Master Silurian was scared. Jonny did not know why The Master so was frightened but he could see he was, and anything that could frighten his master terrified Jonny.

The Master spoke again, quieter now, but with no less intensity. "Jonny, I see you really don't understand, and I must take some of the blame for this myself, but you have no idea, boy, how dangerous it would have been for that crowd to have seen more of your talent tonight. As it is, I am going to have to appear on the stage tomorrow to make them forget about your performance. Much as I am loathe to make that kind of show, it is necessary so they will talk about me, the wise master of the realm, and not you, the boy apprentice.

"Jonny, more than half that crowd tonight don't live here in town, they come from far away, some very far, to our festival. You would be in very great danger if certain people learned of your existence too soon, before you are able to defend yourself.

"Someday Jonny, everyone will know your name, but now is neither the time nor the place. You are not ready. I am not ready, and if things happen too soon, our cause could be lost before it is begun."

Jonny had no idea what cause The Master was talking about, but some of the gravity of what he was saying affected Jonny. "I'm sorry, Master," Jonny pleaded. "I didn't know, I didn't know." Jonny began to cry. He did not know why, and he was embarrassed to do it, but he could not stop.

The Master folded him in his arms and held him to his body. "That's all right, Jonny. It's my fault as well." He sighed, "I guess I'll just have to make sure that my performance is one to remember."

§ § §

The Master's performance more than lived up to his desire. For over half an hour the next night the crowd witnessed pyrotechnics and power such that fifty years later any magic act performed anywhere within hundreds of miles was still compared to it. People told their children and grandchildren about the great show of Silurian as it came to be called. Few even recalled how the night previous a young apprentice had performed.

Chapter 26

"Feldor," The Master asked as he finished his buttered bread, on the last morning of the Harvest Festival. "How do you think the diversion is working?"

"Your performance the night before last was most impressive, Sir. I think without any help that many people would be assuming that Jonny's antics were only a warm-up tactic to draw more attention. I have also had key people inserting comments into the crowds that they saw you at the edge of the scene by the melon vendor's wagon, as well as how you were on the stage for all of Jonny's performance.

"Last night I heard completely uninvolved people making similar comments. So, I believe that by the time the festival is over you will be getting all the credit for Jonny's *tricks*," Feldor said, sitting with a folio in his lap.

"Good. Good. I hate to do this to the boy, but it is just too soon for the idea to get out that there might be another zdrell master again. Jonny is just not ready yet," he said shaking his head.

"Do we have time for him to grow up enough?"

"I don't know. I am not sure how soon the demon wizards will move. They are still cautious, and moving to consolidate, but I think that without some show of force on our part, we will lose too many more wizards to the demon camp," The Master said, staring at the ceiling.

"I think I've got to make at least a token showing at next year's Conclave. If I can have Jonny ready by then, it could be enough to slow their movement. Even seeing it, most won't believe what Jonny does is zdrell, but a few will, and that could be enough to make the demon camp continue cautiously."

"Won't that endanger Jonny," Feldor asked, his face concerned.

"I don't think so," The Master nodded, grimacing. "As I said, most won't believe. In fact, most of them will think I've found some way to do just what we are trying to convince people here. They'll think I've found some way to cheat, in order to make myself look better, because that is just what they would do if they could figure how.

"No, I don't think hardly any of the demon camp will believe if we do an exhibition at the conclave, but those who will believe are the ones I'm trying to reach. The ones who haven't yet fallen in with the demon camp, but feel there will soon be no alternative, they will be my audience. If I can give them an alternative . . . it will go a long way to weakening the demon camp without revealing Jonny's true nature."

"How much of this are you going to tell Jonny?" Feldor asked, his eyebrow cocked.

"Some. Not all. More than I have. Hopefully enough to keep anything like this fiasco from happening again." He rose from his chair, and wiped bread crumbs from his beard.

"Come, friend Feldor. Let us make this last day of the festival a memorable one in a good way."

Feldor opened the door to the study, waited while Master Silurian walked out, then quietly closed it behind them.

§ § §

"Jonny," Master Silurian began as they both sat in The Master's main study. The Master had said nothing more about the show since the night of it. In fact, he had acted as if it had never happened, as though he had planned to perform all along. Jonny knew, now the festival was over, The Master was going to take him to task.

"Jonny," The Master said again, shaking his head slowly, not looking directly at Jonny. "There is much I must tell you. And much that I cannot tell you." He sighed in exasperation.

"You are unique in the world, and that uniqueness has marked you. Whether you wish it or not, the simple fact that you have the potential to become a zdrell master means there are a number of people in the world who will want you dead, as soon as they learn or your existence." Master Silurian's restlessness caused him to stand and pace alongside the table, only occasionally looking at Jonny.

"There has not been a true zdrell master in the world in over one thousand years. I've told you this before, but I'm not sure you understand how significant it is. Feldor has taught you histories of the Great War. Have you noticed how large a part the zdrell masters played, before they were eliminated?"

"Yes, Master. The stories Feldor told us were that a single zdrell wizard was able to defeat entire armies." Jonny paused, a thought he had not allowed to fully form burst into his head.

"Master, are you saying *I* could do things like that?"

"Yes, Jonny, that is exactly what I'm saying, and there are many people who would do anything to keep you from gaining that kind of power."

"But, Master, I'm not like that. I couldn't possibly destroy an army." Jonny could not even imagine having that kind of power. Those things only happened in stories, not in real life, not to him.

"No, Jonny, you couldn't destroy an army, today. But in a few years, with full development of your talent, I believe you could. Now do you understand why your skills must remain carefully concealed until the proper time? Today, there are any number of wizards who could destroy you without a second thought. That is why I have been so concerned with the pace of your training. Eventually, your secret will come out, and if you are not ready to defend yourself, no where will be safe."

Jonny was stunned. He did not know what to say. He just stared blankly at the desk in front of him, not seeing anything.

"What can I do, Master?" Jonny asked weakly, feeling more alone and vulnerable than he had since his parents died.

"Keep doing exactly what you have been, Jonny. Learn. Learn quickly and well and a year from now, you will be in a position to defend yourself. In another two or three years, who can say, you might even be able to take on an army." He said the last words quietly, then continued even more softly, "or even a demon."

Chapter 27

Fall quickly turned to winter, and this one was the coldest Jonny could remember. There was ice on the ground every morning. Jonny was glad his room had a small stove because the storehouse had run out of extra blankets. For the first time since coming to the castle, Jonny had boys other than Roald sleeping in his room because the stove could keep it somewhat warm. Most of the rooms the other apprentices lived in had no heat at all. With the shortage of blankets, Feldor had decided it would be no problem for Jonny and Roald to have roommates. He was older now, so the threat of harassment had largely disappeared.

Jonny still kept strange hours compared to most apprentices and he usually ate his meals with the Journeymen, but having them in the same room with him he started to really get to know some of the boys his own age for the first time. When he came in at night, they were nearly all in bed and asleep, but occasionally there would be one absent, usually for the entire night. That boy would then usually spend the next couple of days in bed. When Jonny asked what was the matter, they would say nothing. When he pressed them, they would say Feldor had forbidden them to talk about it.

The conspiracy of silence bothered Jonny more and more. In the beginning he had assumed that what went on must be some deep magical secret he was not supposed to know yet, but now he knew there was no secret magic, or at least not as far as he could see

Finally, he got up his nerve and went to ask Feldor what he had forbidden the boys to tell him. Feldor's reaction surprised him, though it should not have. He simply said he was acting on The Master's direction, and if Jonny wanted an explanation he would have to ask Master Silurian directly.

Jonny put off asking The Master for several days. He had a feeling that if he asked, he would learn much more than he really wanted to know.

One morning his hesitation left him. He woke to find one of the younger boys who shared his room, Carlik, crying as he got into his bed.

"Carlik, what's wrong? Why are you crying?"

"I'm sorry I woke you, Jonny," the boy said, getting painfully into bed. "I'm still hurting a little," he said with a grimace, obviously moving in pain. "I'll be better soon."

"Carlik, you're hurt! Tell me what happened."

Carlik's look of pain deepened as he shook his head and turned away from Jonny, whimpering softly.

Jonny was mad. Carlik was the smallest apprentice in the castle. Jonny was going to find out who was hurting him, even if he didn't want to tell.

Jonny was about to try and force Carlik to tell when Erlil, an apprentice nearly as old as Jonny, interrupted. "Don't force him, Jonny. He had a hard night, and if he tells you what happened he'll, only get in trouble with Feldor. If any of us tells, we'll get in trouble. If you want to know, you have to talk to Feldor. Don't get us in trouble, please, especially not Carlik, not now."

Jonny was frustrated. "I have talked to Feldor, Erlil. Do you know what he said? He said I would have to talk to The Master."

"So talk to The Master," Erlil said quietly. "You see him every day. We don't."

Jonny was mad, but he knew Erlil was right, so he said nothing until he was dressed. As he left the room, he turned to Erlil and said, "I will ask The Master. You'll see." Erlil said nothing in return.

§ § §

Jonny did not see Master Silurian at breakfast; this was not unusual. He was not in the main workshop when Jonny went there. There were two Journeymen working there but they had not seen The Master that morning either. Jonny knew that the fastest way to find The Master would be to ask Feldor, but he was reluctant to ask him since he knew Feldor would ask why he wanted to see Master Silurian.

This was one of the few times where Jonny was trying to see The Master without being requested. He went around the castle to the several of The Master's studies, but got no response when he knocked at the door of any of them. Finally, after over an hour of searching, he gave in and went to Feldor.

"Lord Feldor, where can I find The Master? I've been looking for him and can't find him anywhere, and no one seems to know where he is?"

"Why do you want to know?" Feldor asked, his brow raised questioningly.

"I just have a question to be answered that only he can answer," Jonny said cautiously.

Feldor looked at him carefully then said, "The Master has gone to Alavar for the day. He will not return until this evening." He looked closely at Jonny, making Jonny feel intensely uncomfortable in the force of his gaze. "Should I tell The Master you wish to speak with him when he returns?" He said it with an edge that told Jonny that if this was not important, The Master would not be happy.

Jonny swallowed, and then said, trying to sound more confident than he felt, "Yes, Lord Feldor, I would most appreciate it if you did." Jonny did not wait to see Feldor's reaction. He turned and walked quickly out of his office so Feldor would not notice his shaking.

Jonny did not know what Master Silurian would say. He only knew that since he had been at the castle, something had been going on he had not known about, that people had been careful to conceal from him, and he seemed to be the only one in the whole castle who did not know the secret. He also knew that it was a terrible secret. He did not know why, but he felt it was something he was better not to know. That is why he had seen things that puzzled him for a long time, but he would not ask. Roald never had told him why he screamed.

§ § §

After dinner, Jonny was in the main workshop reading an Ardalan history book while trying to keep a stick in the air by his worktable. He had just straightened up from picking it off the floor for the third time in a row when he saw The Master standing next to him.

"I see the stick is still giving you trouble, Jonny," Master Silurian said without introduction.

"Yes, Master. I can lift it, or read, but it is so hard to do both at the same time."

"I see." The Master paused and looked at Jonny intently. "I understand you had something you wanted to ask me, that only I could answer. What is it?"

Jonny felt his ears begin to burn, but was determined not to back down. "Could we talk about it in your study, Master?" Jonny asked, feeling foolish.

The Master's brow quirked up, just as had Feldor's. "All right then."

They went to the study Master Silurian kept just adjacent to the workshop. When they had gone in, The Master closed the door and asked Jonny to sit. He took his seat behind the desk and asked, "So what is it that you wish to discuss in private, Jonny?"

"Master." Jonny stopped and swallowed. "I have to know the secret you and everybody else here have been keeping from me."

"What secret?"

"What happens to other apprentices but never happened to me? Where do they go at night? How do they get hurt, and why?"

"Why do you have to know, Jonny?"

"Because, because I can't stand not knowing. I can't stand people lying to me, not answering my questions."

"No one has ever lied to you, Jonny."

"They might not have lied about what happened, only because they wouldn't say anything. But they did lie when they said it didn't matter, that I didn't need to know."

"Jonny, have you ever wondered why you alone of all the people in the castle don't know this secret?"

"Yeah, I've wondered. At first I thought it was just some big high magic thing and eventually when I knew enough about magic I'd learn, but apprentices who've only been here a couple of months know, so I know that can't be it. Then I thought it maybe had something to do with it messing with my talent if I knew, but I don't believe that either."

"Jonny, have you ever thought that maybe we were doing this for your benefit; that you were better off not knowing?"

"I used to think that too, Master, and that's why I waited this long to ask. I'm not stupid. I've known all along there was something people weren't telling me, but I figured you had a good reason for not telling me, but I don't believe that any more."

"What changed your mind, Jonny?"

"Carlik. No, he didn't tell me anything, but he came in this morning hurt and crying, and he wouldn't tell me why. None of the boys will talk, and I can't stand it anymore."

The Master shook his head and muttered to himself. "I knew this would happen. I told Feldor that if you roomed with other boys it would be too much. Well, I suppose you are old enough and you would have to find out one way or another." He sighed.

"Find out what?" Jonny nearly yelled.

"Find out what happens to most apprentices; that which we don't talk about outside the castle, ever."

Now Jonny was more scared than ever before. Maybe they really did feed apprentices' souls to demons.

"I can see by the look on your face that you still do not understand. So, let me ask you a few questions."

Jonny nodded.

"Jonny, what are the basic classifications of magic?"

The question took Jonny off guard. This was one of the more basic parts of his studies. Still, he was not sure where Master Silurian was leading, so he gave the standard answer.

"The basic categories of magic are: material magic, demon magic, divination, power manipulation, and physical manipulation also called sleight of hand," Jonny answered, just as he had memorized in his first months of training.

"Good, Jonny, you have parroted back the answer you were taught," The Master said. "Now, outside of the kingdom, in the world at large, what is the most commonly performed type of magic?"

Jonny was even more confused by this question. Again, he answered what he had been taught. "Demon magic, Master."

"And why is this the case?"

Now Jonny was very uncertain. "Because it's the easiest of true magics for a person to do?" Jonny said this since he had been taught it, but now he felt uncertain with the answer.

"Correct again, Jonny. Now the most important question: of all the types of magic, which one have you not studied at all?"

"Demon magic, Master."

"Now, why do you think this is so? If it is the easiest and you seem to be so gifted, why haven't I had you practicing it as well?"

"I don't know, Master. I never really thought about it before. I guess I just always assumed that because it was easiest you would get around to it sometime, but it wasn't important for me since I was already doing the harder stuff."

"You are right in part, but there is another reason. Jonny, do you know how I feel about demon magic?"

"Yes, Master. I have always heard that you don't like it and you don't like magicians who practice it as their primary mode of magic."

"Do you know why I do not like it Jonny?"

"I just always thought it was because it was easy, and because the demon does the work and not the magician that you disliked it."

"Now we get to the heart of the matter, Jonny. The demon does the work. Does the demon work for free?"

Now Jonny was entering territory where he truly was ignorant. He only knew the most basic concepts about demon magic, and The Master was pushing the edge of what Jonny knew.

"No, Master, I don't think the demon works for free. The wizard must provide him some sort of payment for his work."

"And in what form does this payment come, Jonny?"

"I don't know, Master. I've not learned that part."

"That is the secret, Jonny, how the demon gets paid. Demons want only two things, pain and death. They feed on the pain of others, and they feast on their death. The greater the task a wizard desires a demon to perform, the greater the sacrifice required. If a simple enough task is desired, a demon can be summoned with some minor suffering on the part of the wizard himself, but for any really useful task a good deal of pain is required and the wizard cannot afford to do the suffering himself."

The truth was starting to dawn on Jonny and he was not at all sure he was happy to begin to understand this terrible secret. "So you mean . . . ."

"Yes, Jonny, the apprentices here at the castle suffer. They are deliberately hurt so they can provide the pain the demons require to pay for the magic they do. Young boys experience very intense pain, very easily, so they work best. It is one of the reasons why magicians are apprenticed so young.

"I don't like it, Jonny. I have never liked it, but it has been proven time and again that someone who can successfully summon a demon can perform other types of magic as well, and a person who cannot summon a demon, cannot do any other sort of magic, short of sleight of hand. I use demon magic here as little as possible. Only apprentices who show promise do the magic. The other apprentices undergo their pain, then later, if they prove talented, they give pain to the next round of apprentices. In this system, all those who practice demon magic have already been used to provide pain for spells in the past. They know what they are doing to the apprentices, and what it feels like to be on the receiving end of the knife, so they are as careful as they can be." Master Silurian's face was very grim, leaning intently towards Jonny.

"I don't like those who make demon magic their stock in trade, because to be effective they *must* become numb to the pain of others. Some even come to be like the demons and crave the suffering in their subjects, and the worst regularly feed the demons the lives of their victims. They are murderers, and worse than other killers because they kill only for a temporary gain, and soon will kill again. Demon magic is a bloody business, and that is why I have tried to shield you from it."

Jonny was too shocked to say anything. He just stared at the wall seeing nothing. After several minutes where The Master just let him sit, Jonny finally asked, "Master, do you still do any demon magic yourself?"

"Jonny, it hurts me to hear you ask that, but I suppose it is a fair question. I personally have not performed any demon magic in over eighty years, not since the war to create Salaways. Then it was only because I needed demons to fight the demons of my enemies, and those demons were summoned with the understanding that if they won they would have the souls of the wizards who they fought against.

"No, you have no idea how contemptible demon magic is to me. I still have the scars on my back from the tine knife used on me when I was an apprentice. As old as I am, I still remember the pain I felt. I feel it still."

"Why use it at all, Master?"

"Because I don't know any other way to find out if a boy can do magic, Jonny. I have tried many other ways over the years, none shows talent like a summoning does. You have no idea how rare you are. In all my life I have only known one other boy who could do magic untaught, and he became a truly powerful wizard. Only two now out of thousands and thousands of boys through the years. Jonny, you truly are an exception, and that is why I wanted to shield you from the horrible rite of initiation the rest of the boys must endure."

The Master leaned back in his chair. "Now you know the secret. Now you know why Roald screamed. He was a very sensitive boy, he suffered greatly and the older boys used him frequently until he relived his torments in his sleep. When you came, he was taken out of the rotation, so just by being his friend you did him the biggest favor you could have imagined, though you never knew it. He never told you because of the secret."

"How do they do it, Master? Why don't they run away? How do they keep on staying here, doing their chores when they know that soon they'll be tortured?"

"That is a good question, Jonny. I cannot answer for all the boys, I can just tell you why I put up with it. I did because I hoped that someday it would be me on the other side. Not so I could hurt another boy, but so I could perform a summoning and have it work. After I saw my first summoning, I wanted so desperately to do magic that I was willing to do whatever it took, and I did. You see, I was a boy like Roald. I hurt easily, and that made me a favorite of the apprentices and journeymen. I had to endure more than two years of nearly nightly torture before I got my first chance to perform a summoning, and I had the good luck to have it work the first time.

"So now you know the secret. I will tell Feldor, and I am sure everyone will be relieved that they will not have to hide things from you anymore. I guess I will have to make sure you understand the theory of demon magic, even if you do not actually practice it. You do need to understand how it works. In truth, there is not too much to learn. You'll see." The Master stood up, as did Jonny. They walked out into the courtyard. "Goodnight, Jonny," the Master said and turned back inside to his quarters.

Jonny went up to his room, where for a change everyone but him was already in bed. Jonny lay there for a long time pondering what he had been told, and wondering whether he was happier now that he knew the secret or sadder because he knew the truth.

Chapter 28

Now since they did not have to keep him in the dark, he found he was welcomed into a completely new world of relationships with the other apprentices and even, to a lesser degree, the journeymen. He soon found out that one of the apprentices' major pastimes was gossiping about who was giving and getting the most pain; who had the ugliest scars, and who took the longest to heal.

Even though the boys were still somewhat wary around Jonny, they did not have to maintain the façade that had always been invisibly around him in the past. Jonny had had no idea how much effort had been devoted to keeping him in the dark. As he talked with the other boys, he was astounded the secret had been kept so well, for so long.

Virtually every time apprentices gathered, they talked about sessions, both those on the giving and receiving end of the pain. Generally, a boy had to endure at least six months, but sometimes as long as two years, before he was given a chance to perform a summoning. This was not just out of malice, but because even a boy who was "under the knife" as the saying went, was to observe and learn from the summoning he participated in. In addition, there were exercises a boy could use when under the knife which would help determine if he had any aptitude himself for performing magic.

All the boys were anxious to share their stories with Jonny and he soon came to see why they stayed and put up with the pain. They all desperately wanted to be wizards, many of them just so they would be the one on the giving end. The more he heard from them, the more he admired them, but at the same time was repulsed as they recounted some of the more grisly details of a bad summoning. The only one who didn't want to talk about any of his experiences was Roald. Knowing what he now knew, Jonny wasn't surprised.

Master Silurian also had him divert his studies so he could read more on demon magic. He found that the journeymen had had a whole bookshelf of volumes on demon magic that they had moved into another room before Jonny had been admitted to The Master's workshop. The Master explained that most people learned much about demon magic by experience long before they learned any of the theory. The Master said learning that way limited them, so Jonny would not learn that way, he would learn first from the books and only last by experience.

Jonny now knew why he had never been allowed into the castle dungeons. This was where the summonings were performed. Jonny was both attracted and repulsed at the thought of witnessing a summoning. He was in no hurry to see one, especially as he read more about them.

Demon magic involved only one small part of true magic on the part of the wizard, the summoning itself. A summoning involved opening a portal between our plane of existence and another plane, called the demon world. The wizard then essentially advertised to demons passing the portal what sacrifice he was offering and what the demon would be expected to do to receive it. If a demon agreed to his terms, he crossed over to this world, received the sacrifice, performed the act and then left. Aside from the magic of opening the initial portal, the magician had to attract and then contract with a demon. This was not easy, but it was not genuine magic either.

Apprentices were taught very elaborate forms for contracting with a demon. This was done for their own protection. If a demon passed through the portal without a contract, there was nothing to stop it from doing whatever it wanted and taking whatever sacrifices it pleased.

One of the greatest hazards to a novice practitioner of demon magic was in not clearly stating his offer or securing the contract. If a wizard attracted a powerful demon with an offer that he could not back up, the demon would usually turn on the wizard and consume him. If an offer was improperly worded, a demon would always take the offered sacrifice without giving back what the wizard wanted. Properly binding a demon was an art and was why certain wizards could perform better than others.

Jonny learned that demons were beings of magic. They had immense powers and could do nearly anything in the material world they wanted, but without pain or souls to feed them, they had no reason to leave their world. Pain was like candy to them, wonderful, but it did not satisfy for long. An important part of binding a demon was keeping it from doing things the wizard did not want it to do, and the demon would always look for some way to maximize its return on time spent in the material world. Demons could only enter the material world when summoned and could only stay for a limited time. The hazards of demon magic were great for there were so many ways for a demon to get out of control and most often, it was the summoner of the demon who suffered.

Chapter 29

After over a month of study, Jonny was ready to watch his first summoning. The Master told him it was time; in fact, he said Jonny now knew more about demon magic than some of the journeymen who had trained with him in the past.

Summoning could be done at any time, but it was most easily accomplished near midnight. The lesser demons found sunlight unpleasant and would not appear when there was any chance of being caught in the sun. Jonny was set to watch a journeyman who had just recently arrived perform a medium level summoning. The journeyman's name was Jemeril.

Since this was more than a minor summoning, there would be two apprentices put "under the knife" so neither had to suffer too much. One of the boys, Earlil, roomed with Jonny. The preparations were long and elaborate, but Jonny watched with rapt attention to detail. This was the first summoning Jemeril had done at the castle so Master Silurian was also on hand to watch. Jonny could tell The Master approved of Jemeril's thorough preparations.

Once all the other items were in readiness, the two apprentices were prepared. They both had removed their upper clothing and lay face down on special tables where they were strapped in place by Jemeril. Both of the boys had been through this many times before and were not especially concerned, though neither were happy about it. The both had many scars on their backs from previous trips "under the knife."

The object of putting an apprentice under the knife was to cause a maximum amount of pain for as long as possible while causing as little actual permanent damage as possible. Much had been written in the books Jonny read about techniques to do this. The slow torture had become an art form. A master demon wizard could keep his subject in intense pain for hours at a time. The Master did not allow any to become that proficient at his castle.

The summoning began with the one true bit of magic. Jemeril spoke the words and performed the prescribed motions that opened an initial portal to the demon world. Once the portal was open, Jemeril shouted the initial terms of his offer. He had to speak the demon tongue to make his initial offer, but the binding would be done in Herglish.

Jemeril had secured a fairly large stone, about the size of a man's head and he wanted a demon to transform it into gold. This was one of the more common things done in demon magic and only the quantity of gold being produced made it more than a minor summoning. Jonny had come to understand in his studies that any successful practitioner of demon magic would never lack for money for long.

After a few moments of waiting, a voice answered from the portal. This was Jonny's first time hearing a demon voice. It was pretty much what he had expected, but not entirely. The voice was low and powerful. It was not loud or terrifying, as he had thought it would be. The voice did have an edge of discordance to it that marked it as being not of this world.

Again, Jemeril made his offer of sacrifice in the demon tongue with the task desired. The demon responded, apparently in the affirmative for Jemeril began speaking the words of the binding. His voice had an almost hypnotic quality. Jonny could tell he had done this many times before because he did not hesitate or look down at his written notes. It took him nearly five minutes to speak the terms of the binding. Now it was the demon's turn to act. He could either accept or reject the terms or attempt to modify them.

Much had been written about the situation where the demon attempted to bargain or alter the terms of the binding. The general consensus was that allowing the demon to do this was very dangerous and to be avoided. Even the most skillful demon wizards had come to ruin by being tricked by a demon. Many powerful demon wizards felt they could work with demons who insisted on modifying the terms, because they could get a more powerful demon that way, in spite of the danger.

This demon did not attempt to modify the binding, but accepted the terms and came through the portal. Though the portal was only a circle of light not much bigger than a man's fist, the demon had no problem passing through. When he appeared on the other side he appeared to be large enough that had he had legs, he would have stood over eight feet tall. His upper body appeared to be that of a large muscular man, except his skin was tinted dark blue and he had no discernable lower body, only a grey shapeless fog.

Once his form solidified, the demon glanced around the room then ignored everyone except the two apprentices strapped to the tables. He glided over the tables and hovered there. He looked at Jemeril and spoke only one word, "Begin."

Jemeril went first to Earlil and took his tine knife and began the torture to feed the demon. The tine knife was a strange instrument that had been refined over many years. It did not resemble a normal knife; it was more a metal blade with many long tiny spikes. It was pressed on a tangent to the skin so it was like having many metal splinters simultaneously pressed into them. It was very painful and because only the very top layer of skin was penetrated, not much permanent damage was given. Jonny's knuckles were white as he saw the tines begin to penetrate Earlil's skin and heard his scream, and he did scream.

The one thing all the apprentices agreed on was that it never really got any easier to be tortured. Even though they knew exactly what would happen, it did not decrease the pain or make it any easier to bear. In fact, if a boy started to show more tolerance for pain, he usually stopped being used. This happened with most boys around puberty but with some it came earlier. With most boys at the castle they had either started doing magic themselves or been apprenticed out before their tolerance for pain increased.

Jemeril had promised the demon thirty full minutes of pain. So that neither had to suffer too much, this meant each boy was put to the knife for ten minutes, then five minutes in alternating fashion. The demon appreciated this as well because even though a boy was not actively under the knife he was still in pain so the demon was getting pain from both of the boys at the same time. Jemeril worked carefully, but by the end of the thirty minutes he was sweating profusely, and so was Jonny just from watching the suffering. The demon meanwhile had glowed brighter and brighter as he drank in the pain. He seemed to be very much enjoying the experience.

When the hourglass that Jemeril had been using to time the shifts dropped the last grain of sand, he stepped back from the boys and said, "Fulfill your task."

The demon nodded his immense glowing head and picked up the stone. The stone began to glow and seemed to become somehow out of focus. As the stone glowed brighter the demon's light began to wane. Eventually the stone began to dim and become more solid looking again. As it glowed less brightly, it became evident that it was gold colored, and also smaller.

Finally, the stone looked completely golden and the demon set it back on the table where it had been previously. He turned to Jemeril and said, "I have completed our bargain. I go now."

With that, the demon turned and vanished as suddenly as he had previously appeared. The portal still glowed in the air but Jemeril spoke a word and it too vanished. He visibly wilted once the portal was closed, but he did not rest.

He immediately went to a large jar located on the sideboard and started smearing large amounts of white greasy paste on both of the boy's backs. They both sighed with relief from his ministrations.

"That salve you see him applying," The Master said to Jonny, "is another one of our secrets. It kills pain instantly and greatly speeds healing. Without it, it would take days or weeks for apprentices to heal from a session under the knife. As it is, it only takes a day or two."

"Why don't you share it with the outsiders, Master?"

"There are many reasons, Jonny. There are things mundanes would do with it that would not be good, but the most important reason is it is difficult to prepare. The ingredients are not easily obtained, and it takes time and effort to combine them properly. In time, you will learn how to prepare it yourself. Then you will understand."

§ § §

After watching his first summoning, Jonny felt even worse about demon magic. He felt the pain of the apprentices easily offset the gains from practicing this type of magic. He now understood why Master Silurian was so loathe to encourage its use. He continued his demon studies for two more weeks and attended two more summonings, but then decided he had all he could take of it and asked The Master if he could return to his previous studies.

The Master seemed pleased. He told Jonny that he now knew more than enough to perform a summoning, but that The Master did not see the need for Jonny to do it at this point.

Chapter 30

Returning to his study of zdrell, Master Silurian decided it was time to again have Jonny focus on moving objects. He now wanted Jonny to move large objects. Up to this point, Jonny had never moved anything over ten pounds in weight, and that had quickly tired him. Now The Master wanted him to move much larger and heavier objects.

At first Jonny had very little luck at it, but once again The Master made a seemingly small suggestion that changed everything. He took Jonny out to a dry streambed and blindfolded him. Jonny had been in this area working on developing his zdrell sight before, so this did not surprise him. The Master then had him lift a rock that he indicated, without Jonny ever seeing it with his eyes.

To Jonny, the rock did not seem much bigger or heavier than ones he lifted routinely so he had no problem lifting it off the ground. The Master then had him lift another, then another, and still another. Jonny, using only his zdrell sight, could tell each rock was larger than the last. When seeing things this way, he did not see size the same as with his normal eyes. He could only see how he needed to bend the force lines that held the rock to the ground in order to lift it.

When Jonny had the fifth stone in the air, The Master took off Jonny's blindfold and asked him to look at the rock. Jonny opened his eyes and was so startled he allowed the rock to drop. The stone landed with a great crash on the rocks below and split in half. It had been a rock nearly the size of Jonny and must have weighed well in excess of two hundred pounds. Jonny went over to examine the two pieces, and found he could not lift either one by himself. Master Silurian only smiled and said, "Just as I thought."

"How did I do that?" Jonny asked in pure astonishment.

"How indeed?" The Master replied still smiling, though now Jonny could see that he really wanted Jonny to answer the question.

Jonny thought for a moment, looked at the rock and shook his head in disbelief. "How did I do it?" he muttered under his breath. Walking slowly around the rock then tried to lift it again. It was still too heavy.

The Master said nothing but Jonny could feel his gaze on the back of his head. Finally, Jonny decided to look at the question literally. "I just closed my eyes . . ." he said, closing his eyes. "Then you told me which rock to lift . . . Ah!" he grinned and looked to The Master, who was looking very interested in the lichen on the side of one rock.

"I've got it! I can see the two halves now and they don't look that big or heavy with only my sight. That's it! With my sight things don't look as hard as they do with my eyes open!" He opened his eyes and fairly danced around.

"That's it, isn't it, Master? I'm right aren't I?" Jonny asked, jumping from rock to rock with excitement.

"What do you think, Jonny?" The Master asked, trying to look unconcerned, but Jonny could tell from the quirk of his lips that he was right.

"If you think that's right, Jonny," The Master asked gravely. "Why don't you lift this half of the rock with your eyes open?"

Jonny stopped bouncing around. It was easy to learn the truth of something, to have solved the riddle, but now The Master, as usual, wanted him to prove he really understood.

Jonny took a deep breath and stared at the half of the rock. Immediately his doubts began to nag at his mind, this rock was just too big.

"No!" he said sternly to himself, he closed his eyes to see the rock again with his sight only.

The Master sharply said, "With your eyes open, Jonny."

Jonny opened his eyes, but that quick look with them closed had been enough. Even though his eyes were open, he concentrated on his sight's view of the rock and barely noticed what his physical eyes registered. Looking at the rock this way made it seem not really big at all. He quickly set about bending the force lines the same way he had with his eyes closed.

The rock floated gently up until it was over six feet in the air. "Where would you like it, Master?" Jonny asked, deliberately looking at Master Silurian while still using his sight to keep track of the stone.

"Anywhere will do, Jonny, now you've figured this out. Over there will be fine," he said pointing to a spot about twenty feet away.

Jonny casually looked back to the stone and sent it flying. He let it go half way there and it dropped shattering into several smaller fragments. One of them flew back at him and nearly hit him.

"That will teach you to be more careful, Jonny." the wizard said chuckling. "Don't forget that just because *you* can toss around a stone easily, does not mean it is any less heavy or any less destructive." He paused and then added thoughtfully, "In fact, with stones just that size thrown a bit higher and with not much more force, many a castle has been defeated. No Jonny, your little trick has now reached the point where you are in many ways a force to be reckoned with," he said, shaking his head.

Jonny marveled. He had never thought of his talent as anything but a simple trick, though now he thought on it he realized that what he had done to Gareselin in the market with melons could have been easily fatal if those had been rocks instead. "Wow," was all he said as the implications of all this started to dawn on him.

"Now don't start to get a swelled head," The Master growled. "Your power is great, but you are still a child and worse you have no idea how to defend yourself. I could bend you over my knee and I doubt there is anything you could do about it right now. You still need to concentrate too much. All I'd have to do is break your concentration or take you by surprise and you would be helpless."

Without warning, Master Silurian sprang at him and quickly twisted his arm behind his back while simultaneously wrapping the other arm around the boy's throat. He whispered in Jonny's ear, "lift a rock now, Jonny, even a pebble. Do it, or I'll choke you unconscious!"

"I can't," Jonny croaked, even as he felt his neck squeezed tighter and tighter. He desperately flailed around with his body and mind but he could not focus on anything except the roar filling his ears. The world started to turn red, then black and then he knew nothing until he woke to find himself lying on the ground.

He looked around and saw The Master standing near, looking down at him. "Do you understand now," he asked. Jonny only nodded his head, unsure of his voice. "Do you know why I did that to you, Jonny?" Jonny shook his head no.

"Jonny," the old wizard stated gravely, "you must never forget that no matter how much power you have, no matter what great feats you can do, in one quick moment you can be defeated." He sighed. "I have seen many very promising wizards over the years who have forgotten that lesson, and it cost them dearly. Many times, it cost them their lives. You are just a small boy now, but you must never forget this lesson. We are all mortal, we can only die once, and in many cases, there are no second chances. I had to be sure you understood that, not in your head but in your soul.

"However, you must not take the wrong lesson from this experience. You should not be afraid, for fear will kill you more surely than overconfidence. No, you should learn from this that you must always be alert, be careful, and act without hesitation when you are threatened. It is hesitation which allowed me to immobilize you. You must not be caught. So, I think I will have to reinforce this lesson later, and you must be ready. Do you understand now?"

Jonny nodded, then said, "I think so, Master, but does this mean you will hurt me?" Jonny's voice trembled as he asked.

Master Silurian grinned and shook his head. "No, Jonny, I won't hurt you, at least not more than a bit to help you understand, but you must school yourself to be wary at all times, not afraid, but always looking around," he pointed at the trees around them, "suspecting that something might be coming for you, for someday that will be the truth."

Jonny did not feel reassured. All he said was, "Yes, Master." The wizard nodded.

"Jonny, I'm going to leave you now. I want you to start working on larger rocks this afternoon. I want you to tell me at dinner how big the largest one you have moved was. And it better be at least twice the size of the one you had when you first opened your eyes. Any questions?"

"No, Master," Jonny replied meekly.

"Good, then I'll see you at dinner." The Master turned and left.

§ § §

Jonny spent a good long time sitting and thinking after The Master left. He was not sure if he learned the same lesson from the two experiences of the day that Master Silurian had intended, but he had learned. All afternoon he half expected The Master to pop out from behind a tree and attack him again. Which was probably just what the wily old man wanted, but he did not test Jonny again that day.

Jonny did work at lifting stones the rest of the afternoon. In the end he ended up lifting a stone easily five times the size of the one he had first split. It was a fair sized boulder and there was a family of ferrets living under it, which scattered when he lifted the boulder into the air. Because he did not want to destroy their home, he set the boulder back down exactly where it had been before he lifted it. He also deliberately threw one head sized stone at high speed into another boulder some distance away. A portion of the boulder split away and fell apart while the stone fairly exploded. Jonny was glad he made sure he was well back from where the two came together. Pieces of rock flew for over twenty yards in every direction.

When Jonny reported to The Master at dinner that evening, the journeymen at the table looked on with frank disbelief as Jonny related the size of the largest boulder he moved, the ferrets and the exploding stone. The Master only smiled enigmatically, and the journeymen were flabbergasted that The Master would listen to such outlandish stories.

The next day he had Jonny move several large boulders from the creek up to a spot above the castle where they could be used in case of a siege. Because the process was nearly silent, the only ones who knew Jonny did it were he, The Master, and two of the journeymen The Master had invited to watch. All were sworn to secrecy, but respect for Jonny among all the journeymen increased significantly. Moving the stones became so easy for him that it was easy to think he could terrorize any person he wanted with a stone; but he knew better.

§ § §

The Master had Jonny work at lifting large stones for another few days away from the castle. There did seem to be a limit to the size of stone Jonny could move, but it was quite large, and Jonny was not even sure if it really was a limit or if he just could not find a large enough rock to test him too far. He moved a rock that was the size of a carriage, but could not move another that was smaller. He thought this might be because the smaller rock had been too deeply buried in the ground or was possibly attached to a larger rock he could not see.

Chapter 31
Grimor

"The latest reports have arrived from Skryla, Master," the younger wizard said, as we walked with parchment in hand across the cavernous, room that served as Master wizard Jelnic's study. A large map of the two major continents, Skryla and Gimor, hung from one wall.

"So, tell me what they say, Chiz. I know you must have already read them." The wizard, who appeared to be about forty years old, gestured impatiently at the much younger wizard, who appeared to be in his early sixties.

Chiz, once again, felt a flare of irritation that someone whose lifespan was measured in centuries, could be so impatient. He allowed none of his emotions to show as he complied.

"The last major non-demon wizard in Jolondra is dead, Master."

"So Beldereth finally died? About time." He snorted. "He lived long enough to be quite a nuisance. Died of old age did he?"

"No, actually he died in an experimental accident," Chiz said, face impassive.

"Accident? Did you have a hand in it?" the old wizard quirked an eyebrow.

"Indirectly, Sir. I only arranged for his journeymen to be less, *diligent*, to attending to his late night experiments. One eventually went awry and there was no one to pull him from the noxious vapors and he expired." Chiz spoke evenly, as though reading a crop report.

"Wonderful. You're getting fairly crafty after only a couple hundred years."

"You have taught me to take the long view, Master."

"Indeed, yes, but what of our other endeavors?"

Chiz glanced at the parchment. "With the elimination of Beldereth, Jolondra is no longer a threat. This brings us to eleven of the seventeen Skrylaran city-states that will pose little if any objection to our imminent dominion."

"That assumes," Jelnic sneered, "that they don't see our taking control as an invasion."

"Quite, so, my Master," Chiz said, bowing his head, annoyed at his master's need to point out the obvious.

"And how long until your various intrigues have the continent ready for our, *dominion*?"

"If things continue to plan, five to nine years, barring something unexpected." Chiz looked up, carefully.

"Which states still have a significant number of practicing wizards that refuse demon-work?" Jelnic said, pulling on his beard and staring at the map of Skryla.

"Ardalan, Giltrup, and Floric still have several non-demon practitioners. Chezney has two of note, and then, of course, there is Salaways."

"Salaways, bah!" Jelnic spat as he paced in front of the map. "I should have taken a more direct role in preventing that fiasco. But who knew Silurian could not only conquer the most disputed land in the continent, but hold it, prosperous, for this many years?" He stabbed his finger at the center of map where Salaways lay. "He gives those other fools encouragement to avoid the demon path, and he has a strong enough hold on that land that only journeymen demon-wizards dare spend time there, and I am loathe to have them do it. He has turned some of my most promising recruits."

"Why not move directly against him now, Master?"

"Why?" he whirled to face Chiz. "Why? Because the whole point of these last centuries has been to eliminate other practices of magic without an overt struggle. I have been working on this for over one thousand years, Chiz. I cannot have this, this, Silurian, or his allies interfere when we are so close." He held up his hand with thumb and forefinger held close together to illustrate his point.

"Master, you have told me before, but I cannot see how being somewhat more direct would be a problem."

"Chiz, how can you not see? But you have not lived any time among the Skrylarans. Here in Grimor, the people accept the natural supremacy of wizards and demons. They have had over fifteen hundred years to become accustomed to it. It is not so in Skryla. Wizards there live with varying degrees of welcome, from gratitude to contempt, and demon wizards are held more in the latter category. The rulers of those fractious little states know they need wizards to stay in power, but they are also worried by our power, as well they should be.

"Things are best when wizards rule, but mundanes never believe until we force the issue. We will be vulnerable in Skryla until wizards rule there as they do here. Moreover, we cannot assure our rule until the other modes of magic are subservient to demon work. Have I made this clear yet?"

"Quite clear, Master." Chiz carefully kept his face neutral. He knew he shouldn't goad Jelnic like that, but at times he could not resist. The old wizard was very dangerous, but so was Chiz, and he felt his comparative youth gave him an advantage in dealing with the situation in Skryla. When the invasion was complete, or maybe just before, Chiz would see if the demons would show someone else their appreciation.

Chiz let none of this show as he lay down the reports and left his master muttering, contemplating the map of Skryla.

Chapter 32

The Master put Jonny back into his more regular studies, while he decided where next to develop Jonny's talent. Jonny spent more and more time reading from books written in Klathar. He also took to keeping two or three small pebbles in the air all the time while he was studying, both as an exercise and as a way to be ready when he was attacked.

And he was attacked. The Master had made good on his promise to reinforce his earlier lesson. He had assigned the journeymen to periodically "attack" Jonny to keep him on his toes. All an attack consisted of was them getting Jonny immobilized, without Jonny hitting them with a pebble. It became quite a game, both for the journeymen and for Jonny. Master Silurian made it very clear that no one was to be hurt in any way during the attacks, so the journeymen were careful not to be too rough with Jonny, and he was careful not to hurt them when he hit them with his pebbles.

In the beginning, Jonny rarely was able to stop a journeyman from tying him up, but with time and practice, he found that better than two thirds of the time he could hit them with a pebble before they could immobilize him. Even then, he found he could still hit them after they had him down, but they still counted that as a win for them.

§ § §

After a couple of weeks The Master had a new area for Jonny to study.

"Jonny, I've just obtained an old manuscript that contains some tantalizing concepts I would really like to see you incorporate. According to this manuscript, the world all around us is composed of particles so small that they are invisible to the eye. It also seems that though we perceive things to be solid and still, these little particles are constantly in motion within their realm. When we perceive something to get hotter, it is these little particles vibrating at a higher rate of speed. When we see something cold, it is actually that these particles are vibrating at a slower than normal rate.

"Now, Jonny, we cannot see these particles with our eyes because they are so very small, but, according to this wizard, someone with a sufficiently developed zdrell sight can perceive and influence them, can actually make something get hotter or colder by controlling the speed these particles vibrate. I want to see if you can do this."

"Is that really possible, Master?" Jonny asked dumbfounded.

"I believe it is. I doubt I could do it, but you have already developed your sight to a level I have never witnessed before. I think you should be able to do it, and I think I have worked out a method for you to make it happen."

As usual, The Master had a plan. He first had a series of exercises to help Jonny learn to sharpen his sight so he could see smaller and smaller things down to the level that he could see these particles. Once Jonny could do that, he helped him learn how to control the speed the particles vibrated, and eventually Jonny did.

It took a lot of time and effort, and many days Jonny felt he was making no progress at all. The Master encouraged him and told him to study other areas when he became too discouraged.

Months passed, and spring arrived when Jonny finally felt he had a handle on the technique. He found water was one of the easiest things to change the temperature of, both because of its uniform nature as well as because it was easy to see when it changed temperature. Jonny amused himself by freezing small saucers of water and then thawing them to the point where the water flashed into steam.

Once he finally got the technique down, Jonny found it was not so hard to do. He also found that the easiest way to make something hotter was to steal the heat from the surrounding material. This caused the thing he stole the heat from to get colder, and created the strange situation where he had water boiling in a container that was so cold that ice formed on the outside of it.

Once he figured out how to heat wood, fire was easy to create. A beneficial side effect of learning to see things at such a small level was helping him to learn to better manipulate wood and other organic materials

All of this happened at just the right time. The annual wizard's conclave was held at the beginning of the summer. This year, The Master announced he would take Jonny and have him perform in the apprentice competition.

The conclave was the event of the year. Wizards from all around came to the conclave to share knowledge, trade, and compete. More importantly, this was where journeymen wizards were presented to the council of elders to be declared master wizards. They had to perform and prove they were sufficiently skilled and worthy to have the rank of master.

The apprentice competition was really more a way for the various masters to show how skilled they were by the quality of the apprentices they produced. Great prestige went to the master whose apprentice won the competition. Up until this point, Master Silurian had said Jonny was not ready to perform using his talent. Now that Jonny had mastered controlling heat and cold as well as making objects fly, The Master said Jonny had something to show.

Chapter 33

Jonny was really excited as he, Master Silurian, and nearly all the journeymen from the castle arrived at the conclave. They had traveled north through Kenton and over the high pass in the Crags of Glondor to arrive in the city of Glondor, where the conclave was to be held this year. Its location rotated each year to make equal over time the travel for the various wizards coming from the entire continent.

The conclave created a small city outside the walls of Glondor. There were vendors and people dressed in different ways everywhere, somber colored robes, bright satins, and Jonny counted ten different styles of hats in just the first half hour.

It was very exciting to Jonny, who could only really remember living in Alavar and the castle. He had been born in a small town outside of Kenton, but he did not remember much about it at all. He had never been outside the kingdom of Salaways before, and now he was seeing representatives from all of the seventeen city-states in the continent of Skryla.

Jonny was also very interested in the way people reacted to his master; each was different. Most of the other master wizards were deferential and some were obviously in awe of him. Others who smiled to his face, but Jonny could see that after he left they looked after him with hatred.

When he mentioned this to his master, Master Silurian only chuckled. He told Jonny that since wizards live a long time, there were many opportunities to accumulate enemies. He said he assumed most of the wizards Jonny saw looking askance at him most likely were demon workers and The Master was well known for his contempt of wizards who chose that as their primary mode of magic.

There was so much to see. Hundreds of magician masters, journeymen, and apprentices thronged the grounds. One large segment was devoted to journeymen performing almost non-stop trying to prove they were ready to become masters, so Jonny saw more magic each day than he saw in a typical month at the castle. He saw glyph writers inscribing symbols of power on parchment, wood, stone and metal, and then releasing the power they trapped. He saw war mages demonstrating their fireballs, power lances, and magical shields; amulet makers demonstrating their stored spells; incantationists healing minor wounds; potion makers demonstrating elixirs; diviners foretelling future events.

There were also Elders, master wizards of great renown, who spoke on various aspects of the ten major categories of magic. The whole conclave was closed to non-wizards (mundanes as they were referred to in a derogatory way) so all things could be discussed. Jonny was not surprised, and was actually proud of how his master was considered one of the most important Elders at the conclave. He also discovered, as he listened to the various lectures and watched the journeyman perform, that Master Silurian was one of the few wizards who was conversant with (and had tried to teach Jonny about) nearly all the different branches of magic. Master Silurian was known as an expert in all the branches except divination.

The demon summonings were held in the center of the conclave grounds. This kept them furthest from mundane scrutiny, and because that area was a mild depression in the grounds, it helped cut the sound of the screams. Journeymen who were trying to qualify as masters had to perform at least one summoning in full daylight; a difficult task. Jonny stayed away from that part of the grounds as much as possible, but, centrally located as it was, he found it hard not to cut through occasionally. He always regretted it when he did.

Chapter 34

"Gentlemen," Master Silurian began, addressing the ten other senior wizards gathered in the tent. "I have talked with nearly all of you individually, and I hope to not waste your time here. You all know why you are here," he said, looking slowly around the seated men. "Because you feel as I do about the growing ascendancy of demon magic." He pointed out the door. "You have all seen it. Each year they grow bolder. They have taken of the center place of our gathering; we have been symbolically pushed to the edge." He finished the last and looked as if he would spit on the floor.

"As you say, Silurian," replied one of the seated wizards, Kentaroth. "These things we already know. This is the third conclave they have held the center place. What of it? They are growing, as we wane. There are now nearly three demon wizards for every one of any other branch of magic. What can we do about it? There are more of them; their path is easier," he stared at Master Silurian, daring him to deny his words.

The Master unflinchingly returned his gaze and continued, "Exactly! Their path is easier, for them, but what of their victims?" He held up his hands to forestall their comments. "No. I am not talking about those boys out there, screaming right now. I mean all the mundanes in the land. Most of you are old enough to remember when wizards were admired, as well as respected. Now, because of them," he gestured towards the tent door, "we are barely tolerated and feared rather than respected; considered a 'necessary evil,' or worse."

The assembled wizards muttered, but none denied his words.

Again, Kentaroth, voiced the group opinion. "We like it no better than you do, Silurian, but what can we do? Our magic is strong, but it is not as strong or versatile as demons, at least for destruction and power. Why tell us what we already know? You hinted you had another reason for this gathering. What is it?"

"You are right, Kentaroth. I have two reasons for you being here, the first some of you already know. They," he said, pointing towards the demon end of the camp, "are not content with their gains. They are preparing to move against all non-demon wizards."

Several of the assembled wizards nodded, though many seemed surprised and muttered their disbelief to their neighbors.

"I know this is something of a shock, but talk to me after if you need more specific evidence, but I, and several of you, have gotten enough detail to believe that they plan to move against us within as little as a year, but surely no more than five, unless they are somehow deterred. You need to be prepared, and we need to work together, or everyone in this tent will fail to live past the next decade."

Silence reigned in the tent for several moments, as each contemplated their own situation.

"You said there were two things, Silurian, what is the other?" Kentaroth asked, breaking the silence.

"You are right, old friend. I did say two. The other is tied to the first. I cannot say all I wish, but let me say that I might, and I do say only *might* have found a way to turn the tide against the demon masters."

"Out with it then. Do not tease us, Silurian. What have you found that none of us has discovered?"

Master Silurian allowed his gaze to move slowly over them and then breathed one word quietly, "Zdrell."

Angry mutters and shouts greeted his announcement.

"You don't expect us to believe, that after all these years, you have suddenly unlocked the ancient mystery?" a wizard named Chardis said angrily.

"I do not expect you to believe anything I say," The Master said quietly. "I simply want you to watch the apprentice competition and watch my apprentice Jonny. Observe him carefully, and then draw your own conclusions."

Chapter 35

The apprentice competition took place on the third and fourth days of the conclave. Jonny was one of the last to perform. Apprentices performed in an order based on the seniority of their masters, as well as their master's opinion of the quality of the magic they would perform. Few, except for the five wizards assigned to judge the competition, paid much attention to the first day's contestants. In short order, Jonny understood why. Many of the first several contestants merely opened a portal to the demon world, and then hastily closed it, nothing more. Since this was the most rudimentary magic anyone with magical talent could perform, it failed to impress Jonny, or anyone else.

Fully half of the apprentices entered in the competition performed aspects of demon work. Most did what were called "dry summonings." In this type of exhibition, no demon was actually summoned. A portal was opened and closed, then the apprentice would repeat his offer and contract, as if a demon was present. The success of the performance was judged in the details of the wording and the appropriateness of the offering the apprentice would have made for the task to be performed. It was not much fun to watch.

Jonny was much more interested in the apprentices who performed feats using other branches of magic. The highlight of the first day was a boy, not much older than Jonny, who enchanted a piece of wood and small iron bar so that no matter where the piece of wood was placed, the iron bar would lead the holder of it to the wood piece. It was not very sophisticated magic, but it was much more fun, as spectators went to greater and greater lengths to hide the wood piece so it couldn't be found.

The second day dawned hot, with a cloudless sky. Jonny worried if today there might be apprentices whose skill might rival his own. The first two apprentices both did dry summonings, but they were for the sort of task only a powerful demon could have performed. Had they actually summoned the demons, they would have been dangerous.

The next performer took quite a bit of time because he created a complex potion (showing the judges all steps and ingredients) that would nullify poison. The apprentice then proved the efficacy of his potion by giving a rat poisoned food, causing it to die very quickly. He then poured the potion over the food, fed it to a second rat, who ate without harm. The finale came when the boy took some of the formerly poisoned food and ate it himself. This got the first honest round of applause from the crowd.

Two more apprentices did complex dry summonsings, and they were followed by a pair of apprentices who demonstrated basic war magery. First one, then the other cast basic wizard missiles at a target. Then, the senior boy cast a shield spell while the second cast more missiles directly at him. This got quite a reaction from the crowd, partly because some of the missiles ricocheted rather than burst on the shield.

Another boy drew a glyph that kept unknowing spectators from entering within ten feet of it, no matter how much the crowd urged them. This was followed by an apprentice who cast ball of flame that went over three hundred feet up before bursting; an excellent signal, even in daylight.

The last performer before the lunch break was an older apprentice who seemed to Jonny like he was somehow different from the others who had performed earlier. Jonny could not say why, but the sun did not shine so brightly on this young man. He strode to the stage and bowed to the judges.

"I will be performing a summoning, but it will be live, not dry," he stated quietly with purpose.

There was a murmuring in the crowd. The judges exchanged looks at one another. The head judge spoke. "Apprentice, all summonings with offerings must be cleared in advance."

The apprentice bowed towards the judges and spoke. "I understand. I am not using another for my offering. I will be providing the pain to the demon, myself."

A more profound buzz passed through the crowd. While it was possible for a wizard to both perform a summoning and provide the pain offering, it was almost never done. A single misspoken word could ruin any summoning, and few dared to be distracted by pain while working with a demon. Here was either a very brave, or a very foolish apprentice. By the rules of the competition, the judges could not interfere.

The apprentice bared his upper body, got out a tine knife, and then opened his portal. He opened the portal as quickly and as easily as Jonny had ever seen it done. He then took the tine knife and began to scrape at just above his belly, all the while incanting an open offer.

It took only moments for a demon to come through the portal. The binding was done quickly. The apprentice only asked for the demon lift him up as high as the top of the nearest mountain and then bring him down again. The pain the apprentice was applying to himself was sufficient for the demon and the transaction only took five minutes.

Jonny and the entire crowd were impressed, not so much by the magic, but by the strength of the young wizard in using himself as an offering in a demon summoning. The crowd, Jonny included, gave the apprentice, the greatest ovation yet received.

There was only one apprentice slated to perform after the lunch break before Jonny, and only one after. The first to perform was another boy who looked strange to Jonny. He was the first boy actually smaller than Jonny in the competition. At first glance he appeared very young until you looked into his face, then he appeared to be *much* older than his size indicated.

The boy stepped forward, and in a voice much deeper than seemed possible, announced he would attempt a divination of events which would occur before the close of the competition. This was another surprise for the crowd, which had grown quite large after the lunch break. Divination was the least practiced branch of magic, both because the results were not particularly reliable, and because knowledge of future events was, at best, a mixed blessing.

The boy seated himself on the stage and began an incantation in Klathar. Watching him keenly, Jonny saw changes through his zdrell sight in the area around the boy, but they were like nothing he had ever seen before. For the first time Jonny saw a color in his zdrell vision. Normally all he perceived in his sight was monochromatic, but now he perceived a golden radiance, with no specific source, surrounding the boy.

The boy's eyes, which had been closed from the start of his incantation, snapped open, staring through the crowd. His voice took on a higher pitch and he said, "I see things flying without wings or demons. I see uproar in the crowd, and fire burning a wizard's face. I see a demon laughing." He paused, and shook his head appearing to wrestle with the force of his vision. "Demons fight. Wizard fights wizard. Thousands die . . . so many dead," his voice trailed off to a whisper. The boy closed his eyes, bowing his head, bringing his hands to his face and began to sob.

The crowd sat in stunned silence, not knowing how to react. Finally, a few of the crowd began to applaud, even as the boy's master mounted the stage and led the still sobbing boy off.

§ § §

Finally, it was time for Jonny to perform. He was nervous, but The Master had drilled him enough that he felt that he could do this with his eyes closed if he needed to. He stepped to the front of the performing stage and began his introduction.

"Esteemed judges, masters, journeymen and apprentices, I am called Jonny; apprentice to my master the Elder Master Wizard Silurian. I have for your pleasure and entertainment prepared a series of conjurations, which shall all be performed by the direct manipulation of force lines. There will be no use of demons for any of the tasks I perform."

This brought a surprised murmur from the crowd. Many of them were unfriendly, but others were of frank amazement.

Jonny continued. "I would first like to have a journeyman or master come and verify that all things on the stage are as they appear and that I have prepared no manipulation tricks."

On the stage, Jonny had a large earthenware pot half full of water, a small pot also half-full of water and a wide shallow bowl that was empty sitting on another table. He had a small bundle of fire starting tinder sitting in front of the bowls on the table. A journeyman came from the audience and checked all of the props for hidden wires or strings.

"Would you please dip your hand in the water in both pots and tell me whether they are hot or cold."

This was according to the script. The journeyman did not look happy about getting his hand wet but he verified that the water was regular water, possibly a little cold. Jonny thanked him and he went back to the audience.

"The first thing I wish to demonstrate is the bending of force lines to move an object."

Jonny looked at the smaller pot, and it began to slide across the table. There were immediately cries from the audience. They believed that Jonny was using some sort of manipulation trick to move the pot. Master Silurian had anticipated this, so Jonny continued with his dialog.

"If moving the pot on the table is insufficient to convince, then I will remove it from the table."

The pot floated up free from the table and moved off over the stage until it hovered about six feet above the ground. The comments from the audience grew louder. Several were loudly complaining that Jonny was using some kind of sleight of hand to pass off as magic; others had grasped amulets and were staring intently at the floating pot of water with amazement on their faces.

Finally, one of the complainers said, "I'll prove that he is using some sleight of hand trickery," and he stormed up onto the stage. He passed his hand over and around the pot from every angle and could find nothing. This only encouraged him to greater efforts, all in vain.

Jonny then lifted the pot a bit higher so it was out of the man's grasp, and then started to tip it so the water ran out and landed on his head. The crowd laughed and the man ran off the stage.

Jonny said, "I seem to have lost all the water in my pot. I guess I'll just have to get some more."

Whereupon, the pot dropped down into the larger one and came up again filled with water. The crowd applauded as Jonny brought the pot to hover above the shallow bowl. He then caused it to poor a small amount of water into the bowl. He set the pot back down on the table where it had started. The crowd watched attentively, waiting to see what would happen next.

"Aside from being able to manipulate objects. My master has also taught me to influence their temperature."

With that, Jonny concentrated on the bowl. After a few moments, he used his power to have the bowl float up and over the crowd. After the bowl had hovered for a few moments he had it slowly turn over. The audience had clearly been expecting it, but was even more surprised when nothing came out. He floated the bowl down until it was sitting in the lap of a wizard who stared at it with a look of horror on his face. He was shocked because he could clearly see that the water in the bowl had all turned to ice. He exclaimed and then passed the bowl around for others to see that the water was frozen solid in the bowl, but the bottom of the bowl was warm to the touch.

Jonny was pleased with the effect on the crowd but he had one more thing left to do. "My master says that it is always best to end a show with a bang, so I have one for you."

The ball of tinder which had been sitting on the table slowly rose into the air till it was about thirty feet above the stage, then Jonny focused a bit more on it and the entire ball burst into a large ball of flame which took less than a second to consume itself.

The audience sat in stunned silence for a few moments and then erupted into applause. Jonny left the stage and as he left The Master mounted the stage.

"That is correct gentlemen, none of that was demon magic. All of it my apprentice accomplished through manipulations of the forces available. So, when you are told that significant magic cannot be accomplished without demons, don't you believe it. Thank you."

He left the stage to the applause of the audience, though several in the audience who were not applauding and looked as if they had eaten something very sour; two of them were judges. The Master rejoined Jonny and complimented him on a well-done performance. Jonny basked in his master's approval, which meant more to him than the applause of the crowd, though he had enjoyed that too.

§ § §

Jonny sat in the audience and watched the last apprentice perform. At first he hardly noticed what the apprentice was doing, he was so flushed from his successful performance. His attention perked up when a pair of pain tables were wheeled onto the stage, and apprentices quickly strapped in place, gagged.

The apprentice explained that he would summon a demon, in broad daylight, that would create a pile of four hundred gold pieces. He worked rapidly, applying the tine knife to the two apprentices while performing his summoning. Something about the young man's attitude bothered Jonny. He seemed too casual for performing a sophisticated summoning.

The apprentice worked quickly when the demon appeared as well, running through the terms of the binding faster than Jonny had previously heard done. Then the demon did the unexpected, it asked the apprentice to clarify a term of the binding. Several members of the audience quietly gasped, waiting to see what the apprentice would do. The apprentice did not seem to notice the audience's reaction, and quickly spoke his clarification.

The binding was concluded and the demon waited for the agreed upon pain offering. It took nearly twenty minutes to complete the torture of the apprentices. All the while, Jonny sat and fidgeted. He did not want to watch this part, but he found it hard to look away. He was glad that the boys were both gagged, otherwise he doubted he could have stayed.

Finally, the offering was finished, and the demon began to perform its task. It faded from visible sight, but Jonny was still able to follow its movements, though less clearly, with his zdrell sight. The crowd murmured when the demon seemed to disappear. Several of the wizards in the audience grasped amulets. Within a few moments, gold pieces began to appear on the stage next to the apprentice. At the disappearance of the demon, he had started to look concerned, but when the gold began to appear, his look of supreme confidence returned.

Bit by bit the pile of gold grew, but as he watched, Jonny and those wizards holding amulets, looked more and more puzzled. The demon, instead of hovering over the stage and converting air, or rocks, or whatever substance they had expected into the gold coins, seemed to be flying extremely fast, darting in many directions all over the conclave grounds. At times it would hover over a member of the audience, or a tent, and then it would return to the stage just long enough to drop one, or several gold pieces on the growing pile.

Jonny began to have a suspicion, and from the looks on the faces of several of the wizards who also seemed able to see the demon, he was not alone. Finally, one of those wizards opened the money pouch at his side and stared within. "The demon isn't making that gold!" the man shouted, "He's stealing it! Everyone, check your money."

The apprentice on the stage stood paralyzed, his face ashen. As more and more shouts from the audience confirmed that the demon was indeed stealing the gold still collecting on the stage, he began to panic. The apprentice called out to the demon. It appeared visible again, hovering over the stage. The apprentice spoke, "Demon, I bound you to *produce* a pile of four hundred golds, not steal it."

The demon spoke, its voice booming, "I have produced this unfinished pile, mortal. You did not specify the method. Do you wish me to continue?"

"No," the downcast apprentice replied quietly.

"Then our business is concluded, foolish mortal." The demon laughed as it disappeared through the portal.

The humiliated apprentice turned to the crowd and spoke clearly, if quietly. "I am sorry for my failure." He looked down, and then squared his shoulders and continued. "If any of you have lost golds because of this *demonstration* please come to the tent of my master, Feltran, and I will repay all." He gathered up the gold in a bag, brought for that purpose, and silently departed the stage.

There was considerable confusion in the audience after this last, unexpected, demonstration. The judges were leaning together and whispering in agitated tone.

After several moments of consultation, the head judge mounted the stage and announced that the winner of the competition would be announced the following morning. Jonny got up to leave when he heard a familiar voice.

"Jonny! Jonny, just look at you! You're bigger and uglier than ever. And then you go and put on a silly demonstration like that. No one would believe that you're the best apprentice of Master Silurian." Jonny could see the speaker was laughing and did not mean a word that he said.

It was Eleander, the journeyman who had befriended Jonny when he first came to the castle.

"Eleander," Jonny shouted. "It's great to see you!"

"I'm not called by that name anymore, Jonny, you should know that. I'm called Skylock now, Master Skylock to you," he said grinning.

"Well, *Master* Skylock, did you see my demonstration then?"

"I did, Jonny, and a pitiful thing it was too . . . except in comparison to all of the other ones! That was incredible, Jonny. I wish I had your talent. I see The Master has kept you busy since I left. You've probably got all sorts of new tricks I haven't seen. But it looks like Master Silurian hasn't kept you too busy to keep you from growing. You are at least six inches taller than when I last saw you, even though you still are one of the smallest apprentices here. Of course you probably are the youngest apprentice in this contest so I guess it makes sense."

Jonny beamed. He was so happy to see Eleander, no, Master Skylock again. The Master had gone off somewhere shortly after Jonny's demonstration, so Jonny was only too happy to accompany Skylock when he suggested that they go back to his camp to eat and catch up on what had gone on since they had last seen each other.

Jonny had a very good time talking with Skylock and telling him about all the changes at the castle. He also loved hearing about what Skylock had been doing since he had been awarded master status. Skylock said that he had still not decided on a place to settle down and so had been traveling for most of the last year. He told Jonny about all of the different places he had visited and things and people he had seen.

After several hours Skylock told Jonny he had better head back to The Master's camp otherwise he would get concerned about Jonny's whereabouts. Jonny doubted that, but knew he did need to get back. It was late and he was getting very tired. The excitement of the day had kept Jonny going, but now he felt the fatigue of the day's events set in. He bid Skylock farewell after arranging to meet again the next afternoon.

As Jonny started walking back to The Master's camp he started to realize just how late it was. The moon was out and not many people were walking between camps. In the distance, he could hear the singsong chants of demon wizards performing summonings. There seemed to be a lot of them and the sound of the chants with the soft cries from the apprentices being tortured made the hair on the back of his neck stand up. He started walking more quickly, wanting to get back to the safety of The Master's camp. The Master had told him it was not wise to be out walking late at night and now he understood why.

He was walking down a narrow way between several large tents when without warning he was grabbed from behind. He was dragged into a dimly lit tent and then thrown to the floor.

"Hey," said the young man who had just released him. "You're not Darslom! What were you doing walking out there? Actually, it doesn't matter," he said giving Jonny no time to respond. "You'll have to do. Now take off your shirt and get on the rack. I have to get this summoning going now or I'll miss The Confluence all together."

Jonny was confused, but he saw the rack the young man had pointed towards and he suddenly realized what he wanted. Jonny was to be his sacrifice for a summoning! Jonny started to stammer how the man had mistaken him for someone else, that he could not be a sacrifice, but he was having none of it. He said he did not care who Jonny was, and he had to have a sacrifice for his summoning and Jonny was going to be one whether he wanted to or not. He grabbed Jonny and since he was over six feet tall easily held him immobilized while he pulled Jonny's cloak and shirt off. He then took Jonny and started to strap him down to the pain rack. He let out a surprised grunt when the dim light in the tent caught Jonny's as yet unscarred back.

He took a step back and said, "What's this? You're too old not to have been used before. Why are there no scars on your back?"

Again, just as Jonny started to answer the man continued. "What do I care? It'll just be easier to do you, the demons always like a first timer, not that they get 'em often."

Jonny was more scared than he could remember being. He knew from watching what it was like to be made a sacrifice and did not want to be made one, especially for this man whose name he did not even know. Jonny looked over his shoulder and saw the man hastily arranging things. Then he pulled out a tine knife. This one was bigger by half than any Jonny had seen used in Silurian's castle and now he was even more scared.

As the man began to approach, Jonny could see he was going to do a more controversial type of summoning with Jonny. He would put Jonny to pain and then open a portal. This method was more risky than the summonings which Jonny had already seen, but he knew from the literature that it was also the fastest way to get results. The fresh pain drew the demons very quickly to the portal.

Jonny was tied down so he could not move; all he could see was that huge tine knife in the man's hand. Suddenly Jonny realized, as the man moved to a position behind Jonny, Jonny was not seeing the man with his eyes, but with his sight. With the realization he was using his sight, he suddenly realized what he had to do. He was mad at himself for taking this long to remember.

The knife was already burning clearly in Jonny's sight, so all he did was take control of it and make it fly straight upward through the tent roof and high into the night sky. Unfortunately for the man holding the knife, that meant he too was pulled off the ground and through the same hole in the tent's roof the knife made as it flew upward. At some point he must have lost his grip on the knife because he shortly afterwards came falling back down outside the tent with a great dull thud.

Jonny was still tied to the rack. Using a combination of his talent and wiggling he was able to get free after several moments. He put his clothes back on and ran all the way back to the master's camp without a backward glance.

He did not know what had happened to his would be torturer, but he was mad enough that he did not care. As he ran, he kept a fist-sized rock in his hand so he could defend himself if the need arose.

Jonny got back to camp without further incident and immediately dived into his tent and got under his blankets. He was shaking from exhaustion, fear, and the realization of how close he had come to being tortured and possibly even killed.

He was mad at himself for being caught in the first place, and then for being so slow to remember how to defend himself. He was ashamed at how easily he had been caught, just as The Master had warned him. He resolved that he would tell no one what had happened. As soon as he made up his mind to keep the incident a secret, he relaxed a bit and eventually fell asleep.

Chapter 36

As Jonny woke, he remembered all that had happened the previous day. He hoped this day would be a little less exciting, but he was to be disappointed. The day started normally enough, he ate with The Master and the other apprentices in the group. Jonny prepared all sorts of explanations in case the incident from the previous night came out, but nothing was mentioned. The journeymen were already off preparing for the final day of journeyman competition and the master rank awarding ceremonies. The other apprentices were eating and talking about how much prestige The Master would gain when Jonny won the apprentice prize. Jonny told them he did not think it was a sure thing, but they just laughed. They were sure that Jonny was the only possible choice.

The Master said nothing while they were eating. As he finished, he looked at Jonny and told him to be sure his robes were clean and hanging straight. He did not want to have his apprentice look unkempt before the crowd. It took Jonny a couple of minutes to realize that The Master had in his own way been agreeing with the other apprentices. He thought Jonny would be in front of the crowd to accept the prize. Jonny was having trouble concentrating on that possibility. He was still endlessly replaying the previous night's events.

§ § §

The prize for the best apprentice performance was awarded with much ceremony. The event began at midmorning with each apprentice being called before the judges and having their performance publicly critiqued. It took nearly as long as the competition the day before, and was designed to be as much a teaching experience as an awards ceremony. There was only one award given but the order that an apprentice was called before the judges declared his ranking with the poorest performer being called first. Jonny knew he would be one of the last called, but even so, he waited and listened to the critique and advice the judges gave each contestant. Much of the advice was the same, but occasionally Jonny heard something that made him consider things he had not before.

It was well after noon when the judges got down to the last three contestants. They had not taken any sort of a break before the last three, and they only stopped a few minutes before they again commenced. Jonny was now more than a little nervous. In his heart, he agreed with the other apprentices. He felt his demonstration had been superior to the others, but still he was afraid the judges might see things differently. The third best contender was called, it was the boy who had had the wood button and rod from the first day.

Now it was just Jonny and the apprentice who had done the demon summoning using himself as the offering. Jonny was sweating, and not just from the afternoon heat.

The critique ended, and the next name was called. It was not Jonny! The boy looked back at Jonny with great contempt as he mounted the platform. Jonny seemed to be in some sort of bubble. The realization that he had won made all his surroundings seem somehow unreal. He could not hear anyone, and so he did not hear his name when it was announced. He just stood there stunned. The apprentice standing next to him had to tug on his sleeve. "Get up there!" he whispered. "You've won!"

Jonny went up onto the stage and still was having trouble hearing anything being said. He heard dimly the congratulations of the head judge and the other judges. He saw the crowd cheering for him, but it was all as if his ears were stuffed with cotton, like he was in some kind of dream.

It all snapped into sharp focus and sound when two things happened. First, The Master mounted the stage to the cheers of the crowd and the congratulations of the judges. But the second thing was what brought Jonny fully back to reality. Behind Jonny a man jumped onto the stage with a yell. It was the same man who had tried to prove that Jonny was faking his demonstration the day before. The same one Jonny had poured water on. The man was incoherent with rage. He grabbed Jonny by the throat and shook him.

"Tell me how you cloaked your demons boy!" the man screamed. Jonny could see his eyes bulging.

"Tell me and everyone here how you did it, or I throttle you here and now!"

Jonny could not have answered him even if he had wanted to. The man was holding him so tightly Jonny could barely breathe, let alone talk. Jonny had no intention of talking. The man's enraged face filled Jonny's vision and for the second time in his life, he allowed his rage flow back at the man. This time he did not use a rock. The man had a flaming red beard and hair, Jonny decided to make it really flame. He concentrated on making it get hotter and hotter. It was not as easy to do as with water, but no harder than wood.

The beard began to smolder as well as the man's hair. At first, he did not notice, but when his beard caught fire, he had no choice. He released Jonny and started trying to put out the flames with his hands but then jumped screaming from the stage when he realized his whole head was on fire.

The crowd stood in stunned silence, and then they burst into applause with several yelling their opinions of Jonny's assailant after him. The Master came over to Jonny and very quietly said, "Well done, Jonny. Very well done."

Jonny had rarely seen The Master like this before, so obviously pleased. The look on his face made Jonny feel better than any other thing possibly could. The medallion he received for winning seemed pale in comparison to the warmth of his master's approval.

§ § §

That evening the Council of Elders announced the journeymen who were awarded master status. It was a solemn ceremony where each new master was given a certificate to indicate he had been a judged a master and each was given his master ring. These were special rings that once one person had worn them could never be worn by another. The owner could take the ring off but no one else could put it on, they simply would not go. The magic ring was the surest sign a wizard truly was a master. Certificates could be forged, but a master's ring could not be faked.

After the ceremony was over, Jonny went to meet Master Silurian, who had acted as The Eldest and given out the rings. The Master introduced him to another wizard.

"Jonny, I want you to meet master Gorkonder. Master Gorkonder is one of the finest workers of amulet magic I have ever met."

Jonny blushed and stammered out, "I'm very honored to meet you, Master Gorkonder."

Master Gorkonder bowed to Jonny making him blush even more deeply. "And I am most honored to meet you, young man. I have seldom seen so powerful a display of force manipulation as in your demonstration in the apprentice competition and your encore afterwards."

Jonny did not know what to say, but he managed to stammer out, "Th-thank you, Master. It was nothing."

"Not at all, young man. Your master will not say it, but I will tell you that your talents already exceed several of the journeymen we awarded master status tonight. You are not yet ready to be a master, but when you are, I suspect everyone will know your name."

Jonny was stunned by the compliment. Now he really did not know what to say and Master Gorkonder easily discerned it from the look on Jonny's face. He turned to face The Master.

"He's humble too, Silurian. You have done well, old friend. This one will go somewhere someday. But, I must go. Before I go," he said, turning back to Jonny. "I have something I hope you will find useful. I almost doubt you need it, but I think you may find it helpful. Your master will tell you how to use it."

He handed Jonny a small amulet. It was silver and shaped like a teardrop with runes etched lightly into the surface and seemed to glow from within with a reddish light. It hung from a simple leather thong, which seemed strange to Jonny for something so obviously valuable. Jonny stammered out his thanks and Master Gorkonder left.

"You know, Jonny," The Master said as they both watched Master Gorkonder walk off into the night. "You have just received one of the most important gifts you could have received. This is a demon sight amulet, and Master Gorkonder is the only one I know who knows how to create them. I have known many journeymen who have served him for over a year just to get one. Nearly every master wizard here has one; they are very valuable indeed. You must have greatly impressed him. It has been years since I have seen him give one to an apprentice. Years ago, he gave them to anyone who would ask, but that was long ago. Yes, you must have impressed him greatly."

"But what does it do, Master?"

"What does it do? Why it allows you to see the world as demons see it. It lets you see the lines of force with your natural eyes as well as other things. This amulet will allow you to see the world from a completely different perspective. For many, this is the only way they can see force lines or where to place a portal, or to see through a portal into the demon world. There are many things that can be done with this amulet. I am sure you will learn them with time."

"How does it work, Master?"

"That is the best part of it, Jonny. It is so simple anyone, even mundanes, can do it. Simply grasp the amulet with your eyes closed and then open them while you hold onto it."

Jonny did not wait for further instruction. He grasped the amulet between his thumb and forefinger with his eyes closed. Without loosening his grip, he slowly opened his eyes to see a new world.

Everything around Jonny was tinted red. It was like looking through red colored glass. The first thing he noticed was that while it was full dark outside, it did not look dark at all now. Everything around him glowed with its own inner light. The Master glowed quite brightly and Jonny could scarcely look at some of the rings on his fingers they were so bright.

At first, he was confused at how things looked and he expected to see force lines the same way he did with his zdrell sight. It took a few minutes before he began to perceive them though they looked nothing like the way he visualized them. They were showing as the general colored haze that he saw. He tried moving a rock and saw the haze around the rock clear and understood that it was just a different way of seeing the force lines he was used to manipulating.

Jonny closed his eyes and released the amulet. He opened his eyes and looked at The Master. "Is that really how the demons see our world, Master?"

"Yes, Jonny. That is how they see it. If there were a demon present or a portal open, you would see it very differently than you have thus far. With this amulet, when you look through a portal you can actually see the demon world on the other side. This is a very powerful tool. Master Gorkonder is one of the few left who can create magical objects like this with any kind of ease.

"But enough of this for now, you have had enough excitement for a day. Tomorrow we begin our trip back to Salaways. Best we both get some sleep."

Chapter 37

Three wizards stood on the city walls watching as the last caravan left the now nearly deserted former conclave grounds. The center wizard was of middle height, with blue eyes and red hair cut much shorter than he was accustomed to. His red beard, a trademark of his features for the last thirty years was notably absent.

The taller, dark haired wizard to his right spoke, still looking out over the valley. "That's the last of them." He paused and turned towards the middle wizard. "Not quite the triumph we hoped for, eh, Feltran?"

The middle wizard, Feltran, continued looking out over the valley. "No," he answered crossly, "not the triumph I had planned at all. Blast Silurian!" he said pounding his fist on the top of the wall. "He wasn't responsible for the failure of that fool apprentice of mine, but everything else that has gone wrong can be traced back to him." He spit over the wall. "This conclave has set our cause back at least two years, maybe more. Curse Silurian, curse Salaways, and curse that little rodent of an apprentice of his!"

The two wizards on either side, shot quick glances at one another. Neither seemed willing to say anything, afraid of becoming the target of Feltran's wrath. Finally, one spoke. "Do you think Silurian's apprentice was really doing direct force manipulation?"

"What, zdrell?" Feltran asked, contempt in his voice. "No. I don't believe it. Silurian was running some sort of game there. There was no way that boy was doing anything himself. He hardly even moved or talked, except for that stage prattle. No, Silurian has found some way to do what we saw, while passing it off as the boy. He had to have an accomplice hidden somewhere controlling things. I don't know how, but I know that old man has more tricks than most have dreamed of." These last words were a grudging mutter.

Again, the two wizards flanking Feltran shared a glance. The one rolled his eyes and gave a small shake of the head. They both turned away from the outer edge of the wall and walked to the stairs heading back towards the center of the city. Feltran remained, silently brooding.

§ § §

The trip back to the castle was uneventful. In truth, unless bandits had attacked them, anything would have seemed tame after all that had happened at the Conclave. The journeymen and apprentices treated Jonny with nearly as much respect as Master Silurian, though Jonny could sense that some of the journeymen were frankly jealous. The Master treated Jonny as he always had. The pleasure he had shown at Jonny's performance was displaced by his usual detached manner towards him. Jonny suspected The Master was thinking of new things for him to learn.

He was right.

Chapter 38

When they had returned to Salaways, Master Silurian gave Jonny two days to continue the studies he had been working on prior to the conclave, then summoned Jonny to his main study.

"I have some new things for you to study, Jonny," The Master began. "I suspect you knew this would happen, after your performance at the conclave."

"Yes, Master."

"I think after the incidents there, something should be very clear to you."

"What is that, Master?"

"You are still young, still vulnerable, and will continue to be for some years yet, but you have already made some powerful enemies."

"I have, Master?"

"Oh yes, Jonny, you have indeed. Do you know who that wizard was you humiliated twice, in public?"

"I heard he is called Feltran, that's all."

"Well then, you need to know more. As you may have guessed, he is a demon master. Frankly, he is not that proficient of a wizard, but he is a mouthpiece for a number of other wizards who are quite powerful. By humiliating him, you essentially made an enemy of that group of wizards who rely on demon magic alone.

"In a sense, you have made yourself more my apprentice than any other before. By doing this, you are allied with me, not just because you are my apprentice, but also because you have made enemies of those who despise me. However, there is still a significant difference between you and me. You are a young apprentice, and I am a rather old and respected master. Many, who would not dream of attacking me, would not give a second thought to attacking you. It has already happened twice, eh?"

Jonny had told no one of the first attack, but was not surprised that The Master somehow knew of it.

"Ah, I see. You thought I did not know about you almost becoming an offering? Well, I am glad you came out of that passably, but again you managed to humiliate someone who will not soon forget it. The journeyman who could not complete his summoning because of you, did not achieve master status this conclave. I can assure you he will not forget you either.

"All this brings me to my main point, Jonny. You have a great deal of offensive power with your talent, but you still cannot really defend yourself, not against a determined attack by a master wizard, and that is who you must be prepared to fight.

"From now on I am going to have you focus on learning magics which will enable you to better defend yourself, and the first area that you need to learn is how to move people and animals the way you can move rocks or wood."

Jonny was intrigued by the thought. He had wanted to try it before, but since people were made up of even more complicated things than wood or leather, he had not really wanted to try it. He was afraid it might hurt someone if he did it wrong.

"I see you have thought about this before," Master Silurian stood and paced. "Good. Let's work out how you are going to learn how to do it."

They spent the next couple of hours looking at a couple of the texts The Master had bought at the conclave, books that talked about manipulating force directly and thus were ignored by most others. Jonny found some passages that gave him several ideas and wanted to work on them, but expressed his fears about hurting his subjects. As usual, The Master had a simple solution: use a small pig in the beginning. If the pig squealed too much, Jonny would know he was hurting it.

§ § §

Jonny spent the next two days reading and learning from the books. They were written in Klathar, the High Wizard tongue, which made it slow going, but Jonny was getting better at understanding the language. One of the books mentioned some things Jonny found truly miraculous. The things that could be accomplished with Jonny's talent according to this book made the throwing of stones seem like the most elementary exercise imaginable. Jonny was both excited and awed by the vistas opening to him.

Putting the things written in the books into practice was a different matter. Both books were good for general description, but very poor in detail. There were no exercises to help get from point A to B. Jonny would have to figure those out on his own.

Jonny found very quickly that using a pig as his first subject was probably not the best idea. He found this out when he tried to pick up a small pig with his hands. It squealed, a lot. He was not at all sure how he would tell the squeals of a pig that was just squealing because it was uncomfortable from one being harmed by his magic.

Jonny decided to try something simpler, rats. Rats were easy to come by and they did not make too much noise. More importantly, Jonny figured he would feel much less put out if he hurt a rat rather than a pig.

He started out lifting a cage with a rat in it. This was easy since the cage was metal and wood and Jonny had gotten quite proficient with them. Next, he tried to lift the rat itself.

This turned out to be much more difficult. He tried different things, studied the books, and after a couple of weeks managed to successfully lift a rat. He was glad he had started working with rats because one of his first attempts did something to one of the rats that caused it to die that night. He later determined he had moved the rat's internal organs without moving the rest of it. It was a grisly thought, but Jonny had found yet another way he could hurt others.

After Jonny had gotten the basic technique down for moving a rat, he refined it by making the rat fly around in more and more complicated ways. He also practiced letting the rat run and then snatching it up into the air. When he

141

felt comfortable with rats, he graduated to pigs. He started first with small ones, and in the end was moving around five hundred pound sows.

When Jonny demonstrated to Master Silurian how well he was able to move the pigs, he told Jonny he was ready to move on to humans. Jonny was a little scared to try it after what had happened to the rat, but he knew The Master was right. The Master told him there was a new apprentice who had only been at the castle for a month. He was very small and would be an excellent first subject to work with. The boy's name was Grelnick, his parents had just died, similar to Jonny, and Lord Feldar had decided he would be better used as an apprentice than a slave. The boy had already been under the knife a few times but seemed to have an unusually high tolerance for pain in one so young. The Master felt this would be a good match.

Chapter 39

Master Silurian accompanied Jonny and Grelnick for their first attempt. Grelnick was excited about his being made to fly, even though Jonny warned him that it might hurt. Grelnick said he did not think it would be as bad a being under the knife. Jonny was unsure. He remembered the rat.

The three of them went to the large barn where hay was stockpiled for the winter. It was mostly empty since the harvest was just weeks away, but there were several large piles of hay. Jonny instructed Grelnick to climb to the top of one of the haystacks. Jonny looked at Master Silurian who nodded for Jonny to continue. He took a moment to clear his mind and focus his sight on Grelnick. For a moment, nothing happened, then Grelnick let out a surprised yelp. Jonny opened is eyes and looked at him. He was hanging about a foot above the stack of hay. Jonny looked to The Master and just then heard another yelp from Grelnick. Jonny had lost his hold on him and had dropped him down into the hay. The Master grinned wickedly and was about say something, but Jonny beat him to it by apologizing.

"Apology accepted, Jonny," The Master said, still grinning. "Keep your focus, and do not damage him. Keep working till you can take him from the floor to the hay loft and back down again with your eyes open or closed." The Master left Jonny and Grelnick to work.

It took less than an hour for Jonny to do what The Master had asked. He soon had the hang of moving Grelnick around as easily as he had the rats and pigs. He was ready to give it a rest, but Grelnick had other ideas.

"Do it again, Jonny!" Grelnick kept saying. He was having lots of fun and did not want it to stop. Faster, slower, hovering, spinning, Grelnick kept coming up with new variations he wanted Jonny to try. Finally, Grelnick started to get motion sick from some of the more crazy rides and Jonny called a halt. He was happy with the day's work.

The next day when he and Grelnick went to practice, they had an audience. Word had gotten out about what Jonny was doing and as many apprentices as could sneak off from their duties came to watch.

Jonny picked up where he had left off the day before. Within a short time, the other apprentices were begging for a chance to fly too. Jonny was at first reluctant, but eventually gave in. It was actually good practice since it was a little different getting each person in the air. As Jonny worked with different boys, he learned to more easily compensate for the differences between them.

After lunch, Master Silurian came by to see what was going on, and shut down the show. He said it was good that Jonny had been working with the other boys, but now he wanted Jonny to try some more things. He brought Jonny and Grelnick out into the castle courtyard and asked Jonny to raise Grelnick off the ground. Jonny did. When Grelnick was about twenty feet off the ground Jonny held him hovering there.

"Good, Jonny," The Master began. "Make him go higher."

Jonny concentrated and doubled Grelnick's height.

"Grelnick," The Master called. "Can you see over the walls yet?"

"Not yet, Master, I need to be another twenty feet higher I think."

"Jonny, can you get him that high?"

"I think so, Master," Jonny answered, a little concerned because he knew that if he lost Grelnick now the fall would probably kill him.

Jonny kept pushing Grelnick higher until he called down that he could see over the walls.

"It is so amazing, Jonny. I'm like a bird. I can see everything. I can even see . . ." Grelnick's voice trailed off. He had gone white as a sheet.

"What's the matter, Grelnick?" Jonny called.

"Get me down, Jonny!" Grelnick screamed. "It's too high! Get me down."

Jonny quickly lowered him back down to ground level.

"I'm sorry, Jonny. I'm sorry, Master," Grelnick said, after he stopped crying. "I was just so high. When you were putting me up, I was looking at the walls and the hills and all that stuff. When I looked straight down and saw nothing under me and the ground so far below, I panicked. I'm sorry."

"That's all right, Grelnick," The Master said. "You have been very brave so far. I thought you might get scared when you saw how high you were. You have nothing to be ashamed of. Few grown men would have gone as high as you did."

Master Silurian turned to Jonny. "Try doing the same thing with some of the other boys. They might as well help since they are all watching," he said, waving at the several boys peering out from various hiding places. "You should also try placing them on the archer's walk and getting them down too."

Jonny spent the afternoon putting boys up into the air and placing them at various places around the castle. Many of them panicked when they were no more than twenty feet above the ground. It became sort of a game to see who would crack, and when. When Jonny finally called it quits for the day, he was very tired from the work, but he was now everybody's best friend. The apprentices who previously had held him in awe now practically worshipped him. He was not only a powerful wizard, but he was fun, and he was one of them, sort of.

§ § §

The Master had more ideas of how Jonny could expand his skill, but most of them were unneeded. The other apprentices were continuously coming up with new ideas for things to try, involving them, of course. After a week, Jonny had reached the point where he could do with the boys many of the same tricks he had perfected with knives and coins. He finished by having six boys rotating in the air as if they were all on a huge invisible wheel. When The Master saw it he was grudgingly impressed, but he also called a halt to that trick.

Jonny was feeling fairly pleased with himself, but one look at the glint in the Master's eye told him the fun was over. He was right; Master Silurian once again suggested something that immediately made Jonny want to rebel.

"You want me to what?" Jonny yelped.

"You heard me correctly, Jonny," The Master said unperturbed. "I want you to make yourself fly."

"But, but how can I? I've never done anything to me before. I use my sight, and I make other things move, not me. I don't move."

"That is exactly why I've waited this long before introducing this to you, Jonny. Having you fly has been my objective ever since I saw you first spin that coin. Sit down."

The Master motioned to the chair across from him in his main study. Jonny had been pacing back and forth during the entire discussion.

"Jonny, you have been making others fly for over a week now. Isn't it about time you found out if it is as much fun as they seem to think it is?"

"But, Master," Jonny moaned, "this is different."

"Why?"

"Why? Why? . . . Well because it's me. How can I push me off the ground when it's me doing the pushing?"

The Master stroked his beard. "You know, Jonny, if you were pushing boys somehow up off the ground I would have to agree with you. Then it would be like trying to lift yourself off the ground by grabbing your own hair, but, . . ." He paused and leered, pointing at Jonny, "you don't actually lift anyone or anything else yourself, do you?"

"What do you mean I don't lift anyone . . ." Jonny trailed off as he started to see what The Master meant.

The wizard was grinning like a cat that had just eaten a very tasty bird. "How is it that you lift things, Jonny?"

Jonny thought of the reality of what he did. He did not lift anything, he just manipulated the lines of force that normally held things down so they did not do it so well, so things then just sort of floated up on their own. He did actually help things along the way as well as letting them loose from the force that naturally held them, but it was true he only exerted changes on the force lines, not the object itself.

He said none of these things aloud, but The Master could see Jonny was starting to see how it could work for him to "lift" himself.

"But, Master--"

"No buts, Jonny," he cut him off. "I can see you have the idea. I know it will be very hard for you. This is probably the hardest thing I have ever asked of you, but think of when you succeed. This is the dream of every mortal born to this earth, to fly as the birds, to go anywhere you want. Think on it, Jonny! How I envy you."

"You envy me, Master? But you're the greatest wizard in this part of the world, maybe the whole world alive today."

"But, Jonny," he said slowly, a wistful expression on his face. "I will never be able to fly as you soon will. It is true I have flown by other means, but never like you, and I am too old to master it now. Maybe if I had learned these things two or three hundred years ago, yes I think I could have done it, but not now, no not now." The Master looked at his desk, his eyes seeing something else.

"If it's too hard for you, Master, how can I possibly do it?"

The Master's reverie was quickly broken. Anger glowed from his eyes.

"How? You have already done it! Do you think I could do what you were doing with those boys today? No, don't answer. I'll tell you. I could not do it, not now, not in a hundred years. I still have not even figured out to how to move a rat, Jonny. I do not have your gift; I don't have your talent, not here, not in this area. In potions, incantations, glyphs, and countless other areas I am still very much your master. In this one area, you are already the master, but this is only one small area, and it is not enough.

"So, you must keep growing, keep expanding your abilities. I know where you need to go, but I can only direct you, I cannot lead or even follow. You must do it yourself. And you will.

"Now go. Get over to the barn and do the same thing with yourself that you did with Grelnick. I don't want you doing anything else till you can show me that you can leave the floor. Go!"

Jonny left. In some ways, his world had been turned upside down, but the more he thought on it, the more it made sense that even The Master would have his limitations. So just how was he going to prove The Master right and that he could fly?

He dared not do otherwise.

Chapter 40

The Master was right, in more ways than one. The more Jonny thought on it, the more he realized that since it was not him actually doing the lifting, he should be able to lift himself. But The Master was also right in that he had said he was asking Jonny to do the hardest thing he had ever asked. Lifting others was different from lifting himself in one very big way, his frame of reference. He had not realized it previously, but he had always held quite still when he first lifted something. He did this because he had to manipulate the force lines. When he moved, his relationship to them changed.

Dealing with the change was not easy.

Jonny quickly found he could move parts of himself. He could make his arm or his foot want to fly, but when his main body started to move his relationship with the force lines changed and he lost control.

§ § §

In the midst of Jonny's efforts, time had not stopped. The month of Gnil, the first month of fall, was ending. This meant Mid-fall day was fast approaching, and with it the Harvest Festival. Jonny had no intention of doing anything to call the slightest attention to himself this year.

The one notable event this year was Roald's departure. He was thirteen now and was being apprenticed as a clerk in the city government of Alavar. He had not come to the castle from Alavar, and so could apprentice there. His studies with Feldor made him highly sought after. Roald even had hopes of one day working in the government of Salaways.

Jonny was very sad to see him go, though for the last six months they had only seen each other at meal and bedtimes.

The night before the festival was an unusually somber night for the boys. Roald was packing his things. Roald, who had been a very messy boy when Jonny had first moved in with him, had gradually transformed into a very neat and organized person. Everything he owned was always properly folded and put away. The more he had worked with Feldor, the more he had become like the man. Jonny had joked that maybe Roald wanted Feldor's job. Roald did not think it was a funny comment. He thought he would very much like to have that job, but he did not think Jonny knew how much Feldor did.

Feldor was not just the steward of the castle Salaways. He was The Master's personal representative in the government of the kingdom. In many ways, he ran the kingdom, much as it was run.

The three major cities were mostly self-regulating and the master, who was nominal lord of all Salaways, rarely intervened unless there was some urgent matter that could not be resolved in the cities themselves. When those matters came up, it was Feldor, much more often than the master who intervened. He was a very competent man, and Roald greatly admired him.

"Well, that's the last of it," Roald said as he closed his traveling case. Roald was not taking much. Most of his material goods would be provided as part of his new apprenticeship.

"Yeah, I guess it is," Jonny replied without enthusiasm.

"Hey, don't get so down, Jonny! It isn't like I'm dying or anything. I'll only be in Alavar. You can come and visit me, or I can visit you. It's not like I'm leaving Salaways."

"I know. It's just . . . you're the only real friend I've ever had, and I know how it will be. I haven't been to Alavar since last harvest festival. We'll hardly ever see each other."

"Yeah, I know what you mean. But, we always knew this would happen someday. I'm gonna miss you too, but we have to make the best of it. Please be happy for me."

"I am happy for you, Roald. I'm just going to miss you. That's all."

"And I'm going to miss you too. Let's not talk about this anymore. Friends forever, right?"

"Yeah, friends forever. Even if you do take Feldor's job someday," Jonny laughed.

"Don't you forget it! I will too. You wait and see. But let's just see what fun we can have at the festival tomorrow. OK?"

"OK. We do have to leave early tomorrow don't we?"

"Yeah, let's see who gets to sleep first."

They both got into bed and though neither of them was sure who went to sleep first, neither of them slept for a long time as they thought about the time they had spent together and what the future would bring.

§ § §

Jonny spent the entire Harvest Festival with Roald. They went to all the shows, the soldiers' trials, and ate until they could barely walk. The three days went by so fast, that on waking the morning of the fourth day Jonny could scarcely believe it was nearly over.

Master Silurian presided over the swearing in of the new soldiers, then gave his final speech, and then it was time to go. Roald was all moved in to his apprentice quarters in the government building, excited and happy. They hugged, unselfconsciously, and then Jonny hopped on the last wagon heading back up to the castle. Around him the other apprentices and journeymen chatted happily. Jonny just stared off at where Roald had waved and then gone into the building, long after he was gone.

Chapter 41

Jonny was frustrated. After nearly a week of making no progress at flying, he decided to take a new tack. Master Silurian said he should not leave the barn, but he did not say anything about what he was to do there.

Jonny went back to the basics. He started lifting stones again, only now he did it while pacing around the barn. This was a completely new experience, and a frustrating one too. If he had not already been through this process of trying and failing and then finally learning, he would have given up.

After two weeks, he was finally able to walk slowly and keep a rock in the air. Once he had made that breakthrough, it was not long until he was able to keep several stones moving while he ran in a circle around the barn. It probably looked strange to those watching, and there was always someone watching now.

Jonny's fame was such now that many apprentices took every opportunity to sneak looks at what he did. They all knew better than to talk to him while he was working, but he could tell they were there. That might have been part of the reason it took him as long as it did to do anything, but it also forced him to concentrate more closely on his work.

Every night when he ate, there were always boys who were eager to talk to him. Usually there were questions about his progress, and if he might need a volunteer to be flown around some more. After a day of no progress, Jonny was quite short with some of the boys, but they were used to the abrasive manner of The Master and thought no less of him, even when he yelled at them to leave him alone.

Each night he went to bed exhausted mentally from all the work with so little to show for it. At night, he dreamed that he flew. The way Master Silurian had described it had fired his imagination. Sometimes he really thought he had it figured out, and was only more frustrated when he woke up with no recollection of how he could actually do it.

§ § §

Slowly he made progress. He got better at walking and keeping things moving in the air. He considered using Grelnick as before, but he suspected The Master would not approve. Besides, the requests for being flown were finally starting to die down. He hit upon the idea that maybe he could get himself to fly if he got something else to fly with him aboard it.

One morning he figured he was ready to make the attempt. He got a barrel top that was about three feet in diameter. He practiced moving it from standing and walking. He put a heavy sack that weighed as much as he did atop it, and practiced keeping it balanced as he moved it until he felt he was ready.

As with Grelnick, he took his barrel top and placed it atop a large pile of hay, then he stood on top of it as well. He tried to clear his mind and concentrate, but he was quite scared and could not focus. Finally, he just said to himself, "This is stupid!" Then he focused on lifting the barrel top with him on it.

At first, it did not seem to be working and then as the top lifted he panicked. The barrel top tilted and fell out from underneath him as he lost focus. He was not hurt because of the hay, just annoyed.

His small moment of success did make him want to do it even more. He tried several more times, with mostly the same results. Balancing the barrel top with the force lines and trying to keep his balance on top of it at the same time was just too much. He made some very comical falls, but never succeeded in getting more than three feet above the hay. He supposed this was good because his falls were bad enough that were he higher he could have been seriously injured.

He had scrapes and bruises all over his arms and legs from the barrel top hitting him as he fell off. After landing on his face and the barrel top landing on his back after his thirtieth attempt, Jonny threw off the barrel top in disgust.

"I can't keep this stupid thing balanced, no matter what I do!" Jonny screamed in disgust. He kicked the barrel top, hurting his foot and fell down. Tears of rage came from his eyes.

"If only there were some way I could just stand on something which didn't need to be balanced. Something that would push up just the bottom of my shoes and wouldn't pitch over at the slightest thing . . ."

That got Jonny thinking. "I wonder, . . . I wonder if I could just make my shoes push me up. Hmmm, I would have to balance the pressure between them, but at least I wouldn't have to balance two things at the same time. It just might work!"

Jonny stood without waiting for time to second-guess himself and concentrated on the soles of his shoes and pushed them up. He pushed gently, but he could feel it working. Slowly he lifted off the hay. All his attention was focused on keeping even pressure on both feet, so he really did not have time to be scared. He was using his sight so when he finally looked around he found he was more than ten feet above the hay. It was a good thing the hay was soft because seeing this caused him to lose his focus and fall. He banged himself painfully on the edge of the barrel top, but that could do nothing to dim his enthusiasm.

Sore, he immediately got up and tried again. This time he only let himself go up a foot or so above the hay before he forced himself to be aware of his surroundings. Now that he was ready for it, he was able to maintain better control. It felt like he was standing on the shoulders of an invisible giant and so his balance was still very precarious, but the longer he stayed there the more comfortable he felt with it.

He let himself back down and then lifted himself two more times. After his fourth successful attempt, he was simply too tired to go on. He lay in the hay, covered with sweat and exhausted, but thrilled. He was tempted to run and tell

The Master but he decided he would rather get better at controlling things before he told him of his success.

That night he had a hard time falling to sleep. When he did, he dreamed again of flying, but when he woke up, he knew it was not just a dream.

Chapter 42

Jonny waited nearly a week before he told Master Silurian of his success. The reason for the delay was that progress was still very slow. Any small distraction and he started to fall and when he started, he could not recover. He nearly broke his ankle when he was at the edge of the haystack and a rat moved noisily in the rafters and diverted his attention. He fell hard, but was able to limp away from it.

He did not directly tell The Master he was successful, he only started attending his more usual classes that he had been forbidden to attend until he was successful. Two days after he started attending classes again, Master Silurian entered the barn where Jonny was still trying to perfect his technique.

When The Master saw him demonstrate what he had accomplished, he seemed pleased, but he quickly cut to the heart of the matter.

"When you lift, you are not lifting yourself. You are lifting your shoes, aren't you, Jonny?"

"Yes, Master. How did you know?" Jonny asked, amazed that he had seen it so easily.

"It looks as though you are standing on something, something unsteady at that. I was fairly certain that if you had been lifting your whole body that you would not look like that. Still, what you have accomplished is impressive. Keep working at it."

The Master left and Jonny felt even more frustrated. The Master was right again. He needed to make his body fly, not something under or around it, but the body itself. That was what he had done when he made the other boys fly, why not himself?

Jonny answered his own question. He had not really tried to move himself the way he moved the boys since he had hit on the idea with the barrel top. He sat and closed his eyes and used his sight to see his body the way he used it on others.

He had gotten better and better at seeing with only his sight. As he turned it on his own body, he saw himself as never before. He had no idea how long he examined himself from a completely different perspective. He could sense the flow of the blood through his body and many other things he could not easily describe but he was able to sense how his life force interacted with the force lines around him.

He wondered why he had never done this before, but even as the thought occurred to him, he realized that even a few weeks earlier he could not have done it. He had needed to be able to externalize his point of view with his sight, and he had only learned to do this as he had learned how to use his sight while moving.

Almost without thinking, he released the force lines holding his body down and he slowly floated upward. He felt his reference shift, but was not troubled by it. He opened his eyes and saw he was only inches above the hay, but he did not try to go higher.

The feeling of being suspended was euphoric. It was totally unlike what it had felt like when he was pushing his shoes up. Here, balance was not an issue. His body was just too light to be held down. He was not being pushed up at all, he just was not being held down.

Jonny stayed floating like that for quite a long time, enjoying the sheer joy of the experience. He let himself back down and pondered on his other major problem. He was still just as vulnerable as before to falling if his focus failed. As light and easy as what he had just done felt, he was actually now a little scared. He knew that with no effort on his part, he could float very, very high, and if for some reason he was distracted, he could fall and most likely the fall would kill him. This thought made him realize he had to find something he could do about that.

§ § §

Jonny spent the rest of that day cautiously experimenting with this new way of flying. He was certain that this was what Master Silurian had intended for him to learn how to do. It felt so right, but even now when he should be jumping for joy, he was consumed with fear that he could fall. He decided he had to talk to The Master about it.

Jonny did not get to talk to The Master until the afternoon of the next day. It was the first day of the month of Pastran, the first month of winter. He was now fairly used to the procedure of inquiring after The Master and knowing he would either be told where he was or that The Master would find him. Since he had all that time, he attended his other neglected study sessions and continued to experiment. He found his initial thought was correct; he could go as high as he wanted, or dared. He had been careful, but even so, he had two near falls that scared him even more.

When The Master arrived, Jonny was back to where he had been when he first succeeded, floating some inches above the pile of hay. Jonny saw The Master and tried to gently glide down to him. He mostly succeeded, even though the movement was not nearly as smooth as Jonny wanted.

"I see you have discovered how to move yourself instead of your shoes," Master Silurian commented with a smile. "I am glad you have got it. So why did you need to see me?" he asked with a quirked eyebrow.

"Master. . . . I know how to, to move myself," Jonny said uncertainly. "But I don't know how not to fall."

"Ahhh," The Master said with a happily surprised look on his face. "You thought of that, have you? I was afraid the thought would not occur to you until you had broken a leg. Not falling, yes there is a trick. If a rock you are moving falls because you get distracted, it does not scream out in pain. You have no idea how it worried me when you were doing all those tricks with the other apprentices, that you would be distracted and I would have a dead apprentice on my hands. Thankfully, all the training I had you do with inanimate objects paid off, you did not drop any of them. Now you are worried about dropping yourself. Good!"

"So what do I do, Master?"

"What do you think, Jonny?"

This was not the answer he wanted to hear from his master. Even so, he had half expected it, so he tried some of his thoughts.

"Well, I guess I'd somehow practice learning to ignore distractions, or learn how to catch myself, but I don't know how I'd do either of those things, Master."

"You are on the right track, Jonny. Let us see if I can help you come up with some ways of working on this.

"How does a baby learn to walk?"

The question took Jonny off guard. He scuffed a foot and stared at the floor, not sure where the question applied.

"Uh, I guess first it learns to crawl, and then pulls itself up on stuff, and then it starts to walk."

"Mostly right, Jonny. But let's not worry about the crawling and clinging stages, you have already progressed beyond that. What happens when the baby first starts trying to actually walk? Does it do it perfectly at first?"

Jonny was now starting to get an idea where The Master was going.

"No, it falls down a lot at first." Jonny laughed remembering babies he had seen playing near their parents' stalls in the market. "They fall down a lot. It's pretty funny to watch sometimes."

"Right, Jonny, now here is the big question. Does the fact that they fall a lot in the beginning keep them from eventually learning how to walk?"

"No, Master, they just keep trying till they get it figured out, but, Master what I'm doing is different. If I fall, it could really hurt me, it could even kill me. It scares me just thinking about it."

"Again, Jonny, you are right, but you are coming at this the wrong way. How is it those babies you saw fall over and over again were not hurt?"

"They were hurt sometimes. Sometimes they would sit there and just bawl."

"And then . . . ?"

"Then," Jonny said, hating what he had to say. "They would get up and try again."

"Right, Jonny, they would do it again. That is where what you are doing is different. Those babies could not fall far just by trying to walk. You can. However, no one said you had to fly high in order to learn what to do. When I came in you were floating just a few inches above the hay, can you do the same while standing?"

"Sure," Jonny said, and proved it by lifting a couple of inches off the floor.

"Good, now you need to act just like those babies. Don't fly high, as a matter of fact, I want you so low that unless people see you move they would have a hard time telling that you are not touching the floor. I want you to practice this a lot. It takes months for babies to go from being able to toddle unsteadily to being able to run around easily. It may take as long for you to do the same, but I do not think it will. We will see.

"That's just the first part of the exercise. I have several other ideas as well . . ." and The Master proceeded to outline what he needed to do.

Chapter 43

When Jonny was learning to make himself fly, that was all he had been doing. Now Master Silurian had him working in completely different ways. The Master had him spend two weeks where Jonny was in the air for every waking moment he could manage it. Not far in the air, just an inch or two. If that was all he had been doing, Jonny would have been terribly bored.

Boredom was not a problem.

For the first few days, Master Silurian detailed Jonny as his official messenger; in addition to catching up on all his other studies. He would send Jonny all over the castle and surrounding grounds with messages from The Master, and from Feldor. Once again, Jonny found out how a lot more went on in the castle than he had known about. He became privy to information he never would have imagined previously, and was even more impressed with what The Master and Feldor did in running the castle and kingdom. There were so many details just to keep the castle running and supplied, let alone all the affairs of Salaways.

At first Jonny found it hard to stay airborne for more than a half hour at a time, but gradually he was able to go longer and longer without having to come to ground. The Master even had him attending classes and eating his meals while floating.

All of this gave him ample opportunity to practice getting back in the air after the inevitable loss of concentration and fall to the ground. Jonny grew less and less easily distracted, and better and better at keeping himself in the air while concentrating on other things. Mid-winter day came and went.

The Master then had Jonny focus on reading while floating. This would not have been so bad except Master Silurian figured Jonny had not been studying enough in Klathar, the High Wizard tongue. Reading those books would have been difficult in any circumstance, but doing so while staying in the air made it doubly difficult. At least the reading was interesting once he figured out what it was about. The Master had him study more about materials magic, amulets, glyphs, and most intriguing, books on zdrell manipulation.

Jonny read these books late into the night. The most annoying part of them was how they described things from a theoretical point of view, or described accomplishments, but few gave more than the vaguest instruction on how to actually accomplish the wonders they described. When he asked his master about it, he simply said that was the way with most books on magic. It is much easier to write of things than to do them, and you have to both do and understand a thing well in order to actually explain the process to someone else. Even in the Klathar, many parts of magic were very difficult to describe.

One day, three weeks into Chule, the first month of the year and second of winter, Jonny was reading in the Journeyman's study, floating just above a chair, when Master Silurian entered.

"Jonny, you seem to be doing much better at staying in the air."

Jonny nodded, but made sure that he did not allow himself to drop.

The wizard continued, "Your birthday was three days ago and you are small for a thirteen-year-old. A growing boy your age needs physical exercise, and I don't believe you are getting enough of it."

"How can I, Master, if I'm always to keep floating?"

"How indeed? I have a simple plan. I want you to climb the stairs, on your feet, to the top of each of the five turrets of the castle and then float down them again, five times a day."

It was pure torture for the first week, but Jonny knew better than to argue. By the end of the second week of this regimen, he actually looked forward to it as a way to get a break from his studies.

§ § §

Soon, The Master decided Jonny was ready for another twist. He brought Jonny back to the barn where Jonny found a bigger than usual pile of hay.

"I want you to fly up to the loft, Jonny," he began.

Jonny flew up and waited for the next instruction.

"Now, jump down into the pile of hay."

Jonny was puzzled, but stepped off the loft and began to float down towards the pile of hay.

"No, Jonny," The Master said, irritated. "I did not say fly, I said jump. Just like any of us earthbound mortals would do it."

Jonny was more puzzled, but floated back up to the loft and jumped off. It was a strange feeling. He had almost forgotten what it felt like to fall like a stone. He almost stopped himself reflexively, but let himself fall into the hay. It was strange but not unpleasant since the hay was soft and deep.

"Now, Jonny, I want you to get back up to the loft and jump again, but this time when you are half way down I want you to stop your fall."

This did not sound too hard to Jonny since he had already nearly done just that. He flew up to the loft and jumped, his anxiety at stopping himself did not let him get control until his feet were just beginning to touch the hay. Master Silurian did not seem to mind and had him try it several more times, each time at a different height. It went fairly well until The Master once again pulled a switch.

"Jonny, I want you to go to the loft and wait till I tell you to jump."

Jonny went up and waited, then The Master yelled out, "Grelnick!" Before Jonny knew what was happening, he was being pushed by the young apprentice off the edge of the loft. It was totally unexpected, which was clearly The Master's intention. Jonny hit the hay before he had time to figure out what was happening.

"Well, Jonny, I can see that you still are not reflexive enough at recovering from a good distraction," the wizard said chuckling. "I think you and Grelnick have some work to do."

The Master looked up at Grelnick. "You have my permission to try anything you can think of to see if you can get Jonny to fall as well as you did that time, Grelnick. Start off easy, but I want to make sure that this is as automatic for Jonny as not falling when you step in a crack is for you."

He looked back at Jonny. "I will expect a full report this evening," he said and left.

Grelnick once again proved a very resourceful boy. Every time Jonny was sure he could not be surprised into falling, Grelnick proved him wrong. It was a good thing the hay was soft because Jonny fell many times, but just like a toddler, each fall only increased his determination. By the end of the day, he was bruised, sore, scratched, tired, and had straw all through his hair and clothes. But in spite of Grelnick's most strenuous efforts, he had not fallen once in the last hour. He decided that they were done and headed up to his room to bathe before having dinner with The Master.

It seemed that Master Silurian was not content to let things lie. After dinner, where Jonny had reported his progress to The Master, he was walking back up the stairs to his room when a hole suddenly opened in the wall next to him and he felt himself thrown out twenty feet above the courtyard. He was bone tired and looking forward to collapsing into bed when it happened. Even so, he transitioned from falling to floating seamlessly. He did not even bother to look at how it had happened or if his master was watching, he would not give him the satisfaction. He just flew in the window of his room and went straight to bed, smiling.

§ § §

The next morning The Master said nothing about the previous night's incident, but Jonny could tell by what he did not say, that he was very pleased with Jonny's progress. Unfortunately, the way Master Silurian chose to show his pleasure was nearly always to increase the difficulty of the tasks he asked Jonny to do.

He told Jonny to work through the morning again with Grelnick, but what he did not tell him was that he had spread word to all at the castle that it was now open season on Jonny.

The morning had been mostly easy, so Jonny was just a little suspicious after lunch when Feldor put him back on messenger duty. He quickly found that everyone in the castle was trying to do what Grelnick had done the previous day, and there was no easy bed of straw to fall on this time. Everywhere Jonny turned there were apprentices, journeymen, and servants trying to surprise him into falling. He was back hovering at only an inch or two off the ground, so when he did fall it was more embarrassing than dangerous, but it soon became the biggest game in the castle.

Everyone was trying to distract Jonny, but he soon got into the spirit of the contest and was having as much fun at not falling as they were in trying to make him fall. Even Feldor got into the act. While Jonny was truly surprised that he would try, the surprise was not enough for him to fall.

This went on for three days before The Master called a halt. He said Jonny was ready for the next phase. Jonny too was ready because he was really getting tired of not having any peace. He accomplished very little the day before, because everywhere he turned there was yet another hopeful contestant in the "make Jonny drop" game.

"Jonny," The Master began, the morning he had called off open season on Jonny. "I know I have pushed you pretty hard, but realize all this is for your good. It is necessary that your reactions be reflexive if you are to survive. But, I think you are ready for the next step, I really do."

"So what is it, Master?" Jonny asked breathlessly. Jonny had several ideas but he did not know which direction The Master would choose to go.

"The next step is simple, Jonny." He paused, "Leave the ground and fly like a bird. You have proven to me and I am sure to yourself as well that there is no danger of you losing concentration and falling more than a few feet. Since you are safe to do that, there is no longer any reason you should stay so close to the ground."

Jonny was stunned. It was more than he had hoped for. He had assumed that it would be weeks or months before The Master would let him get more than a few feet off the ground. The Master was still talking.

"Jonny, I want you flying over the castle walls. I want you soaring like an eagle, eventually even as high as an eagle. I want you to show us all what you can do. There is only one thing I want to caution you about; those outside the castle must not see you. As it is, I am going to have a hard time trying to keep this a secret, but as long as you are not seen by anyone but those here; I think no one will believe it. In some ways I think if it were me, I would not believe it."

"But why, Master?" Jonny asked, confused.

"Jonny, Jonny, you are so young, you know so little of the world, and I think that is why I love you all the more."

Now Jonny was stunned. "Love?" That was the word he had used, but Jonny had never once thought he was anything more than a student for The Master, a special student, but love? Jonny did not understand, but decided he would have to think about it later, as The Master continued to explain.

"Jonny, you saw just a small bit of the jealousy that your talent and skills engender when we were at the conclave. You probably were not aware that you were the talk of it, were you? I have since heard how your demonstration has been talked about across the continent and more than half the world away.

"It is natural for you not to see this as astounding, but there has not been a wizard who could fly as you now do in nearly seven hundred years. The last one I am aware of who could do it was a very old master. He only did so rarely, but his power was such that he was over one thousand years old when he died. Many have thought magic of the type you wield had forever left the world.

"Even without the ability to fly, you are already able to fight as most wizards only can by using demons. Think what a large boulder dropped on an enemy castle or army would do. You can already move a stone larger than most siege engines. Now combine that with the ability to fly, and think of the jealousy that will arouse. I have tried to shield and prepare you, but many people will want you dead, and soon. That is why, Jonny, it is imperative you develop your talents as quickly and as completely as possible. That is why we must keep your ability to fly secret outside the castle, a little while longer."

If Jonny had been stunned by The Master's earlier comment, this nearly made him faint. Now, all of The Master's constant pushing and testing, now it made sense. Fear, yes, fear made sense. The Master was afraid for Jonny, not of what Jonny could do, but what others would try to do to Jonny if he was not ready.

Also now, Jonny saw The Master's actions in a new light, as being motivated by something better and more noble than Jonny ever could have conceived earlier. Yes, love, that was the word.

The Master had been treating Jonny like a father treats a son he loves, and knows he must discipline if the boy has any chance of growing into a man of strength and character. All this made Jonny incredibly grateful, but he knew he could not, should not, say it.

All he said was, "I understand, Master. I will be careful." Then Jonny left The Master's study, but he was not the same boy who had entered it. He had grown, and this had nothing to do with magic.

Chapter 44

Jonny did not immediately go out and fly as Master Silurian had said he could. Instead, he climbed all five of the castle's towers for exercise and to warm himself from the early spring chill, but his mind was elsewhere. When he reached the top of the last tower he did what he had never done before, he stepped off the edge and floated down outside the castle walls. Then he hiked up to the grove of trees above the castle where he had always liked to play with Roald. The days of Gost, the first month of spring, alternated between cold and rainy and clear with a bite in the air. The previous day it had rained, and today there was not a cloud in the sky, but Jonny was glad for the heavy coat he wore.

He sat on a rock and thought, his bottom gradually going numb. He thought about all the things that had happened to him in his life, all the pain, and lately all the joy and he wondered, why me? Why am I special?

He could come up with no answer. After some time, it could have been hours, he was not sure, he determined he was unlikely to find out any time soon. So, he left the questions for later. There was something The Master was preparing him for, something big. The more he thought of it the more sure he was that all this was preparation for something more significant than just defending himself, and that it would affect more than just Jonny.

It was too big.

Jonny knew his master would tell him when the time was right, when he was older and could do something about it. . Knowing Master Silurian loved him only increased his confidence in him. Now was not the time; Jonny could feel that too, and in a sense it made him happy.

He was just a boy, and he felt very young. Now, he was happy to put all these questions in the back of his mind, and concentrate on learning the best he could now and letting the future wait.

When Jonny came to this resolution, it was like waking up from a long night of sleep. Without really planning it, he was drifting towards the tops of the trees. Most of the trees near the castle were just coming back into leaf and the trees were a painfully bright green in the early afternoon sun. He remembered The Master had said, "Fly like a bird," so he decided that is just what he would do.

He flew until he was above the tops of the trees, casting a shadow on the green canopy, then he flew horizontally dipping and soaring, staying within ten feet or so of the tops of the branches. He was flying faster than he ever had before, and he was not scared. Actually, this was the most wonderful feeling he had ever felt. He flashed fast and smooth through the air. His eyes started to water, his cheeks and ears burned with the cold, he was moving so swiftly, but the faster he went the faster he wanted to go.

Flying above the treetops, he was weaving higher and higher in the hills that provided the backdrop above the castle. The trees and rocks became a gray and green blur below him until finally they suddenly dropped away beneath him.

Realization struck, the ground had dropped away because he had reached the top of the mountain ridge. He saw patches of snow along the ridge, the only place it fell in this part of Salaways He whirled and looked back at where he had come from and was stunned. He had gained over three thousand feet in elevation and covered perhaps four or five miles, all in a few short moments.

He floated, awed by what he had just done with so little apparent effort. Then he could not contain it any longer and he shouted for joy. His voice echoed down the canyons. He could see the castle below. Much further he could see Alavar and the river Neem, glittering in the afternoon sun.

He rose higher in the air, until he was several hundred feet above the ridge. It felt like he was much higher because of the way the ground dropped away from the ridge. He was flying like an eagle now, and as if drawn by the thought Jonny saw the form of a hawk circling in the thermals below and to the left of him. He yelled again, but the bird was either too far away, or simply did not care about the strange character that had intruded into its domain.

The cold began to seep into him. For a moment, he wanted to fly all the way to Salaways and visit Roald, swooping in on the unsuspecting city like a great bird, but then he remembered he had to practice but also remain unseen. Immediately, he allowed himself to drop until he was again just above treetop. He doubted anyone could have seen him, this far from any settlement.

He grinned as he thought that as long as he stayed fairly low he could go as fast as he wanted. He launched himself forward at breakneck speed, heading down the hill. He flew faster this time than he had going up the hill and he went in a nearly straight line instead of the random path he had followed up the hill. Faster and faster he flew, squinting against the wind roaring past him.

The castle grew rapidly, and in less than two minutes, he had come to it. He slowed, and then rose to circle a hundred feet or so above the battlements and yelled as he circled. For a moment, nothing happened, and then some apprentice carrying a load of boxes towards the kitchen looked up and saw Jonny. He yelped and dropped the boxes. Jonny laughed. In moments there was a crowd looking up at him. Everyone was shouting and pointing then Jonny recognized Grelnick who shouted up at him, "Is that you, Jonny?"

Jonny laughed again, "Who else would it be? Do boys usually fly over the castle walls?"

That got a laugh from the crowd and Grelnick said, "Nope, no boys, just crazy 'prentice birds!"

That got everyone laughing, and Jonny allowed himself to slowly float down. When Jonny was just ten feet above their heads, he reached for his pants like was going to take them down and said, "Grelnick you better watch your tongue or I'll do to you what birds do sometimes when they fly overhead!"

Grelnick covered his head, looking scared and said, "Sorry, Jonny, I was just funning. I didn't mean it."

"I know Grelnick, so was I," he said with a laugh and dropped the last few feet to the ground.

A cheer went up from the assembled apprentices and there were many congratulations for Jonny. Just then, Master Silurian walked up and the crowd dispersed more quickly than it had appeared. The Master was smiling. He motioned Jonny to follow him and asked Jonny to tell him about where he had been and what he had done.

Jonny told The Master about the whole flying adventure, but not the brooding he had done before. He could not help but bubble with enthusiasm as he described flying fast and free as a bird. The Master was obviously pleased, and even more so when Jonny told him how he had caught himself when he had wanted to fly into Alavar.

"So, you did remember?" Master Silurian asked, leaning back in his chair and staring at the ceiling. He didn't wait for Jonny to respond. "Good. Good, but I must know one other thing: did you ever close your eyes while you flew?"

"No. Master, why would I?"

"Why indeed?" he said still looking at the ceiling.

"Think on it, Jonny. When next you fly, do it, but take care that you are high enough to recover."

Jonny was about to ask him what he would have to recover from, but Master Silurian cut him off, and then outlined a few more things for Jonny to try, as usual.

§ § §

Pleased with Jonny's progress, The Master allowed him to enjoy it, for a few days. He kept thinking up new twists like flying with his eyes closed and relying on his sight, using the demon amulet to see by, flying face up, face down, feet first, and several other things. He never let Jonny stop studying other things too. He allowed Jonny no more than half a day flying, the rest of the time he was reading the increasingly ancient tomes The Master had found written about zdrell, learning history and trying other types of magic. Jonny had gotten quite good about reading Klathar, the High Wizard Tongue, and Master Silurian slowly conceded there probably was not another magician in several hundred miles who could read it as well as Jonny and himself. Understanding zdrell helped in understanding Klathar, as that language was formulated by the zdrell masters. Some of the journeymen would occasionally ask Jonny for help in deciphering a tricky passage in their own studies.

§ § §

"Jonny," Master Silurian began gravely, a week after Jonny had begun flying. "I know you have been enjoying your new freedom, but I am afraid we do not have time to dwell at this level. We need you to develop some new tricks soon or you will be in mortal danger before you are fourteen."

163

This took Jonny back. He had managed to forget, or at least ignore the warnings given him before he had started flying free.

"What do I need to do, Master?" Jonny asked, clearly puzzled. "I've tried flying every way you or I could think of. How can I get better without letting outsiders know I can fly?"

"That is just it, Jonny. Flying is no longer the issue. You do that perfectly. What you need now is a means to defend yourself. Have you thought what you would do if an archer shot at you while you were flying?"

"No, I guess I hadn't. I guess I'd just move away from the arrow."

"Jonny, guessing is not good enough. We are going to have to find out."

"What, you mean you're going to have people shoot at me while I'm flying?" Jonny asked with alarm.

"No, not at first, but, yes, eventually I will have archers shooting at you."

Chapter 45

Jonny started again on a new twist on his skill. It started simply with Grelnick throwing a beanbag at him while he hovered. Jonny first practiced avoiding it by dodging, then by deflecting the bag, and finally by taking control of it and flinging it back at Grelnick.

Once Jonny mastered that, he progressed rapidly. First, stones were thrown at him, one at a time, then in multiples until he was deflecting as many as twelve incoming stones at a time.

Then, just as promised, Master Silurian had archers shooting at Jonny. They were using blunted arrows at first, which flew a little slower than normal, then they started using arrows with normal weight, but blunt tips. In each case, once Jonny got the hang of working with new restrictions, he learned how to handle them. The inevitable bruises he acquired only spurred him to learn faster.

Jonny found out that no matter how he tried, he could not seem to focus on more than about twelve incoming objects at a time. This was a good number, but he already saw that in a full-scale battle there could be hundreds of arrows pointed at him.

Defense alone would not be enough, so The Master had him practice throwing things at his attackers while he was flying. This was only an extension of deflecting things and again made for a fun game.

The Master knew that no matter how many objects Jonny could control at a time, there would always be the possibility of even more coming after him, so he had Jonny work on defenses other than just controlling things. He introduced Jonny to a spell that created a bubble of force around a person.

It was very difficult and took Jonny nearly two months before he could invoke it and remain airborne. It was an incantation with a gestural component, but by using his zdrell sight he was able to cast it without speaking aloud and reduced the gestures to a few quick finger flicks, but it required enough concentration that for a long time he despaired ever being able to do it and fly.

Master Silurian also started him working on amulet magic, since amulets could store spells which could be invoked without the user having to spare mental energy to maintain them. The spell he thought Jonny should first commit to an amulet would be an invisibility spell. This spell would be valuable since no one shoots at a target they cannot see. More importantly, an amulet spell could remain active while Jonny slept, and since Jonny must sleep, it seemed wise to be protected when he would otherwise be defenseless.

§ § §

Amulet magic was a whole new area for Jonny. He found he enjoyed it, even if it was difficult. First, the amulet had to be fashioned, and The Master explained that while it was possible to use a pre-existing amulet, it was much better if the spell caster had personally fashioned it. So Jonny learned how to shape the metal necessary and how to inscribe it with particular tracings that would allow it to capture and hold his spell.

It was work unlike anything Jonny had done before, and for the second time in his life, Jonny found he both liked and had some talent for it. He was able to make an amulet that Master Silurian pronounced serviceable on only his second attempt. The Master had journeymen who had taken years and many attempts before they had succeeded in creating even one usable amulet. Jonny had succeeded in just under three weeks. There probably would have been considerable animosity towards Jonny for this feat, but after Jonny's ability to fly, many assumed he was gifted in all areas, even though his teachers in other branches of magic knew better.

Jonny could tell The Master was both surprised and pleased, but he was not sure why. He had never had time to pay much attention to the specific exercises The Master had the other journeymen do. He also felt he should not have needed two attempts. It was only months later that one of the journeymen told him of the magnitude of his achievement.

After The Master pronounced the amulet serviceable, he went about instructing Jonny in the art of storing a spell within it. This process, unlike producing the amulet itself was more a matter of perseverance than skill, he explained. First, Jonny must be able to cast the spell perfectly, and then he must cast the spell *into* the amulet. That was what was so hard about creating a serviceable amulet, it had to be made so the spell would be absorbed by it rather than be affected by it. He must then repeat this process over and over. Each time the spell must be perfect, as though Jonny were actually using it and he must use his full concentration and mental energy. He had to keep doing it until finally, at some point, the spell became part of the amulet.

Once that happened, there was a single binding spell which permanized it. There was no set number of times needed before the spell stuck, but it was never a small number. Master Silurian said that if it happened in less than one hundred attempts it would be unusual and Jonny could never manage more than three repeated castings of the invisibility spell before he was too tired to continue.

§ § §

Mid-summer's day came and Jonny started a new routine. He continued flying, studying, and two or three times a day casting spells into the amulet.

Jonny got very good at casting the spell. He even used it several times to play pranks on the journeymen and some of the apprentices.

One day, he spent nearly an hour terrorizing a materials magic class: moving items, bumping students into each other, and generally creating a fuss. The journeyman teaching the class left the room screaming that the class was unteachable. He tried the same thing in an incantation class, but the journeyman there knew a counter spell and he found himself suddenly visible, embarrassed and in trouble. The Master wouldn't let him fly for three days afterward.

He found he could actually cast the spell while flying, but it was very hard to maintain. He looked forward to when he would have the amulet finished.

"Master," Jonny asked one day as he entered The Master's study to get another zdrell book. "How will I know when the spell has finally stuck in my amulet?"

"You will know, Jonny," was all he said, and gestured for Jonny to leave.

So, Jonny kept at it. He kept a log of how many times he had cast the spell. At times, he looked at it and wondered if he would ever be done.

Occasionally, when he had finished the spell, the amulet was glowing softly. Jonny wondered if that meant he was finished, but the other journeymen assured him that when it did happen it would be much more dramatic. They would not tell him what to expect either, but the few who had experienced it agreed with The Master that Jonny would know when it happened.

Jonny was also practicing flying with the shielding spell in place. It was a lot of work and tired him quickly. In some ways, it was easier to try to deflect many incoming objects than it was to maintain the spell. He wondered whether it was worth it. Master Silurian assured him it was.

Chapter 46

Master Silurian walked into his private apartment tiredly. His wife, Alira, sat at a work table rearranging some herb seedlings. She looked up at him and looked down with a smirk.

"Are you going to tell me what happened at the Conclave, or are you going to make me guess," she said, not looking up.

"Oh, I'll tell you, dearest, but I would hazard your guess would be nearly the same as fact." He crossed the room to sit in his "thinking chair," a rocker by the fire.

"Don't flatter me, old man. Just spit it out." She smiled, still not looking up.

Master Silurian settled more deeply into his chair. "As I'd guessed, the demon masters reasserted themselves after their *little embarrassment* last year with Jonny. Skylock wrote that they were feeling their oats so much that they have started to try and influence the council of elders to keep non-demon journeymen from being confirmed masters. That caused quite a stir, and they had to back down. Nevertheless, it is my experience that when something like this comes along, the first time everyone hears of it, they are shocked, the next time, less shocked, and before you know it they accept it as if it always been the way of things.

"The lines are being drawn. I am glad I was there at the last conclave to try and organize the other wizards. Skylock said there was a similar meeting this time, though some took my absence as a sign I was afraid. Thankfully, Skylock was there with my message, though I'm not sure if there weren't more than a few of the old fools who will read it as cowardice. I haven't attended more than one conclave in five for the last hundred years. You'd think they would know by now," he said with a harrumph.

"You certainly seem to care about the opinions of these *old fools*, Silurian," she said, smiling at his consternated expression.

"I only care, because they are all that stand between us and becoming like those poor souls in Grimor. Skylock says he is seeing the signs everywhere he goes. Demon wizards are so prevalent that in many of the cities the people think all wizards are demon wizards. Only fifty years ago, demon wizards were the exception, now they are the rule."

"Yes, just as you predicted."

"Sometimes I hate being right. Have you heard anything from your letter?"

"No, and I really didn't expect to hear anything. You know I was cut off from the sisterhood when I married you."

"Yes, but don't they see the danger? Just because weidges are women, and wizards are men, don't they see that all people will suffer if demons get control of everything?"

"You are talking to the wrong person, Silurian. I chose you over the sisterhood nearly a century ago, because I believed in you. I still do, but they trust no man, wizard that is."

"It all seems so futile. Each group is so set in its ways, they would die rather than change, and that is just what it will come to if something doesn't change soon. I don't know what I would do if I didn't have Jonny to give me hope. If he can only live long enough to develop his talents, it might be enough to buy us the time necessary to get people working together. The demon masters and Grimor won't wait."

"So, how is he progressing? I saw quite a group of apprentices throwing rocks at him the other day. He looked to be enjoying it, though I can't guess why," she said, getting up and moving her chair by Silurian's.

"Oh, he is progressing quite nicely. He might even be able to withstand an attack by anything less than a full regiment. But mundanes are the least he has to worry about. He needs to be ready to battle other wizards, and I have a few ideas on what to do about that."

"Silurian, please, just don't kill him with all your helping him to stay alive."

"Yes, dear one. I'll try to keep that in mind."

Chapter 47

One day in Clost, the second month of summer, The Master called Jonny into his study and announced that it was time to for Jonny to try out his skills in a more realistic environment.

"Jonny, this is to be a mock battle. You will use all your skills and knowledge to defeat three journeymen."

Jonny was scared. It must have showed on his face.

Master Silurian waved his hand, placating. "Don't be upset, Jonny. Not three weeks past I had archers shooting at you. Those arrows were real, and this battle is real, but it is about learning. If you lose, you will not die, soon that may not be the case. If you lose, you may even learn more. The experience will do you good, win or lose. The one piece of advice I will give you is that stealth and guile are often more important than strength and power."

The mock battle was to be staged at an old cabin in the woods above the castle. The Master told him he could have the help of up to three apprentices or one journeyman.

The task would be a simple hit and run. The three journeymen would be guarding an item in a cabin away from the castle. Jonny needed to retrieve the object and return to the castle with it in his possession.

The only stipulation The Master gave was that no one, Jonny or his opponents, was to do any physical harm to the other side.

Jonny thought for a long time and decided that his only ally would be Grelnick. Jonny had worked with him more than any of the other boys and felt he could trust and rely on him to do what he needed.

Jonny had a week to prepare, but he was not allowed near the cabin. Meanwhile, the journeymen worked feverishly on their preparations. Jonny had no idea what they were, but he expected they would be impressive.

The night of the battle arrived. Master Silurian had decreed that the encounter would take place at night so that all would have to rely on other than simple physical senses. The item was a marker amulet, one that glowed like a bright light to magical senses.

Jonny flew, holding Grelnick, to within one hundred yards of the cabin, then set him down.

"Grelnick, I'm going to fly high over the top and see if I can get an idea of the layout. Stay here till I get back."

"What if you don't come back," Grelick said nervously.

"Stay until sunrise. Go back to the castle if I don't show."

Jonny was familiar with the area from all his flying trips, but he wanted to see what his opponents had done to prepare. He went straight up very high, and drifted slowly over the cabin. The amulet was indeed a searchlight to his sight, and even brighter when he looked using the demon amulet.

Something large flashed past him. Jonny did not know what it was, but he did not stay around to find out. He flew a half-mile away, high, then circled back low to Grelnick. He told Grelnick what the layout was and outlined his plan. Then they started their assault.

§ § §

Jonny knew that trying to get the amulet directly would never work. The spell he had dodged as he had looked had been very powerful. Master Silurian had said guile, or trickiness, would work better than power, so he would be tricky.

Jonny used Grelnick as a decoy. He flew him low and fast over the top of the cabin. From inside shouts came and several spells flared in the night. Grelnick was hit repeatedly with spells. The voices inside grew louder as Grelnick continued to circle the cabin. The journeymen were yelling at each other, each blaming the other for their spell not knocking out "Jonny" though it was really Grelnick. Jonny was pretty sure poor Grelnick was unconscious, but the journeymen had no way to know Jonny was making him fly, while not flying himself.

Meanwhile, Jonny crept close to the cabin and was able to look in a window opposite to where he had Grelnick flying and simply reached in with his zdrell and floated the amulet quietly out and into his pouch. The three journeymen were still focused on Grelnick, and blaming each other. None of them saw him until he had the amulet and was already leaving. One ran outside looking for him. After three steps, he was in the air, pulling the unconscious Grelnick behind.

§ § §

They flew back to the castle and The Master received them with great joy and not a few harsh words for their opponents who Jonny had so successfully distracted. When Jonny later found out the strength and potency of the spells that had been used on Grelnick he was very glad he had opted to follow The Master's suggestion for wit over power. He knew he could never have withstood those spells and was nearly downed by the first spell that passed him by.

For their part, his three opponents gave him their hearty congratulations, but Jonny could tell they were quite annoyed to have been beaten by a thirteen-year-old boy, no matter how talented. All three soon left to begin their separate journeys to the wizards' conclave the following year, where they hoped to be confirmed masters. They all left, The Master said, much wiser for the experience.

Jonny himself could not make up his mind how to feel about the experience. On the one hand, he had felt excited and flushed through the whole escapade. On the other hand, he felt like it had gone too quickly. Looking back it all seemed like a blur. Lastly, below it all, he felt like on some level he had cheated. Sure, they had nearly gotten him with that first spell, but other than that, he had successfully tricked them into wasting their efforts on Grelnick. It just didn't feel like it had been an honorable fight.

When Jonny explained his feelings to The Master, a few days after the encounter, the old man had started to laugh, but seeing Jonny's scowl stopped and explained.

"I'm sorry for laughing at you, but I forget sometimes how young you are, and how old I am. You must understand this, Jonny, there really are no "honorable" fights. Yes, there are those who follow the rules, and those who use treachery and betrayal, but even fights that follow the rules are truly not things of honor. The best fight is the one that doesn't happen. Among true men of honor, disagreements can and should be resolved without direct conflict. Fights happen when one of the parties decides their way is the only way, regardless of others."

Jonny sat, trying to grasp what his master was telling him, but he just couldn't wrap his mind around it.

"Master, are you saying there is no honor in battle?"

"Yes, Jonny, that is just what I'm saying, though you will find few who would agree with me."

"But, Master, are you saying that if you fight, you are not honorable?" Jonny could not believe that.

"No, Jonny. There are many times when one is forced to fight. They say it takes two to fight, and that is true, but it only takes one to decide to fight. It is the one who decides to make the fight inevitable who is less than honorable. To defend yourself or those dear to you from an aggressor can be very honorable."

"But, didn't you just say—"

"Here is the important point, Jonny, when a fight is forced upon you, then you must do all you can to win, and win in a way that minimizes the casualties of the fight. That is why what you did in that test was well done indeed. By avoiding a direct conflict you shortened the battle and increased your chances for success."

Jonny's head was swimming, trying to grapple with this different way of seeing the test. Master Silurian sat and watched him, saying nothing for several moments. Finally, he spoke.

"One last thing to consider, Jonny, and then you need to get back to your studies. Winning a fight means making hard choices. You and Grelnick both knew that he was going to take the brunt of the attack so you could get the amulet unnoticed. That was a hard choice for both of you, but you made it and Grelnick was brave enough to accept it. In the future, you will need to make similar choices with more dire consequences. Understand, the best path is rarely the least painful, for you and others."

Jonny left The Master and went off to study, but his mind was not on his studies for several days. He kept replaying The Master's words, and thinking about this test, and wondering what other tests he would face, and if he would be brave enough to choose the right course.

He didn't know it at the time, but he would be tested again very soon.

Chapter 48

Not long after the three journeymen left, a few weeks before mid-fall day, a new one came to the castle. This was nothing unusual. Master Silurian had a very impressive reputation. He was known as one of the most powerful wizards in the continent, possibly in the world. It was also well known that he had almost nothing to do with demon magic, but had a very good command of the various other sorts. He was considered preeminent in force magics but also knowledgeable in nearly all the other branches of magical study. Because of this, there was a steady stream of journeymen who came to study with him.

This new journeyman was different. He already had something of a reputation, and when Jonny first saw him, he knew why. This man, and he was a man for he was nearly twenty years old, carried himself like a master, not like a humble journeyman. He was tall and had dark hair that fell to the middle of his back and a long face with a prominent nose. He went by the name of Flask. He said he had chosen it because he was a vessel that yearned to be filled with all the knowledge he could find. He did not dress like a journeyman either. He wore a rich brown cloak, a shirt of finer material than most traders owned, and rode in on a fine roan horse.

The other journeymen said he could have been confirmed a master two years ago, but had deliberately avoided the wizards' conclave so he could continue to acquire experience and knowledge as a journeyman. Once he was confirmed a master, no other wizard would be obligated to teach or mentor him as they were while he remained a journeyman. This fact was lost on most journeymen, who only aspired to the title of master, not realizing that once attained it effectively cut them off from much of the instruction that was a journeyman's due.

There was no doubt Flask was a cut above other journeymen. He had traveled widely, having finished his apprenticeship when only fourteen. He had studied with many of the most renowned masters in the continent and had quickly learned from them and then moved on. He, like Master Silurian, was reputed to be skilled in several different disciplines, but unlike The Master, he was known to be fond of demon magic, though he had sworn not to practice it while studying with Master Silurian.

Jonny quickly saw that The Master was not entirely pleased to have Flask studying with him. The journeyman's well-known affinity for demon magic, as well as his fame and ego, were not to The Master's liking. The apprentices and the other journeymen did not share this opinion. They all flocked to him and tried to become his friend, to bathe in the reflected glow of his presence.

Jonny, sensing his master's reticence stayed aloof as well. He sensed there was something very strong and very dangerous in Flask.

The Master had instructed everyone in the castle that Flask was not to be told of Jonny's abilities, especially flying, until The Master decided whether he could trust him. Even so, Flask quickly determined that there was something special about Jonny, not from what he saw him do, but from the way everyone treated him

Jonny tried avoiding Flask as much as possible, but since he studied in the same room with the journeymen (the only apprentice to have that privilege), and ate in the same dining room, it was not entirely possible. When Flask asked the other journeymen why Jonny was given journeyman privileges, they only said that Jonny was The Master's star pupil or that Master Silurian had decreed it. Jonny could see that no matter how much others tried to play down Jonny's importance in the castle, Flask would not give up until he found out what they were all hiding.

One afternoon when Jonny was studying a new book The Master had recently acquired, in the journeymen's workshop, Flask entered and came over to Jonny.

"Boy," Flask began, addressing himself imperiously to Jonny. "Run over and get me a large saucer of water and place it here on this worktable," he said pointing to the work table next to where Jonny had been studying.

Activity in the workshop stopped. All eyes were on Jonny to see what he would do. Flask was perfectly within his rights to ask any apprentice, even Jonny, to fetch and carry for him if he was not already engaged in another task for The Master. But Jonny was no ordinary apprentice and had not been treated like one for years. There was not another journeyman in the place who would dream of demanding that Jonny do their dirty work for them. They knew what Jonny could do, Flask did not, but he clearly wanted to find out.

Jonny looked up slowly from his book, stood up, and walked over to where the crockery was kept, took out and filled a saucer and brought it over to the table. As he was approaching the table, Flask, seemingly accidentally, stuck out his foot just far enough so Jonny would trip on it. But Jonny had spent too long playing the game of not being surprised and simply stepped around the foot as though he had not seen it and set down the saucer. When he finished, he walked back to his table without saying a word, or even looking at Flask.

This was obviously not the reaction Flask had been expecting. He looked for moment as if he was going to try something more, but then a thought apparently occurred to him. He turned to one of the journeymen who was watching and spoke.

"Chandar, isn't it?" he asked.

"Y-yes," stammered the journeyman.

"Have you ever seen a map made from water before?" Flask asked, clearly inviting all around, and knowing they had not seen anything like it before.

"N-No," Chandar stammered his reply.

"It's really quite interesting," Flask said smugly. "I'd be happy to show you how it's done, if you're interested."

Chandar was plainly interested, as was every other journeyman in the room. Jonny was interested too, but he tried not to show it since he knew that had been Flask's intention all along. Chandar and the other journeymen gathered around the table blocking Jonny's view, but he closed his eyes so he could concentrate his zdrell sight on what was happening.

Flask took some powder he did not name and sprinkled it on the surface of the water in the saucer. He then made some gestures and spoke a short incantation, and the water in saucer began to move and have a texture. It formed into a three dimensional map of the area surrounding the castle. The powder he had sprinkled on the water somehow gave it depth and shading. Everyone was impressed, and stated their approval. Jonny too was impressed, but he also noted that Flask had not really explained how it was done.

§ § §

So it went for several days. Flask would at least once a day treat Jonny as though he were a regular apprentice. Each time Jonny would respond only as an apprentice might. He never got mad or was in any way disrespectful. As soon as he finished whatever task Flask had asked him to do, he went back to his studies and ignored Flask. Flask for his part would try and do some little feat to draw a reaction from Jonny, and though Jonny did not want to show it, he quickly saw that Flask was indeed a very talented magician.

The annual Harvest Festival came and went. Jonny got into town and saw Roald, but otherwise just watched the events, taking care not to draw attention to himself. Flask, took care to be seen doing small bits of magic among the crowds. He never did enough to be considered a performance, but very much enjoyed the attention of the crowds.

After the Harvest Festival, someone must have talked. Several of the Journeymen had been up late the previous night talking and joking with Flask, so it was hard to know who had said what, but someone had told Flask that Jonny was truly very talented. That morning when Flask had entered the workroom he walked right over to Jonny, who was again studying in one of the books.

"So you're something special, are you?" Flask challenged.

"What do you mean?" Jonny asked quietly.

"It's obvious isn't it? After all, you're the only apprentice I've ever seen who's treated like he was a master. So what's so special about you that no one will tell me about?"

"I know a few tricks," Jonny answered calmly. He didn't feel calm. He was reflecting on how Master Silurian had said that it only took one to start a fight, and how he might have one whether he wanted one or not.

"A few tricks, eh? Well what are they? What's so special?"

Jonny looked at him steadily. Outside he was calm and serene; inside he was very frightened of this imposing figure. "I'm afraid you'll have to ask Master Silurian. I'm not at liberty to say."

Flask looked angry, but then he nodded slowly. He changed his tactics again.

"Look," he said conspiratorially. "I won't tell anyone, promise. Can't you show me anything, just a little something? Just a trick or two?" he cajoled.

Jonny lifted his eyebrows, and then shrugged his shoulders resignedly.

"All right, I'll show you a trick, but I doubt you'll be impressed," Jonny said sounding bored.

Jonny had discussed Flask's attempts with The Master and they had decided that the best way to deal with Flask was to give him what he wanted, but not nearly all Jonny could do. Since he still saw Jonny as an apprentice, he would be impressed by any of Jonny's skills. Hopefully, he would think that what Jonny showed was all he could do. At least, that was the plan.

Jonny fished his lucky coin, the first one he had ever spun, out of his pocket. He placed it on edge on the worktable with his index finger on top. Closing his eyes he set the coin spinning then removed his finger. It sat spinning steadily on the table.

"Nice bit of manipulation that," Flask chuckled. "I looked carefully and never saw you start it spinning."

This rankled Jonny, he was not doing simple sleight of hand; this was real.

"That's because I didn't use my hand. It's not manipulation!" Jonny said testily. In spite of all his attempts to keep calm and uninterested, Flask was getting to him.

"Really," Flask grinned. "I saw a trick almost exactly like it done at a fair not six months ago. I couldn't see him flick it either."

Jonny was getting madder. "But did it keep spinning like mine has?" he challenged.

"Hmmm, now that you mention it, his did seem to slow a bit faster than yours is, but he didn't have a nice fat heavy coin like yours either," Flask smirked.

Jonny was losing the calm that he had so carefully cultivated being around Flask. Flask's insults really hurt Jonny; hurt him most because he knew he could not show him the full extent of his power. Here was the first magician he had encountered who had failed to be impressed by this trick. Flask not only was not impressed, but was also ridiculing him, comparing him to a country sleight of hand artist. He decided he had to show him more.

"But, could he make it spin faster?" Jonny asked, gritting his teeth to make a show of the effort it was taking.

It was not an effort. The real effort was in not taking it and flying it down Flask's throat, as he wanted to do.

As the coin visibly increased its speed, Flask's smirk faded somewhat. Jonny wanted to grin when he saw Flask surreptitiously grab at an amulet that Jonny assumed was a demon sight amulet like the one Jonny had. He wanted to laugh aloud when he saw the smirk fade completely as Flask tried vainly to see how Jonny was making it happen.

"How are you doing that, wart?" Flask demanded.

"It's just a trick," Jonny said. "Anyone could do it," he added smugly.

Now Flask was the one losing his control.

"I said, how are you doing that? I can see the force lines bending, but you used no incantation, no materials, nothing. You just looked at it and now it's spinning," Flask shouted.

"I told you, it's just a trick I can do," Jonny said, matter of factly.

"No you don't," Flask growled. "You're not getting off that easily. You're telling me, or you'll wish you had!"

Jonny was scared, but then he looked around the room. All work had stopped. Every journeyman in the room was watching. As Jonny looked at them, Flask too suddenly became aware of the aucience. The look of hatred left his face as though it had never been there. He looked around at all the other journeymen and smiled.

"You boys were right," he said in a jolly tone. "This Jonny here really is something special. You're lucky to have him here," he said moving over to wrap an arm around Jonny as if they were the best of friends. As he did this Jonny realized just how much bigger Flask was than him, the top of Jonny's head did not even reach his armpit.

"That's really a good trick, Jonny, I'm sure your master is pleased with you," Flask enthused. Then he said, speaking out of the side of his mouth so only Jonny could hear.

"I meant it, Jonny. You'll tell me on your own or I'll beat it out of you."

He let go of Jonny and stepped away. "Most impressive, yes most impressive," Flask said, speaking for his audience again. The coin was now spinning so fast that it appeared to be an indistinct gold ball. Jonny decided he had better make it clear that he could do more.

"Heads or tails, Flask?" Jonny asked as Flask was about to turn and go.

"What?" Flask said, caught off guard.

"I said you should call it Flask, head or tails?"

Flask was nonplussed. "Uh, heads, ah yes, always heads."

"Right then," Jonny said and looked hard at the coin which suddenly came to a complete stop still balanced on its edge, then gently fell over to land tails side up.

"I guess today's just not your lucky day, Flask," Jonny said unable to keep the smirk out of his voice or off his face.

Flask's face flamed bright crimson. He again looked like he was going to throttle Jonny, but slowly wrestled control back. Jonny had never seen someone who was so obviously upset exert that kind of control. In a way, it was more frightening than the rage had been.

"So, that's the way it is then," he said through gritted teeth, "So be it. I challenge you to a duel."

"Oh you do, do you?" The Master suddenly boomed out. No one had seen him come into the room; all had been so intent on the conflict between Jonny and Flask.

"You challenge my apprentice?" The Master said, mocking. "I thought that you were upset over the fact that I was treating him like a journeyman, and here you are challenging him to a duel. A duel can only take place between equals. Are you suggesting that this boy is your equal, or possibly your superior, Flask?"

Flask was speechless. He tried to reply but nothing came out. "I, ah, I, ah, that is, ah . . . I meant, uh . . ."

"What you meant," Master Silurian went on implacably, "was what you said. You do consider little Jonny here your equal, and your rival. You have no right whatsoever to challenge him to a duel, in fact I should have you thrown right out of here for your impertinence."

Flask started to stammer some sort of a reply, but The Master cut him off.

"Yes, I really should have you thrown out of here right now, but I will not, because I really think you need to have your pride shrunk a size or two. I also think Jonny here is just the person to do it for you." He turned to Jonny. "What do you think, Jonny? Do you want to accept this overblown windbag's challenge, or shall I throw him out on his ear like he deserves?"

Now it was Jonny's turn to have difficulty speaking. "Ah, um, M-Master, I guess I'd like to accept his challenge," he said quietly, very much aware that the eyes of everyone in the room were on him.

"So be it then," The Master said, looking at Flask, "Tomorrow at noon in the field north of the castle. Open duel. The only restraints I will apply is that this is a duel until one is incapacitated or yields, not to the death. Also, no demon magic is allowed. That should not bother you, Flask, since you agreed to forego demon magic while you were here at the castle. Do you both accept the terms?"

They both agreed, then Flask glared at Jonny and left the room.

"There's one to watch, Jonny," The Master said looking where Flask had gone. "You have pricked his pride. He will be no easy opponent. He is more than a match for most so-called masters out there."

"How can I hope to beat him, Master?" Jonny said, starting to get really scared as the full import of what he had just agreed to sank in.

A wizard's duel was no small thing. Like sword duels, they were frequently a matter of life and death, or at least a matter of honor. Even with the strictures The Master had added, this could still mean a whole world of hurt to Jonny.

"Ah, it shouldn't really be too difficult, Jonny," The Master added distractedly. "You have seen most of what he can do. He really is a fairly competent wizard, and much more broadly versed than most wizards today, but even he is still greatly dependent on demons for anything really powerful. He cannot use them, so I do not think he should be too great of a challenge.

"In fact, you have a great advantage on him," The Master said now grinning.

"What's that, Master?"

"Well, you know pretty much what he is capable of, but he still has no idea what you can do. That coin trick really threw him, but I seriously doubt he has thought about the implications of what it will mean. No, you really are the one who has the advantage, but you must be very careful. I am sure this is not his first duel so he will have more than a trick or two up his sleeve too. It should be fun," he added, grinning a grin that did nothing to reassure Jonny.

§ § §

The Master had been correct in saying that this was not Flask's first duel. The other journeymen told Jonny that Flask had been in fourteen previous duels, and had won them all. Worse, was that four of those opponents were now masters, and Flask had beaten them nonetheless. This did nothing to boost Jonny's confidence.

Jonny believed he could win because The Master thought he could. In a way, this was more exciting than the earlier battle had been. This was real, and Jonny decided he would prepare for it as he had the previous conflict. He would think of things that he hoped would catch Flask off guard.

The trickiest part was that The Master had again cautioned Jonny against revealing the full extent of his talent.

"I know this is unfair to you, Jonny," Master Silurian had told him, "but if he knows you can fly, it would be no time at all before many people we do not want aware of your ability would know. No, I hate to say this, but it would be much better for you to lose than for Flask to find out all you can do. In some ways, losing would be the best thing you could do. But I can't ask you to do that. I just want you to know what the stakes are here."

Jonny decided he would treat this purely as an educational experience. If he could win with his magical hands tied behind his back, well and good, otherwise he would just do the best he could.

Chapter 49

The whole castle was in an uproar over the duel. Jonny was surprised to find that there was almost no one who wanted Flask to win. Most of the journeymen there felt that Jonny, though only an apprentice, was one of their own. Many admired Flask, but they were also jealous. The Master was not the only one who wanted to see Flask's ego deflated.

The apprentices were totally on Jonny's side. He was their hero. Just the fact that Flask considered him worthy of a duel had elevated Jonny to godlike status in their eyes, and he was what they all secretly wanted to be, a kid who could show the big people who was boss.

Jonny got little sleep that night. He tossed and turned, coming up with plans and then discarding them. Every time he thought he had something that would work well, he found himself wondering if he was showing too much, or if Flask would have a simple defense. It drove him crazy, and he finally fell asleep just before dawn.

§ § §

Grelnick shook Jonny awake. He told Jonny it was just two hours before noon. Jonny could not believe he had slept that long. He did not feel like he had slept at all. Grelnick helped Jonny get some late breakfast and filled him in on the mood in the castle. Apparently, Flask, though he had told everyone this was no contest, was taking no chances. He had been holed up with another journeyman making plans for much of the night. Other than that, everyone in the castle wanted Jonny to win, but many were not expecting him to. There was fierce wagering going on and there had even been fights among some of the apprentices as to whether anyone should bet against Jonny. Jonny almost asked, but decided it was better if he did not know what the odds were against him.

Jonny was resigned to his fate, he would probably lose. He could not anticipate everything Flask might do. Several of the plans he had worked out the night before he thought might work, but he was not going to commit himself to any of them until he saw Flask's reaction. He didn't think it would be enough.

Time passed very slowly, and very fast at the same time. It seemed to Jonny like noon would never arrive and that it was upon him before he could possibly be ready no matter what he did. He was not feeling happy. He felt like a man condemned to be hung at dawn who sees the sky getting lighter and lighter. He only hoped it would be over quick.

§ § §

As the sun reached its zenith, the whole castle flowed towards the north field. It was rare when everyone in the castle congregated for anything, but they were there now. Jonny, Flask and Master Silurian were at the center of the unruly mob. The Master had everyone fall back to give them room. There was much jockeying for position on the rocks at the northern edge of the field, which afforded the best view.

Flask looked every inch the master wizard. Even though his robes still marked him as a journeyman, he somehow managed to wear them so that they appeared more fine and noble. He stood tall, his hair perfectly in place, a gleam in his eye.

Jonny looked every inch the young apprentice. He had changed into fresh clothes, but he looked uncertain and small, especially when compared to the radiant Flask. Jonny did not look happy, but neither did he look beaten. There was a subtle but clear sense of resolve that surrounded him. It looked like this whole duel was a farce, which Jonny could not possibly win, but there was something about him that belied the first comparison. Flask saw it too.

They both stood about thirty feet apart facing each other. The Master once again reiterated the rules: a battle of honor, not injury, no demon magic, and finished when one of them yielded or was incapacitated. He raised his large staff and let it drop, the signal to begin.

Both Jonny and Flask began to invoke spells rapidly. Jonny used his shield spell, which he hoped would give him time to figure out what Flask would try to do and counter it. Flask began gesticulating and then pointed his index finger at Jonny. From the end of his finger sprang three small white globes, flying straight at Jonny. Luckily, Jonny had finished his shield spell in time and the three magic missiles bounced off it harmlessly. Jonny had seen Flask demonstrate the magic missiles before and expected Flask to use them.

Now that the initial exchange was over Jonny was not sure what to do next. Flask gave him a mock bow.

"Well done, apprentice. A fine shield spell," Flask began, "but what are you going to do now? You can't keep the shield up forever and I doubt very much you can do anything offensively while you have it up."

Jonny said nothing, then closed his eyes and reached out for a rock with his zdrell and sent it flying right at Flask. The rock impacted a shield surrounding Flask and bounced away into the audience.

"Oh my," Flask said smirking. "I seem to have a shield as well. Too bad, I don't have to concentrate to keep mine up. Good try though, I am impressed."

Jonny had expected something like that, but seeing it made his stomach tighten wondering how he could win.

At just that moment, Flask unleashed another salvo of three missiles that again rebounded off Jonny's shield. Some of the good humor left Flask's face when he saw that his diversion had been foiled and Jonny still had his shield firmly in place. Jonny responded by throwing three more rocks at Flask who could not help flinching even though they were repelled by his shield.

A cheer went up from the crowd.

"So you want to play rough, do you?" Flask said, all traces of good humor gone.

He began an involved incantation that Jonny had not seen before, but he could see the force lines moving strongly so he decided it was time to act. Jonny reached out again and started moving as many bits of rock and dirt as he could at once and poured them over the top of Flask's shield. This had two effects. The first was that it temporarily made Jonny invisible to Flask. The second was that at least some of the dirt got through Flask's shield. The shield spell had to allow air to pass through or the wizard would die if he used it for any length of time. Dust and dirt that mixed with the air were able to pass through. This was the one thing Jonny had been able to test since the duel challenge had been issued.

Flask roared with rage and was soon coughing and choking. His incantation disrupted, and curses were clearly heard between his coughs. The crowd roared with laughter and even Jonny smiled a little. He felt like he might have a chance, but now he had a new worry because a side effect of throwing the dirt was that Jonny had been unable to maintain the shield spell. He was now very vulnerable and knew it. Jonny took advantage of Flask's continuing partial blindness to run around behind him. Jonny could see Flask was now livid with rage and he worried about The Master's ability to stop him if he tried to kill Jonny.

"Running won't save you now, you little offspring of a dung beetle," Flask screamed, and threw two more magic missiles at Jonny. Jonny was ready, and intercepted the missiles with rocks that exploded with their impact. Bits and pieces of the rocks did reach him, stinging his face.

Jonny's nerves sang. Either of those could have killed him. He wanted nothing more than to fly right out of there, but knew he could not. Could The Master save him from Flask's wrath? He doubted Flask would even let him surrender.

Then something even scarier happened. Jonny was again throwing dirt and rocks at Flask and running to be behind him when he heard Flask's voice call out in the demon tongue. Jonny was not sure, but it sounded like part of a summoning.

Jonny immediately grabbed his amulet to be able to see where the demon was coming from, but no demon came. This puzzled Jonny, he had stopped running to scan the sky in all directions. It appeared to puzzle Flask even more. He obviously expected something to happen that clearly was not happening. Then he began to curse, ignoring Jonny.

Jonny decided it was time to try the best thing he had thought of the night before. He knew he could not let Flask see him fly, but there was nothing that said he could not make Flask fly, just a little.

Jonny reached out into the force lines and felt Flask's body. The shield kept material and magical objects out, but it could not keep out the natural lines of force. Jonny bent the lines so Flask began to float free of the ground. When that happened, Flask panicked.

At just the moment when Flask was flailing about the most, though he was only inches off the ground, Jonny brought him back down, hard. He landed flat on his back with a resounding thud. His head hit the ground and he lay there dazed, nearly unconscious.

The crowd erupted with cheers. The Master stood up and declared the duel over and Jonny the winner. Several journeymen went forward at The Master's direction, helped Flask to his feet, and escorted him through the surging crowd.

Jonny was instantly surrounded. Before he knew what was happening, he was hoisted up on the shoulders of the jubilant crowd and carried in triumph back to the castle.

Chapter 50

A celebration the likes of which Jonny had never witnessed overcame the castle. Jonny was shocked because he was the cause of it. It seemed that everyone had to touch him, to congratulate him, to tell him how great he was. It could have gone easily to his head, except that Jonny did not feel like he was really awake. It was more like he was in a dream and at any moment he would wake up to find he was the one knocked unconscious in the duel.

He kept waiting for the moment when he would wake up; it never came. His face hurt from the smile that had not left it since he had heard The Master declare him the winner. He only wished Roald could have been there to share in the celebration.

Uncharacteristically, The Master allowed the celebration to continue the rest of the day and into the night. The party and good feelings continued on, but not Jonny. He was too tired. Jonny found that between his previous sleepless night and the sheer letdown of the duel being over, he felt like a wrung out floor rag. He managed to last until dark, but then crawled up to his room and was instantly asleep.

The next morning, Jonny found that the surprises had not stopped. The previous afternoon The Master had quietly, while the celebration went on, found out the full details of what had happened in the duel.

The Master had suspected that Flask might do something outside the rules laid down for the duel. He had instructed one of the other journeymen to watch Scarflag, the journeyman who had been preparing with Flask for the duel. Flask had been much more impressed with Jonny's coin trick than he admitted to anyone. He knew he could win against Jonny if he could use a demon, but he also knew that there was no way Master Silurian would allow him to perform a summoning. So he had arranged to have Scarflag perform an open summoning with an apprentice already under the knife and then pass control of the demon over to Flask if the duel appeared to be going against him. Scarflag had already waylaid an apprentice and begun the summoning when Feldor had appeared to stop the attempt and confine Scarflag. When Flask spoke the command that he assumed would bring the previously summoned demon to him, nothing happened and Jonny was able to use the moment of surprise to bring Flask down.

At noon, just one day after Flask's defeat, The Master had all the apprentices and journeymen assemble in the castle courtyard. Flask and Scarflag were standing next to Master Silurian and Feldor. The Master called Jonny up to stand with them though he had not told Jonny what was going on. The news of Flask's attempted cheat in the duel had turned the mood ugly in the castle.

The Master began speaking, going over the rules that had been set for the duel, how Flask and Scarflag had attempted to cheat, and how they had been foiled. He then went on to explain the gravity of violating the rules of a formal duel; that a master could lose his mastership if judged guilty, and that a journeyman could be broken back to apprentice. He allowed the implication hang for several moments, and then he turned to face Flask and Scarflag and announced that he would not be renouncing either of their journeymanships. There was an angry grumble from the crowd, but The Master held up his hand and the crowd quieted.

"I have not finished decreeing my judgment," The Master said, his voice echoing over the silent crowd. "Flask and Scarflag are to leave this castle and my kingdom immediately, and while I will not mention this matter to the council of elders, all of you bear witness to the facts of this case. These men have dishonored themselves, and you all are witnesses."

"There is one more thing. Both Flask and Scarflag have agreed to publicly apologize to Jonny and admit their guilt to him, and that he is, even now, a greater wizard than either of them."

The crowd was thunderstruck. Jonny was stunned beyond words. First Scarflag came to stand before Jonny, asked his forgiveness and told him that he was the greatest wizard he knew besides Master Silurian. This was embarrassing for Jonny, but it did not prepare him for what came next. Flask, looking much less proud, strode before Jonny with a little of his former grace and then went down on one knee with his head bowed. Jonny's mouth dropped open at the incredible sign of respect.

"Jonny, I have wronged you," Flask began, not looking up. "I have wronged you greatly and it is only because of the great mercies of Master Silurian that I am not now an apprentice. In truth I would gladly be your apprentice, but I am not worthy."

Jonny could not believe what he was hearing. In his wildest fantasies, he had never dreamed of something like this happening. He almost started to speak, to deny what Flask was saying but The Master laid a hand on his shoulder to stop him.

"I truly am not worthy, Jonny," Flask continued. "You have taught me a great lesson in humility. I haven't slept since last night, and I now see the fool I've been. I have been arrogant and proud. I can only hope that you can forgive me and that someday I can meet you again when we have both put this far behind us."

Flask stayed with head bowed on one knee, waiting. Jonny wondered what he was waiting for then he realized that Flask was waiting for him, as was everyone else.

"I f-forgive you, Flask," Jonny said, his voice breaking. He could not think of anything else to say.

"Thank you, Jonny," Flask said, still not looking up. "You are already more a man than I."

With that, Flask got up, picked up his traveling case and began to walk out of the castle. The crowd parted and no one said anything until he had left the castle.

Something was bothering Jonny about the way Flask left, but he could not figure it out, then it came to him.

"What happened to Flask's horse, Master?"

"He left it for you," The Master replied. "That was not one of my conditions to him, but he said he felt he needed to give you something more than just an apology. I am still not sure how much of that apology was an act, but he seems to be truly penitent. It is hard to know what he really thinks, but I do believe, Jonny, that you have given him the greatest shock of his life. If he actually learns from it, he will be a much better man for it."

The crowd broke up with everyone talking quietly. It seemed that no one talked of anything else for weeks afterwards.

§ § §

Jonny went back to his previous routine, but he could tell things had changed. He felt isolated again. He had proven to everyone that he was beyond them. They could not treat him as one of their own, yet he was still an apprentice.

Two weeks after the duel, The Master called him into his main study.

"Jonny," he began, "after the duel, it is a pure farce on my part to call you an apprentice, and everyone here knows it. However, I have a problem; you are not yet fourteen years old. If I make you a journeyman, you will become nothing but a target, and I do not think you or I want that. I also think it is time that you studied with someone else. Therefore, I have come up with a plan, and I want to see what you think of it. The decision is yours. Whatever you decide I will abide by your choice."

"Yes, Master," Jonny said with some fear. "What is your plan?"

"Jonny, you showed real talent in the creation of your amulet. I told you of this earlier. I have since thought that it would be valuable for you to gain more experience in the fashioning of similar artifacts. Unfortunately, there is no one within a reasonable distance who has any greater expertise than I in the fashioning of amulets. Frankly, my talents only slightly exceed yours at this point. I feel with only minor training you will easily surpass me in this area as well."

"So," The Master continued, holding up a hand to forestall Jonny's protest, "I propose that you be apprenticed to Kason, the master jeweler and armorer in Alavar. He knows nothing of magic, but there is little known in the working of metal in weapons and jewelry that he does not know. He can teach you the things that can be done with metal, and you can take what you already know in magic and combine them. Not only that, but a little hard physical work will do you good, put some muscle on you," he laughed and smiled.

Jonny sat and considered. He did not say anything for several moments and Master Silurian started to look impatient.

"So, what do you think, boy? Will you do it?"

Jonny still said nothing for several more moments then slowly replied, "If you think it is best, Master, I'll do it."

"What's the matter? I thought you would be excited to get out of here where everyone treats you like some holy thing?"

"It's just, Master, that, I thought I was *your* apprentice," Jonny answered not willing to meet his master's gaze.

"And you will continue to be my apprentice, my boy, at least as far as you and I are concerned. I am not turning you out, if that's what you are thinking. No, I am giving you a rare opportunity to explore some new areas. If this works out you should become a journeyman in both magic and jewel craft, a combination I do not think I have heard of in more than a thousand years.

"The only thing I am waiting on is for you to complete that invisibility amulet. Once that is fully activated I think it will be time for you to go."

"But, Master, I've cast the spell into it so many times I think I must do it in my sleep. Will it ever be done?"

"Yes, Jonny, sooner than you think."

As usual, Master Silurian was right. Two days after Jonny had his conversation with The Master, the amulet was done. When Jonny cast the spell into the amulet the final time, there was no doubt it had taken.

As Jonny finished casting the spell for the one hundred and eighty third time, it happened. The amulet, which up to this time had only glowed briefly as he finished the spell, began to glow like a burning ember. The glow increased and the force line etchings in its surface blazed with light. When Jonny looked using his sight, he could see that there were force lines tightly concentrated in the center of the amulet and branching out like some sort of spider web away from the amulet.

The effect did not last long, only moments, but there was no question that something within the amulet had changed. Jonny thought about going to get Master Silurian to verify that this was not another false alarm, but he was sure it was not. And besides, he wanted to cast the binding spell before the amulet changed again.

Jonny had practiced the binding spell and it, too, went quickly. After he finished the spell, the amulet now appeared as it had before he had done any magic on it, but now when he picked it up, he felt the weight of the spell. All he had to do was think and the spell activated. This, though, was different from casting the spell. He did not have to exert any effort to maintain the spell. In fact, he had to deliberately think again in order deactivate it.

Jonny was elated. He ran to show The Master, who was suitably impressed. He was even more impressed when Jonny told him it had taken him *only* 183 casts in order for it to take. Only then did he tell Jonny that his first amulet had required him nearly 400 casts before his spell had taken. Now it was Jonny's turn to be impressed by his own accomplishment.

§ § §

"He did it again, Alira," Master Silurian said as he walked into his wife's greenhouse, where she was tending her herbs.

"Who did what, Silurian? Did Gorlick not shoe the black mare properly? I keep telling you we need a real farrier up here, not some old, broken-down—"

"No, Dearest. This has nothing to do with Gorlick. It is Jonny," he said, coming to stand by her side as she fussed with her plants. She still hadn't looked up from them.

"What did he do?" she asked, extracting a weed.

"He finished his amulet," Master Silurian said with glowing pride in his voice.

"Weren't you expecting that?" she asked distractedly, examining the leaves of one of the plants with a scowl.

"Yes, yes, I was, but he finished it in under two hundred casts," he enthused, pacing.

"Is that really significant?" she asked, scraping at the bottom of a leaf. "I never understand you wizards. When I make an amulet, well, if I have to cast the spell more than once, I've done something wrong, haven't I?"

"That's something completely different, and you know it," he said, waggling his finger at her. Her head was still down, but a grin tugged at the corner of her mouth. "A weidge's amulet is made of living things, the magic is already in them. Your 'spell' only preserves them beyond their normal life. It is nothing like storing magic in an inanimate object."

"I'll never understand why wizards are so bound to working with 'dead' objects," she said, still grinning. This was an old and well-worn argument, but there was no rancor in it.

"You know our magic is different, dearest, and you know exactly how difficult it is to create an amulet. You've lived here too long for it to be otherwise, so don't pretend to misunderstand how great Jonny's achievement is."

"Yes, I know, Silurian," she turned and looked at him now with full attention. "So, what will you do with him now?"

"It is nearly Mid-winter day. After that, I will send him to Kason."

"So, he has agreed," she said slowly, smiling.

"Indeed, though I could tell he was less than enthusiastic about it. He has no idea what it will be like working with a wizard as an apprentice."

"And you do?" she laughed softly.

Now Silurian smiled. "True enough, I never know quite what to expect with Jonny, but the one thing I'm sure of is that he will excel. This work with the amulet proves it. If he only achieves the least of what I expect, he will surely be the best wizard at creating amulets born in the last two hundred years. Beyond that," he paused and looked off into the distance. "Beyond that, who knows? For the first time since the Great War there could be new objects of power. All the greatest zdrell masters created them. If we are very lucky, perhaps Jonny too could produce them, maybe even a line-cutter. Wouldn't that set the demon masters back?" he snorted.

"Silurian, you put too much on the boy," she said, shaking her head.

"Maybe, but since the last line-cutter was destroyed three hundred years past, the demons have grown in power and control. To have a weapon the demons fear," he said wistfully, "would change everything."

"I will say this, Silurian, going to Kason will be certain to be good for the boy."

"Why do you say that with such conviction, Alira?"

"Because it will get him out of this castle, and away from you," she said, with only slightest hint of a grin.

"Hmmmph," he grunted. "You may be right, old woman. You may be right."

Chapter 51

With the completion of the amulet, there was nothing left to hold Jonny to the castle. The Master completed the arrangements he had worked out previously so Jonny could become Master Kason's apprentice following Midwinter day. The whole affair was highly irregular, but everyone in the castle had become used to how the normal rules did not apply to Jonny . . . everyone that is except Jonny. He still felt like he was somehow breaking his apprenticeship, even though Master Silurian reiterated he had not, and required that Jonny return and report to him monthly.

So it was, that in the coldest days of winter, Jonny left the castle Salaways to live in Alavar, slightly more than three years after he had arrived. He went as he had come, in a carriage accompanied by Lord Feldar.

His reception by Master Kason was a cordial one. Master Kason was one of the leading masters in the city, even in the kingdom. Even so, having a new apprentice delivered personally by the Lord Chancellor of the kingdom was an occasion. Jonny suspected that the quarters he was given were almost certainly not the usual apprentice quarters; in fact, he guessed they had either belonged to one of Kason's family, or been quarters for visiting guests. Several days later, talking to the other apprentices, he was able to confirm his guess.

§ § §

Master Kason did not seem quite sure how to treat Jonny. Jonny was certainly the age of an apprentice, and Master Silurian had left instructions that Jonny be treated as a normal apprentice, but Jonny and Master Kason knew Jonny would never be treated like one.

The next day after his arrival, Jonny dressed and presented himself to his new master to begin work.

"I'm told you've had some training in metalwork previously," Master Kason began.

"Only a little, master. Just enough to enable me to produce this," Jonny said pulling his amulet from under his shirt and showing it to the master metalworker.

Master Kason looked closely at the amulet. "Not bad. A bit rough and unfinished but not bad at all." He continued looking at it. "Do you mind if I look at it more closely?"

"Not at all, master," Jonny said, removing the thong that held it from around his neck.

Master Kason took the amulet and put it down under a glass that enlarged his view of it. He grunted. "This is enchanted, then?" he asked.

"Yes."

"And I suppose these lines scribed into the surface have something to do with that?"

"They do," Jonny said, offering nothing more.

"And I suppose you aren't about to tell me what this amulet does?"

"I will if you require it, Master, but my uh, Master Silurian said it was best if I didn't discuss what it does unnecessarily, since anyone can make it work if they know the proper keyword to activate it."

"You mean I could use this, thing, to do whatever it does, if I knew the code word?"

"Yes, Master."

"That is potent magic indeed that can be used by one of us non-wizarding folk. I can see why you don't wish to reveal it, and I certainly won't force you. I grow more uneasy with this arrangement all the time. How can I treat you like a common apprentice if you are already wizard enough to do things of this sort?"

"I don't really know, Master, but I know that I can work and that there is much you can teach me. Try to forget where I come from and treat me just as an apprentice and I think we can make this work."

Jonny really did want to succeed. In just the time he had been there, he had seen weapons and jewelry of a level of artistry that it made him ache with desire to learn how to create the same himself. Once again, Master Silurian had proved to be correct in what Jonny needed to develop the talents he had.

"Well then we shall give it a try," Master Kason said smiling and giving Jonny a warm pat on the shoulder.

"How old did you say you were?" Master Kason asked.

"Nearly fourteen, sir."

"That old eh?" he grunted. "I'd have not guessed you at more than twelve and scrawny at that." Jonny cringed. "Don't worry, son," he said smiling down at Jonny, "We'll soon put some meat on those bones and many a lad doesn't begin to really grow till after his fourteenth birthday. No, don't worry, you'll grow soon enough. And even if you don't, a jeweler doesn't need muscle or size, but precision. From what I see with this amulet of yours," he said handing it back to Jonny. "I'd say you already have more than your share of precision. With a little training, you could become a worthy artisan regardless of your magic.

"Are you ready to start work then?"

"Yes, Master Kason," Jonny replied eagerly.

"Then, the first thing you need to know is that here only the customers call me 'Master Kason.' You'll call me Master, or just Kason, it's what all my workers do."

"Yes, M-Master," Jonny said, unsure what name to use.

"That'll do, son," Kason said grinning, "That or Kason is fine. Now how much do you know about getting the different metals ready to be used . . . ."

§ § §

Jonny's education began anew. Kason was a patient teacher. He or one of the journeymen explained to Jonny each of the various processes going on in the shop. Kason's was one of the few places that did both armory and jewelry. He had many orders from far and wide for weapons that were more for show than for use: Jewel encrusted swords, daggers, armor, and the like. But Kason's craftsmanship was such that even ornamental weapons would also serve as well or better than any plain weapon if called into battle.

Jonny had never worked so hard in his life. Even before he was apprenticed to The Master, when he was living as a slave, Jonny had not been so tired at the end of a day. In the beginning, Jonny mostly observed what his new master, the various journeymen, and apprentices did. He observed while hauling materials, holding pieces while they were hammered on, and cleaning up after the very messy business that was metalwork.

No matter what the weather outside, it was hot in the workshop. In the winter when Jonny began, it was comfortable, but as the weather turned, it grew more and more furnace like.

Kason insisted that Jonny learn every aspect of trade, from the converting of ore into metal, all the way to tempering and polishing the finished product. It was hot, sweaty, dirty work, and Jonny loved it. He learned to work wearing nothing but the heavy protective leather apron that wrapped to cover his behind, gloves and boots that were needed to protect his body from heat and flying ash and metal.

Kason's prediction that Jonny would put some muscle on his frame was soon verified, but it was not a painless process. For the first three weeks Jonny worked in the shop, he awoke each morning barely able to move from the stiffness in his abused muscles. It generally took him most of the morning to get over being stiff. Soon after, he was usually in simple pain from performing some new chore his muscles were unaccustomed to doing. In those first three weeks, he wondered if he would ever be able to move again without pain. But Jonny was young, and after those first weeks, he was better able to bear the pain, and it troubled him less and less.

Chapter 52

When Jonny returned to the castle to make his first progress report to The Master in five weeks, forty-five days, after he had begun his new apprenticeship, he was surprised by how much he had changed. Jonny knew that he was getting stronger, but he did not really think much about it. He was shocked by how everyone else at the castle reacted. Every person who saw him stopped and gawked. At first Jonny thought that they were staring at the metal worker's apprentice clothes he wore, but he soon realized it was not only that, it was something about him. Finally, he could not take it anymore since everyone looked, but no one said anything to him.

"Just what is it you're staring at?" Jonny yelled at Carlik, when he saw the young apprentice.

"Well, it's, ah, ah . . . you look so different, Jonny," Carlik stammered.

"What do you mean, different? It is it the clothes? What?"

"Well, no, um, it's not the clothes, Jonny, you just . . . just look different, really different, that's all," he said and ran off.

Jonny was annoyed. He did not know what was different, but it bothered him to come back to the place he thought of as home and have everyone treat him like a person returned from the dead. He had only been gone a month, five weeks. He was not that different. Jonny was even more shocked when Master Silurian also gave him the same strange look.

Now Jonny was mad.

"What is it?" he demanded. "Everyone in here looks at me like I have leprosy or something. I can understand them being put off, but not you, Master. What is it?"

The Master said nothing for a moment, just looked at Jonny and then brought him over in front of the full length mirror he had at one end of his study, a mirror which Jonny had seen himself in many times before. He simply said, "Look at yourself, and tell me what you see."

When Jonny looked, he finally understood. While the jewelry shop had a full-length mirror, it was for customers and Jonny had never bothered to look at himself in it. In fact, he had not really looked at himself other than in the reflection of polished metal for the last 45 days, now he saw. Now he understood.

If he had been walking down the street and seen his reflection, he would not have recognized it for him. He was not any taller, but nearly everything else about him had changed. Where before his skin had always been pale, now it was a burned brown, rough and chapped. Where before his face had been soft and very childlike, now it had edges, and creases. There was something, a look of someone older, much older.

But none of that could compare with what he saw of his arms. His arms had always been thin scrawny things, now they had muscles, real muscles. His skin looked stretched tight over the arms and the muscles were very clearly visible like cords under the flesh. The muscle continued up his shoulders and neck to the edges of his jaw. He stared down at his arms and hands as if he had never seen them before. It was a shock.

"Now do you understand?" The Master asked quietly.

"Yeah, I guess I do. I really do look different don't I?

"I guess that's what Master Kason meant when he said he thought that you'd see my progress right away."

"I would guess that would be the case," The Master chuckled. "It never ceases to amaze me how rapidly it can happen to a boy when it's time."

"Time for what?"

"Time for his body to begin the change from boy to man. You are well on you way, Jonny, well on you way, indeed. You may even be taller than me by this time next year."

Jonny, who was still a foot shorter than The Master, could not believe that he would ever be two feet taller, but then, looking at this person he saw in the glass, he decided The Master might be right. That would be strange.

Jonny was eager to tell The Master about all he had learned. They talked for hours and Master Silurian was very impressed by all Jonny told him. He had a sort of half grin on his face that Jonny had only rarely seen.

The Master wanted Jonny to stay the night, but Jonny said he had promised to be back that evening, so he compromised by staying for dinner. After dinner, in order to get back in time he used the amulet to become invisible and flew nearly the whole way back. Jonny gloried in the freedom of it and vowed that he would not allow himself to be so caught up in his new apprenticeship that he would not take time out to practice his other talents. He had spent the whole month without using magic once and now remembered how much fun it could be too. Best of all, magic did not make his muscles ache.

§ § §

The next day as Jonny was going about his work. He was again struggling under the weight of a bucket of slag from the forge he had been cleaning, when he suddenly remembered his vow of the night before. He set down the bucket and laughed.

"What are you laughing at?" one of the journeymen asked.

"I just . . . it's just that I remembered I've been working too hard," Jonny said still laughing.

"Looks to me like you're not working hard enough!" growled the journeyman. "I've got work to do that's waiting on that forge. Now get to it and finish cleaning it."

Jonny probably would have been mad, but he was still laughing at himself. He answered in mock seriousness. "Yes sir, right away, sir. Anything you say, sir."

The journeyman obviously could not make up his mind whether Jonny was mocking him or not. He looked ready to scold Jonny further when the heavy bucket Jonny had been hauling suddenly left the ground of its own accord and floated towards the slag pit.

Work in that part of the shop came to a sudden halt as everyone watched the bizarre phenomenon. Jonny had been doing such a good job of playing the part of an earnest apprentice that everyone had nearly forgotten just who, and what, he was. Now this floating bucket forcefully reminded them.

Kason came in and was about to reprimand his workers for the sudden stoppage until someone pointed and he saw what they were all staring at. Unlike the others, he did not act as if it was something strange. He just looked for a moment and then yelled, "What are you all staring at? I see no dancing girls. I see a bucket of slag getting dumped. Get back to your work."

He came over to Jonny who was now looking a bit sheepish. He stood by him watching until the bucket had dumped its load and returned to Jonny's feet.

"Nice trick, that," he said, still looking out towards the slag pit, "but I think you'll need to be a bit more subtle in the future. I don't think Master Silurian wanted most people to know you were anything other than an ordinary apprentice."

"Yes, I guess you're right, Kason," Jonny said. He had gotten used to calling him that since everyone else did. "I'll try to be less obvious, but I just remembered last night that I can do things different from everyone else."

"That's surely true, boy, but we don't want to raise any jealousies or let any of my customers know. The lads here were sworn to secrecy before you arrived so I don't think they'll talk, but there's nothing to stop the town gossips if someone sees something like this."

"I'm sorry, master," Jonny said contritely. "I just wanted to get the job done a little easier."

"Well, you still can, I'll wager. Couldn't you still hold the handle of the bucket, even if you're not holding the weight?"

"Yeah, I could," Jonny said, brightening.

"That would do it, I think. Besides that, it wouldn't make the other lads feel bad. They don't have to know how heavy the load feels to you. That gives me an idea. How heavy a load can you lift like that?"

"I'm not exactly sure. I once lifted a stone as big as a carriage, so I guess I could probably lift something quite heavy."

"A stone as big as a carriage? Gods, boy! You're not just saying that?"

"No, Master, I wouldn't try to joke about that."

"Well," Kason said rubbing his hands, "Well then, this could be very useful indeed. You've seen us struggle with the iron when it comes in or when we have to cast a large piece. We have to use block and tackle or get several of the larger lads to work together. If you could lift something like that all by yourself and position it where we need it, you could save us a lot of work."

"I'd be happy to help, Kason. It'll be fun."

"Fun, he says," Kason said shaking his head in wonder. "Fun! Well, the fun you need to do is finish getting that forge cleaned. There's work to be done, and mind you, remember what I said about being careful."

"Yes, Kason, I will!" Jonny said, happily getting back to his work.

§ § §

He got quite good at using just enough lift in his work so that he was able to get things done rapidly, but it did not appear to anyone watching that he was doing anything unusual.

In the days that followed, Kason was good to his word. When anything bulky or heavy needed to be moved or positioned quickly, he had Jonny take care of it. It was a great help to everyone in the shop and the other workers' attitudes towards Jonny changed quite a bit. Where before they had treated him mostly like any other apprentice, now they still had him doing apprentice tasks but treated him with a much greater deference. They still kidded with him, and included him in the banter, but Jonny could sense they were a bit wary, almost afraid, though they tried to pretend they were not.

After a few weeks, everyone adjusted to Jonny's new place. The fear receded, and they mostly were just glad for how Jonny made their work easier.

Jonny proved to be a very quick study. In short order, he moved from observing to participating in the creation of the armor, weapons and jewelry that were Kason's business. Jonny was still too small to be able to work on the larger pieces, but it quickly became apparent that Jonny was quite good at working the smaller blades of knives and daggers. The blades he forged took an edge quickly and were of an unusually high quality.

After only five months, just more than half a year, Jonny's blades were considered the best produced. His daggers were even better than the best Kason could produce. Because they were apprentice work, they were priced accordingly, and sold as fast as they were produced. Kason quickly decided that they should not be sold as apprentice work, and priced them higher, but they still sold just as rapidly.

Kason decided Jonny was ready to begin making the more ornamental style of weapons he was known for. He showed Jonny how to include jewels, scrollwork, inlay, and etching without reducing the utility of the weapon. Jonny did not have a very good feel for the design, but he could execute anything Kason directed him to do. The blades Jonny now produced were of the sort purchased by nobility and rich traders, and still they sold rapidly.

§ § §

A noted and rich duelist came to Kason to request a special weapon. He had heard about some of the blades Jonny had produced and wanted a blade of exceptional quality. He wanted the blade to be different in that he wanted it to be somewhat ornamental, but to be even more than commonly good for fighting, since that was his profession. Kason spoke with Jonny about it, and together they decided that if Jonny forged the blade himself and then worked with the engraving that he could make it perform somewhat better than a normal blade.

Jonny spent a long time working on the blade. It was to be a dirk, longer than a normal dagger but not long enough to be considered a sword. He spent several days working on the engraving, trying to use his zdrell sight to make the engravings follow the force lines in the metal. It was his first deliberate attempt doing this, though when he looked back he realized he had been doing it unconsciously on a more limited basis before. The engravings followed no established pattern, but they caught and held the eye.

The duelist was pleased with the blade, and commented on the unusual engravings. Kason assured the man that the engravings were not just for looks, but that they would enhance the performance of the weapon.

One month later the duelist returned and could not say enough about the blade. He said it was the finest weapon he had ever used. He said that he had had more success with it than any other he had ever seen. He said that in one duel he had actually sliced through his opponent's sword while parrying it. The sword had been of fine steel, but had divided as easily as if it had been made from butter. He desperately wanted a sword made after the same fashion.

Up to this point Jonny had never made a blade larger than a dirk. He had finished and ornamented full swords, but he, though much stronger, still lacked the sheer mass and physical strength necessary to pound a large enough piece of metal into a sword blade. He was willing to try it, but Kason felt it was still too early for Jonny to attempt such a large project, especially for so important a client. They compromised with Kason doing the initial work and Jonny doing all of the finishing work.

Jonny worked for several days on the etchings. Once again, the blade looked like no other. It took and held an edge so keen that Kason actually seemed a bit frightened of it. Because of its exceeding sharpness, they had to abandon their standard scabbard for the blade. It simply cut through them. They switched to a wooden scabbard, which usually was used with more common swords. The duelist was at first offended that the sword was placed in such a common scabbard, but after he saw the blade he decided that a more common scabbard was actually a good idea, so as not to attract undue attention.

The duelist paid three times more for the blade than had been paid for any other sword that year, and said he counted it a bargain. The fame of the duelist's sword and dirk soon brought in even more customers, and Jonny was working full time to produce blades of all types as fast as he could.

§ § §

When Jonny went back to speak with The Master just after Mid-fall's day, six months after he had begun working with Kason, he had grown four inches taller since the start of his new apprenticeship.

"Jonny, I've heard quite a bit about your work lately. The blades you are making for Kason have gotten quite a reputation," Master Silurian began, after they were both seated in the study. "Have you learned about things other than just blades?"

"Oh yes, Master," Jonny began enthusiastically. "I've learned about lots of things, armor, jewelry, and tool making too. But lately, I have been doing a lot on blades. Kason just gets more and more orders for them."

"Yes, I'd imagine he would. It's not every day you can pay for a regular blade and get an enchanted one," he commented dryly.

"Enchanted, Master? I've done no magic on those blades. I've only given them etchings to enhance the natural powers of the metal."

"And exactly what do you call an enchanted blade? No wait, do not answer. Jonny, a blade that is 'only enhanced' as you say is most certainly an enchanted blade. Remember your types of magic. Anything that interacts with force lines is, by definition, magic. What you have done is the best kind of magic since it does not require a wizard to use it. Or at least that is the way the people who have been buying those blades feel."

Jonny was once again surprised that what he thought of as a simple thing turned out to be significant magic. He started to say something, but The Master shushed him.

"Jonny, have you learned anything really new in the last few weeks?"

Jonny began to respond by telling him of all the small techniques he had refined and discovered in the last few weeks, but Master Silurian again cut him off.

"That is good, Jonny, but all that you have said is not anything fundamentally new, not like in the first few months."

"Yes that's true, Master, but there's so much to learn. I feel like I could keep learning new things there for years."

"Yes, yes, I'm sure that is true, but that is not why I sent you there. I sent you there to learn in a new area, and to apply those skills to your art. I also sent you there to give you some time to grow up a bit. It seems to me that you have pretty much done all those things.

"You are fourteen and a half and you have started to grow quite a bit. You are not a little boy anymore and we do not have time to wait until you have learned everything there is to know with Kason. I think it is time to consider you getting ready to move on."

Jonny was stunned. "Move on, Master? How could I, I've only just begun, there's so much I don't know."

"There will always be much you do not know, Jonny. There is still much I do not know, and I speak with over three hundred years experience. No, I will speak to Kason and we will see if we can't set up a task for you that will serve as a journeyman project in both arts, metal working and wizardry."

"But, Master, how could I possibly be a journeyman metal worker. That takes years!"

"How many apprentices, or journeymen there besides yourself create weapons that have men from half way across the continent coming to buy them?"

"Well, ah, it's really Kason's weapons they're buying," Jonny said staring at the floor.

"No, you know better, Jonny. They are your weapons they are buying."

"But I'm still not big enough to forge a proper sword by myself."

"Have you tried lately? Tried doing it using your powers?"

Jonny paused, and then mumbled, "No."

§ § §

A few days after Jonny had returned from the castle, the whole of Kason's shop was in an uproar as Master Silurian himself came and visited. Kason and Jonny both showed him around and The Master spent quite a bit of time examining the blades and other things that Jonny had made. He and Kason then went into Kason's negotiation room and spoke for over two hours. Everyone was asking Jonny what was going on, but he said he did not know.

When they finally emerged from the room, they did so only to invite Jonny to come in with them.

"Jonny, sit here at the table with us," Master Silurian began, motioning him to a chair. "I believe Master Kason and I have agreed on a project which will be of sufficient difficulty and quality that it will constitute a journeyman project for both of us."

"What is it, Master?" Jonny asked trembling with excitement and sudden fear.

"Well it is not just one thing," Kason continued. "We want you to make four items, the sum of which will show your mastery of the basics of both our arts."

Jonny waited expectantly.

"For mastery of using force manipulation, Jonny," The Master continued. "I want you to make a ring which can focus force lines, the same way you have been doing with the blades you have been making. But there will be one difference; I want you to forge it without using your hands."

Jonny was confused. "How can I do that, Master?"

"How indeed?" The Master said grinning. "How do you move things without touching them, Jonny?"

"Oh," Jonny said, starting to understand. "Like that."

"Yes, like that," he agreed. "I also want you to make a second ring after you have made the first. I want you to do it differently, but use the force lines there as well. Use what you learn making the first ring to make the second. I want you to make it as a ring that does not concentrate power, but can disrupt it. I cannot tell you more; you will have to determine how to do it yourself."

"The third item is my contribution," Kason continued. "I want you to make a sword. A full sword, on your own without any help from start to finish, and I want it to be beautiful. I won't say more than that. I have come to trust your judgment on what constitutes a beautiful sword and you've had enough practice that I've no doubt it will be wonderful. More importantly, Master Silurian has said that he will cover the costs of all the materials, and that no expense is to be spared. You will be able to use any materials that you feel are appropriate. I have rarely had that opportunity myself; you are lucky."

"And the last item?" Jonny asked expectantly.

"The last item is for you to decide," The Master said. "My only requirement is that it contain both beauty and power. I am sure you will know what to make when you come to it."

"How long do I have?" Jonny asked.

"As long as you need, one month, six months, a year, it does not matter. What matters is that it is your best work. That is what a journeyman's project is all about. These will be your examples to show off what you are capable of producing," The Master finished quietly.

Master Silurian had said something that struck Jonny. He could not believe it. He had to ask.

"Do you mean that I am to keep these items?" he asked, unable to believe that that could be what they meant.

"Yes, you do, Jonny," Kason replied. "Normally a journeyman's project is paid for out of his wages so that when he is done, he will own the work. As I've already said, Master Silurian has said he will pay for the materials, so you are freed from that burden. It is a very, very great gift."

Jonny was speechless. For a long time he said nothing, could say nothing. For so long he had wanted to own just one of the simpler blades he had been making, now The Master would be allowing him to make and keep four items all of great worth. He finally choked out "Thank you, Master," but could say no more.

"You are most welcome, Jonny," The Master said beaming. "You have certainly earned this, and I dare say you may need these items sooner than you think."

Jonny did not know what to make of that last comment, but his gratitude was so great he thought he would explode.

"One thing, Jonny," The Master interrupted Jonny's thoughts. "You are to work on this project no more than two days in nine each week. You are still to work and learn all that you can from Master Kason, and I will continue to expect regular progress reports."

"Yes, Master, yes," Jonny gushed. "I'll do just as you say. I'll do everything I can to make you both proud."

"Do good work," Kason said gruffly, "that's all we ask."

Jonny promised he would.

Chapter 53

It was agreed that in order to avoid arousing jealousy among the other apprentices and journeymen, Jonny was not to announce that the projects he would be working on constituted a journeyman project. As far as any of the other workers knew, the items Jonny was making were a special order from Master Silurian.

Jonny spent two weeks experimenting, trying to figure out exactly how to forge a ring without using his hands. Master Silurian had said that Jonny was limited to working two days of the nine in a week on the project. Kason held him to his word and worked Jonny harder than ever on those other days. Kason opted to have Jonny work almost exclusively on enhancing blades and armor. Jonny got quite proficient at quickly adding a bit to the natural strength of a well-crafted item. That little bit extra made the weapons much more valuable but did not greatly expand the time needed to create them. Kason knew he did not have years to milk Jonny's talents so he worked him all the harder.

On the third week after he had been given his charge, Jonny was ready to begin the first ring. The air of late fall was chill. He had experimented and worked things out in his mind and was feeling confident he could make it happen. He decided that this first ring would be made of gold, since gold had such a low working temperature. He also knew that it would be easy to start over again if his first attempt did not turn out properly.

Jonny worked at one of the jewelry forges off in the corner of the shop. He made sure that no one was watching. He was unsure enough of himself that he did not want any distractions.

He started with a small rectangular piece of gold, commonly used to make rings. He lifted it with his zdrell and brought it to the hottest part of the forge Using his zdrell sight, he could see the metal take on the heat and soften, then begin to flow. As the metal became fluid, he reached out with his mind to bend it round until it formed a circle. Then he set the circle spinning in the midst of the heat. As it spun, he felt it become more and more uniform. He could no longer tell where the two ends had originally been He moved it to a slightly cooler part of the forge and felt the metal begin to harden. As it hardened, he moved through it with his mind, removing any imperfections or inconsistencies.

He felt for where the natural force lines intersected it and enhanced those parts of the ring. Without planning it previously, he began to shift the actual structure of the ring in a manner very similar to what he did when he inscribed the blades of weapons. This though was at a deeper level, and subtler in its execution. The ring continued to cool and Jonny worked more and more near, but not on, the surface of the ring. Jonny planned to scribe enhancement lines in the surface of the ring as well, so he did not attempt to alter the surface.

At last, Jonny could tell that the ring had cooled to a low enough temperature where it could touch things without being marred. He gently allowed the ring to come to rest on a work cloth where it glinted brightly. Because physical implements had never touched the ring, its surface was as bright and polished as a well-finished piece. As bright as it was to natural eyes, that was nothing compared to how it glowed when Jonny looked at it with his zdrell sight. It fairly radiated force lines. It strongly reminded Jonny of how his amulet had looked when his spell had finally taken. The ring though, did not have the fragility about it that the amulet had had. Jonny knew that with the amulet he had needed to quickly cast the binding spell, or the whole thing would collapse. With this ring, he did not sense this at all. It seemed like it could stay like this forever.

Jonny knew one more thing when he looked closely at the ring. It was not done. He could sense it, and he knew what he needed to do. He needed to give it surface etchings, as he had with the swords. But that evening he was too drained to finish.

He started early the next morning and worked most of the day. Finally, at near normal close of day, he was done with the etchings, but had one more thing to do. He took the ring and lifted it again with his mental touch alone. He brought it to a small cauldron filled with liquid silver. He dropped the ring to where its bottom edge just touched the liquid surface. He set it slowly spinning, so that as the ring rotated the silver was drawn into the etchings. In just a few moments, all the etchings were filled with silver. Jonny withdrew it and allowed it to cool slowly.

The previous day the ring had been bright when viewed with his sight, now the ring was nearly blinding. The etchings had done as he had anticipated, and even more greatly enhanced the power focusing nature of the ring. To a pair of natural eyes, the ring was dazzling as well. It was a simple gold band with silver inlay, but the overall effect of its perfection and the way the silvered etchings flowed, captured and held the eye.

Jonny knew he had done something important. He knew he could not leave it in its present state. Hoping he was not making a mistake, he cast a binding spell on the ring, the same as he had with the amulet. Immediately the ring's aspect changed. Where before with his sight Jonny could clearly see the ring connected to lines of power in all directions, now he saw nothing. Now all he saw was that the ring glowed with an inner light, but its connections were not visible. Jonny was unsure if he had done the right thing, but he knew he could not have left it as it was. That much visible power was sure to attract some sort of unwanted attention.

To the natural eye, the ring was still a thing of great beauty. When he showed it the next day to Kason, the master metalworker was extremely impressed. "It is a wonder, Jonny; I've never seen its like. I'd sell my whole shop to have one like it."

He turned it over and over and ran his finger around the inside of the band. "Still, it is a thing of power. Even a poor mundane fool like myself can see that. No, on second thought, it is not for the likes of me. You keep it, and do not show it to anyone else in the shop, for a time. Yes, that would be best."

Kason instructed Jonny that he should immediately go and show the ring to The Master. Jonny had wanted to do just that, but had not wanted to ask. He borrowed a horse and rode to the castle, tired and happy.

Chapter 54

Jonny entered the castle just before noon. Master Silurian was unavailable, so Jonny had lunch with the journeymen, as had been his custom. He was surprised at how many different journeymen were present from when he had left. Fully half of the journeymen were new, and they gave Jonny curious glances. The journeymen who knew Jonny had no such reserve, and welcomed him with great enthusiasm. He had a good time getting caught up on all the gossip of the castle, but he could still see that there were some of the new journeymen who kept looking at him in less than friendly ways.

Jonny's interview with The Master did not last long. He examined the ring and was clearly impressed. When he put the ring on his finger, a look of great surprise filled his eyes.

"Jonny, have you tried this ring on?" The Master asked with awe in his voice.

"Yes, Master," Jonny replied quietly.

"How did it affect you?"

"I'm not sure I can put it into words, Master. Mostly, everything just seemed much clearer."

"My boy, that is one of the greatest understatements I believe I have ever heard. The inrush of power I feel is tremendous. I do not think I have felt this strong in two hundred years; that is if I have ever felt this strong. This ring is wonderful, Jonny. You have once again exceeded my expectations. If we had not already set the ground rules, I would say this ring alone would fulfill your journeyman assignment."

Jonny was embarrassed. He had never heard, or thought it possible to hear, The Master be so effusive with praise. The Master's eyes glowed brightly. He looked down sadly, as he took off the ring and placed it back on top of the sack Jonny had brought it in. He looked somehow smaller than he had moments before.

"It is a pity to take it off. I wish I could wear it always."

"Then wear it, Master, keep it. I can always make another!"

"No, Jonny, this is part of your journeyman project, and I feel," he said, as a faraway look came into his eyes, "that you will need it. Yes, wear it as you work on the other items. It will increase your abilities and the quality of your work. But remember to take it off sometimes, so that you do not become dependent on it, for that is the danger of an item such as this. It can cause you to believe that all this power is within you. It is not, it is the ring."

Now Jonny was almost afraid to take back the ring, afraid of what he had created. Master Silurian saw Jonny's fear and reassured him.

"Don't be too concerned, Jonny. You should be proud of what you have done. I doubt a ring of this power has been created in the last hundred years or more anywhere in the world. There are much greater magical devices in existence, but most are of ancient date, made well before the Great War."

"Do not be afraid of what you have created. You will do better still, but always remember that the power an item such as this confers is only with you as long as you have it, and a ring like this would be a very great prize to many. My best advice is that you wear it most of the time and that you deliberately tarnish it so that it will seem less valuable. It is a great shame to do that to such a beautiful thing, but better that than to have jealousy and the greed of others take it from you."

§ § §

Jonny left soon after he finished talking with The Master. He wore the ring as he rode back to town and it did make everything much clearer. Without any effort at all, he perceived things the same as when he concentrated on his sight, but he also saw things with his natural eyes much more clearly. He felt the power, and on a whim lifted himself and the horse off the road into the air for several yards. The horse did not enjoy the experience much. It was so much easier to do than if he had not been wearing the ring that Jonny laughed nearly the whole way back just thinking about it.

When Jonny mentioned Master Silurian's idea to tarnish the ring to Kason, the man looked as if he were going to be ill, but he finally agreed with the wisdom of the action. Sullying the ring turned out to be more difficult than either of them had anticipated. The ring was so finely made that dirt and grime just flaked off it. Finally, they came upon the combination of coating the ring with oil and metal filings and then heating it until the oil burned and charred on its surface. This left a fairly solid coating that mostly obscured the ring's beauty. Jonny had to be careful when he took it off for the inside of it quickly polished itself again, but the outer portion maintained its disguise.

Chapter 55

Jonny had several weeks of work for Kason before he could begin on the next ring. Kason worked Jonny very hard, but while wearing the ring Jonny rarely tired, and was able to work very quickly. Even the other workers noticed Jonny's new ability to work long hours without apparent fatigue. He also noticed that even now in the middle of winter, he didn't get as cold. Jonny knew it was because of the power he was getting from the ring.

He quickly came to understand why The Master had cautioned him against relying too much on the ring. When he took it off, the whole world seemed flat and colorless and he got tired so quickly. Jonny began thinking of the ring as his "power" ring. When he thought of it in his mind, that is what he called it.

When the week was up, Jonny was eager to begin work on the second ring. He did not really know what he was going to do with it, but he knew it should be very different from the power ring. Still unsure of what direction to go with this ring, Jonny settled on this ring being the exact opposite of the first.

Where the first ring had been made of fine materials Jonny decided this would be made of coarse but strong ones. He used a remnant of steel that he had used in a sword earlier in the week. He took the metal and heated and beat it into a strip as though he were making a very small blade. He dropped the metal into the forge and pumped the bellows until the metal was white hot then he used his power to fold it into a circle as had with the first ring. However, with this ring once he had it rolled to perfection, he dropped it straight into the water to quench it.

With his enhanced sight Jonny could see the metal getting stronger from being quenched, but also losing connections to the force lines around it. As soon as he saw it, Jonny knew what he would do. Where the first ring drew in and concentrated power, this one would disrupt and drain it.

Jonny heated the ring again and began to make subtle changes in its structure. He doubted he would have been able to do work this subtle without the assistance of the power ring. Again, he quenched the ring and Jonny could feel the rightness of the changes he had made. The ring was now a dull gray in color, almost black, and it seemed to take light in and give none back. It had no reflection or luster. Jonny had to use his hardest, sharpest scribe to make his etchings, and even so, it was very difficult work.

When he finished his work, Jonny was almost afraid to put on the ring. It had a presence, a weight about it that was somehow oppressive. Two things happened when he put it on. It felt like Jonny had taken off his power ring, even though he had not. He felt more tired and less clear-headed. Jonny also felt that the lines of power feeding into his power ring more acutely, and he was certain that if he concentrated, he would be able to break them, to destroy the power of the ring.

The ring frightened Jonny, and he quickly took it off. He knew that in some ways, this ring was more powerful than the first, but it was a power of destruction. Jonny put it in a leather pouch and took it to Kason to show it to him. When Kason saw it, he too was clearly disturbed by it.

"This is a curious thing of power Jonny. I'll not hazard to try it on, nor guess what it does, but it has a dark beauty to it. In truth, this is what I always imagined a wizard's ring would look like. Guard it well, for I don't think it would do for it to get into the wrong hands."

Chapter 56

Master Silurian was not there when Jonny went to the castle the next day to show him the new ring. Not only that, but Jonny noticed that even more of the journeymen and apprentices were new and did not know him, and those who did, did not know him well. Nearly all his old friends were gone.

Jonny entered The Master's workshop to find only two journeymen there, neither of whom he knew.

"What are you doing in here?" the bigger of the two asked. "This area is off limits to all but magicians and journeyman."

"I'm Jonny. I was looking for Master Silurian."

"He's not here today," the shorter journeyman said. "He had to go to Sharafleg on business."

Jonny was disappointed and about to leave when the taller journeyman suddenly looked at Jonny with new interest.

"Are you 'The Jonny,' the one everyone is always talking about, the one that everyone says can do more magic than most masters?" he asked with a sneer on his face.

Jonny was not sure how to answer. He thought about just leaving, but decided he had better at least answer the question. "Yeah, I guess I am the one everyone talks about."

"I don't believe it. You don't even look like you're twelve. There's no way even half of what they say about you could be true."

This was a lie. While Jonny was still a bit small for his age, he had grown considerably and could possibly be taken for thirteen, but never younger than that. Jonny could sense that things would only get worse, so he said nothing and turned to go.

The tall journeyman clearly was not happy with Jonny's lack of response. "Hey, I didn't tell you, you could go. Master Silurian left me in charge and you haven't asked my permission to leave."

"May I go," Jonny said staring at the floor, knowing what the response would be.

"No you may not. In fact, I want you to come over here right now. Tillock help him if he can't see the way."

"I'm not so sure this is a good idea," the shorter journeyman said.

"Now, Tillock, just do as I say. It's a fine idea. The Master left me in charge, so that means that any apprentice or journeyman here has to do what I say, isn't that so?"

"Well, yeah, but I don't think this is what The Master meant, Surlant. He just had to name someone to deal with small things since both he and Lord Feldor are gone. We could get in trouble if you do something to The Master's star apprentice."

"Nonsense. He is still an apprentice, and has to do what I tell him, and he will," Surlant said with an ugly edge to his voice.

By now, Jonny had come over to stand by the two journeymen. He avoided eye contact, hoping that he could quickly do whatever stupid task or scut work Surlant seemed to have in mind.

"Why don't you show us some of your wonderful talent?" Surlant said.

Before Jonny could do or say anything he continued.

"No, I know just the thing. You'll watch me do some real magic, in fact you'll help. Someone told me you've never been under the knife. That means you can be a very big help in the task Tillock and I were just about to do."

Both Tillock and Jonny were shocked by what Surlant was saying. Jonny had never been under the knife and had no intention of experiencing it now. Tillock too was clearly alarmed by what Surlant was suggesting.

"I don't think this is a good idea at all, Surlant "

"I don't care if you think it's a good idea or not, Tillock, you'll do as I say. I'm in charge! Now start an open summoning and I'll get our apprentice here ready."

Before he had even finished talking, Surlant had grabbed Jonny by the back of his neck and bent him over a work table. In no time, he pulled Jonny's shirt up over his head.

"Look at this Tillock. Not one scar. This really is his first time. It will be easy to get a big demon to come for this."

Jonny knew he could easily focus enough energy to hurl Surlant across the room, but he hesitated. Even though Jonny knew The Master would never approve of Surlant's conduct; Jonny technically was still bound to follow Surlant's orders.

Tillock meanwhile had been chanting the spell for an open summoning. As soon as the opening appeared, Surlant applied his tine knife to Jonny's back and began to chant his offer in the demon tongue. Jonny cried out in pain and tried to get up, but Surlant was much bigger and had no trouble holding him all the while continuing his chant.

The pain from the knife was incredible, and Jonny's resolve to just let Surlant have his way was quickly fading. He reached out with his mind and got a good hold on the knife. He was just about to fly it across the room, with or without Surlant, when a large demon came through the portal.

The demon was much larger and more powerful looking than the one that Jonny had seen the other times he had watched a summoning. The demon hovered over Jonny, clearly enjoying his pain, when suddenly his aspect changed. Where a moment before the demon had been enjoying Jonny's torment, now it looked as if someone had pricked it in a sensitive place with a pin.

The demon roared in rage.

"You dare to bring me here promising a sweet taste of pain and a small task, when you actually plan to do me hurt?"

"No, no I have no desire to hurt you," Surlant stammered, clearly afraid and uncomprehending of what the demon was talking about.

"You deny you have a line cutter here in this very room, ready to destroy my lifeline while I am engaged in this 'task' of yours?"

"A line cutter? I don't even know what a line cutter is, let alone how to hurt you, your magnificence," Surlant said, panicking, and obviously ignorant of what the demon was talking about.

"You lie! You ignorant human filth. You think me some fourth circle fool who does not know treachery when he sees it, but you will learn. You brought me here with the words of your contract. You have broken the terms. It is now void, and I am free to show you what I think of human scum like you!"

The demon moved towards Surlant, rapidly growing in size until it barely fit in the room. It opened its now enormous mouth and in one swift motion bit Surlant in two. Blood sprayed everywhere, but not for long. The demon just as quickly opened its mouth again and ate the rest of him. The demon chewed and swallowed and then turned to face Jonny and the petrified Tillock.

The demon hurled bolts of energy into the floor in front of both Jonny and Tillock. The floor cracked and the table Jonny was bent over began to smoke from the heat. Jonny was certain that the demon was about to kill them too, when it stopped and smiled a gruesome pointed-tooth smile.

"Remember, mortals," it said its voice like boulders rolling in a raging river. "A contract broken is a terrible thing." Then it laughed and continued laughing as it shrank and disappeared through the portal.

§ § §

For a long time afterwards, neither Jonny nor Tillock moved or said a thing. They were both too stunned by what had happened to know what to do. Finally Tillock turned to Jonny and said, "Do you know what the demon was talking about; a line cutter?"

"I'm not sure," Jonny said, "but he might have been talking about my new ring."

Jonny took out the ring and showed it to Tillock. He explained what he had been able to do with it. Tillock was clearly impressed by the ring, and thought it might be what the demon meant.

It was all very unclear to Jonny who had little experience with demons.

The Master explained it to him when he returned that evening with Lord Feldor, after they had been informed of what happened to Surlant.

"It is in the nature of demon magic, Jonny. As you have already been taught, each summoning is a very specific contract between the caster and demon. The demon agrees to provide certain services in return for certain rewards, usually pain, provided by the wizard. The danger in all demon magic is when the contract in the casting is done incorrectly. Usually this simply means that the demon finds a loophole that allows it to take the reward without doing the work, but part of the contract is that the demon shall not be harmed by the caster or any of his associates."

"Most wizards think of this as a mere formality because there is generally so little that a mortal can do to harm a demon, but there are exceptions.

"Each demon has a lifeline that secures it back to the demon world. The lifeline is what allows the demon to return even should the portal the demon entered through close; it is also its source of power. If a demon's lifeline is cut, unless it can find a way to return, or find some other source of power, it will begin to weaken and can eventually die. To have its lifeline cut is the greatest, and almost the only, fear that a demon has while it is in this world."

"This ring," The Master said, holding it up and examining it in the light, "has the power to cut a demon's lifeline. It is a powerful object indeed. The demon thought it was being led into a trap. As far as it was concerned, the summoning contract was invalid, so it was free to take any retaliation it saw fit, and you saw the end of it.

"It always amazes me," Master Silurian said, leaning back and still gazing at the ring, "how many so-called wizards forget that working with demons is making a bargain with a being who is held in check only by the slimmest of threads: a demon cannot break its word. What you witnessed today is what happens when that thread is broken."

Jonny knew he would never forget what he had seen that day. He also had a new reason to be glad his work did not involve him with demon magic. He felt bad about Surlant.

Surlant had succeeded in hurting Jonny, but no one deserved to die like that. Jonny felt even worse when The Master told him that the demon had not just consumed Surlant's body, but that the real reason he had eaten him was to obtain his soul. Consuming the soul of a mortal was the one thing that demons craved above pain. It all made Jonny feel terrible, since his ring was the cause of the demon's rampage. Everyone told him that it was not his fault, but Jonny could not shake the feeling that somehow it was.

He stayed at the castle that night. He couldn't eat anything. Even the sight of food made him feel sick. His mind cycled over and over with the images of the demon's huge mouth biting Surlant in two. It was only with the help of a sleeping draught that he was able to have some relief from his pain.

Chapter 57

When Jonny returned from the castle, he had lost much of the enthusiasm for his journeyman project. For several weeks, he did not take the time he was allotted to work on it. Things had not turned out as he had thought. He had hoped to create things of beauty and light, and now the whole thing had resulted in death.

After seven weeks, three weeks past his fifteenth birthday, Kason came up to Jonny and asked him when he was going to begin the next part of his project. Jonny tried to be vague and put him off, but Kason would not have it.

"Things haven't turned out like you wanted, lad, but that is no reason to give up. That is just how life is. It is part of growing up, and good you've learned it this soon."

Kason paused for several moments looking at the anvil to the left of where Jonny was standing, and then he continued. "Your next part of the project is my contribution. You'll not disappoint an old man will you? It is only to create a sword, a fine and worthy sword. It does not even need to be magicked, it only needs to be your finest craftsmanship, nothing more, but nothing less."

Through the whole exchange Jonny said nothing, could say nothing. Kason waited several moments for Jonny to respond. Jonny would not even look at him. Jonny could tell Kason was angry with him, but he could not respond. All he could think about was the demon biting and the blood spraying everywhere.

Kason's face reddened with anger. "If you won't say anything, that is your privilege, but if by tomorrow you haven't begun work on that sword, you'll not be welcome here till you do!"

He turned on his heel and stormed out of the workshop. All work momentarily stopped, and everyone stared at Jonny, since Kason's last words were shouted louder than the noise of the workshop. Jonny felt their eyes on him, but he only looked at his hands, put down the piece he had been working on, and walked slowly out of the workshop.

§ § §

Jonny walked for a long time. He knew Kason was right. The Master had told him many times that his gift was powerful and that many would fight and die over it. But this was real. The harder he tried not to think about what had happened the more the images invaded his mind.

Jonny knew he would have to work this out for himself. He walked out of town to the south along the river that formed the main trading artery of the kingdom. He stopped and sat on the riverbank, throwing stones into the river. Almost without trying, he started assisting the rocks as they flew. He pushed each rock further until they were flying clear across to the other side of the river, over forty yards away.

He stood up and knew what he wanted to do. He wanted to fly. The sun had just set, and the river was temporarily empty of traffic. He knew that if he flew as high as he wanted he would be visible to any observer for miles--unless he used his invisibility amulet.

As soon as he thought that, another thought struck him, and he knew he had to get back to the workshop fast. He realized that he still had the ring that the demon had called a line cutter in his belt pouch. He realized that the ring would be as visible to a demon as he would have been if he had decided to fly into town at this time of night without using his invisibility amulet. He had to find some way to hide the ring or destroy it, or it would be his blood and soul that would be consumed next.

Jonny did end up flying back most of the way, but not high, as he had first planned. He flew just a foot or so above the ground so that someone who saw him from a distance would think he was just running fast. He ran the last quarter mile when he got back to where there were people and he could not fly without attracting attention. For some reason he could not explain, he did not feel safe using the invisibility amulet.

While he was running and flying, an idea formed of what he had to do to hide the ring. Jonny knew that the demon ring, as he now thought of it, dispersed the lines of force in the opposite way that his power ring concentrated them. He needed something that would isolate it from any lines of force, and he thought he knew how to do it.

Jonny took two small round thin pieces of metal, usually used for armor and shaped them till they were both concave and came together to form a type of locket. He soldered a simple hinge and clasp on them. When it was done, he put the ring inside and looked at it using his demon sight amulet. The ring was still clearly visible through the metal.

Jonny began to work, scribing on the inside and the outside of the locket. He etched lines on the inside that cancelled the lines on the outside. He kept using demon sight to check his work; it got dimmer and dimmer. The scribing in and out nullified each other and cut the interior of the locket off from the outside world completely. In time, even using demon sight, he could sense nothing from within it. Jonny put a thong through a small ring he had soldered to the locket and hung it around his neck, next to his two amulets. Finally, Jonny felt he could rest.

§ § §

Creating the locket, and the fear that prompted its creation, pushed Jonny out of his fog. He no longer felt trapped by that horrible experience. On the contrary, he now felt some of the urgency that he had often seen in The Master. The ring marked him, and he felt certain that if a demon would kill someone for having it, then it would search and kill more readily someone who had created it. He felt sure his locket would hide it for now, but he really did need to do more to be prepared. A sword, a powerful enchanted sword, would be just the thing to help him feel more ready for the conflicts he now felt certain would come.

Jonny did not sleep; he began work on the sword. Jonny had learned quite a bit about making swords in his time with Kason. He knew the different ways to form and temper a blade, but up to this point, he had never started from a raw bar of metal. Someone else had always done the initial forming. He had started from scratch on smaller blades, but Jonny knew this had to be a large sword.

In short order, he was sweating and straining as he struggled to form the large piece of metal. He knew that if he wanted to have the blade he planned that his physical strength was not up to the task. It was then that he remembered his power ring. He had not worn it since before his encounter with the demon. He put it on, and the surge of raw power and vitality that hit him was phenomenal. He reached out with his power and began to form the metal with his mind. He still used the hammer to help form and shape the blade, but now he used the hammer in strategic places to speed the process he was driving primarily with his mind. In no more than an hour after he had put on his ring, the rough blade was finished. Jonny knew it would be his finest work yet.

Chapter 58

Jonny was frustrated. The initial work on his sword had gone quite well. Kason had seen his progress and tried to act unimpressed, but Jonny could tell the master metalworker was excited by what Jonny had accomplished. Now nothing seemed to be working. Having formed the basic blade he now wanted to breathe life into it, the way he had with his two rings, and it just was not working and Jonny could not figure out why.

After two days of frustration, Jonny decided he needed to consult with The Master and see if there was something fundamental that he was forgetting.

Jonny flew up to the castle after dark with the unfinished blade. He surprised several apprentices as he landed in the courtyard and asked for The Master. None of them would speak, but they pointed towards The Master's north study.

Jonny entered the room and set the blade down on The Master's desk.

"There's something wrong with it, or with me, Master, but I can't see what I need to do to make it right."

Master Silurian said nothing at first. He picked up the blade and examined it carefully, then closed his eyes and breathed in and out very slowly. He opened his eyes and took one hand and reached into his shirt and touched one amulet, then another.

"Yes, Jonny," he said nodding slowly. "There is something missing in this, but," he paused, shaking his head. "When you do work it out, this will be an awesome weapon of power. The power is already there, you have done that properly, but it is trapped."

"How do I let it out, Master?"

"How? You alone can discover that. I am not even sure how you put it there in the first place. Did you have on your ring when you formed it? No don't answer, it is obvious you did."

He paused, shaking his head again and then grinning. Jonny never liked to see that grin.

"No, Jonny, you will have to work it out for yourself. I cannot help you here."

"But, Master, I don't know what to do! Surely you know something, have some idea I can try, something."

The wizard smiled sadly. "Jonny, I honestly would help you if I could, but I was not joking when I said I do not know how you have trapped power in this blade. I have some suspicions, but I would have to study it for years to be sure. You have gone beyond me again with your zdrell. I can only perceive it dimly."

"So what do I do, Master? I've already tried everything I could think of. I was hoping you could tell me."

"Jonny, I cannot tell you how to solve this problem, but I can give you something to try."

"Anything, Master."

"Well, whenever I get into a situation like the one you are currently in, and I have been there many times myself, I leave the problem alone and work on something else."

"You mean you just give up?"

"No, I mean I lay the problem aside and work on something totally unrelated. It has to do with the way the mind works, Jonny. Even when I am not working on a problem, part of me knows it is there and will keep thinking about it while I work on something else. Many times working on something I think is unrelated will give me that critical insight that allows me to go back and solve my original problem."

"So you're saying I should just leave it alone and do something else?"

"Yes."

"But what would I do?"

"It does not matter, but it is best if it has little or nothing to do with your problem. Seeing this blade makes me want to see if you can do something for me."

"What, Master?"

"I want you to make me a ring. I want you to make a ring that will hold power like this blade is doing. I saw an amulet like that long ago. The amulet's owner was a very old powerful wizard, and I have no idea who has it now since he died over one hundred years ago, but I believe you could create one like it for me. It would be very useful."

"Yes, Master, I would be happy to help," Jonny said, pleased to have a task to take his mind off the unfinished sword.

"Tell Kason this is an official commission and not part of the journeyman project, since you are making it for me. Oh, and one other thing, the amulet I remember seeing had crystals of some sort, they may have been quartz or diamond, embedded in the metal. I am not sure if they were essential to the amulet's power, but they may have had something to do with it. I unfortunately did not have much time to study it, but I do remember that clearly."

Jonny thanked his master and was about to leave when The Master looked up and said, "Where did you put the line cutter?"

The question took Jonny by surprise, he had not thought about the ring, or the demon, for a few days.

"It's with me right now," Jonny said, reaching in his shirt to pull out his holding container.

"Extraordinary!" The Master said when he saw the container and Jonny opened it to show him the ring.

"This container completely shielded the presence of your line cutter. I had no idea what you had done with the ring; I half feared that you had destroyed it. I have a container like this, but you created yours all on your own. The container I have is over two thousand years old. It is one of the most valuable magical items I own. Jonny, you never cease to amaze me. After seeing this, I have no doubt that you will be able to create a magical storage ring for me."

216

"Thank you, Master," Jonny said, flushed with embarrassment.
"No, Thank you, Jonny"

Chapter 59

The new commission from Master Silurian was just what Jonny needed. He had noticed as he had worked on the sword that somehow it took energy and held onto it. It was not what he had been trying to do so he had mostly ignored that aspect of it. Now he turned every form of sight he possessed on it trying to see how it worked so he could duplicate it in the ring for The Master.

At first he thought of making The Master's ring out of steel as he had with the sword, but since he had also made the demon ring of steel he was leery of doing that. He also had no idea how to easily embed jewels of any sort in a steel ring.

In the end, he decided to use a silver alloy commonly used for jewelry where durability was also a factor. He also decided to use very small chips of diamond. He had seen before in working with other jewelry that small diamond chips seemed to sometimes act as mirrors for reflecting force lines as well as light.

His initial process for forming the ring was similar to what he had used in the previous two rings, but as the ring began to cool he added several diamond chips so that they were nearly invisible, submerged in the metal. As soon as he had done this, he saw that they did indeed seem to have a reflective property for the force lines. He kept the ring hot enough that he could keep rearranging the chips and modifying the structure of the ring until it felt right.

When he finally sensed he had it right, he set the ring down on a cloth to cool and looked up. To his surprise, it was dark and no one else was there. He had no idea how long he had been working on the ring, but it obviously had been several hours. As soon as he thought of it, he realized he was very hungry and needed to go to the toilet very badly.

After he had taken care of his bodily needs, Jonny went back and looked at the ring. He put it on and focused some of the power he had from the power ring at it. The energy disappeared into the ring without a trace. Even so, while wearing it, Jonny could feel the energy was still there. He focused more energy at the ring and again it was absorbed.

Now came the test. Jonny focused his attention on the ring and attempted to release the stored power in it. Here was where Jonny found the diamond chips mattered. Pushing his awareness along the imperfection provided by one of the chips Jonny found it easy to release the power. He used it to heat one of the forges that were standing empty. In no time, the forge was blazing with heat as though it had been stoked for hours.

Jonny was impressed. He had not realized how much power he had placed in the ring or how easily it could be released. Best of all, Jonny now knew what he needed to do to finish his sword. He was very excited and wanted to show this new ring to The Master, but figured that he needed to get some rest. He hung the new ring on the thong with his amulets and fell into bed.

It was nearly noon when he woke. He still had no idea when he went to bed, surely sometime after midnight, but before dawn. He got a piece of bread and went in search of Kason. When Kason saw him, he at first looked irritated, but then his face lit up.

"Did you finish it?" Kason asked.

Jonny nodded.

"Let's have a look at it."

Jonny took the ring off the thong and put it in Kason's hand. Kason looked at it closely, and then took it out to look at it in the light.

"Oh Jonny, 'tis very good," he said with wonder in his voice, "but there's something strange about it. I can't put me finger on it. It doesn't, doesn't seem like anything's wrong, more like there's more there than you can see. Is that part of the way it's supposed to be?"

Jonny nodded again.

"You've done well, lad. Each time you do something, I think I've seen it all, and then you do something I've never seen before. Things will get dreadfully dull once you've left us all behind. Now go and show this to Master Silurian. I know he'll be pleased. Tell him I'll discuss payment with him later."

§ § §

Pleased was not the word to describe The Master's reaction, overjoyed was closer but still inadequate. When Jonny handed him the ring, he was immediately taken by the look of it and told Jonny so, then he closed his eyes and focused his attention on it. He stayed that way for several minutes, long enough that Jonny began to get worried, but then he opened his eyes and there were tears beginning to flow from them. Jonny was about to apologize when The Master smiled the most brilliant smile Jonny had ever seen on his face, and then began to laugh.

"Jonny, Jonny, Jonny," The Master said still chuckling. "I tell you next to nothing, ask for something no one has been able to create since the Great War, ask the impossible of you, and instead of failing you have returned with an object of power that is almost certainly many times more powerful than the Amulet of Karaken!"

Master Silurian leaned back and started laughing again. Jonny did not know what to do. He was happy The Master was pleased with his work, but he was afraid of this reaction. There was an almost maniacal edge to his master's laugh. His concern must have showed for when The Master looked at Jonny, he controlled his mirth with visible effort.

"Do not be afraid, Jonny," The Master said. "I have not gone insane. It is just that once again you have succeeded beyond my wildest dreams. For nearly two hundred years, I have sought an object like this. The ability to store energy in an object and have it ready at need was one of the greatest accomplishments of the zdrell masters. I cannot tell you the number of uses this has. One of the greatest limitations those of us who shun demon magic face is that there are certain magical operations that require great power; you know this from your studies. Without an object such as this, the only non-demon way of doing those things was to find several wizards of comparable skill and technique to pool their talents. You already know how difficult it is to get more than two wizards to agree on what to eat for lunch, let alone work together on a common cause; it has been very rare indeed. So, there are many great works I have wanted to try for years. I have been unable to do, so many, so very many things, because I lack the strength.

"When I first saw the Amulet of Karaken I was jealous, but had I known that I would not see its like again for over a hundred years, who knows to what extremes I might have gone to get it. It is probably best I did not know. Now you come to me with an object you have created yourself that I can already tell is superior in every way to that amulet. What can I say?"

Jonny did not know what to say either. Once again, he was both happy and irritated by the way The Master had kept him in the dark about the difficulty of what he had attempted. Had he known the magnitude of the challenge, he would surely have been intimidated by it. Even so, it still rankled.

"Nothing to say, Jonny?" The Master said with a smile.

"What can I say, Master?" Jonny said and shrugged. "I guess, I guess I did good. I'm glad you're happy."

"Happy? Jonny, happy does not even begin to express the way I am feeling right now. For the first time in many, many years I believe that I'm feeling hope, hope that this age might not see the end of free humans in our world."

Jonny was more confused than before, and it showed on his face.

"Jonny," The Master began. "There is so much you do not know, so much I have not told you about this world we live in, and I guess now I can put it off no longer. With your ability to create objects like this, you will become involved all too soon. In fact, you are already involved, whether you know it or not.

"You know I have had a sense of urgency about developing your skills for some time, don't you?"

"Yes, Master. I always knew there was something big you thought somehow involved me. Sometimes I wanted to ask you, but other times I was afraid you would tell me. I really started worrying when I found out what you had been hiding from me about going under the knife."

"Yes, I can see how finding out a terrible truth would make you reluctant to learn another one. Unfortunately, this truth is many times more frightening than that one, though they are connected.

"Most people believe that the Great War was fought over whether the Grimoridans could extend their empire to our continent, Skryla. That was the publicly announced reason, but it was not the main reason for the war. I believe you were taught this much in your history lessons."

Jonny had been taught a lot about the Great War, but he still felt like it was so far away he did not really know much about it. It was mostly referred to obliquely by people when they said things like, "Don't forget that Skryla isn't

Grimor, not that the Grimoridans didn't try to crush us, but we showed them and we'll show them again if we need to!" The Great War had been long enough ago that it was mostly the subject of epic stories, but he had been taught how it was the beginning point for the current political situation.

The Master continued, "Jonny, few people realize that the Great War was fought to eliminate zdrell from the world. The demons and their wizards had eliminated all the zdrell masters in Grimor in their consolidation of that continent. The Great War was their pretext for eliminating the zdrell masters in Skryla, and they were successful. Once the last zdrell master in Skryla was dead, they abandoned their attempt to conquer this continent within three months, though they had been fighting for nearly twenty years. That was the real reason for the war, and that is why you have been in danger almost since the moment you became my apprentice, even though you did not know it."

Jonny was both amazed and confused. "But why would anyone care about me, Master? I'm no zdrell master, I'm just a kid, a nobody."

"Jonny," The Master said, smiling sadly. "You are so much more than a nobody. You may only be ranked as an apprentice, but you are already a zdrell master, and what frightens and heartens me most is that you are already stronger and more gifted than most of the masters I have read of. And you are still just learning to use all that you can do. You could ultimately become one of the most powerful wizards this world has ever seen."

Jonny just shook his head. "I could never be greater than you, Master." No matter what The Master said, Jonny would not believe he could be greater than his master.

A look of irritation passed across Master Silurian's face. "I tire of this absurd worship you seem to have for me, Jonny. I am only a man and you have already surpassed me in so many ways I can hardly name them."

"But you know so much more than me, Master!"

"Yes, yes, I do know more than you, and that is why you must understand that I know I, with all my vast experience, can never hope to accomplish so much that you do easily. I could never, listen closely, *never* could I have created this ring, yet for you it was only a few days work. That, Jonny, is power!"

Jonny was ashamed, proud and humiliated all at the same time. He was ashamed because he had contradicted The Master needlessly, and made him admit his limitations. He felt a little proud because he had heard The Master's words. The tiniest possibility that he could become a truly great wizard, even surpassing The Master, was intoxicating. He felt humiliated because of the previous two things and because The Master had needed to shout at him to get him to listen. His emotions were in such turmoil; he was powerless to say anything.

The Master, too, said nothing for several moments and then he shook his head and said, "Jonny, Jonny, do not worry. Here you have brought me the greatest gift I have ever received and I have burdened you with nothing but more cares. Go and use what you have learned here and finish that sword. Do not forget you still need to make one more thing. That was the agreement. In many ways you have far surpassed it, and I almost, almost, want to release you from it. Whatever you make I am sure it will be wonderful and surprising."

Chapter 60

Jonny walked from the castle back to town. He could easily have flown. He longed to fly, but even more than that, he needed time to think. With everything The Master had told him, his head was spinning. It took him over three hours to get back to his quarters at Kason's. In that time he thought of many things, but now, even more than earlier that night, he realized that he was in very real danger. The demons and those who used them would come for him, would stop at nothing to destroy him, as soon as they realized he existed. Jonny knew he had to be ready, because he felt sure that they would come looking for him very soon.

§ § §

One of the things Jonny decided on his long walk back was what he would work on next. He knew he had to finish the sword. He knew it would be very valuable in defending him against demons, but he felt that he needed something more before he attempted to finish it. He needed to use some of the insight he had gained in creating the ring for Master Silurian as well as the two previous rings and the sword. He felt he needed to create yet one more ring that was the sum of all he had learned.

Jonny began work on the new ring the next night, after he had told Kason about The Master's joyous reception of the ring and then spent the day working on mundane projects. Jonny knew this ring would be different. He wanted to make something using zdrell that could be made no other way. He did not make this ring out of a single piece of metal or alloy. He carefully trimmed four pieces of heavy gauge wire, each from a different metal: gold, silver, copper, and iron, and laid them down at the edge of one of the jewelry forges.

The forge was cold.

Jonny closed his eyes and using only his zdrell vision to see them began to heat them with his mind. He wanted to form and join the different pieces of metal in a way that could not normally be done. Each metal had a different melting point and other characteristics. He heated each wire until it was nearly liquid and then wove them together and rolled them into a ring.

It was taxing work, the hardest thing Jonny had ever attempted. He could not have done it without the power ring to give him the additional strength and control. Jonny started to really understand what The Master had meant earlier when he had said that there were certain operations that a single wizard just was not powerful enough to accomplish. Creating this ring was taxing Jonny to his very limit.

Finally, he could sense it was done. He allowed it to cool and then opened his eyes to see what he had created. It was strange to look at because the different metals were clearly distinct, but you could not say from looking at it where one ended and the other began. The different metals flowed together in a spiral throughout the length of the ring. It was a very odd mix. Still, looking at it Jonny could see that it lacked something; then it came to him, he needed the diamond chips he had used with The Master's ring. But he was too tired now. It had taken too much out of him just to get this far. The final additions would have to wait.

§ § §

Jonny did not wake until midmorning. When he went out to Kason and showed him the results of the night's work, Kason looked puzzled.

"'Tis passing strange, Jonny," Kason said, turning the ring over and over in his hand. "I'd have said it wasn't possible to make metal do this, but clearly you have. I suspect though that for any but you, it still is impossible."

Kason shook his head. "You've passed me, boy. There's little more I could teach you when you can make things like this. I take it, this is the last item for your journeyman project?"

"Yes, Kason. It is, but it's not done yet."

"Not done? What more will you do to it?"

"I'm going to add diamond chips to it like I did with the ring for Master Silurian."

"How will you—no never mind. I've no idea how you made this thing. You shouldn't have been able to do it, so how am I to understand how you'll change it."

"It was hard to do, Kason, but you can easily understand what I did. I just heated each of the wires to just below their melting point and pushed them together. Keeping them all at just the right temperature was the hard part."

"You . . . had them all at their own melting points, at the same time? No boy, I don't get what you did, even though you tell me, much less how. All I can say is: it must be magic."

Jonny could see that Kason was right; he would not be able to understand what Jonny had done. Jonny was not even sure he could explain it with words himself. He had just done what seemed right. There was no other way to put it. Once he had started, he had just felt a sense of rightness as he had worked to bring the whole thing together. Now, for the same reason, he knew he still was not done and that he needed the added changes the diamonds would bring.

§ § §

Jonny did not finish the ring that day, nor the next. He really had not realized how much making the ring had taken out of him. Every time he took off his power ring, he felt so drained and tired that all he wanted to do was sleep. He did sleep a lot those days and it was not until the third day before he felt recovered enough to attempt to finish it.

Again, he waited until after the normal close of business to begin his work. This time Kason asked if he could be present to watch. Jonny was very happy to consent. Jonny prepared six small chips of diamond to embed in the ring. He did not know why he chose six, except that it felt like the right number.

He moved again to a cold jewelry forge and brought the ring into the air and set it spinning slowly. He reached out and heated the metals that made up the ring and then pulled the first chip to it. He waited until he found just the right place where the pieces of metal came together and fit the chip into it. It was like finding the missing piece to a puzzle. Once he found the right spot, it slipped below the surface of the ring with almost no effort on his part. As the piece fit home, there was a brief flash of power from the ring. Kason cried out in surprise, but Jonny had somehow known this would happen and felt energized by the wave of power.

Jonny continued working, fitting the remaining chips into the ring. As each found its spot, there was another release of power, each one slightly stronger than the previous. When he was about to fit the final piece in place, Jonny told Kason to shield his eyes.

This time the flash was much stronger, but Jonny was ready. He soaked in the power using his power ring and then channeled it back to the new ring. Without waiting for it to cool, he reached out and put the ring on. It should have burned him, but it did not. As soon as he put it on, he felt the whole world change.

He could see in ways he had never before imagined. His zdrell vision was there, and at a much greater level. He also could see much that before he had only seen when using the demon sight amulet, but where with the demon sight amulet things had a fuzzy, indistinct look to them, now he saw those things with razor edged clarity.

When he looked at the new ring, it was like looking into the sun. The power and energy channeling through it was incredible, but he instinctively knew that it did not have to be that way.

With a thought, he commanded the ring to be still, and it was. Just like snuffing out a candle, now the ring appeared to be nothing more than metal, though Jonny's enhanced perceptions continued.

Then he remembered Kason.

The master metalworker was half hiding behind one of the workbenches.

"What have you done, Jonny? That ring was glowing like the sun and you just reached out and put it on. For a moment, you looked like a picture of one of the gods or demons. You were glowing just like that ring." Kason said with awe in his voice. "Now you're not glowing, but what are you, boy?"

"I don't know Kason. I don't think I am, myself, any different, but with this ring I don't think things will ever be the same."

Neither spoke for some time. Reluctantly, Jonny removed the ring. The world snapped back to its normal, seemingly dreary look. The effect scared Jonny, but he knew what he had to do next.

He took off the power ring.

For the first time since he had begun his work that evening, Jonny realized the workshop was dark and he had been working without any lights. He saw Kason had a small lantern on the workbench by him, but its light barely reached where Jonny stood.

With an effort, he brought back his zdrell sight, but it was such a pale thing compared to what he easily had with the power ring and was not remotely close to what he had with the new ring on. He used his sight to look at the ring and it still looked like nothing more than plain metal. With his other rings and amulets, there was always a sense of magic about them when he looked at them with his zdrell sight, but not with this ring. He had told it to be still, and it was.

Now that Jonny thought about what it had been like to wear both rings, he knew that this new ring was very different from his power ring as well as from the ring he had created for The Master. The power ring gave Jonny direct access to the power in his surrounding environment. Like a man taking a small commission on a sale of a large parcel of land, the power ring took a small portion of the power all around Jonny and gave him access to a piece of it.

This new ring was something different altogether. Jonny could tell that it did more and less all at the same time. He could tell that he could use it to store power, much the same as the ring he had created for Master Silurian. He could also tell that it too could tap into the ambient power around Jonny as his power ring did, but at a much higher level. He knew he could pull the power from things, more than just the ambient power that all things radiated into the environment, but the power that held them together. It was a great and terrible power that the ring possessed, yet it was not evil. Jonny felt this ring could control, or master, the power anywhere he could perceive, and with the enhanced perceptions Jonny had while wearing it, there was little he could not perceive.

Jonny feared this ring, feared it for what it could allow him to do, and what he might become if he did some of the things it made possible. He was not at all sure he was ready, or that anyone could be, for this much power.

Unlike his power ring, Jonny was not afraid of this ring falling into someone else's hands. He knew that it would only work for someone who understood how to see with zdrell. As the ring was now, he doubted anyone but he or possibly Master Silurian would be able to do anything with it.

He resolved not to use the ring too much. He already knew that the enhanced perceptions he had when wearing it were too intoxicating. It would be much too easy to become completely dependent on it, much more so than the power ring.

In his mind, he was already thinking of the ring as the *master* ring. It gave him mastery and control over all power in his reach. He felt that one day he would be ready to wear it all the time, but not now.

Chapter 61

The demon lord came through the portal into Jelnic's work room. Before the wizard could speak, the demon spoke in his booming voice.

"Whatever the reason for your summons, Jelnic, you will hear me first."

Jelnic was puzzled, as well as irritated. He sat for a moment with his mouth half open wondering if he was wise to allow this breach of protocol. He decided to hear the demon out before he decided if the reason justified the slight.

"Say on, Karth. What is so urgent?" he said with a slight wave of his hand.

"There is another line cutter abroad in the land."

Jelnic tried ineffectually to hide his surprise and irritation.

"How can that be? I eliminated the last line cutter over three hundred years ago. Who claims this line cutter exists?"

"A third circle demon was summoned and immediately detected it in the room where he arrived. He eliminated the foolish wizard who summoned him, but the line cutter remains."

The demon floated there, waiting for Jelnic to respond. Jelnic wished the demon who reported the line cutter had eliminated it itself, but, of course, demons were powerless (or claimed they were) to destroy the one thing that could harm them.

"Where was this?" he asked.

"In Salaways, in the castle of the wizard known as Silurian."

"Ah, Silurian. Strange that a third circle demon would be summoned there, he has always opposed us, but I guess that it was not Silurian that did the summoning?"

"It was not."

"Well, Silurian has always been fond of poking into unlikely places and finding things. He must have found some hidden cache," Jelnic said, almost talking to himself.

Focusing his attention on the demon, he continued. "I will have the line cutter found and destroyed, if you will take a message for me to Feltran in Skryla. He can find someone with the appropriate skills to find and destroy the line cutter. I was going to have you take several messages to Skryla, this will only be one more."

"I will do this for you, Jelnic. Do not forget your charge. It is only to keep zdrell out of this world that I have lengthened your pitiful mortal life," the demon rumbled.

Jelnic was irritated by the demon's tone, but he had not lived this long by being too impatient.

"I do not forget, demon. I will act to eliminate this threat to you and your brother demons. Here is the message you must give to Feltran. Say to him . . . ." Jelnic told him the message to relay to Feltran, and also gave him several message scrolls he had originally summoned the demon to give to various wizards in Skryla. After that was done, the demon left.

Sitting alone at his desk, Jelnic's anger cooled. He thought over how this would affect his plans for the coming invasion of Skryla. It could easily upset the timetable he had spent the last hundred years putting into place. He turned it over in his mind, wondering how any zdrell cache could have escaped his notice.

Finally, he smiled. He had been working by subtle means for decades with little outward to show for it. Perhaps a little action would give him a chance to see something happen directly. It might also give him an excuse to remove Silurian. Salaways had been a thorn in his side since Silurian took over. This might just be the chance to pluck it out.

Chapter 62

Nearly a week after he had completed the master ring, Jonny still had not gone back to work on his sword. He also had not put on the master ring again. Kason knew that Jonny was not working on the sword, but said nothing to him. In fact, Kason said very little to Jonny at all. Jonny could see that what Kason had seen the night Jonny finished the master ring had affected him even more than it had Jonny.

Jonny didn't want to work on the sword because he knew that to do the things he needed to complete the sword would require him to put on the master ring, and he was afraid to do it. The ring scared him, even though he knew he had created it. It scared him most because he was afraid that if he put it on again he would never want to take it off.

Jonny thought about talking to Master Silurian about it, but for some reason was reluctant to do it. He felt he knew what The Master would tell him, besides he did not want to admit he was scared.

§ § §

Jonny went nearly two weeks before he finally decided he could put it off no longer. He heated a forge at the end of a late spring day, got the sword and all his tools ready, and put on the ring.

He felt his perceptions shift, and the world became much more profound and intense. When he looked at the sword, he could clearly see the power trapped in the blade, but now he could also clearly see the pathways he needed to create to channel and control the power. He placed the blade in the fire and watched until it was the right temperature, and then he pulled the blade out and began to work rapidly. In less than five minutes, he was able to do what he had been unable to do earlier while working for hours.

He spent the next several hours working on the hilt and the guard of the sword. Previously he had done all his magical work with swords directly on the blade. On this blade, he knew that the pommel, hilt and guard had to all be one piece with the blade rather than separate pieces as in other swords.

The hilt of this sword would link the wielder directly to the blade. Jonny knew this was important for this sword would truly be a line cutter. With it, Jonny would be able to cut lines of force with the same ease that shears cut fleece from a sheep.

Jonny was still working on the sword when the other workers came into the workshop the next morning. They neither spoke nor disturbed him and he was completely oblivious to their presence. Finally, just past noon, Jonny noticed the sun was up and that the other workers even existed. He looked up at them, smiled, waved a greeting, then wrapped up the sword in a cloth, and walked out of the workshop. He relieved himself, then went to his room and lay down; still holding the cloth wrapped sword, he slept for two days.

§ § §

With the sword completed, Jonny had technically completed the terms of his journeyman project and could, by presenting his items to The Master and Kason, claim the title of journeyman.

Jonny was reluctant to do it.

Though he knew he had more than fully proven his right to be a journeyman, he knew that on doing so everything would change. He was not at all certain he wanted things to change more than they already had.

Jonny also knew that he needed to make one more thing before he presented his projects to The Master. He had completed the sword, but as with the power ring and the demon ring, it radiated power to any who could see it. When Jonny looked at it with his zdrell or demon sight, the sword blazed with a fire of power. He knew that if he were to safely keep the sword, he had to find a way to hide its power the same as he had with the demon ring.

He determined that the best way to hide the sword was to make a scabbard that would obscure its power. Jonny knew that it could be no ordinary leather scabbard, so after some thought he opted to make a wooden scabbard similar to the one he had made for the duelist's sword. This time, since he was not working in metal, he would have to carve the wood to channel the force lines to obscure the power of the sword.

This turned out to be a complicated task. It took him four attempts, and as many weeks, before he had finally created a scabbard that would hide the nature of the sword. In the end, it was only when he added some metal bands to the outside of the scabbard that Jonny finally achieved the balance he required. By the time he was finally finished, he determined that whatever his gifts were, working with wood was not one of them. The scabbard was an odd, unsightly thing, with crude, rough carvings, but that actually was an advantage in hiding the nature of the weapon it concealed.

§ § §

With the scabbard completed, Jonny felt somewhat safer, knowing that sword was now not so actively advertising its presence to anyone with eyes to see its power. Jonny also knew that the time had come for him to present himself to his two masters to gain his status as a journeyman.

He thought he would approach Kason first, and then Master Silurian.

"I wondered when you'd be talking to me, lad," Kason said when Jonny came to him. They were both in the negotiation room where Kason normally received clients.

"It's past time, and you and I both know it."

"Yes, Master Kason," Jonny replied, unwilling to meet his eyes.

"Boy, you know how little I like it when you call me that."

Jonny only answered, "Yes, Master."

"I'm no master of yours, boy," Kason grunted. "But I'll have your journeyman certificate writ before the even."

Jonny heard the dismissal in his voice and left. He was sad that Kason was so short with him, but he did not think it was anger Kason was feeling, but more an irritation that Jonny would be leaving him soon, with the loss of income that would entail, or possibly it was fear.

Things had never been the same between them since that night when Jonny had finished the master ring. The other workers in the shop had felt it too, and some had secretly rejoiced. Kason never tore into Jonny, as he had so many of the apprentices or journeymen, for some mistake. Partly this was because Jonny so rarely did anything that could earn Kason's wrath, but Kason had always treated Jonny differently, and though the others knew the reason for it, that did not stop them from resenting it. Now that Jonny seemed to be less than fully in Kason's good graces, the other workers were actually treating Jonny better, though none dared ask what Jonny he had done to earn Kason's ire.

Jonny enjoyed the improved camaraderie, but it made him both happy and sad since he knew he would be leaving soon.

Kason was good as his word and handed Jonny his certificate before the evening meal. Normally the awarding of journeyman status was a great cause for celebration in the shop, but since no one but Kason had even known that Jonny was working on journeyman projects, he also told no one of Jonny's change in status.

That suited Jonny just fine. Being a journeyman would only have meaning as he worked in other places. Even if everyone were told about Jonny's new status, his work there would scarcely change. He had been doing journeyman and master level work for some time. No one really treated him like an apprentice any more anyway, so it mattered little to Jonny if they knew.

Jonny knew that it would change things quite a bit when he presented himself to Master Silurian. For that reason, and for other reasons that he felt, but could not explain, he delayed going to see The Master.

Chapter 63

Boregond

Master Boregond hated to travel. No, that was not true; he hated to travel by mundane means. He traveled quite a bit by means of demon magic and found it most refreshing, but he was not doing that now. He was traveling by carriage on a hot dusty road and was not enjoying it one bit.

The roads had gotten much better since they entered Salaways. He hated to admit that Silurian did a better job at keeping his kingdom in good repair than most, but it was true. Moreover, it was all because of Silurian that he had to travel in this slow uncomfortable way, Silurian and the demons.

Boregond was in Salaways because a demon reported that he had been summoned by a journeyman of Silurian's who had possessed a line cutter. The demon had not destroyed the line cutter, but had killed his summoner, even though the summoning wizard had claimed not to know anything about it. Now Boregond had to find out about this line cutter. If he could find it, he had to destroy it.

He also had to find out what other devices Silurian might have found. The only known line cutters in existence had been made before the Great War. If Silurian had found an unknown cache of ancient artifacts, there was no knowing what he might have acquired in addition to the line cutter.

It was the uncertainty of thiswhole affair that made it necessary for Boregond to travel by these unsavory means. Until Boregond could find and destroy the line cutter, no demon would risk itself in the artifact's presence.

Boregond was reminded again how only those who worked with demons were aware how truly fickle and skittish they were. The only reason anyone worked with them at all was that in spite of being skittish, they were immensely powerful and could, when properly bound, provide astonishing services for those who knew how to handle them.

Only one thing frightened demons--death. They were effectively immortal, and were so powerful that few things could harm them in any way, let alone kill them. Line cutters were one of the few artifacts that had the power to harm a demon, and for that reason Boregond had been charged by no less than Supreme Grandmaster Jelnick, the oldest and greatest demon wizard in the world with finding and destroying this line cutter.

Boregond had this dubious honor because he was the demon wizard closest to Salaways who also possessed expertise in other branches of magic, since demon magic would not be available to whomever went to recover the line cutter. The demons had made it clear that it was the humans' job to eliminate the threat of a previously unknown line cutter. So, in spite of the inconvenience, here he was.

Boregond had not always been a demon wizard. He had even, over a century earlier, been a journeyman who studied under Silurian, so he knew and understood him better than most. Boregond had only adopted demon magic as his primary mode when he had seen that method triumph consistently over other types of magic, both in his duels, and in the contests of others. In spite of this, he knew that the other branches of magic could be very potent, especially in an old master like Silurian.

Boregond knew he could not approach master Silurian directly about the line cutter. Silurian knew where Boregond's loyalties lay, and he would be no direct help at all. Therefore, Boregond exited the carriage at Alavar not as Master Boregond, demon master, but as master merchant Carson, come to Alavar to explore new sources and markets for his trading business.

He was certain that the line cutter had to come from some previously unknown cache of ancient artifacts. If Silurian had a trove such as this, Boregond was certain the traders of the city would be the first to know about it, because there would be much in the find that did not interest Silurian, but would be sold to help support the costs of running the kingdom. Traders were always interested in items pre-dating the Great War.

§ § §

At first, his efforts seemed to be fruitless. Though he met with many of the great traders of the city, and hinted broadly that he had heard of ancient artifacts recently originating from Alavar, no one seemed to know what he was talking about. The more he pushed, the more baffled his listeners became.

After five days, Boregond was nearly ready to despair when he met for luncheon with the last of the heads of the great trading houses of Salaways, a Master Zolic. At first, his inquiries were met with the same sort of bafflement he had encountered earlier with the other traders, when suddenly Master Zolic leaned back and laughed.

"Ah, Master Carson," Zolic said, still chuckling. "I now know of what you're hinting. You keep asking about artifacts of ancient date, when in fact what you are looking for are items newly made here in Alavar, which most outside of our fair land believe must have been made in the old days. Nevertheless, I can tell you, without a doubt, they are not ancient at all. They are made right here by our master metal worker Kason, and I will tell you they are the equal of anything made by the ancients.

"No doubt," Zolic continued, "they are sold by others outside of Salaways as ancient artifacts. If it were not for the sheer volume produced by master Kason in the last year, and the fame they have gained on their own, I think I would be tempted to do the same. Look at this," Zolic said, placing an ornate dagger on the table between them.

Boregond looked, and was impressed. The dagger was beautiful, finely wrought, and with an obvious air of utility as well. More than that, the blade was etched in a pattern he had never seen before. With a shock, he realized that the etchings were not purely decorative. They definitely added the slightest bit of magic to the blade, a magic that Boregond had only seen before in ancient artifacts.

233

Zolic smiled broadly, as he watched Boregond's reaction. "Beautiful, isn't it?"

"Yes," Boregond said, not taking his eyes off the dagger, "it is."

"That's what you've been looking for, isn't it?" Zolic said.

"Yes, I believe it is. I believe this might just be what I was looking for," he said, handing the knife back to its owner.

"Yes, well I expect you'll want to go and see Master Kason about acquiring one, or a shipment, for yourself. I only wish I could say that I had the exclusive contract to trade his wares, but I don't. It never used to bother me before, but with the fame his work's been getting of late, I greatly wish I had pursued that sort of arrangement with him earlier," Zolic said wistfully.

"It is true, you can't always win," Boregond said with a type of joviality that he did not feel.

"True, true, but that doesn't mean you can't try," Zolic said laughing also with forced humor.

§ § §

The dagger Zolic had shown Boregond concerned him greatly. His thoughts spun. How could an artifact, made in the style of the ancient zdrell masters, look as though it had been forged in the last year? Had Silurian found some way to reach back through time and obtain work created thousands of years earlier? No, that was impossible; if Silurian had that kind of power, he would not content himself with simply bringing things forward in time. He would bring a zdrell master himself. No, no all this was impossible, but then how had the dagger come to be?

Boregond puzzled over it for some time in his rooms. The only possibility that he could see was that Silurian had somehow found one of the caches of the ancients, which were rumored to be sealed so that items stored inside did not age. Things that were stored for three thousand years could look the same as the day the cache was sealed. He was not pleased with this explanation either, but it at least fit the facts. If Silurian had found a cache that contained a large number of weapons, what better way to distribute the items without drawing attention than to give them to a contemporary weapons maker to distribute as his own work. It would also explain the sudden appearance of a line cutter.

Boregond would have to pay a visit to Master Kason.

Chapter 64

Jonny saw the stranger step down from a carriage that had stopped near the workshop, late in the morning of a mid-summer day. He appeared to be a fat wealthy merchant of the type that had been visiting the shop with greater and greater frequency as the fame of Jonny's weapons had grown.

Jonny would not normally have paid him more than a glance, but there was something familiar about him. Jonny kept watching the supposed merchant as he continued to rearrange some of the items in the display area. Then he had it; it had been long ago but Jonny could not forget this man. He was the demon master Boregond; even though he was dressed and playing the part of a merchant, Jonny was certain it was him.

Boregond had already glanced at Jonny once or twice but had not really seen him; there was no trace of recognition in his gaze. Jonny understood that. Master Boregond looked unchanged from the last time Jonny had seen him, but Jonny now bore little resemblance to the scrawny scared little boy he had been the last time Boregond had seen him. At nearly fifteen and a half, he was fully two feet taller now than then, and still growing rapidly. His hair was still red, but now more the color of tarnished copper.

Jonny was puzzled that Master Boregond was not wearing his master magician's robes. He was a vain man, even in the robes of a master trader that much was obvious, so why should he not be actively advertising his status as a master magician? The only thing Jonny could think of was that Boregond must not want Master Silurian to know he was here and what he was about.

Boregond and Kason were already involved in conversation. As Jonny watched, they moved, carrying one of Jonny's enhanced daggers into the negotiating office where Kason discussed important deals. It was not long before they emerged. Both of them looked angry and Jonny saw they were heading for him. He was not at all sure what he was going to do when they got to him.

Kason got to him first. "Jonny," he said gesturing with the dagger. "Please tell this *gentleman* who made this weapon. He seems to think that you are incapable of having crafted any part of it!"

Jonny hesitated, unsure of what to say. He knew what Kason wanted him to say, to take credit for the blade, but he also knew that Kason did not know who Boregond was or what his real reason for being there might be.

"I would say," Jonny began carefully, "that I was the one who worked on this blade."

Jonny could immediately see that his answer pleased neither Kason nor Boregond. Kason was obviously mad because Jonny had not plainly defended his work. Boregond looked as though he sensed evasiveness in Jonny's answer and he was upset, but for different reasons.

Kason was not about to allow Jonny's abilities to be slighted.

"Jonny, tell this man that you didn't just work on this blade but that yours is the only hand that's ever touched it, that before you started, it was an unformed lump of metal and now it is as fine a blade as ever this man's seen!"

"Sir, Master? . . . ," Jonny began.

"Carson, Master Trader Carson," Boregond said.

"Master Trader Carson, I would say that I am the only person here who has ever worked on this blade."

"As I thought," Boregond said. "You say you are the only one here who has worked on this blade, but you do not say who might have worked on it before it came here."

"Are you daft, man?" Kason yelled. "He said he was the only one that worked on it. Before it came here it was a lump of metal, nothing more."

"You sir, are the one who insists that it was a lump of metal. Your young man here has not said that. In fact, he has been very careful not to say what state it was in prior to coming here."

Kason was turning red with rage, but Jonny held up his hand to signal him to back down. Kason looked closely at Jonny, and then with great effort held his tongue.

"Why do you think that I could not have produced this blade?" Jonny asked mildly.

"First, because you are so young, but more so because this blade has been magicked. I've seen its like before, but no wizard has lived that could produce one such since before the Great War."

Jonny was not shocked by this comment, but he could see that Kason was. Master Silurian had said as much to Jonny previously, but had apparently not shared this insight with Kason. Now Jonny understood fully what Boregond was asking, and in many ways he was more worried than he had been when he thought it had been a simple dispute.

"So you believe, Master Wizard Boregond, that we are receiving blades from somewhere else, and that these blades have been magicked and stored for more than a thousand years and we have been taking them and turning them into finished weapons and selling them as if we had made them wholly ourselves?" Jonny asked quietly.

Both men now were shocked. Both showed surprise when Jonny used Boregond's name, but Kason showed even more surprise and indignation at Jonny's telling of Boregond's version of events.

"Yes, I'd say that's just about exactly how I see things," Boregond said. He continued low and dangerously, "But I want to know how you knew my identity."

Kason's jaw just hung open. He obviously wanted to hear Jonny's response too.

"You probably don't remember me, but I was an apprentice at Castle Salaways the last time you were there. I remember seeing you, but I doubt you would remember me. I was quite a bit smaller and younger then too, so I doubt I look much like I did then." Jonny said.

"And now you've been apprenticed to Master Kason?" Boregond asked.

"Yes. I've worked for Master Kason now for some time, and he's taught me much. In fact, he just recently awarded me journeyman status."

Jonny knew that he had to get Boregond away from Kason quickly. He now knew the assumptions Boregond was working under, and he did not want to give Kason a chance to question them any further. For that matter, he knew that Kason was very upset by the deception Boregond had already used with him by posing as a trader.

"Master Kason," Jonny said, trying desperately to get Kason to go along with him. "I think it would be wise if Master Boregond and I were alone to talk of this business. I think there are things he wishes to discuss that he does not want most people to overhear."

Jonny could see that Kason was about to explode, so he hurried on.

"Could we possibly take a walk down by the river for a time, so that we could discuss these things in private?"

Boregond saw where Jonny was going and jumped in. "That is, if you can spare your young journeyman for a short time, Master Kason," Boregond added in a conciliatory tone.

Kason looked back and forth between them with something like loathing and said through gritted teeth, "Yes, we can spare him for a short time, though I don't know why I should allow any courtesy to a man who hides his true identity from me for any reason."

With that, Kason turned and stomped back into his office and slammed the door.

Chapter 65

Jonny was careful to talk only of the weather and other pleasantries while he walked with Master Boregond through town and down to the river. Boregond played his part as well and did not try to steer the conversation to more serious matters until they were on the outskirts of town walking along the side of the river. Jonny was afraid, but was doing everything he could to appear calm and in control.

Once they were in an open area with the river on one side and open fields on the other, with no one else in sight, Boregond stopped and faced Jonny.

"Now, boy," Boregond said, steel behind his words. "I've been patient long enough. Tell me where those enchanted blades are coming from. Tell me where Silurian gets them, and I'll make you rich beyond your wildest dreams. You'll never have to work another day in your life."

Jonny tried to appear unaffected, though he was not, not by the offer of riches, but by the unspoken 'or else!' in Boregond's words.

"I would tell you, Master Boregond, if I could. But I can't."

"You can't, or you won't? What did Silurian promise you?"

"Master Silurian has promised me nothing other than what he's promised all who work for him."

Jonny could see the rage building in Boregond. He was frightened by it, but he knew he needed to get Boregond to react before he realized who and what Jonny was.

"Then let me tell you what I will promise you," Boregond said, menace in every word. "I will promise you that if you don't tell me all I want to know, and tell me quickly, you will never live to see the sun rise again!"

Jonny believed him. He was scared, but he knew there was much Boregond did not know. He tried to tell himself that this was no different than his earlier duels, but he knew there was no one to make sure the rules were followed here, worse, he doubted there were any rules.

"I told you I can't, because you've already been told where those enchanted blades came from and you didn't believe."

"You claim you've created them?" He snorted derisively. "My patience grows thin boy. There's not a master wizard alive today who could do what's been done to those blades, let alone a rejected apprentice."

Boregond clearly did not believe Jonny's claim, but he was still not quite ready to attack. Jonny had to goad him into acting before he realized what Jonny could do, and prepared to defend against him.

"You fool," Jonny said with contempt he did not feel. "Whoever said I was a rejected apprentice? I am Master Silurian's star pupil. It was I, and I alone who made the blades you've seen. You don't remember, but I was the one who made you leave castle Salaways in disgrace the last time you were foolish enough to come there!"

Jonny could see that his insults had hit their mark. Boregond was clearly enraged, but he also was still in control.

"Yes, now I do remember you. You were right earlier, you look little like the beaten whelp you were then, but I still remember how Silurian used you to stage that trick to humiliate me. Silurian thinks himself the only one capable of power in other branches of magic. He thinks that those of us who use demons as our primary mode are helpless without them. Well, you shall see just how wrong he is, before you die!"

Jonny had been holding himself ready for this moment, without hesitation invoked his invisibility amulet, and started to run as lightly as he could into the field.

"Ha! You think a simple invisibility spell will save you? I see you still; you little rabbit. That spell does make you a bit harder to see, but it also marks you for the magic I will send your way."

Jonny ran over a natural levee separating the river from the fields and turned to face Boregond who was walking rapidly after him.

"Which of the five amulets you wear will you use to show me your power, Master? Or maybe you'll use one of the two rings you also wear or the one hidden next to the amulets beneath your shirt?"

Boregond was obviously taken somewhat aback by Jonny's knowledge of the magic he carried. Jonny had made a point of using his sight to its fullest while they had been walking to the river. Boregond fairly reeked with magical items. He also knew that even if Boregond had used his demon sight amulet on Jonny, all he would have seen was the invisibility amulet and power ring. Jonny's other two rings were concealed within the cancellation locket.

Boregond may have been put off by Jonny's knowledge, but the taunts had been effective in making the man not consider the full extent of Jonny's power.

"You tell me," Boregond said bringing his right arm back and throwing it forward as if he were pitching a rock at Jonny. Midway through the throw, a ball of energy appeared within his hand and flew at Jonny.

Again, Jonny was ready and had invoked his shield spell, the same one he had used in his previous duel. The ball impacted the shield and failed to break through, but exploded with a great detonation. If Jonny had not been feeding additional power from his ring into the spell, it would not have held.

"Impressive, young fool. Your shield held that time, but can it hold against this," Boregond said as he threw a small black ball at the ground just outside Jonny's shield. Almost immediately, the ball began to throw off great clouds of smoke.

Jonny knew that the smoke would get through his shield, so he quickly concentrated on the ball and sent it flying over the levee and into the river. Jonny knew that if he stayed on the defensive he would lose, so he rapidly sent three fist-sized rocks flying at Boregond. They rebounded off a shield that Boregond must have invoked from an amulet. Once again, Jonny cursed himself for not having taken the time to create a shield amulet himself, since the effort of throwing the black ball and the rocks had taken enough of his concentration that his own shield spell had dropped.

Jonny did not wait for Boregond to realize that Jonny's shield was down and jumped straight into the air.

This had the desired effect. For a moment, Boregond was stunned by Jonny's action. The only problem was that Jonny was not sure what to do to press his advantage. Then he remembered his last duel and reached out to pull Boregond off the ground.

The old wizard was very annoyed by Jonny's tactic, but he did not panic.

"No more playing boy!" he shouted and activated a pair of amulets.

Immediately Boregond was surrounded by green translucent sphere. Jonny lost his hold on him and the sphere settled gently to the ground. As soon as it touched the ground, a whirlwind sprang up around it. At first, it was only a few feet taller than Boregond, but each moment it grew wider and taller. The wind of it was now picking up small rocks and throwing them, and not just in random directions, but right at Jonny.

If Jonny had not spent hours defending against just this sort of attack, he would not have been able to stand against the assault. As it was, he was able to move the rocks with relative ease, so that he was in no danger. He tried turning the rocks back and sending them at Boregond, but he quickly found that once a rock entered the whirlwind it was grabbed and whipped around and thrown back at him. So Jonny settled for pushing the rocks enough that they flew harmlessly past him. Jonny knew that he would have to do something else soon.

With every passing moment, the whirlwind was getting bigger and stronger.

Jonny looked around and saw a large boulder several yards away. The farmers probably thought it too large to move when the field had been cleared. Jonny thought it might be a good thing to throw at Boregond, but for now it would provide enough shelter from the rocks leaving the whirlwind that Jonny would have time to think. Jonny flew over, took shelter on the lee side of the rock, and turned his attention back to finding a weakness in Boregond's attack.

Jonny focused first his zdrell sight, then his demon sight on the spell Boregond was using. It was unlike any spell Jonny had ever seen. He could see the power being used and the force lines being warped, but the manipulation looked like no sort of magic Jonny had previously witnessed. One thing was sure; the spell's power kept growing. The whirlwind was now over one hundred feet high and grew taller and wider each moment. Larger and larger rocks and pieces of dirt were tearing loose and being thrown by its power.

Jonny considered flying away. He knew that he could get away, but he also knew that now Boregond knew who and what he was that he would never get another chance like this. Boregond had not believed that Jonny could have been the creator of zdrell objects so he had not been prepared to duel with a zdrell wizard.

Now he knew.

If Jonny ran now, there would surely be another conflict, but Boregond would not come alone and he would be prepared. Jonny had to win this duel now, so he stayed.

The problem Jonny faced was that the cyclone that Boregond had conjured was both an awesome offensive and defensive spell. The sheer quantity of debris that the cyclone was now throwing made it both a devastating weapon as well as blocking anything Jonny could think to throw at it. The boulder that Jonny was hiding behind was taking repeated hits from rocks thrown against it and the wind was starting to make it rock back and forth with the force of the gales.

"That's right you fool!" Boregond shouted over the wind. "Hide like the scared little rabbit that you are! See how your foolish zdrell tricks stand before a real power!"

Jonny knew he had to do something fast. He realized that the magical cyclone shared something in common with a natural one; it had an empty center. Jonny figured that even Boregond would be hard pressed to throw rocks straight up. He waited for a momentary lull in the barrage and leapt straight up heading for the top of the whirlwind.

Boregond roared with rage when he saw where Jonny was headed, but he could not do anything to stop him. Jonny was able to hover in place above the top of the cyclone. It was tricky staying away from the main turbulence, but Jonny's practice again paid off. Jonny could tell that this maneuver would gain him some time but it was not going to do anything to stop Boregond, who was already doing something else. Jonny tried conjuring some magic missiles, but nearly fell from trying to split his concentration. The missiles bounced harmlessly off the green sphere surrounding Boregond. He had to come up with something better to attack Boregond.

Then Jonny remembered the master ring. He flew a bit higher and pulled out his canceling locket. As soon as he opened it, Boregond roared again.

"You do have the line cutter with you! Now I will kill you and retrieve that infernal device as well."

Jonny fished around in the locket to get the master ring, but it was hard to get it and at the same time maintain his position above the whirlwind. Just as he was slipping the master ring on his finger, a burst of wind knocked his hand and sent the demon ring, the line-cutter, flying. He almost flew after it, but decided that if he survived he could retrieve it easily enough. If he didn't survive, it wouldn't matter.

Jonny had considered trying to use the line cutter to disrupt the power of Boregond's spell, but the wizard's lack of concern for its power had made Jonny go ahead with his choice of the master ring. As soon as he got it fully on, his perceptions shifted and he was able to see the power that made up the cyclone's spell much more clearly. It was immensely powerful, but it did not use power the way Jonny did with his zdrell. The spell was somehow converting all of the energy bound in the matter around Boregond into pure liberated energy. Jonny suspected Boregond was using only a tiny fraction of the available power, but even so, it was stunning to behold. Jonny could see that the cyclone rather than being the primary reason for the spell was a side effect of the energy Boregond's spell was releasing.

Just in time, Jonny moved aside to avoid a bolt of that pure energy that Boregond projected at him. To Jonny it looked like Boregond had only limited control of the power he was unleashing. With his enhanced vision, Jonny could also see that if the spell were even slightly unbalanced it could easily destroy the wielder. As soon as Jonny realized how fragile the spell was, he knew what he had to do.

He was about to act when Boregond released another blast at Jonny. This time Jonny did not completely get out of the way. His whole left side felt as if it had been set on fire and he felt himself falling. He struggled to maintain his altitude, but even as he struggled to stay in the air he felt himself starting to black out.

He was falling; all he could hope to do was control where he hit.

With one last burst of will, he aimed his fall straight at the green sphere that protected Boregond, this was the last thing Boregond had expected, so he did not hurl the next bolt of energy at Jonny that would surely have killed him. Instead he diverted the power into the energy shield so that when Jonny hit it, he bounced.

Jonny was thrown laterally over twenty feet from his impact with the shield, but that actually was a much softer landing than Jonny would have had without it. He had been over two hundred feet in the air when he had started to fall. The impact also shocked Jonny back awake. He landed in a heap, but did not even try to get up.

Without even moving his head, he reached out with his zdrell and grabbed the boulder he had been hiding behind earlier and threw it in a high arc at Boregond.

Boregond saw the boulder coming and sent a blast of energy at it that caused it to explode into thousands of fragments. But Jonny had expected that and had been using all the enhanced vision the master ring gave him to watch the flow of energy in Boregond's spell as he destroyed the boulder. As he watched, he saw what looked like a weak spot in the spell. Jonny knew that if he could find just the right place to push with the master ring he could collapse the spell, but he also knew he would have just one chance.

Boregond was greatly enjoying himself now.

"Did you see that, you little zdrell mouse! Your boulder did you no good at all. I destroyed it easier than swatting a fly. Now it is time to swat *you* and end this whole affair!"

Jonny needed to keep Boregond talking. He was almost certain he had found the weakness in the spell, but he needed a few moments more to be ready. If Boregond struck too soon, Jonny would have no way to exploit the spell's flaw.

"You are right, Master Boregond," Jonny yelled above the noise of the storm. "Your power truly is awesome. I have never seen anything like it. How do you do it? Could you tell me how that amulet works? Even with demon sight I can't understand it?"

"Now you are right to be awed by this power, zdrell gnat. I will tell you just enough so that you will appreciate your dying all the more. Zdrell was not the only magic lost in the Great War. This amulet and its magic was old before the Great War. The demons would kill me if they knew I possessed this, but they don't and never will, unless they try to attack me. It is good to have something that can cause the demons to fear. It is the most powerful magic that there is, but sadly it is too powerful for most things, it has no finesse and is difficult to control. But I am master of it, and now no more talking. Time for you to die!"

Jonny could see the power gathering for the bolt of energy that would kill him. The time Boregond had been talking had given Jonny a handle on the flaw. He just hoped it would be enough. He reached out and began to pull at it with the master ring. He felt the power building as Boregond prepared to release the bolt. Jonny pushed and pulled frantically at the fabric of the spell but still it held.

Just as Boregond pointed to release the energy at him, Jonny felt the spell give. When it gave, it went all at once. Boregond no longer had anything holding the energy in check and no way to control it.

The bolt meant for Jonny detonated at the end of Boregond's arm, vaporizing it and much of his head and shoulder. It was a nearly silent explosion coming from inside the center of the vortex. Boregond's body fell to the ground, as did all the debris that had been contained in the cyclone. Rocks and dust pelted Jonny, but within a few seconds, the air was undisturbed as if the cyclone had never been.

Chapter 66

For several minutes, Jonny could do nothing but lie there. His left side still hurt abominably. He almost blacked out again, but willed himself to stay conscious. Slowly he got up and walked over to where Boregond's body lay. It was a terrible mess. If Jonny had not already been suffering from shock, he would have been sick. As it was, Jonny felt a strange curiosity looking at the wreck of the man who had nearly killed him.

Jonny figured that between the explosions and magical cyclone someone would be sure to investigate fairly soon, and he did not want to be around when they arrived.

Jonny was about to turn and leave when he remembered he had to retrieve the line-cutter. That made him think of the magical items Boregond had been wearing. The ring on the wizard's right hand had vaporized along with the rest of that arm, but the ring on his other hand and the amulets were still there.

Jonny felt somewhat squeamish about taking them, but he was certain that was how Boregond must have acquired them in the first place. Jonny quickly bent and took the items and put them in his belt pouch and left at as quick a walk as he could manage. He then remembered the invisibility amulet, which was still active, and slowed. Walking was still painful, but he made sure he walked just off the path.

Within five minutes, Jonny saw a large group of curious townspeople and a detachment of the town guard coming down the path. Jonny moved off to the side and waited for them to pass. As soon as they passed, he saw there were more coming behind them. Even with the invisibility spell, Jonny did not think that he could get back into town without running into someone, and there were sure to be questions, as beat up as he was. He was also really feeling the pain of his injuries. He had to fly.

After resting for a moment, Jonny took to the air. Following the initial effort, he found it was actually much easier to fly than it had been to walk. He started out flying to Kason's shop, but the more he thought about it, the better he thought it would be to just go back to the castle. If he had been walking, he could not have gotten there in his present condition.

As it was, he was barely able to make it far enough land in the castle courtyard. No one saw him land with the invisibility spell in place, so he just seemed to appear out of the air when he dropped his invisibility spell.

He found that while flying his whole side had stiffened up so he could barely stand. He knew he looked mangled, so when a startled apprentice saw him appear, he almost laughed. Jonny could feel his consciousness fading again so he croaked, "Get The Master," then slumped to the ground.

§ § §

It was dark outside when Jonny woke up. He was in a bed. A candle burned at a table beside it. He recognized the room as one of the rooms where sick boys were kept at the castle. The Master's wife, Alira, sat in a rocking chair beside the bed, weaving with a finger loom. She had not seen him wake.

He tried to sit up and found that his whole left side felt on fire when he moved.

"Hush, don't try to move," Alira said. "Silurian will want to know you're awake."

Jonny was confused, then he remembered how he had gotten there. He also found that he was wearing nothing but a nightshirt. All his clothes, rings, and amulets had been removed. This realization shocked him, but even as he tried to move, the pain rose up again and he passed out.

§ § §

There was sun shining in the window when Jonny next woke. The Master was sitting in a chair by the bedside reading. He put down the book as soon as he saw Jonny was awake.

"So, Boregond finally bit off more than he could chew," the wizard said, smiling.

Jonny was confused. How could Master Silurian know what had happened?

"No, I used no magic," The Master said to Jonny's unspoken question. "The news is all over Alavar. Everyone knows that there was a deadly wizard's duel outside of town. What they do not know is that I was not involved, and they do not know the identity of the loser. Only you and Kason knew who he really was, and I want to keep it that way for a bit longer.

"There will be trouble enough when the news of his demise gets back to his masters. I have no desire for them to find out any faster than need be. As things are, I think it will be at least two weeks before anyone suspects anything, and hopefully, it will take even longer before they send anyone to investigate. There should be plenty of time for you to heal and get away."

Now Jonny was even more confused. "Why do I need to get away, Master? Almost until the very end, Boregond didn't believe that I could be a zdrell wizard?"

"Yes, that was a good thing you did by allowing him to think your zdrell enhanced blades came from some ancient cache. No, you need to leave so that when they do come looking for Boregond's killer, I will be able to say under oath that I did not do it, and have no idea where the wizard in question might be. Besides, you are a journeyman now and it is high time you started on your journeys."

Jonny was stunned. "How can I be a journeyman, you've never given me my license."

The Master laughed. "Truth be told, Jonny, I was within a day or two of doing just that when you took matters into your own hands."

It seemed like the more The Master talked, the less Jonny understood. "How did I take matters into my own hands, Master?" he asked, hoping that he would finally figure out some of what Master Silurian was saying.

"Jonny, I know you are still recovering from your wounds, but surely you remember that there are two ways you can be awarded master status. First, by passing the tests by the board of elders, or second, by defeating an acknowledged master in single combat."

"Now this second way is not very common, but every year there are certain journeymen who become masters that way, primarily war mages. I do not think I have ever heard of an apprentice being advanced to master that way, but technically, it should be possible. So, in a way, I could say you have qualified as not just a journeyman, but a master wizard."

Jonny did not know what to say, did not know what to think. How could he be a master?

His master took pity on him. "Don't fret, Jonny. Even though technically you could claim to be a master now, that would make even less sense than if I had made you a journeyman two years ago. No, I have already prepared your journeyman's license with no mention of this incident. No one needs to know about this other than the two of us. Now, tell me from the beginning to the end all that happened."

Jonny told The Master exactly what had happened from the time Boregond had shown up at the metal shop until Jonny landed in the castle. When he was finished, The Master looked very thoughtful.

"I will have to think on this. I would not have thought Boregond capable of this kind of subtlety. I will also want to look closer at the rings and amulets you took from him. That was very wise of you to do, and your just spoils from the duel. Now put on these clothes, go, and get yourself something to eat and come and talk to me when you are rested and ready to talk more. You have been asleep for nearly two days."

Until he started to eat Jonny had not realized just how hungry he was. His side was still tender but it felt much better than it had the last time he had been awake. He took his time eating. Occasionally one of the other journeymen would come into the room, but none of them did more than glance at him. After he finished eating, he went back to his room intending to rest for just a few minutes before talking to The Master. As soon as his head hit the pillow, he was asleep. The Master had to wait until the next day to talk to Jonny.

Chapter 67

Jonny woke the next morning a little ashamed that his nap had once again gone on all night, but he felt much better. He was hungry again so went back to the journeyman's mess for breakfast.

As soon as he came in the door, the previously noisy room went silent. There were twelve other journeymen at the tables and all of them were looking at Jonny. Jonny stood there wondering at their reactions. He did not know these journeymen, but somehow they knew him. Finally, one of the journeymen started clapping. Within seconds, all of them were clapping. Jonny just stood there until they stopped and then went to get his food.

As he sat down to eat, the journeyman who had started the clapping came over to sit by him.

"You probably don't remember me, Jonny, but I'm called Carth. I came to work with Master Silurian just two weeks before you left to apprentice with master Kason. I'm the only journeyman still here from before you left, but we all know about you. We all know, or at least we think we know what you did to that demon master Boregond."

"How do you know about that?" Jonny asked.

"Well, all The Master will say is that Boregond was killed in a duel, and that he had nothing to do with it. We figure you are the only other wizard around here that could possibly have taken on Boregond and lived to tell about it. Did you know that he killed more than thirty wizards in duels and wars?"

Jonny just shook his head. He was glad he had not known.

"I'll let you eat now," Carth said. "I just wanted to let you know that we're all behind you. We think it's great that one of The Master's students would be the one to take out Boregond."

"Thanks – I guess," was all Jonny could say.

Jonny ate in silence for a time, but he could see that everyone was still watching him, though not directly.

Apparently, Carth could not contain his enthusiasm and had to keep talking to Jonny.

"So have you picked out your new journeyman name yet? Or is it a master name since you defeated a master?"

"Ah, no, I mean, I'll just be picking out a journeyman name, I'm no master, and I haven't really thought of one yet," Jonny answered hesitantly.

Actually, this was not entirely true. In the time Jonny had worked his journeyman projects, he had thought of dozens of names. He had listened to the names of travelers from distant lands. He had played with combining sounds; he had tried many names on for size. What was true was that he had come to no final determination and he had not thought about names at all for the last several days. Carth's question now reminded Jonny that he would have to decide, soon.

Jonny finished eating. He could tell that the journeymen in the room all wanted to ask him questions, but they were uncertain how to approach Jonny, so they just waited. Jonny did not want to talk right then, so even though he felt bad about it, he just waved and left the room.

§ § §

The castle still felt like home, even if many of the faces had changed. Jonny went to Feldor's office to find out where The Master was only to find that he was in the study where he had told Jonny to meet him the night previous.

When Jonny entered the study, The Master looked up in his usual distracted way and said, "So what name do I put down on this journeyman license?"

Jonny laughed, thinking that The Master had asked the same thing that the journeymen had wanted to know. "I'm not sure yet, Master."

Master Silurian waved his hand impatiently. "Come on, boy, we do not have time for this. You have had months to choose a new name. What will it be?"

"Well, I've been considering Cheklith or Eril."

"So which is it? Do you want me to pick?"

"I'd like to know which you think is better," Jonny said hopefully.

"Well, I don't much like either, but I don't like Checklith at all. So if you are asking me, then my answer would have to be Eril; why did you like it?"

"It is Klathar for the verb 'to seek.'"

"So it is. Though it is also a girl's name in the kingdom of Espilona, if I recall correctly.

"That's why I was hesitant to take it. What do you think, Master, is it still a good name?"

"Doesn't matter, doesn't matter at all what I think, boy," The Master said while writing on a parchment. "There it is: your journeyman license, Eril."

"But, but, you just said."

The Master cut him off. "I said I did not care for either of them. You asked which one I liked, I told you, and you must like them, otherwise you would never have told them to me. Therefore, I have written it down, and now it is official. You are now a journeyman. Congratulations, Eril," he said standing up and giving the still drying parchment to Jonny.

Jonny was bewildered. This was happening too fast. For years, he had dreamt of being a journeyman, and now he was one. But there had been no ceremony, no formal presentation as he had seen with the few other apprentices he had seen advanced. Again, The Master seemed to be reading his thoughts.

"Sorry about the lack of ceremony and all, Jonny, I mean Eril, but there is no time to waste. I have received news that someone has already figured out that the dead wizard was Boregond. I doubt you have even a week before some of his people come looking for you. I need you to be back in town tonight and on the road in no more than three days."

"I have Feldor working on arranging things with Kason. Here," he said handing Jonny a heavy pouch of coins, "is enough money for you to be able to travel and get any of the things you will need along the way. And here are your rings and amulets back," he said giving Jonny back his belt pouch.

"The shield spell amulet should be most useful. I would keep it on all the time if I were you. I'm also very impressed with that new ring, though I'm not sure what it does, I gather it is some sort of zdrell device."

"Yes, Master. I call it the master ring. It was what finally allowed me to defeat master Boregond."

"Yes, I'd rather thought that from what you said. The amulet that Boregond used to conjure the cyclone is in there too, though it looks to me like you fairly well destroyed it. I would like to study it sometime, but for now, I think you should take it with you and study it yourself. I am most interested in what Boregond said about the magic it used. I have only heard the barest hints of something like this before. I had always assumed that they were only rumors. Now I wonder how many of the things I dismissed over the years were real."

"Thank you, Master. I don't know how I can repay you."

"Jonny, I mean Eril, it is I who will be forever in your debt. The money is nothing. If we had more time I would do much more, but we do not. You need to know that you will have to travel in disguise. The people searching for Boregond's killer will be looking for a master wizard, they might even suspect an unusually talented journeyman wizard, but they most certainly will not look twice at a journeyman jeweler."

Master Silurian sat back and smiled with a twinkle in his eye. "The best part of it is that it won't be a lie. You are a journeyman jeweler and arms smith, as well as a journeyman wizard. It just shows that long range planning sometimes works out even better than I anticipated."

Chapter 68

The Master had indeed planned it, and it seemed that he had also planned many other things, for when Jonny arrived back at Kason's workshop he found much had been prepared there too. Kason was beaming as he showed Jonny all the things he had for him.

"I'm sorry we can't have a big send off party for you and all like I'd planned, Jonny, I mean, Eril, but the trading caravan Master Feldor has booked you with leaves tomorrow. Master Silurian thought it best if the lads here thought you just went back to the castle, not that you're leaving Salaways."

"Master Silurian has once again shown how generous he is. Here, just look at this," Kason said pointing to a newly built wooden chest. "This has everything you'll need to open a jewelry shop anywhere you go. It's a full set of tools, and they're of the finest quality too. Frankly, lad, I'm jealous. I've always wanted a fine set like this myself, but I could never bring myself to buy a new set of tools when the ones I had were good enough. But these are fine indeed. I do envy you, boy."

Jonny/Eril was amazed at the tools. One of the main reasons a journeyman waited to become a master was because he lacked the funds for a full set of tools of the trade, and here The Master was supplying him with everything he needed and of the highest quality. In a way, it frightened him.

"Yes these are fine tools. You'll want to guard them carefully," Kason said, echoing Jonny/Eril's thoughts.

"But you have that magic sword to help you, not that you need a sword to defend yourself, eh?"

Eril grinned, but after his encounter with Boregond he was not at all certain that he did not need all the help he could get.

"Thank you, Kason," Eril began, but Kason cut him off.

"Boy, you've made me more money in the last year than I made in the previous ten, and I think you'll keep making me money for at least another ten. It will take me that long at least afore I've sold off the last of your weapons, and by that time I'll be turning this shop over to someone younger.

"Now come see what else Master Silurian and Lord Feldor have gotten for you," he said, as he led Eril around to the back side of the shop.

Eril saw a pack mule tethered by a traveling case.

"That case has clothes for a journeyman jeweler. Do y'know one?" he asked with a lopsided grin. "Oh, and the nag there is to carry your tools and the case. And you have your own horse to ride."

"Yes," Eril said distractedly, still in shock looking at the case and mule.

"One more thing. The caravan you will be with, the head guard for it is none other than Carthic, that duelist who's crowing to everyone about the dirk and sword you made for him. I almost ought to pay him for all the fame he's brought me. Though I couldn't 'ave done it without your work. Lord Feldor has talked Carthic into giving you fencing lessons while the caravan travels."

Kason sighed and shook his head. "I will miss you. boy, but your master and Lord Feldor have made sure you got a proper send off."

§ § §

After sleeping one last time in his room at Kason's, Eril was up early to join the departing caravan. In order to remain inconspicuous, The Master could not be there to see him off, but Kason went with him and introduced him to the caravan master. He gave Jonny/Eril one more bundle, which he said contained two unfinished swords and four unfinished daggers.

"You'll be wanting these to use to keep in practice and to prove to any new masters just what you can do," Kason said with a grin. "I think you'll also want to work more on the looks and less on the magic, if you catch my meaning."

Eril did understand what he meant, but he was very grateful nonetheless, and said so. Kason said he could stay no longer and gave Eril a big hug. This surprised him, but made him very happy.

"I'll miss you, boy. When you come back, make sure you stop by and tell your old master what you've done."

"Yes, Kason," Jonny said, fighting back tears. "I'll miss you too. I will never forget you and all you've taught me. You've been like a father. I'll miss you very much."

"Enough of that, boy. No tears. I'll not have us bawling like a couple of babies. Do good. You're a good lad. Make the world a better place. Gods protect you, son."

Kason did not wait for Eril's reply. He turned and walked rapidly away and did not look back. Before he had turned, Eril had thought he had seen a tear starting down the grizzled face.

Eril too was on the verge of tears as he secured the bundle to his mule. He soon heard the command for the caravan to get under way. He quickly walked over, got on his horse, taking the lead for his mule, and started out with the rest of the caravan, away from all he knew, and into a new life.

Postlude

The runner entered the audience chamber still puffing with exertion.

"What is this message that is so urgent that my meal must be interrupted to receive it?" asked High Demon Master Jelnick, in ill humor.

"I know not, My Lord," answered the runner. "I know only that Master Feltran said it was most urgent and that I must not delay in bringing it to you for any cause, or I would find myself sacrificed to a demon at his next summoning."

"Hmmm, and you made the journey from the coast in under four days?" Jelnick asked, reaching for the message. The messenger nodded vigorously in agreement.

"I wore out eight mounts getting here, My Lord. I have not slept the entire time."

"Yes, yes, commendable. I'll be sure to tell Feltran of your devotion," Jelnick said unfolding the message.

"Let's see what is so terribly urgent," Jelnick said, beginning to read the message. He furrowed his brow in concentration and grunted as he read. He read all the way through and then looked more closely at the message and shook his head.

"You've done well, and I suppose this message warrants your speed. I thank you. You may go."

As soon as the messenger left and he was alone in the chamber, Jelnick grasped the ring on his right hand and said "Karf." In moments, a yellow light characteristic of a portal began to glow in the air in front of Jelnick. Shortly, the demon he had summoned appeared.

"What do you wish, Jelnick? I see no sacrifice," the demon said with a voice like a distant thunderstorm.

"I only need to keep you and your lord Kelf informed of a possibly significant event. It seems that Boregond has gone and gotten himself killed."

"Was he not assigned to destroy the line cutter?" the demon asked.

"Yes, yes he was. That is why I called. I have only now just received word from Feltran. I am not entirely certain his demise is connected with his errand, but it seems most likely. No one directly saw his end, but Feltran's spies were able to confirm that he was killed in a duel with another wizard, and that the wizard in question was definitely not Silurian. Silurian claims no knowledge of who killed Boregond or where he might be, which is to be expected, but he also made very clear that he does not have a line cutter.

"I am sure there is deception here on some level, but it looks as though this may be more complicated than I had first thought."

"You must deal with it then," the demon said. "You are the one who has been charged with keeping zdrell users and their artifacts from this world. You have been afforded much power and a longer life than any of your fellows to accomplish this."

"Yes, that's true, and for over one thousand years I have performed that task flawlessly. Do not you and your fellows feast daily off the bounty of this world? Have any of your brothers been killed or even threatened in that time?"

"One thousand years may seem long to you, human, but never forget that to demon kind it is but a short time, no matter how it seems to you. You must deal with this threat quickly, and completely."

"And I will, I will," Jelnick said. "Rest assured that I will devote all my resources to removing this threat."

"What will you do?"

"For the moment I will continue the search for the line cutter and for this unknown wizard who defeated Boregond. I will send spies to look for him, and one of them will have an amulet I have not used for many years. It detects line cutters from a distance and can lead the user to one. I am loathe to let it out of my presence, but as you remind me, I am over one thousand years old and as yet I see no reason to go searching myself."

"So you do nothing yourself?"

"On the contrary, I have told you what I am doing. When this line cutter is found and the wizard who defeated Boregond, then I, personally, will act and this annoyance will be eliminated."

"Do not forget your obligations."

"I never do. You demons for all your long lives are amazingly impatient. In less than ten years, conditions will be right and the second Great War will begin. Those foolish Skrylarans will soon be brought to heel. They still think they won the first war, not that I simply had our forces withdraw. They are so much more fractured now, and half of the kingdoms will fall to us without even knowing they are conquered. Those that remain will face the united might of Grimor. You and your brothers will feast on the souls of the conquered.

"All is going as planned. Patience. I will find and eliminate this wizard and line cutter, then there will be nothing to stop us from ruling this whole world and you from feasting on its inhabitants for another ten thousand or one hundred thousand years!" Jelnick said laughing.

"May it be so," the demon said, turning to the portal to leave. "I will inform Lord Kelf," the demon said and vanished.

"And I will ensure that nothing interferes with my plans," Jelnick said to an empty room.

About the Author

David K. Bennett first discovered his love for all things SF first by watching Star Trek TOS as very young boy. He fell in love with the works of Ray Bradbury in fifth grade and read voraciously for many years, flirting with the idea of trying his hand at writing, but never committing. He was always making up stories, but never wrote them down or felt they were compelling. Then, in the fall of 2000 he conceived a story which demanded telling and would not leave him alone until he wrote it down. After receiving encouragement from various friends and family who told him that this story was something worthwhile, he wrote what you now have in your hands. Life happens, so it has been a long time coming.

If you enjoyed the book please, please, please, please (am I begging yet?) leave us a review on Amazon, GoodReads, or wherever you got this book. The success of this book and series very much depends on your reviews and feedback.

If you want to learn more about the world of Zdrell, please join us on www.zdrell.com, where you can find additional comments and announcements. Consider joining our mailing list to hear about the latest news and get pre-release and free stuff.

Thank you very much for reading!

David K. Bennett, Simi Valley, CA, October 2018